RECKLESS

RECKLESS

a REWIND novel

CAROLYN O'DOHERTY

Printed in the United States of America
ISNB: 978-1-7366628-0-9 (paperback)
ISBN 978-1-7366628-1-6 (ebook)

First edition
10 9 8 7 6 5 4 3 2 1

Cover design by Barbara Grzeslo
Cover photo Mark Owen/Trevillion Images

The text is set in Janson MT.
The Dr. Ellery narratives are set in Century Gothic

Happy are they who die in swaddling clothes,
And wretched they who die in utmost age.
"Blessed is he who is not born," 'tis said.
And even though the errant crowd may hold
That for long ages Fame may still endure,
What is it that so highly is esteemed?
Time in his avarice steals so much away:
Men call it Fame; 'tis but a second death,
And both alike are strong beyond defense.
Thus doth Time triumph over the world and Fame.

—Francesco Petrarch

01 ◀◀

THE U-HAUL'S ENGINE SHUTS DOWN WITH A RATTLING COUGH. I lift my head off KJ's shoulder, instantly alert, and blink into the absolute darkness filling the back of the truck.

We're free.

The words pop into my head, bringing a burst of happiness that explodes inside me like my own private fireworks. The murmur of tentative voices rising through the dark confirms that this isn't a dream. We did it. KJ and I rescued all twenty spinners from Portland's supposedly secure Crime Investigation Center and brought them here, miles from where we started, to the brink of a new life. A safe life, where no one will control us or our time skills.

"You awake, Alex?"

KJ's whisper is so close to my ear that his breath tickles my neck. I reach through the darkness and find his hand. When I touch it, his fingers twine with mine.

A loud creaking sound comes from outside as our driver, Yolly, climbs from the truck's cab. Seconds later, she yanks the rear roll-up door partway open with a deafening clatter. Normal darkness, the kind lightened by moon and stars and streetlamps, floods our cave-like space. In the soft glow, I can make out the outlines of the kids KJ and I rescued, curled together like puppies on a patchwork assortment of pillows and blankets. At the lip of the truck's bed stands Yolly, her round form a solid mass of reassurance.

"Everyone OK in there?" she whispers—an unnecessary courtesy,

1

given that all the people clustered around me are wide awake.

"We're great." I crawl toward the opening, KJ at my heels.

"Wait here," I tell the other spinners as I squeeze my way through them. "KJ and I will make sure everything is safe."

"What about us?" asks Aidan. "We're just supposed to stay wedged in here?"

"Yep," KJ answers.

Aidan mutters, "So they think they're in charge now?" to his buddy Raul, but neither of them gets out from under his blankets.

I swing myself out of the truck, wincing a little when my feet hit the ground. It's been a long night. The short nap I snatched on the hour-long drive over here is holding back the worst of my exhaustion, but it hasn't erased the headache beating a persistent drumroll inside my skull.

KJ clambers out behind me, stretching his long body like a cat and darting quick glances at our surroundings, presumably searching—as I am—for a sign of someone about to attack. No one appears. The night smells like diesel and hums with quiet. To our right are a handful of long-haul trucks, their slumbering forms blocked from the freeway by a stand of tall pines. To our left, empty parking spots face a low concrete building. A sign hung near the door proclaims MEN over the blue-and-white image of a person in a wheelchair. There's a soda machine next the building and a display of maps and tourist information. I can't read the notices from here, but if we're in the right place, they'll be telling us about the wonders of Oregon's Columbia River Gorge.

"Is the guy you're meeting here?" Yolly asks, peering across the dim lot. She's parked the U-Haul in a spot at the end, as far as she could get from the lights.

"He should be," I say. "This is the Moose rest stop, right?"

"Memaloose," Yolly corrects me.

The word slides from her on a heavy sigh, and I study her more closely. Yolly looks as tired as I feel. Her full lips are pinched, and there are cavernous

2

circles under her eyes. A twinge of guilt dims some of my happiness. What has Yolly been thinking about as she chauffeured us on this midnight drive? Does she regret what she's done? Yolly is an adult and an employee of the Center. If they figure out that she helped twenty spinners escape, she won't just lose her job. Yolly will go to jail.

"I don't see him," I say, pushing my guilt aside to answer her original question. "But I'm sure he's on his—"

A car exits the highway, heading in our direction. KJ yanks down the truck's roll-up door and pulls Yolly and me behind the vehicle's bulky mass. All three of us peer around the side to watch as the car's headlights grow bigger. A familiar thread of worry worms its way up from the back of my mind. What if this is a trap, and instead of coming here to take us to a spinner refuge, Miguel actually works for the Center? What if it's the Center's director, Dr. Barnard, or my former time agent, Carson Ross, who leaps from the oncoming car, bringing with him the leashes that prevent us from freezing time? Or worse, what if the car is full of wipers?

I clench my teeth, willing the fear to go away, which only sort of works. Knowing that freezing time for extended periods causes paranoia doesn't stop my alarm bells from clamoring.

"You think it's Miguel?" KJ asks me. He shoots a quick glance at Yolly, and I know he's thinking the same thing I am: *She shouldn't have turned off the truck.*

"Why don't you wait in the cab," I tell Yolly. "We'll go talk to the driver, and if he's not who we think, or if he does anything threatening, you drive everyone else away. OK?"

Yolly's eyes go wide. "You don't think something's going to go wrong, do you?"

A quiver of fear prickles my scalp. Of course I do.

The lights of the car swing to one side, and a compact blue Honda pulls into a spot three spaces over from us. The prickles on my head spread, and every hair on my body turns into an antenna. I take a deep breath and force myself to smile at Yolly.

"Nothing is going to go wrong," I tell her. "It's just in case."

Yolly makes her way along the side of the U-Haul and climbs back into the cab, her hesitation clear in the half-hearted *thunk* of the door closing. I scan the darkness beyond the restrooms. If this is a trap and Yolly somehow manages to get away, where could she possibly take our friends?

The Honda cuts its headlights, and the engine dies.

KJ grabs my hand. "We should check it out."

"Right," I whisper. "I'll do it."

He nods. I adjust my focus inward. Time drifts through me—minutes, seconds, instants—all sliding forward into the unknowable future. I reach out with my mind. To me, time is not an invisible force; it's a weave I can grab hold of, made up of a million endless strands. I lock onto them and drag the world to a halt. At least that's my intent, but when I close my mental grip, time slides through my grasp like so much confetti. I try again. Nothing.

"You do it," I whisper to KJ. "I can't."

He doesn't look surprised. I've frozen time so often tonight that I literally passed out from the strain before we left the Center; it's hardly shocking that I haven't built up enough strength to do it again. It is worrisome, though. We're not safe yet, and traveling without any time skills makes me feel as exposed as a snail without its shell.

A frown of concentration drags KJ's dark eyebrows low on his forehead. For an instant, I worry that he, too, will fail—KJ held time nearly as long as I did tonight, and bringing someone into a freeze with you is always harder than stopping time alone—but then I feel the familiar shift in the quality of the air as the world stills. The highway turns into a parking lot of unmoving cars filled with equally unmoving people. The wind stops tugging at the pines, stranding their branches in mid-sway. The moon's rays, no longer moving, dim slightly as every atom freezes. In the U-Haul's cab, Yolly sits like a mannequin, head turned as she squints blindly at the blue car.

"How long can you hold on?" I ask KJ.

"Five minutes?" His teeth are gritted. "We better hurry."

The two of us walk quickly around the truck and approach the small car. In the utter silence of the frozen night, the scuff of our sneakers against the asphalt seems loud. KJ's pulse beats like a trapped bird under my fingers. We're perfectly safe right now in this paused oasis, but if the person in that car is not who we think, we're in trouble. The U-Haul isn't going to win in a real-time chase.

We reach the Honda's window and lean forward as one.

Miguel sits in the car's front seat, his body twisted toward us, one hand on the seat belt's release button, the other on the door handle.

"It's him." My words are nearly lost in a sigh of relief.

Miguel looks exactly like he did when we met him yesterday back in Portland: slim, with dark eyes and equally dark hair that falls all the way to his shoulders. He's even wearing the same type of clothes, the sporty kind that suggest he's prepared to set off a twenty-mile hike at a moment's notice.

KJ bends lower and peers through the window into the car's back seat. "He came alone."

The words don't calm me as much as they should. I chew my lip and study the pale-faced girl reflected in the car window. The recently dyed red bob makes the image unfamiliar, but I recognize the distrust in her expression. Are my nerves rational caution or freeze-induced paranoia?

The headache behind my eyes gives an especially vicious pulse as the happiness I woke up with shatters in a burst of fury. I am so tired of living in a constant fog of dread and fear; I'm tired of running, and hiding, and always trying to think two steps ahead. I rub my forehead. I want to crawl back into the U-Haul, curl up with my friends, and let someone else figure out what to do next. Except there is no one else. There's just KJ and me and this single moment offering a temporary shield from whatever comes next.

5

"Do you think you can rewind a little?" I ask KJ, pushing aside my anger to focus on the problem in front of us. "We should check and see if Miguel sent someone ahead of him. You don't have to rewind very far; we only called him an hour ago."

KJ gives a curt nod, his eyes growing unfocused as he sinks his thoughts into the instant that's locked all around us. He grasps hold of the frozen strands of time and starts to pull them backward. The past unrolls around us, the images like the faint reel of a movie played jerkily in reverse. A shadowy copy of Miguel's car detaches from the solid real one and backs onto the freeway, followed not long after by the U-Haul. KJ pulls the strands harder, increasing the rewind's tempo. Shadows flicker over the ground; trees bend in nonexistent breezes. We hear vague echoes of the world's former soundtrack, the noises unintelligible since they're playing backward. Only two vehicles arrive. One holds a tired-looking family, all of whom stagger in and out of the bathroom before returning to the freeway. One of the long-haul truckers stumps toward the restroom as well. We follow his shadowy form and discover no more nefarious activity than the un-purchase of a soda from the machine. The man returns to his truck, and we watch the memory of the vehicle's arrival as its misty shape eases out of the parking spot and rolls backward onto the freeway.

"That's long enough," I say. KJ is panting slightly, and there's a sheen of sweat coating his forehead. "I checked the trucker's watch. He got here right when I called Miguel."

KJ stops the rewind, and the frozen moment we inhabit spreads around us, silent as a held breath.

"We want to do this, right?" he asks, wiping his forehead with the back of his hand. "We're sure we trust him?"

"He's the best chance we have," I say.

"If we *are* wrong"—KJ gestures toward the U-Haul—"whatever happens to them will be our fault."

"We did the right thing." I roll my shoulders to ease the tension that's

6

squeezing them toward my ears. "We don't know what's going to happen at the refuge, but if we'd done nothing, they'd have been taken to the Central Office in the morning and killed."

My words would probably sound more convincing if my hand wasn't squeezing his so tightly. KJ nods anyway. His ability to hold time is obviously nearly drained.

The two of us retreat to our hiding spot behind the U-Haul. The metal side gives slightly when I prop my tired body against it. This exterior isn't as hard as it looks; it would take minimal effort to crush what's inside.

KJ releases the time strands. Lights brighten, and there's a slight loosening in the air that proves the world is moving forward again. KJ is still clutching my hand, almost certainly due to his own nervousness more than my reassurance. I raise my eyebrows in a silent question. KJ's throat works as he swallows. Hand in hand, we step out of the van's shelter and into the parking lot's muted light.

The door to the Honda pops opens.

"Glad you made it." Miguel's greeting is so instantaneous that I suspect he, too, froze time to check us out. The idea is disconcerting. It was only eleven days ago that I learned spinners aren't doomed to die in their teens. Miguel is the only adult spinner I've ever met, and the concept is still hard to accept.

"Hi," I say, as KJ and I move toward him.

Miguel smiles. It's a tight smile, very different from the eager enthusiasm he showed at our first meeting. Of course, it *is* past midnight. Like me, I'm sure he'd rather be asleep right now.

"Where's your ride?" he asks.

"Right here." I gesture to the truck.

"You came in a U-Haul?"

I think he's going to say more, but just then, Yolly jumps from the cab. Miguel tenses. Yolly walks in our direction, eyes narrowed as she sizes up Miguel just as obviously as he's assessing her. When she reaches us, she puts a protective arm around my shoulder. She'd probably put one around KJ's, too, except that he's a foot taller than she is.

"I'm Yolanda Richardson," she says. Her voice is mama-bear gruff, and her body feels warm where it touches mine. I lean against her. I may have rolled my eyes at her relentless cheeriness while we lived at the Center, but she has proven to be one of the few people in my life I've been able to count on, and knowing we'll part soon makes me sad.

"Yolly," I say, "this is Miguel, the man I told you about. He'll take us the rest of the way." I turn to Miguel. "Yolly is the matron at our Center. She knows the truth about what they've been doing to us. Without her help, we never would have gotten here."

Miguel holds out his hand to Yolly. "Thank you."

He speaks with a slight drawl that makes everything he says sound soothing. Yolly releases her grip on my shoulder to shake his hand.

"There aren't a lot of Norms who are willing to help spinners," Miguel says.

Yolly looks at her feet. "Anyone would help, if they knew what was really going on. I can't believe I worked there so long without suspecting anything."

"The Center is very good at what it does," Miguel says. "Especially when it comes to covering up its crimes."

"I wish I could at least quit," Yolly says. "There would be some satisfaction in knowing I walked away. But with the Center closing tomorrow, I guess I don't have a job there anymore anyway."

"It's closing tomorrow?" Miguel frowns. "I thought it was open until the end of the month."

"They changed their plans," Yolly says. "Having four spinners escape last week caused quite a ruckus at the Central Office. And then when Alex got caught and broke out *again* . . ." She shrugs. "The order to close came down yesterday. Dr. Barnard told the press they'd found mold in the building and they needed to evacuate everyone."

"That's why we had to get them out," I say.

Miguel's frown deepens.

"Get who out?"

My stomach lurches. Miguel looks from me to KJ.

"Do you mean you managed to get your friend, what's her name . . . Shannon out of the Center?"

The temperature in the parking lot drops about ten degrees. KJ flinches and drops my hand. Yolly sniffs.

"No." I slide the hand KJ abandoned into the pocket of my jeans. "Dr. Barnard took Shannon to the Central Office yesterday morning."

The words fall from my mouth like hailstones, hard and painful. I shift my weight so I'm no longer pressed against Yolly. She adored Shannon. I don't deserve her comfort.

"I'm sorry," Miguel says.

"We'll get her back." KJ lifts his chin. "Once we get settled, Alex and I will go to the Central Office and rescue her."

Miguel shakes his head.

"You can't get into the Central Office," he says. "It's Fort Knox over there."

"We'll find a way," KJ says.

"There's no point." The expression in Miguel's eyes softens to pity. "I know this is hard to accept, but it's our reality. Spinners that go to the Central Office don't come back. Your friend has been there almost twenty-four hours. Our local Central Office, the one in Tacoma, has been working on a top-secret research project for years now, and from what we've managed to find out about their methods, I doubt there's anyone left to save even if you could get in. You're going to have to let her go."

KJ's whole frame slumps under the older man's words. Yolly lets out a stifled sob. Miguel turns his attention to me.

9

"So who *did* you manage to get out?" he asks with the forced cheer of someone working hard to lighten the mood. "I thought your other friend was already outside with you."

A thumb whose nail I've already chewed to the quick is somehow back in my mouth. I'm looking at Miguel's car, that compact little vehicle, which is starting to grow much larger in importance.

"We didn't save Jack," I say. "We saved everyone else."

Miguel's body goes so still I might have stopped time.

"Excuse me?" he says.

The phone call we had an hour earlier flashes through my head. It was brief.

Me: Miguel? This is Alex. We've decided to accept your offer. We have a car. Just tell me where to go.

Miguel (surprised): You're driving?

Me (extremely tired and rather impatient): Not me—we've got a driver. Someone we can trust.

Miguel: (starts to say something)

Me: You said the refuge is east of us, right? Where can we meet you?

I'm pretty sure that was it. No mention of the U-Haul. Or why we had a U-Haul. Or what was in the U-Haul.

I study the Honda again. The very small Honda.

"We couldn't save Shannon," KJ says, "but we did free our other friends."

"You brought"—Miguel puts his hand against his head like it's hurting him—"*all* the kids from the Center?"

"Yes," I say.

"They're in the back of the truck," Yolly adds. "We should probably let them out. They'll be wondering what's going on."

"What about their trackers?" Miguel manages.

I reflexively touch the back of my neck. The small incision where

Shannon took my own tracker out a little over a week ago has pretty much healed. There's only a narrow scar to mark the place where the tiny device used to sit beneath my skin—a device that allowed the Center staff to know when I froze time and also to pinpoint my location.

"We're not stupid," I say. "Yolly cut them out."

Miguel seems to have regained his bearings. The hand that was clutching his head is now at his side, balled into a fist. He and KJ are both standing with their chests out, shoulders back, in that aggressive posture boys seem to be born knowing. Not that either of them is a boy. KJ is eighteen, two years older than me, and Miguel must be in his thirties.

The throbbing in my head grows stronger.

"When I offered you sanctuary," Miguel says, his friendly drawl now clipped, "I told you we don't help spinners escape."

"You didn't help them escape," I say. "We did. All we're asking for is a place to stay for a while."

Miguel winces. "The refuge's survival relies on the fact that no one knows we exist. If a few of you manage to get out on your own here and there, great, we'll bring you in, but a whole center of, what, a dozen spinners?"

"Twenty," KJ says.

"Twenty." Miguel shakes his head. "We don't have room for that many people. Plus, an escape of that magnitude can't be covered up. They'll be looking for you."

His words, with their hint of refusal, sting like a lash.

"We couldn't just run away and leave our friends behind to die," I say at the same time KJ snaps, "If you don't want to help us, fine. We'll find a way to survive on our own."

Miguel rubs the bridge of his nose and lets out a very long sigh.

"No, no," he says, "I didn't mean that. It's just . . . things are . . . complicated these days, and this isn't going to help." He shakes his head. "I need to make a phone call." He turns away from us and heads back toward his car, dialing a cell phone as he walks. I catch him muttering, "We have a problem . . ." before he moves farther away and I can't make out anything else.

"We don't need him," KJ says, kicking at some loose gravel. "We can all just go on the run."

Out on the freeway, a passing truck lets out a long mournful wail, and my small store of energy seems to seep out with it. We can't all *go on the run.* Beyond those trees is a lonely road barreling into unfamiliar darkness. How could we possibly hide out anywhere with twenty other kids, almost half of whom aren't even in their teens? Jack, KJ, Shannon, and I barely survived a week on our own.

I put my hand on KJ's arm. "We do need him."

KJ kicks the gravel harder, sending a small rock skittering across the asphalt.

Yolly, who has been following the conversation with wide-eyed concern, gestures to the back of the U-Haul.

"Do you think I should . . . ?" she asks.

"Yes," I tell her. "They'll be wondering what's going on. And we *are* at a rest stop. Everyone should take advantage of it."

Yolly retreats to the truck, and I pull on KJ's arm until he faces me.

"We can't ask more than this from Yolly," I say, too softly for her to hear me. "It's not fair."

"I know." He jerks his head toward Miguel's hunched back. "It's just, he could have saved Shannon when we first met him, and he chose not to because they *didn't want to interfere.* And now, when we're the ones who took the risk to get them out, they're saying they don't want us . . ."

"They're not saying that." I hope I'm speaking the truth. "And KJ"—I tighten my grip on his arm until he meets my eyes—"Miguel couldn't have saved Shannon. Even if he'd agreed the minute we asked. She was already in the Center by then, maybe even on her way to the Central Office. If we'd shown up, it just would have meant Barnard had three new test subjects instead of one."

12

KJ yanks his arm away from me.

"You can't know what would have happened if we'd tried," he says. "Now she's dead, and it's all because of me."

Something hard pinches my insides. We both know I'm at least as much to blame as he is for Shannon's fate. If I'd done a better job of convincing her the threats against us were real, or if either of us had told her that her romance was over before she caught KJ and me kissing, maybe she wouldn't have run back to the Center. She'd be with the rest of us right now. Safe. Alive.

The back door of the U-Haul slides upward with a bone-shaking rattle, followed shortly thereafter by thumping noises as twenty bodies tumble from their crowded nest.

"Where the heck are we?" Raul calls, much too loudly. KJ spins on his heel and strides off to the bathroom. I'm tempted to run after him, but I catch Miguel's harried glare and instead hurry over to where Raul is standing, now surrounded by the other spinners, rumple-haired and gazing around with befuddlement.

"It's only a break," I tell them, suppressing the image of KJ's taut shoulders moving away from me. "We'll head to the refuge soon. There's a bathroom over there, and water. Just keep it down, OK? We don't want to wake up any of the truckers."

General muttering meets this announcement, but at a noise level that is blessedly low, and the group moves in clusters toward the toilets. Aidan and Raul stop by the water fountain, talking in low voices. Little Joel hovers nearby, his forehead creased in a way that makes me worry about what he might be overhearing. Yuki and Angel, the two oldest girls, shepherd a group of Youngers around to the women's side of the building while casting nervous glances into the darkness. Ten-year-old Emma and her roommate, Molly, drape a blanket over their shoulders and huddle together on a bench, both of them staring around at the unfamiliar scene.

Their confusion makes my heart hurt. I've lived with these kids and

13

others like them for my entire life. We've shared meals and dorm rooms, watched television together, bickered over chores, and played games in the gym. All of us were raised thinking that the Center was our protection against the prejudice of outsiders, our safe haven in a world that mistrusted us and considered us freaks, and the place that would take care of us when we fell victim to the dreaded time sickness. And then I learned that nothing I believed was true. The Center had lied about the extent of our time skills; they'd lied about the inevitability of our early deaths; they'd turned out to be the ones who were *causing* the sickness that was killing us. Without KJ and me, the twenty people at this lonely rest stop would still be in the Center, hours from being turned into test subjects for Barnard's endless research. I should feel proud of what I've done, but all I can think about is how much we don't know and how far we still have to go before any of us are truly free.

"I need you to tell me exactly how all of you escaped."

I recite the mechanics of our night's adventure while Miguel paces in front of Yolly, KJ, and me. The other kids are in the truck again. The back is open, but they have strict instructions not to make any noise.

"Did anyone see you while you were in the Center?" Miguel asks when I stop talking.

"Agent Ross did." The words taste as sour on my tongue as the memory feels in my brain. "And Jack. They were waiting inside to ambush us, but we got away."

"We tied them up," KJ adds before Miguel can ask. "When they were frozen. We left them handcuffed and locked in the janitor's closet."

Yolly gasps. Miguel rubs his forehead and swears under his breath.

"I'm sure they'll figure out a way to get out," I say, irritated by the implication that we made a mess of everything. "And neither of them is going tell anyone what happened. Jack won't, obviously, because he's a spinner, but Mr. Ross won't either, or he'd have to explain what he was doing there in the

14

first place."

Miguel does not look convinced. He turns to the Center's matron.

"Yolanda," he says, "I'm afraid you're going to have to come with us."

"What? No!" The words burst from my mouth so loudly that Miguel scowls.

Yolly takes a step back. "I can't do that."

"We made up a cover story," KJ says, "to explain why Yolly rented a moving van. She'll be fine."

Miguel shakes his head. "Yolanda will *not* be fine. The wipers aren't stupid. The coincidence of you getting into the Center with Yolanda's key card and her renting a U-Haul is too big to ignore." His gaze moves across our faces; Yolly looks scared, KJ as mutinous as I feel.

"I'm also going to need your cell phones. We can't have anyone tracking us."

Yolly puts a protective hand over her pocket.

"I destroyed my phone before I left Portland," I say. "And Yolly has done enough for us. I told her bringing us here was all we needed her to do. I promised."

"That was not your promise to make," Miguel says. "I'm sorry, but this isn't optional. The wipers don't play around."

Wipers. The word raises hackles on the back of my neck. Automatically, I glance over my shoulder and squint into the dark spaces between the trees.

Yolly frowns.

"What are wipers?" she asks.

"The Center's private security force." Miguel's voice is grim. "It's who they use to find spinners who escape."

Yolly's frown deepens. "But you all control time. Can't you just freeze everything when you see one coming and run away?"

"Sure," Miguel says, "if we see them. The thing is, it's impossible to

15

know who's a wiper. Plus, they have tools—chromoelectronegators—that block our access to time if we're near them. We can sense one if it's turned on—their emanations make us feel intensely afraid—but wipers are cunning. They'll surround a spinner first and then turn on their chromoelectronegators to create a fence we can't get through. By the time we realize they're there, we're helpless."

"But that's illegal!" Yolly says.

The smile that twists Miguel's mouth is bitter.

"Our judicial system and our nation's Centers have a very intimate relationship. Any time a free spinner disappears, the incident is explained away or the investigation is somehow botched. No one—spinner or not—who has been caught by a wiper has ever been seen again."

Yolly hands over her phone, looking queasy. Her horror adds another measure of guilt to the looming tower this conversation has already built. As much as I will miss her once she leaves, I don't want *this* for Yolly. She chose to help us because she thought it was the right thing to do. She doesn't deserve to have her life torn to shreds.

"Yolly just has to lay low for a few weeks, until this blows over," I say, sliding my arm through hers and giving it a squeeze. "Right? The Center runs on a shoestring. The wipers won't track us forever."

"The Center is funded with public dollars." Miguel snaps open the back of Yolly's phone and pries out the battery. "Kronos is not."

A chill that has nothing to do with the weather slips through the weave of my sweater. "What's Kronos?"

"They're the organization that oversees the Centers, and the Central Offices, and the equivalent organizations all over the world." Miguel drops Yolly's phone on the ground and grinds it under his heel until all that's left is a pile of crushed metal. "They're named after Chronos, the Greek god of time. Kronons are fanatics who have been around for centuries and work toward a single goal: the control and suppression of spinners."

16

The asphalt beneath my feet feels like it's tipping. Why have I never considered there might be a mastermind behind the Center's dark work? In retrospect, the existence of an organization like Kronos seems blindingly obvious. How else could the world have managed to control us for so long?

"They have money?" I ask.

"Kronos has made a number of savvy investments over the years," Miguel says. "They also have influence. Members of Kronos have infiltrated the highest level of governments around the globe. They own many of the major media outlets and spend huge amounts spreading anti-spinner propaganda."

The ache in my head sinks down into my bones. The doubts I'd been struggling with a few minutes ago about whether my fear was real or freeze induced now seem laughable. Not only is fear appropriate, it turns out I wasn't scared enough.

"Why haven't we ever heard of—" KJ starts.

Miguel holds up a hand. "Now isn't the time to explain." He points to KJ and me. "You two, go join the others in the back of the truck. Yolanda, take my car and follow me. I'll drive the U-Haul. If anyone stops me, you just drive on, OK?"

"Where exactly are we going?" Yolly asks.

Miguel straightens from where he's been scraping up the shattered bits of Yolly's phone. "It's better if nobody knows until we get there," he says. "Just in case we don't make it."

Yolly follows Miguel to his car. KJ and I walk to the truck. KJ is frowning at the ground, like he's working hard to figure out some complex puzzle. The muscles in the backs of my legs feel tight with the urge to run. I want to tell KJ that I'm scared. I want him to hug me and say he loves me and that together we can overcome this new challenge, but the other spinners are waiting for us. They're expecting me to show them that I know what I'm doing, that everything is going to turn out all right.

We reach the lip of the truck bed and face the twenty pairs of eyes

17

gleaming from the dark interior. I hoist myself inside and scan their nervous faces, counting the ones that are here and remembering the ones that are not. Calvin, who died less than two weeks ago at the Center's hands. Jack, who abandoned us to work for Ross when he thought we were doomed. Shannon.

Exhaustion washes through me. I thought I understood the threats against us. I thought wipers were the worst thing we had to fear. Now it feels like I'm starting all over again with a brand-new enemy about whom I know absolutely nothing.

02 ◄◄

DR. MARGARET ELLERY SITS ALONE IN THE BACK OF THE MERCEDES. Outside, summer sun scorches New York City's streets. People bow under the stifling humidity, trees droop in the heat, and although she cannot smell it from her sanctuary, Dr. Ellery suspects the air is tinged with the scent of rotting garbage. Even the cars flowing past the Mercedes's tinted windows seem to move listlessly. Dr. Ellery observes the city's suffering with detachment. Inside her car, the air conditioning is turned up high enough to bite.

The Mercedes glides across the Brooklyn Bridge, moving away from the congested city and into the sedate streets of Brooklyn Heights. Traffic thins; the buildings grow shorter. They are getting close. The car signals, turns, and stately brownstones begin to appear outside her windows. Dr. Ellery brushes a speck of lint from her tailored slacks. The conversation before her is one that could change the course of human history, and she does not approach it lightly. The Order of Kronos has nine trustees, but she knows the only decision that matters is that of the man she is about to visit, the oldest and most revered member of their ancient organization: Antonio Romano.

Dr. Ellery marshals arguments in her head. She has been working on Project Zed for eight years, overseeing countless experiments, collecting people she trusts, and placing them in positions of power. The next step seems obvious to her, but she knows there will be resistance. As devoted as she is to her organization, she understands that many of her fellow Kronons are ruled by fear. Fear of decisive action, fear of change, and most of all, fear for their own futures if the cause to which they have devoted their lives becomes irrelevant. Which is why it is her job today to prove that inaction is a greater threat than moving forward.

The Mercedes makes its final turn onto the street that houses their destination. The area seems unusually quiet, maybe because the sweltering weather has driven everyone indoors, or maybe because the righteousness of her organization's mission hangs over this particular neighborhood, its significance discouraging the shrill cries of children and daily life's more frivolous pursuits. Jogging. Dog walking. Maybe Mr. Romano, a man who has dedicated his life to containing time deviants, has himself created a kind of eternal pause within the bustle of this vast city.

Dr. Ellery shakes her head to dispel this uncharacteristic fancy. Time operates no differently here from anywhere else on earth. The street outside is merely a street. The neighborhood is only a place. Antonio Romano is just a man.

The Mercedes slows to a stop in front of a discreet building indistinguishable from the ones surrounding it. Exiting the car's back seat, Dr. Ellery is instantly engulfed in sultry heat. She walks swiftly, her shoes—low-heeled, sensible, and expensive—making soft tapping noises as she strides up the brownstone's front steps. The door opens for her before she reaches it.

"Dr. Ellery," a man says, bowing slightly as he lets her pass.

"Charles."

Inside, heavy drapes are drawn against the afternoon sun, muffling both heat and sound. Dr. Ellery removes her sunglasses, and Charles ushers her down a dimly lit hallway to a study. The room looks as if it belongs to an earlier age. It's paneled in dark mahogany and has an ornately carved fireplace and thick carpets of deepest red. Dr. Ellery steps inside, inhaling the sweet scent of pipe smoke lingering in the still air.

"Margaret."

Antonio Romano struggles up from one of the leather armchairs set before an unlit fire. His body is frail, and his once-tall frame is bent like an old tree.

"There's no need for you to get up," Dr. Ellery says, striding across the room.

"You are my guest." The hand Mr. Romano holds out quivers with tremors. "I always rise to greet my guests."

The two shake hands, and Dr. Ellery takes the opportunity to study him more carefully. Mr. Romano has aged in the two years since she last saw him. His skin has reached near translucence, and his white hair sprouts from his head in thin tufts, exposing patches of pink skull.

"Thank you for agreeing to meet with me," she says.

"The pleasure is mine." Mr. Romano waits for Dr. Ellery to sit before resuming his own chair. When he does, a small cat, black as a shadow, leaps up to settle in his lap.

"It is always better to have important conversations in person," Mr. Romano says. His English, while flawless, carries a lilt that indicates he is not a native speaker. "I have never completely trusted telephones, and email is worse. There's no guarantee of privacy."

Dr. Ellery acknowledges this statement with a small nod. Mr. Romano offers her tea from an antique silver service laid out on a table between them. She prefers coffee but accepts a cup anyway, refusing both cream and sugar, then waits while Mr. Romano slowly pours his own. The creamer wobbles in his hand, and she stifles her impatience as he painstakingly stirs in three cubes of sugar.

"I have spoken with the other trustees," Mr. Romano says when he finally settles back into his chair. "Your proposal, this Project Zed, is raising a lot of concerns."

"The world is changing," Dr. Ellery says. "We can no longer control spinners with our usual methods. It is critical that we take a more decisive step."

Mr. Romano sips his milky tea. "Does not every generation believe that their situation is more important, more dire, than those that have come before?"

Dr. Ellery decides to treat his question as rhetorical. She swallows some of her tea, using the brief pause to school herself so her voice remains neutral. Emotion never wins an argument.

"The goal of Kronos has always been to protect the world from spinners. As I laid out in my proposal, recent technological advancements, combined with the groundbreaking research completed by Dr. Jeffrey Barnard of the Northwest Central Office, add new weapons to our arsenal. It is finally within our power to end this scourge entirely."

Mr. Romano sets down his tea and steeples his thin fingers beneath his chin. "I must tell you that I find your proposal extreme."

His tone is mild, but his eyes, encased in their web of wrinkles, are sharp.

"Project Zed will be effective," Dr. Ellery says.

"I do not question its efficacy, only its morality."

The teacup in Dr. Ellery's hand rattles against its saucer. *Morality?* The word seems as old-fashioned as the room's ancient furnishings. There is nothing moral about creatures who are able to spy, steal, even kill completely undetected.

"Project Zed," she says, "will, in one fell swoop, achieve what generations of your family and so many others' have devoted their lives to: the total elimination of spinners."

A small frown deepens the lines on Mr. Romano's forehead. It's not disapproval; it's the frown of an academic considering an ideological puzzle.

"Am I correct," he says, "that your sister was a spinner?"

Dr. Ellery starts. The unexpected reference releases a burst of memories from the darkest corner of her mind, flashing visceral postcards from her past: the series of dingy rooms, none inhabited long enough to feel like a home; her mother's desperation as she demanded ever-stricter levels of vigilance; the countless nights spent scuttling through mean streets to escape yet another one of Clarissa's impossible-to-explain outbursts.

"Yes." Dr. Ellery touches the tender spot on her side, the one her doctor thinks might be an ulcer. "There was an error with my sister's test when she was an infant. At age five, her symptoms emerged. My mother chose to hide her rather than turn her in."

"She was successful for a surprisingly long time. I believe your sister was fourteen when our agents finally got hold of her."

A final memory worms its way into Dr. Ellery's mind: her twelve-year-old self, feet planted on the stained linoleum of a temporary kitchen, informing her mother that Clarissa was gone.

"Gone?" her mother gasped. "To a *Center*?"

An agonized wail split the air, and her mother collapsed, sobbing on the floor. Margaret, terrified the neighbors would call the cops, patted her mother's trembling shoulder.

"At least we can settle in one place now," she said. "We won't have to run anymore."

Her mother raised her head, revealing a bone-white face Margaret barely recognized.

"You still have *me*." Margaret patted her mother's shoulder again. "Now we can be a normal family."

Her mother turned away. Her face showed no sign of secret relief; her eyes had gone dark, their bright spark lost to the empty stare she would wear for the rest of her life.

Dr. Ellery clears her throat.

"It was for the best," she says.

"Still, that must have been difficult for you."

The condescension—or is it pity?—in the trustee's voice steels Dr. Ellery against the onslaught of the past. The only effect her life experience has on her is to deepen her dedication to Kronos.

"Spinners are damaged," she says in a curt voice. "They are violent creatures who bring nothing but destruction to everyone around them."

Mr. Romano taps his fingers together in a gentle rhythm. "I'm sure your personal history brings a . . . unique perspective, but I think we must ask ourselves whether elimination is truly Kronos's ultimate goal. Some of our historians argue that this organization was founded to control and protect, not destroy."

The change in tone from personal to professorial relaxes the tension around Dr. Ellery's spine. She sets her teacup down

24

on the silver tray, arranging her arguments in carefully ordered lines before she speaks. The tea set, she notes, is etched with a scythe, one of the symbols associated with the god of time, and the familiar emblem further bolsters her determination.

"Kronos has been killing spinners since the first century," she says. "You know our origins. Spinners were working together, using their power to gain control over the governments of every single European nation. If we hadn't killed those power-hungry monsters, humanity would have become little more than serfs reduced to serving a mutant race."

"Possibly," Mr. Romano acknowledges, "though history is a complex web. We do know those early eliminations were selective. We only removed the spinners who used their power to control others."

"Complete elimination was not an option when we were founded," Dr. Ellery counters. "We couldn't test people's blood to determine if they carried the trait until 1912. And even if we could have, limited transportation would have made finding all the spinners impossible. The technology we have today was unimaginable to our founders, and thus their vision was likewise constrained."

"Constrained or not, Kronos has successfully kept spinners under control for centuries using primarily containment and propaganda. No spinner could gain a position of power today; our agents are trained to recognize the signs of abuse. More importantly, the public, even without knowing the true extent of their skills, is almost unanimously against them. To admit that you have the condition is to be instantly ostracized."

"Trusting the general public to enforce our objectives is not reliable." Dr. Ellery lifts the teapot and refills her cup even though it is only half empty. "These days, the world celebrates diversity and prides itself on rooting for the underdog. There are hundreds of blogs devoted to spinner rights and even more ranting about government conspiracies and cover-ups."

Mr. Romano runs a hand over his cat's inky fur and offers Dr. Ellery a patronizing smile. "Sympathy for spinners is a fad that will soon pass."

Irritation ramrods Dr. Ellery's spine.

"And what if that doesn't happen soon enough?" she asks. "I know you are aware that the CIA's interest in our operations has intensified dramatically in the last year."

"The CIA has always tracked us, but they are never going to act. They understand the role we play in the containment of spinners."

"Kronos's methods of containing spinners may be privately sanctioned by the world's governments, but given that our strategy includes killing children, they will deny any knowledge of it the moment the public turns on us."

The phrase *killing children* sounds particularly jarring in their elegant surroundings. Mr. Romano doesn't react, but the cat looks offended on his behalf, staring at Dr. Ellery through narrowed eyes.

"Your concern for Kronos is a credit to you," Mr. Romano says, "but it is unnecessary. We have the situation completely under control."

"I'm afraid the CIA would say that the hundreds of rogue spinners living free in the world proves otherwise."

Mr. Romano gives the small, appreciative laugh of someone acknowledging a well-made point in what he clearly sees as an enjoyable debate.

26

"I have come to believe that spinners are not fundamentally evil," he says. "Unfortunately, the power they wield carries such dangerous potential that it is our duty to control them to ensure the world is protected. But if a few of them slip through our net, I see nothing wrong with allowing them clemency, as long as they don't use their skills in a way that disturbs the peace."

Unsaid words clog the back of Dr. Ellery's throat. Mr. Romano is wrong. Spinners *are* wicked. They are deceitful and violent and dangerous. How dare he speak of *clemency*? Was her mother offered clemency? Was she? No—her miserable childhood happened because Kronos allowed one of the vile creatures to "slip through their net."

Dr. Ellery brings her cup to her mouth and studies the old man across from her as he placidly strokes his cat. Antonio Romano has guided Kronos for over fifty years, almost longer than Dr. Ellery has been alive. Respect for him saturated every part of her training as she moved up through the ranks of this venerable organization. And yet . . . Dr. Ellery's eyes travel over his palsied hands, noting the legs whose shriveled condition is not entirely masked by the smooth lines of his trousers. Time marches forward—or it should—and no one, not even Antonio Romano, can hold it back.

She clears her throat again.

"You've heard that an entire Center full of spinners escaped in Portland two days ago?" she asks.

"Yes. I gather it was rather cleverly done. Executed by a girl, I think."

Dr. Ellery grimaces. Alexandra Manning isn't *clever*; she is dangerous. Only a few days before the breakout, she nearly killed Dr. Barnard in a car crash, and since then there has been a string of suspicious robberies, not to mention the unsolved murder of that rogue spinner, Austin Shea. The Manning girl's capture was high on Dr. Ellery's list of priorities.

Mr. Romano, perhaps mistaking her anger for concern, adds, "I'm sure they'll be collected soon. They *are* only children."

Frustration makes her next words sharp.

"The children who escaped in Mexico last spring weren't rounded up for almost six months. We're still cleaning up all the havoc they caused. And what about the breakout this summer in Moscow? Those spinners weren't children."

Mr. Romano's hand pauses in its rhythmic caressing of the cat, who lifts its head and stares at Dr. Ellery with a doleful expression.

"Moscow was"—he pauses—"an unfortunate incident."

"It was more than unfortunate," she says. "There were twenty-seven fully functioning spinners in that facility. Those monsters murdered all eight of their guards when they escaped, plus three wipers were slaughtered before they were recaptured."

Mr. Romano sighs.

"Allowing spinners to fully mature is of course frowned upon, but we all know there's nothing new about them being used occasionally for select activities. Even your North American division has sanctioned limited access to spinners during times of war. The Cold War was primarily waged with their assistance."

"This was not an example of spinners protecting national security," Dr. Ellery says. "The Moscow office has been selling them to the highest bidders for the last twenty years—guerilla fighters, agitators in some of the world's most dangerous countries, people involved in the drug trade."

"We all agree that these actions were inappropriate, and the trustees have assigned new people to manage that office. But the breakout in Moscow was an anomaly. It is hardly prudent to change our entire organizational strategy based on an aberration."

A flare of pure rage flushes Dr. Ellery's neck. How can Mr. Romano not see the risks? Once one Center succumbs to the temptation of selling spinners, what's to stop another one from doing the same? Spinners are too damaged to be allowed use of their full powers. For any reason. The fact Mr. Romano is not outraged implies the whole organization is growing complacent. This cannot be allowed to happen. If Kronos loses its focus, the entire world will collapse into anarchy.

Dr. Ellery draws a steadying breath, looking for an argument that will have more of an effect.

"I'm afraid," she says, "that the CIA does not agree with your assessment. Nor does the KGB."

Mr. Romano's frown returns, and this time, the crease is more concerned than academic.

"What do you mean?"

"The intelligence community has always worried that we have what they call 'undue influence.' They have held their concern in check only because they rely on us to control the spinners, but these recent mass breakouts have led the intelligence agencies to question our competence. The escape in Portland may have been the final straw. That 'clever' girl who spearheaded it exposed her full abilities on numerous occasions, including at a busy hospital, at least two retail establishments, and to a time agent named Tito Marquez, who spoke publicly

29

about what he saw. The sheer number of exposures in such a short period of time, plus our failure to recapture the girl in question, has significantly eroded the CIA's confidence in us. I have personally seen a classified CIA memo discussing the establishment of a new international intelligence cohort that would manage the spinners without our assistance."

The room grows quiet. The cat, perhaps sensing that it no longer has its master's attention, stands up and leaps lightly to the ground. Mr. Romano shivers, as if the loss chills him.

"Kronos has kept the world safe from spinners for centuries," Mr. Romano says. "It's our sole reason for being."

"That's not how the cohort sees it. They see us as a covert society with the power to sway every government in the world. To them, we are a threat, and they intend to bring us down."

Mr. Romano's frown deepens. "They don't understand the danger. If the strategy to control spinners isn't unified, it is guaranteed to fail. Only one country needs to stumble for the entire system to collapse." He runs an agitated hand through his sparse hair. "We'll have to explain it to them."

"Explain it how? These people don't understand our mission. Bureaucracies managed by spies are by definition distrustful, and they are quick to assume the worst about us. The cohort knows how many influential people—senators, judges, intimate friends, legal advisors—owe their positions to us. If we try to stop the cohort from taking over management of the spinners, they will see that as further evidence of our lust for domination. And you are right about what would happen next. If our system collapses, everyday people will learn the truth about what spinners can do *and* about our methods of containment. Not all of them will consider our strategies necessary. More spinners will be allowed to grow up, which inevitably means more of them will escape. Eventually, spinners will once again connive their way into positions of power. And what of us? If spinners are set free, who do you think will be their first target?"

The old man's fingers stretch toward his lap, presumably seeking the comfort of his absent feline. His hand hovers vaguely before settling like a wilted flower on his thin knee. Dr. Ellery leans forward, pressing her advantage.

"The time for change is now. Kronos cannot continue operating the way we have in the past, or we will face ruin. Federal agents *will* descend on us. Do you want to be the one who presides over our destruction? Our legacy is in your hands. We have the tools we need to end spinners. All you have to do is authorize Project Zed."

Antonio Romano droops in his seat, as if all the accumulated years of his long life weigh on his shoulders.

"Very well," he says in a heavy voice. "I will speak to the other trustees."

Dr. Ellery bends her head toward the tea set to hide the triumph she knows must show on her face. She has won. She prepares a fresh cup of tea for Mr. Romano, then pours another for herself. On impulse, she adds a single lump of sugar. After all, celebration is in order. Project Zed is about to become a reality. Starting tomorrow, the wheels will be set in motion, and soon after that, spinners will cease to exist.

03 ◄◄

THE HALLWAY IS LONG AND MAZELIKE. THERE ARE IDENTICAL branching corridors every few feet, and in between them are endless rows of closed doors. Somehow, I know that behind one of them, Shannon is lying unconscious on a metal slab. Her body is limp, and there are wires sprouting from between the strands of her long blond hair. Is she already dead? I try to run, but my legs aren't working. Every step feels like I'm pulling my feet through glue. Tears drip down my cheeks, and suddenly Ross is there, hovering by my side like a smug ghost. *I don't understand why you're so upset,* he says in his most reasonable voice. *Isn't this what you wanted? Shannon's gone, and now you have KJ all to yourself.* No, I say, or try to, but like my legs, my voice isn't working, and no matter how I struggle, I can't make a sound. Ross's lips stretch into a smile. He reaches out one hand and lightly brushes the tip of my nose.

My eyes jerk open, and I spring to my feet, time snapping to a halt before I consciously consider stopping it. A tiger-striped cat hovers in the air inches from where I was lying, its tail stretched out behind it in a startled puff. The frozen bodies of my friends lie around me, all safely slumbering in the basement of Miguel's refuge, a multi-acre property way out in Eastern Oregon called Goat Hill Farm.

I drop back down to the floor, rubbing my skull in the spot where a headache offers up an aggrieved pulse. The jolt of waking to an adrenaline burst is getting depressingly familiar. Even after three days here, it seems like all I ever manage are short naps interrupted by startled awakenings.

I let time go, releasing the cat to complete its frantic scramble, and scan the sleeping shapes until I find KJ's. He's curled on his side at the other end of the room, wrapped in a green-and-white blanket stamped with the logo of the Portland Timbers soccer team. KJ's hair used to be one of his defining features, long waves that flopped over his forehead and that he would toss back with an impatient flick of his head. Recently—was it only five days ago?—he buzzed his hair short in an attempt to elude the wipers. The new haircut exposes the long line of his neck, as well as the puckered edges of the still-pink scar where Shannon cut out his tracker.

I watch the rise and fall of KJ's chest as he sleeps. I wish I could translate that steady rhythm into some sort of emotional Morse code that would tell me everything in his heart. Our time here has been a mix of hectic and surreal: hectic as we figure out how to manage an overstuffed household, surreal as we all struggle to come to grips with this new reality. The constant upheaval has meant that KJ and I have spent zero time alone together. Does he miss me as much as I miss him? Sometimes when he looks at me, I see so much sadness in his eyes, and I worry the shadow of Shannon's death will always hang between us.

The soft creak of the wooden floorboards over my head tells me that Miguel's wife, Lisa, is already hard at work preparing breakfast for our uninvited horde. I push away my blankets, eager for a distraction from my troubled thoughts. Miguel left almost as soon as we got here, driving off into the night to get rid of the U-Haul, leaving Lisa to carry the burden of our unexpected arrival. Helping her is both the right thing to do and the perfect antidote to my uncomfortable thoughts.

I climb the stairs and push open the basement door. The cat appears from nowhere to slither between my ankles, nearly tripping me as I step into the sunny kitchen. Lisa—a short woman with gray-streaked hair pulled back into a ponytail—stands in front of a griddle flecked with pancake residue and sizzling bits of bacon. On the counter, a huge bowl of batter stands ready to feed the sleeping masses. Lisa's head is tilted toward the phone she's holding, but at the sound of the door opening, she puts it down and looks up.

"Good morning, Alex!" she says. "You're up early. Come join the kids, and I'll make you some pancakes."

She waves her hand toward the scarred wooden table in the center of the room where her two children are already eating. Jeremy, who's eight, wears pajamas printed with red fire engines that clash with the screaming orange of his hair. His sister, Rosie, is a chubby two-year-old with a head full of curls only a shade darker than the deep brown of her skin. Both of them are looking at me with identical expressions of frank curiosity.

I hover on the threshold.

"Sorry," I say. "I can go back downstairs if I'm interrupting."

"Don't be silly." Lisa's smile is friendly. "I'm glad you're here. We haven't had much of a chance to get to know each other. Take a seat. The Aclisote chart is on the table—you can go ahead and measure out your dose yourself."

Jeremy scoots his chair over to make room for me. I edge my way toward the table, feeling suddenly shy. Whenever I stumble on Lisa with her kids, I'm overwhelmed by their casual domesticity. It's not just my continuing amazement that there are adults who can manipulate time; it's also that the spinner gene is linked with infertility, and I'd never considered that people like me might adopt children and create real families.

"Is Miguel back?" I ask, suffering a fresh wave of gratitude-laced guilt over everything Miguel and Lisa have done to help us.

Lisa shoots a quick glance at her phone.

"Not yet," she says. "He had a few things to take care of. He should be back soon, though."

I sink into the chair next to Jeremy, pretending I believe that the extra cheer in her voice isn't a cover for worry. In the middle of the table is a red lacquer tray with a pitcher of orange juice, a stack of small plastic cups, an

34

eyedropper, a bottle of Aclisote, and a slim notepad that lists our dosages, each carefully calibrated by Lisa. I pick up the bottle and unscrew the lid, breathing in the familiar sickly sweet scent. It still feels strange to me to take the stuff on purpose, even though I know the doses are way, way below the lethal amounts we were getting at the Center. KJ and I are taking the minimum that'll keep the paranoia that comes with freezing at bay. The others are taking slightly more, enough to suppress their true skills so that everything they do in frozen time goes back to the way it was when the freeze ends. None of them knew that changing things in frozen time was possible until KJ and I got them out of the Center, so they don't feel the loss, although Aidan often complains that it's unfair. Lisa insisted, though—she said she couldn't manage so many kids transitioning at the same time. It's probably a wise decision. When Jack first gained full control of time, all he wanted to do was play tricks on people, which was super annoying, though admittedly sometimes funny.

Jeremy leans across the table while I'm squeezing two drops of Aclisote into a cup of juice, smiling to myself at a memory involving Jack and a bunch of disappearing bananas.

"Did you come here from a Center?" Jeremy demands.

The memory vanishes as quickly as the stolen fruit. I swirl my cup to mix the liquids.

"Yes?" The word comes out like a question. I've spent my whole life hiding the fact that I'm a spinner, and even here, in a place I know is designed to help us, announcing my association with the Center feels like a confession. The little boy doesn't seem to notice my hesitance; he just nods solemnly.

"Jeremy," Lisa calls from where she's pouring batter onto the hissing griddle, "don't pester her."

"I wasn't pestering." Jeremy stuffs a bite of pancake into his mouth. "I was meeting her."

"It's OK," I say, even though that's not completely true.

Jeremy fixes his eager stare on me again.

35

"Did you work with the police when you were at the Center?"

I swallow my juice in a two long gulps to stall answering. Rewinding crimes was the thing I liked best about my previous life, mostly because I loved working with Carson Ross. He told me we were partners, and for a while he convinced me that even when we broke the law, we were still the good guys. He was lying, though. Good guys don't pick locks, or steal evidence, or kill helpless spinners sleeping quietly in pools of frozen moonlight.

"Yeah," I tell Jeremy. "I worked with the police. We all did."

The boy's eyes go wide. "What kind of cases did you rewind? Were they really gory?"

"Jeremy," Lisa chides.

"I don't mind." I think back on the missions I've rewound, settling on a nonviolent one that is likely to appeal to an eight-year-old. "I worked on the Sikes case," I tell him. "Have you ever heard of him?"

"He's a robber." Jeremy's face glows. "A really famous one."

I lean toward him, lowering my voice like I'm sharing a big secret, which, in fact, I am.

"I know who Sikes really is," I say.

"You do?" Jeremy is breathless with excitement. "Who is he?"

I hesitate, but only for a second. I can't help feeling a tinge of malicious pleasure at blurting out this huge discovery in casual conversation. Ross would be furious.

"It turns out Sikes is just a regular guy named Matt Thompson," I tell Jeremy. "He owns a bar in Portland."

Jeremy's little body wriggles at this revelation. Even Rosie claps her hands, though she can't have a clue what the conversation is about.

"Sikes finally got arrested?" Lisa asks, deftly flipping a row of pancakes. "That's big news. I can't believe I missed it."

"He hasn't been arrested yet," I say. "And I'm pretty sure he's fled town by now, so he probably won't be anytime soon." I don't add that Sikes ran off

36

because I mistakenly thought he was a spinner, so I warned him the police were closing in. "But my former agent, Mr. Ross, should be announcing that the case is solved any day now."

And he'll be celebrated for it. My pleasure in making Jeremy happy wilts. The thought of Ross being hailed as a hero makes me want to puke.

"I'm going to be a private investigator when I grow up," Jeremy announces. "Like my dad. He says if I practice my time skills a little bit every day, then we can be partners."

My head swirls like I stood up too fast.

"You're a spinner?" I ask.

"Of course." Jeremy sounds surprised.

"Everyone in our family is a spinner," Lisa says, setting a plate heaped with steaming pancakes and crispy bacon in front of me. "When our kids' birth parents learned their infants had tested positive for chronotin, they found a way to smuggle them out of the hospital so they wouldn't have to be raised in a Children's Home. Jeremy's birth mother even visits us sometimes, doesn't she, sweetheart?"

Jeremy nods. "She brings toys."

Lisa's words bounce around my brain, and I have to struggle to pair the sounds with their meanings. Birth parents. Smuggled babies. Families. Rosie and Jeremy were born with the same genetic marker I was, but they've been raised here, in a real home, with actual parents. An emotion somewhere between jealousy and longing burns the back of my throat, and I busy myself cutting up my breakfast.

"Mommy." Rosie holds up her fingers. "Sticky."

Lisa scoops up the toddler and carries her over to the sink. I watch them through my lashes. Lisa croons to her daughter, who giggles as she splashes her tiny hands in the water. The tightness in my throat turns painful. I know this scene is normal, even mundane. I've seen ones like it on TV a thousand times, but I've never seen *real* mothers and daughters together. In my entire life, I have never spent a single minute with a family, and right now that lack feels like an abyss.

A metallic trilling sound cuts through Rosie's laughter. Lisa secures her daughter on one hip and reaches over to pick up her phone. When she sees the name on the screen, she frowns.

"Max?" she says as she walks out of the kitchen. "What's going on?"

Jeremy tugs on my sleeve. I tear my eyes away from Lisa and Rosie's retreating forms to focus on him.

"Alex?" he asks. "How long are you going to stay?"

"I don't know." I nibble a piece of bacon. "How long do your guests usually stay?"

Jeremy scrunches up his face, considering. "Most people only stay a few weeks. Dad finds them permanent places through the spinner network. Vivian, though, was here when I was born and she lived with us until I was five. And Jasper and Tyrone just moved out last month." Jeremy runs a finger over his plate, coating it in syrup. "I heard Mom talking to Dad last night on the phone. I think they're going to ask you and KJ to be our new foster siblings."

The center of my chest feels like someone hollowed it out with a spoon. For a split second, it's like I'm in a rewind, except instead of looking into the past, I am seeing a vision of the future. My misty shape drifts around the room, claiming each domestic item as her own: the countertop dotted with splotches of batter, the windowsill's collection of pine cones and plastic army men, the pantry door with its haphazard assortment of butterfly decals that looks like a preschool art project run amok. In my fantasy, I feel the warm weight of little Rosie snuggling in my lap as I read her a book and catch the scent of cookies baking in the oven. Chocolate chip, my favorite, which Lisa is baking just for me.

The cavity in my chest expands so much I fear my ribs won't be able to contain it. I force my attention down to the solid reality of my plate and concentrate on keeping the fork in my hand from shaking. Hope is a dangerous emotion for someone like me.

"Do you like having foster siblings?" I ask, making dead sure my voice sounds neutral.

"Sure." Jeremy licks the syrup off his finger. "Tyrone's my favorite. He taught me how to do *this*." The boy sits very still for a second, and then his body shifts ever so slightly at the same moment my plate of food abruptly jumps to the other side of the table. I blink from the transported plate to Jeremy's beaming face. He must have frozen time, moved the plate, and then returned to virtually the same position.

"That was good, wasn't it?" Jeremy crows. "You didn't even see me move."

"Very good," I agree, reaching over to reclaim my breakfast. The trick, while clever, is not what surprises me. It's his obvious pride in his abilities. My relationship with freezing is so much more complicated. Most Norms flinch when they find out what I can do, and my skills have always felt tainted by their disgust.

"That's really impressive," I tell Jeremy. "I couldn't control time nearly that well when I was your age."

"It's 'cause you were taking too much Aclisote. We only take a little bit. Tyrone told me no one in the Centers even knows that they can change things in frozen time."

Jeremy states this as if the lie I accepted as fact until just a couple of weeks ago is obviously absurd. I chew on another piece of pancake.

"Where is Tyrone now?" I ask.

"College," Jeremy says.

The fork in my hand tips, sending the pancake speared on its tip back onto my plate with a syrupy splat. Just going to a real *high school* is something I've dreamed about in the hopeless way Norm girls dream they might somehow meet their favorite movie star or win a national singing competition. I've even fantasized about getting snubbed by the popular clique, missing out on prom,

39

getting cut from a drama production. Every slight that Norms cry about in movies and books seems like a blessed touchpoint of a shared reality I will never taste.

"Spinners can go to college?" I ask.

Behind me, the door to the basement bangs open. I spin around in my chair, time at my fingertips, to find KJ on the doorstep, panting slightly and looking so disheveled he must have raced up here as soon as he woke up.

"There you are," he says. "I was afraid . . ." His words trail off as he takes in the tranquil scene. "Never mind."

Lisa comes back into the kitchen. The welcoming cheer is gone from her face, and she's got her phone clutched against her chest like she's using it to keep something inside her from exploding. KJ and I exchange worried glances. Without a word, I get up from my chair and cross the room to stand beside him.

"It's time to get dressed," Lisa tells her son. She sets Rosie on the ground. "Can you take your sister? The two of you can watch a video in your room for a while."

"But, Mom . . ." Jeremy whines.

"Now!" she snaps. Rosie whimpers. Jeremy slides off his chair and takes his sister's hand, leading her out of the room with a confused backward glance at his mother.

"Should we go, too?" KJ asks.

Lisa startles like she has only just noticed he's there.

"No," she says after a moment. "Sit down. You two need to hear this."

KJ and I sit side by side. I realize I'm still clutching my fork, and I set it down on top of my half-eaten breakfast.

"Is everything all right?" I ask.

Lisa squeezes her eyes shut, then opens them again.

"That was Max on the phone."

"Who?" KJ asks.

"Max. She's an operative with the CIA. She passes on information about

40

Kronos whenever she hears something that might threaten us."

The shock on KJ's face mirrors my own.

"The *CIA* helps *spinners?*" he asks.

"Max does," Lisa says. "The CIA in general is only interested in Kronos."

"And you trust her?" KJ asks. "Is Max a spinner?"

"She's a Norm, but yes, I trust her. Max has proven herself our ally a hundred times over."

This conversation feels like a digression. I tap the table to refocus their attention.

"What did Max say?"

Lisa's eyes dart to the window. "She said that Kronos has the refuge under surveillance."

The pancakes sink like clumps of lead into the pit of my stomach.

"Do they know we're here?" I ask.

"Not yet."

I stand up. My legs are shaking, and I brace myself on the back of the chair. "This is because of us, isn't it?"

Lisa shakes her head. "It's more complicated than that." She looks from me to KJ. Whatever she sees on our faces must convince her we can handle the full story, because she puts the phone down on the table and drops into a chair. "What do you know about the Society for Spinner Rights?"

"I used to think they were just advocates for better living conditions at the Center," I say. "But Miguel told us that some members do more than that, and that he works with them."

"Right," Lisa says. "The Society has a lot of eyes and ears out there, and they pass on information when they hear about wild spinners—people like you who've escaped from a Center, or spinners who somehow never got identified in the first place. Miguel is what they call a trawler. He's the guy who goes out and finds the spinners and, if they want help, brings them somewhere safe.

41

When Max called, she said . . ." Lisa's mouth trembles, and she fumbles in her pocket for a tissue. "She said that Kronos managed to infiltrate the Society. Last night, the names of all the trawlers were leaked to the wipers."

The word *wipers* hangs in the kitchen like a rotten stench.

"Do the wipers know Miguel is a spinner?" KJ asks.

Lisa shakes her head. "I doubt it. Virtually all the Society members are Norms. Kronos probably assumes that Miguel is just a sympathizer."

"A sympathizer who helped twenty-two spinners escape," I say. "If someone at the Society gave Kronos the trawlers' names, they must have also told them what they were doing. They're going to know Miguel contacted KJ and me."

"Kronos doesn't know you're here," Lisa repeats. "If they did, the wipers would be doing more than surveilling us."

"Sure, because they think we're with Miguel. Which means he can't come home."

I know I'm right. Lisa's not meeting my eyes; instead, she's staring past my shoulder and out the window over the kitchen sink. I follow her gaze. There's a tree growing out there. I can see its leaves fluttering slightly, brushed by a passing breeze. Someone has hung bits of paper from some of the branches. I picture her out there with Rosie, the two of them decorating the tree together, enjoying the simple—and to me, unimaginable—pleasure of a quiet family life.

"We should go." I stand up. "We're putting you all in danger."

"Go where?" Lisa clasps her hands in front of her. "No. Goat Hill Farm is a spinner refuge. It's what we do. Kronos would be looking for Miguel even if you hadn't escaped."

Her words lack conviction. I remember Miguel's anger at the rest stop. *An escape of that magnitude can't be covered up,* he'd said. *They'll be looking for you.* I also think about the basement where we've been sleeping. There's a pantry down there with a large supply of food. The stockpile would keep Lisa and her kids fed for months, but this many of us will blow through it in a week.

There's no way she can buy the quantities we'll need without raising suspicion. And that's assuming they can even afford to.

"What if the wipers don't leave?" I ask. "Miguel will have to keep laying low. How will the refuge support itself?"

"We'll manage," Lisa says. "It will be harder now that Austin's gone, but . . ." She catches herself, obviously regretting the admission of doubt. "We'll be fine."

A whisper starts in the back of my head, soft and insidious, like the hissing of a snake. I desperately want to ignore it. I don't.

"By Austin, do you mean Austin Shea?"

Lisa gives me a startled look. "Did you know him?"

I open my mouth but find no words. Austin Shea was the spinner who stopped time so Sikes could steal things. No one knows that, though. No one except KJ, Carson Ross, and me.

"What does Austin Shea have to do with the refuge?" KJ asks.

"He was one of our main benefactors," Lisa says.

KJ gulps. The whisper in my head grows to a roar. It's nothing like a snake now; this is a dragon, powerful and deadly. The sunny kitchen fades, replaced by silvery night and a gaping wound staring up at me from a frozen man's neck.

Lisa's eyes narrow. "Did you work on his case?"

"No." I can't breathe.

"But you knew him?"

"Sort of." The room is contracting around me. "I killed him."

Lisa's face pales.

"You what?"

I grip the back of the chair in front of me. My legs are shaking so badly I can hardly stand.

"Alex, you didn't kill him," KJ says. He turns to Lisa. "Carson Ross killed him. Alex had no idea what he was planning when she agreed to help."

43

"Austin died in frozen time?" Tears glisten in Lisa's eyes.

I wobble over to the sink and press my hands against its cool surface.

"Carson Ross figured out that spinners can change things in frozen time," KJ says. "He wanted Alex to work for him, so he took her off Aclisote and tried to convince her that using her skills to get things—information, access, revenge—was OK if it was for the greater good. Alex saw through him, though. It's the reason we ran away when we did."

KJ's explanation barely penetrates my brain. His words are just static that can't compete with the horrifying thoughts bouncing around in my head. I didn't just kill a spinner; I killed a man who supported one of the few places that keeps us safe. I might as well be working for the wipers.

"It's not just the murder," I say. "Miguel can't come home because we're here. The wipers are watching this place, and eventually they're going to see something. I've put all of you in danger."

"We'll warn the other kids," KJ says. "Tell them they can't leave the house."

"That's not going to be enough."

My voice cracks. I fix my gaze out the window to keep the tears burning my eyes from leaking out. Now that I'm closer, I can see that the bits of paper on the tree are little snowflakes, each one as unique and delicate as their natural inspiration.

"Sweetheart." Lisa comes over and puts her arm around my shoulder. "None of these things are your fault."

I shrug her hand off. Lisa's words are nice, but the reality is much clearer than her kindness.

"I have to fix this," I say.

"Alex." KJ sounds tired. "You can't fix everything. Haven't you been paying attention? The Central Office, Kronos—this thing is bigger than us."

The paper snowflakes twist in the breeze. How little it would take to tear them off. One strong gust, and each fragile piece would be destroyed.

44

I turn my back to the window.

"What if I can lure the wipers away from the refuge? As long as they think Miguel has something to do with our escape, they're going to be watching this place, but if I give them another lead, make them think the spinners are somewhere else, maybe they'll go away."

"How could you possibly do that?" Lisa shakes her head. "KJ is right. This thing is bigger than you. Free spinners have been fighting this fight a long time. We'll work this out, too."

Sun streams through the window behind me. The kitchen smells like sugar and bacon. I picture the living room and the soft armchair with the patchwork pillows where I spent an hour yesterday, curled up reading a book. Was Jeremy right when he said Lisa and Miguel were planning to invite me to stay? Something deep in my chest splits open with a terrible yearning. I let the longing fill me for just a second, and then I push the hole closed again and straighten my shoulders.

"I'm going back to Portland."

KJ inhales sharply.

"No," Lisa says.

"Think about it." I lace my fingers together to keep the tremors running through them from betraying me. "The wipers must know I was the one who got everyone out of the Center. If I go back to the City and talk to one of them, they'll think we never left. Then they won't be after Miguel. He can come home, and you can move all the spinners to new homes just like you planned."

"That's a crazy idea," Lisa says. "How will you talk to a wiper and not get caught?"

"I'll figure something out."

Lisa shakes her head again, this time so vehemently a strand of hair slips loose from her ponytail. "You're a child. You can't do this alone."

KJ stands up and walks to my side. "She won't be alone," he says. "I'll go with her."

Tears blur my eyes.

"You don't have to," I say. "This only takes one of us."

"Of course I'm going with you." His voice is soft but steady. "I promised, remember? Whatever comes next, we'll face it together."

KJ's shoulder brushes mine, and I blink my tears away. A nobler person might fight harder against his offer, but I am much too grateful—and afraid—to be that noble.

"You're both being ridiculous," Lisa says. "I'll put the word out on the network. We'll find another way to handle this."

"Don't you see?" I tell her. "There is no other way. The wipers will only leave the refuge alone if they believe my friends and I are still in Portland."

"But it's too dangerous," Lisa says. "The fact that you kids avoided the wipers for a week is a miracle. What are the chances you'll be able to do that again?"

I lock eyes with her. "What are the chances any of us will survive if I don't?"

Lisa hesitates, which is the only answer I need.

04 ◄◄

THE DRIVEWAY LEADING OUT OF THE REFUGE IS BUMPIER THAN I remember, or maybe it's that this trailer is bouncier than the U-Haul. The tires seem to snag on another pothole with every rotation, making the trailer's ten nonhuman occupants bleat and stamp their sharp little hooves, sometimes on my feet.

It was Lisa's idea for us to leave the refuge hidden in the back of a goat delivery truck. In fact, once she finally agreed that my misdirection strategy had merit, she designed our entire exit plan. Goat Hill Farm really does have goats, which Lisa rents out to people around the state as natural weed control. This delivery was set up a month ago, so even if the wipers are monitoring the farm really closely, having a truck drive away from the refuge won't raise any red flags. They're more worried about someone sneaking into the refuge anyway. The driver—who has no idea we're in here, since KJ and I climbed inside during frozen time—is scheduled to arrive in Portland around eleven a.m., spend a few hours settling the animals, then check on a different herd on the other side of town before bringing the empty trailer back to the refuge. Lisa says that as long as we're at the head of the Springwater Trail no later than four forty-five, we'll be able to catch a ride back. If anything goes wrong, we're supposed to call her, and she'll put us in contact with Miguel, who is hiding out with a spinner friend in a Portland safe house.

The truck slows as we near the end of the driveway. I peer around the goats, trying to catch a glimpse of the outside world through the round air holes in the trailer's sides. Since we heard about the surveillance yesterday morning, Lisa has left the premises twice—once on the pretext of picking up some goat feed, and another time to take her kids to the library. Both times, she's pretty sure she was followed, and she also said she saw a car parked not far from the refuge's front gate. I hold my breath, listening for a voice demanding that the driver stop. It doesn't come. The truck accelerates, and we rumble our way down the road.

"Think we're clear?" I ask KJ. Like me, he's craning his neck to see outside the trailer, probably with as little success. We're wedged too deep in the middle of the shifting animals to see more than streaks of light.

"I think so," KJ says after a few more minutes pass without incident.

I wriggle my back to keep the truck's hard side from digging into my spine. Successfully sneaking out of the refuge brings relief, but I can't say it makes me happy. I close my eyes and let images from our first few days there play on the insides of my lids: sprawling in a field with Yuki, idly arguing about which Disney film is the worst; listening to Kimmi and Emma shriek as they ran through a sprinkler that was supposed to be watering Lisa's vegetable garden; picking blackberries with KJ and Aidan; Yolly teaching me how turn the berries into pies.

The truck hits another bump. I bang my head, and my eyes pop open, the happy memories slipping from my mind as gently as a sigh. Were those sweet days of previously unimagined freedom heralds of our future? Or were they merely glimpses of an alternate reality we will only briefly get to visit?

A curly-haired goat with short horns wedges itself between KJ and me, then kneels down to rest its head on KJ's lap. KJ scratches the white patch on the goat's chest. The creature wags its tail.

"Shannon would have liked hanging out with the goats," KJ says. "She always wanted a pet."

Even with wind roaring around us, the back of the truck seems to grow quiet. I glance over at KJ. His eyes are extra bright, and the smile tugging at the

48

corner of his mouth is wobbly. A tangle of emotions twists inside my heart: sadness, jealousy, guilt.

"Do you miss her?" I ask.

"Of course I do." KJ sounds surprised. "Don't you?"

"I . . ." Jealousy flashes to the surface first, but the emotion is swallowed almost immediately by twin flushes of guilt and shame. Guilt at the part I played in Shannon's ill-fated return to the Center, shame that I am selfish enough to resent KJ's grief over a person we both grew up with. I drop my eyes back down to the goat.

"Yeah," I say. "I miss her."

Sadness overwhelms my less admirable emotions. During the last few weeks of her life, my relationship with Shannon was tense, but it wasn't always like that. Shannon and I were roommates at the Center, and while we weren't exactly bosom buddies, you can't live with someone for five years and not share a bond. Shannon put aside books she thought I'd like from the donation boxes that arrived sporadically, snuck toast out of the cafeteria for me if I overslept, and stuck up for me when Jack or Aidan teased me about my love of police work. I sat through countless hours of listening to her predict contradictory futures for me the year she learned to read tarot cards and stroked her back when she cried over yet another broken heart. Last winter, when Raul taught us all how to play gin rummy, Shannon and I kept a tournament going for months, sitting on her bed after lights-out, playing by the yellowish glow of the streetlamp that shone through the window of our dorm.

"The Youngers would be a lot happier about being stuck in that basement if she were here," I say. "She was always so patient with them."

KJ nods. "I worry about the Youngers. Especially the girls. To Emma and Molly and even Kimmi, Shannon was like a favorite big sister. With everything that's been going on, I'm not sure they've really absorbed the fact that she's gone yet."

Has KJ? I study his profile as he stares moodily over the packed-in

49

animals. I know KJ loves me, but he cared for Shannon, too, and the combined weight of sorrow and guilt makes his shoulders slump.

"Shannon would want us to go back to Portland," I say, swallowing down the lump in my throat. "She'd tell me I was crazy at first, but eventually she'd come around. Shannon loved those kids, and she'd support any plan that kept them safe."

"Yeah." KJ keeps his gaze locked on the blurry landscape outside. "You're probably right."

I rub a hand through the sleeping goat's rough hair, pushing away my sadness and trying to focus on the day ahead. Shannon used to say that you should visualize your goals if you want to reach them. I hope she was right, because I've visualized our plan so many times it's etched into my mind like a scar. KJ and I will get to Portland around noon. Once there, we'll go to a Rite Aid we found online that's near the goat drop-off site and buy a prepaid cell phone. Then I'll call the Center's former director, Dr. Barnard, and set up a meeting, claiming that our situation has gotten out of hand and that I'm willing to give him the location of the other spinners in exchange for a promise that KJ and I will be allowed to remain free. When I meet with Barnard, I'll convince him the other spinners are nearby, then pretend to have second thoughts, freeze time, and run away.

Neither Lisa nor KJ was happy about the idea of me coming face-to-face with Barnard.

"It's better than meeting with a wiper," I argued.

"He'll bring a chromoelectronegator," KJ said.

"So? It's not like I have to talk to him in frozen time."

"Why not just approach a random cop?" Lisa asked. "Wipers work really closely with the police; they'll be scanning every report, looking for a sign of you."

"Sure, the wipers would find out eventually. But the cops I know aren't always great about turning in timely paperwork, and we need the wipers to

50

leave the refuge *today*."

Lisa sighed in resignation when a loud crash from under our feet underscored the urgency of my argument. The other kids had been confined to the basement and the barn for twelve hours by then, and to put it mildly, confinement wasn't going well.

The goat lying between KJ and me resettles itself, shifting its bulk so it's mostly resting on my thigh. I frown at it. Our plan does have one flaw I didn't mention to the others: if we convince the wipers that the escaped spinners are in Portland, it puts Jack, who really is in the city, at higher risk of getting caught. KJ would say it's Jack's own fault, since he's the one who chose to betray us for Ross, but I still wish there were some way I could warn him. Jack is impetuous and selfish, but he's also funny, brave, and often generous. I know he made a terrible choice, but he made it for the same reason I've made a lot of questionable decisions lately: he wants to live.

I sigh. My internal debate is pointless since I have no way to contact Jack. And except for that one potential consequence, our plan is a solid one, with very few places where things might go wrong. I jiggle my leg in an effort to dislodge the resting goat, trying not to dwell on the fact that every plan I've made since we first left the Center, however solid it seemed at the time, has somehow gone sideways. The beast stares at me with its weird rectangular pupils and refuses to budge.

"Alex," KJ says, breaking a silence that has carried us off the country roads and onto a much smoother highway, "how much do you think about the future?"

I give up on the goat and consider KJ's question. Conversation is a much better way to pass the time than wondering how many "very few" is and picturing all the different meanings of "go wrong."

"Not much, I guess. I think I'm still focused on just surviving every day."

"I've been thinking about the future a lot." KJ pushes aside a goat that wants to nibble on his sweatshirt. "Did you know that Houdini was a spinner? Or that spinner doctors save people's lives every day?"

"Nope."

"Lisa told me. She said there are more than a hundred free spinners in the US alone, and most of them live regular lives, completely undetected by the Norms. There are spinner social workers and lawyers, actors and schoolteachers. Some of them never use their skills, and others use them all the time."

KJ waves his hands while he talks, something he always does when he gets worked up. My own imagination must be stunted. Rather than the open vistas of possible futures, all *I* can visualize are the immediate steps of this one day, as if our plan is a mountain and I can't see past the long hike that's required to reach the top.

"Are you thinking about careers?" I ask, making an effort to match his enthusiasm. "Jeremy told me about a spinner who went to college."

"I'm not thinking about me, I'm thinking about them—all those free spinners out there in the world, living regular lives. It makes the stakes of what we're doing seem so much higher." I frown, and KJ's hands stop their animated waving. "I don't know. Maybe I'm not making any sense."

Beams of light flicker through the cloistered truck. A combination of drifting goat funk, dust, and crushed hay make the rays look thick and murky.

"I think I know what you mean," I say. "It's like, if I get caught by the wipers, I'm just a girl facing the early death I always expected, but if Miguel gets caught, it's a much bigger deal. He's got kids and a wife and a whole community. He matters. He *exists* in a way I don't."

KJ frowns at me.

"That's not what I meant at all," he says. "Of course you exist. And you matter to *me*. I'd care if you died. A lot."

I drop my gaze. In the cloudy light, my arms look ghostly.

"I'm not saying I want to die. I'm just saying it's different."

52

The pause that follows feels strained. I pick a piece of hay out of the hair of the goat in my lap. I thought I was agreeing with KJ, but instead I've made him mad, and I'm not sure why.

"Do you ever think about us?" KJ asks. "You know, you and me, as a couple?"

I sink my fingers into the goat's hair. The truck has picked up speed now that we're on a highway, and the wind whistling through the gaps is cold.

"What *about* us?" I ask.

"I feel like so far, we've only ever really thought about us in the short term. Which makes sense, since for most of our life that's all the time we thought we had. But if it's true that we might have decades ahead of us instead of months, that changes things."

The goat's hair is short and not particularly warm.

"Are you saying you want to take a break?" I struggle to keep my voice steady. "I know you blame yourself for Shannon running off. If you need some time to sort that out and you want to be just friends for a while—"

"No!"

KJ turns his body so that he's facing me, then waits until I raise my head.

"I'm sorry if I've seemed distant recently," he says, "but I promise it has nothing to do with Shannon."

Our gazes lock, and my heart turns over in my chest. KJ's eyes are shadowed, and his cheeks are still hollow from his recent illness, but he is staring at me with an intensity that makes his whole face glow.

"I love you," he says. "You are the most important thing in the world to me. The possibility that we could share an actual future makes me unbelievably happy."

My doubts dissolve into the wind that's gusting through the truck. The world fades—the funky goat smell, the thundering traffic, the flickering, dust-dimmed light—everything except KJ, who grows larger in their absence, until the whole world is just him and me, bound together in this private shelter.

53

"I love you, too," I tell him.

He gives me a smile so sweet I feel like I'm melting. I trace the ridge of his nose, relishing the softness of his tawny skin. KJ's lips part under my touch, and I lean toward him.

KJ raises a finger and lays it against my mouth.

"The problem," he says, "is that thinking we might have a future also terrifies me, because it means I have so much more to lose."

I kiss the finger touching my lips.

"It means there's more to fight for."

"Fight." KJ repeats the word in a way that makes it sound like I've just confirmed his worst fear. He sits back, away from me, and crosses his arms over his chest.

"What do *you* picture when you think about the future, Alex?"

"I . . ." I struggle to conjure an image, but all that pops into my head is that allegorical mountain with a rough-hewn trail winding up into an empty sky. "I don't know."

"That's what scares me. I think there's a part of you that doesn't believe you're going survive very long, and it's making you reckless."

Fear invades the murky air. Fear about the risks of today's plan. Fear that I've hurt KJ. Fear that he's right.

"I thought you agreed we have to do this," I say. "The wipers need to think we're in Portland if we want them to leave Miguel alone. This is our best option."

KJ lets out a long, rattling sigh. "I do agree with you. I just worry."

"We have a plan." I rest a tentative hand on his leg. "It's not even that dangerous. One quick meeting, and we're done."

"Do you promise?" KJ unfolds his arms and captures my hand between his own. "Promise that after you talk to Barnard, we'll stop fighting? We'll go back to the refuge and let the free spinners handle things from now on?"

The truck downshifts in a way that makes the engine whine. How can

I promise that when we have no idea what will happen next? Miguel and Lisa have been wonderful, but we don't really know them. If things get worse, why would they choose to protect twenty random spinners over their own family? And what about Yolly? We've already put her in a terrible position. When will she decide she's given enough and move on?

The hand KJ is holding is starting to ache from the strength of his grip. I look at him, taking in his shorn hair and strained face. His sneakers are worn from running after me and my endless plans. KJ is the one person in the world whom I trust absolutely. If he thinks we can count on the free spinners, if he thinks the future is going to work out, there has to be a chance that he's right, doesn't there?

"Alex?" KJ prompts.

"I promise," I say.

KJ's smile is so radiant that it almost erases my doubts.

"When we're back at the refuge," he says, "what do you say we try this whole boyfriend/girlfriend thing again? Do it right. We can even take things slowly."

My answering smile is shaky.

"You mean like a normal couple?" I say. "One that isn't running for their lives?"

KJ stretches over the lolling goat until his face is inches from mine.

"How about, when this is all over, I ask you out on a date?"

His breath smells sweet, and my love for him fills my veins like warm honey. I put my arms around his neck, wishing I could sink into him and wrap myself in his goodness and his faith.

"I'd like that," I say.

KJ's lips meet mine, and I melt into the kiss. Or almost melt. As blissful as it is to kiss this beautiful boy, there's a part deep inside of me that stays locked up tight. It whispers in my head, a persistent gnat warning me that this future KJ is planning—the one that involves us being a normal couple on a date—is

55

not going to happen *when* this is all over. It's going to happen *if.*

05 ◀◀

TWO HOURS LATER, WE'RE STANDING ON A TENNIS COURT AT Irving Park, a place full of wide-open fields that we decided were perfect for meetings where you don't want anyone to sneak up behind you. We've arrived before making contact with Barnard so he won't be able to set a trap for us—a strategy that didn't take weather into account. Portland has welcomed us back with its trademark fall rain, and the tennis court smells like wet pavement and is soggy with puddles.

I heft my daypack higher on my shoulders, peering through the drizzle to make sure we're alone. The daypack feels heavy even though there's not much in it: a just-in-case change of clothes, a small bottle of Aclisote, and some cash. Lisa gave us fifty dollars before we left. I wanted to refuse it, but couldn't think of an excuse to do so that didn't involve confessing that not only am I a murderer, I also stole thousands of dollars, a few hundred of which are still in a side pocket of the daypack. I feel bad about keeping it, but tossing it out seems stupidly wasteful. Money always comes in handy.

KJ takes out the phone we bought. It's a silvery-pink color, the case smooth and unscratched.

"You want me to make the call?" KJ asks.

"I got it."

KJ hands me the phone, then pulls a crumpled piece of paper from his pocket and reads off Barnard's personal cell phone number, helpfully provided by Lisa's CIA friend, Max. I dial before I have time to think too much about what I'm doing.

"Barnard here."

The sound of his voice triggers a surge of hatred so strong it momentarily chokes me. The last time I talked to the Center Director, he was explaining to me, coldly and logically, how he was planning to kill me. To hear him now, speaking with his familiar inflection of distracted self-importance, makes me want to reach through the phone and scratch his eyes out.

I swallow my anger and force myself to focus on the plan.

"Dr. Barnard? This is Alex."

"Alexandra?" A scrabbling sound makes me suspect he dropped the phone. "How did you—"

"I'm calling to make a deal." I let my words tumble over each other, using my hatred to color them with frantic urgency. Barnard is well aware of the heightened fear and paranoia caused by too much freezing, and he is more likely to buy my rather thin story if he assumes I'm going crazy. "The other spinners, they're getting out of control. None of them will do what I say, and I think the wipers are getting close. I see them *everywhere.*" I manufacture a small sob. "We aren't going to make it. There are too many of us to stay hidden."

"Where are you?" Barnard asks.

"Here."

"You're in Portland?" Barnard's voice rises with surprise. "I thought you left in a U-Haul."

"We tried! Do you know how hard it is to move twenty people when you're being watched?"

KJ, who has been rocking nervously on his heels, slides my hood away from my ear and leans his head against mine. I turn the phone in his direction so we can both listen.

"Why are you calling me?" Barnard asks.

"I want . . . I want KJ and me to be safe."

Silence. I picture Barnard frowning behind his wire-rimmed glasses.

58

He, too, must be remembering our last meeting and my loudly voiced distrust of him and the Center. I launch into my prepared speech, hoping the rush of words will erase any suspicion.

"I know you think I'm too dangerous to walk free, but the other kids, their skills haven't evolved. I've been giving them Aclisote—not a lot, just enough so that the things they change in frozen time don't stick. So if they go back, you won't have to kill them, right? I mean, they'd at least get to live as long as they usually would?"

Even though I don't mean any of the words leaving my mouth, it's hard not to feel like a traitor saying them. I'm counting on Barnard's belief in spinners' natural deceitfulness to make me sound convincing.

Based on his response, either I'm a better actress than I think or my faith in his prejudice is well placed. "Of course the other spinners will be fine if they come back," he says. "You know, a lot has changed since you left. Even you would be offered other options."

Options? I want to snap. *What, I'd get to choose whether I died from an Aclisote overdose or as a lab rat in one of your experiments?* KJ, probably sensing my barely controlled rage, rests his hand on my back.

"No," I tell Barnard, letting the slight pressure of KJ's hand steady me and keep me on script. "Not me. But the others . . ." I take a theatrically deep breath. "If you get the wipers to stop chasing KJ and me, I'll tell you where the other spinners are hiding."

"I can do that," Barnard says, too quickly for it to be anything but a lie. Now that I know Kronos is pulling the strings, I doubt Barnard has the power to make that decision even if he wanted to.

"Where are they?" Barnard asks.

KJ gives me a silent thumbs-up.

"I'm not telling you over the phone," I say to Barnard. "You come here, and I'll take you to their hiding place."

"Come where?"

"Irving Park. Meet me in the middle of the baseball field in half an hour."

"Half an hour?" He makes a *tsk* noise with his tongue. "That's impossible. I have a very important event scheduled this afternoon."

I make a what-the-heck face at KJ, who shrugs.

"What's more important than collecting the twenty spinners you lost?" I ask Barnard.

Someone in the background says something before he can answer. Barnard puts a hand over the receiver, so the only words I catch from his muffled answer are *almost ready.*

"Look," Barnard says into the phone. "There is no way I can be there this afternoon. What if I send someone else?"

KJ shakes his head so vehemently our foreheads crack together. *Wiper,* he mouths. I nod.

"I'm not talking to a stranger," I say.

"I'll send someone you know."

I hear rustling noises, followed by the click of a door shutting. Whatever this "event" is, it must be starting soon.

"Who?" I ask.

"How about the chief of police?" Barnard says. "Obviously, he cares about the spinners."

"The chief of *police?*"

It's our turn to hesitate. KJ raises a questioning eyebrow at me. Through the phone, I catch the distinctive ding of an elevator.

"Yes or no, Alexandra," Barnard snaps. "If that won't work, we'll have to do this tomorrow."

"OK, yes," I say. Waiting another day is not an option. "We'll be there."

Barnard hangs up. KJ and I stare at each other.

"What kind of event could Barnard be going to that matters more than getting all the spinners back?" KJ asks.

I shake my head. "And since when does the chief *obviously* care about spinners? The one time I met Chief Graham, he barely managed to look me in the eye."

"Maybe the chief is the only other person who knows all the spinners escaped."

I rub the rain-splattered phone against the damp cotton of my sweatshirt.

"Do you think he'll really show up?" I ask.

KJ shrugs. "Does it matter? Making the offer could be enough for him to believe you're in town."

"Unless Chief Graham does come and I'm not here." The phone isn't getting any drier; all my wiping has only turned the screen blurry. "Barnard already sounded suspicious when I claimed we hadn't left the city."

"You're probably right." KJ sighs. "Let's go scout the park."

Irving Park is big—three or four city blocks long on each side, with lots of tall trees. Besides the tennis and baseball areas, there's a basketball court, a dog park, and a playground carpeted with wood chips. Thanks to the rain, the place is mostly deserted.

KJ and I search the entire area before choosing a spot to hide out while we wait. The only other people are at the dog park, where a wiener dog and a lab are playing tug-of-war with a moss-covered stick. The dogs' owners are both men wearing jeans and fleece jackets. One of them is tapping on a cell phone while the other watches the romping dogs with a fond expression. KJ and I edge around them and head down a short, steep hill on the east side of the park. Here there are no trees, only a big field, the grass marked with lines that allow it to be used for baseball, softball, or soccer.

"This should be safe," I say, even though nothing about this plan feels very safe. "We can hide over there while we wait for Chief to show up."

I gesture to a line of bushes that separates the field from the houses on the other side. The two of us stroll across the open space with self-conscious

61

casualness. The walk, though short, seems like it takes an eternity. Every drop of rain feels like the prick of someone's watching eyes, every rustling branch the approaching feet of a garrison of wipers. It's a relief to turn around when we reach the bushes. The field behind us remains empty, as is the street running along the far side. KJ and I unsling our packs and shove them and ourselves into the bushes, taking shelter behind their concealing leaves.

Then we wait. And wait. And wait some more. Time seems to be snagged because it moves forward at a snail's pace. Other than one of the dog park guys strolling by, his wiener dog trailing after him on a leash, we see no one. Water drips onto my jeans from the shrubs. I shuffle backward in hopes of finding a dryer spot, only to wedge myself into an even soggier bush behind me.

A police car rolls down the street, moving at the slow crawl of a driver searching their surroundings. I hunker down low enough that my leg cramps.

"Look." I point. KJ leans forward. The two of us are squashed so close together I can smell the eucalyptus scent of the refuge's shampoo in his hair. Yuki claims eucalyptus is relaxing. It's not working.

The car pulls over to the curb.

"Let me go with you to talk to him," KJ says.

"No," I say. "We already decided I'd talk and you'd be lookout."

A man in a blue uniform steps out of the car and strides onto the field. The cramp in my leg gives an aggressive spasm that lands my butt on the damp earth. I've only seen Chief Graham a few times, mostly on TV, and I'm not sure I'd recognize him from this far away, but I know the person rapidly closing the distance between us.

"That's Ross," I gasp.

"What?" KJ squints at the blue-clad figure. "Are you sure?"

I nod. Of course I'm sure. This is the man who inhabits my nightmares. I know his confident swagger. I know the way he uses charm like a weapon. I know how his thoughts twist through his calculating brain.

"We need to leave," KJ says. "If that's Ross, then he could have brought

Jack."

Jack! I crawl to the edge of our hiding spot and peer out. KJ lays his hand on the bare skin at the back of my neck. Time stops.

"We can call Barnard again," he says into the abrupt stillness. "Tell him we don't trust Ross, so the deal's off. The fact that we know who he sent will be enough to prove we were here."

Through the bushes, I can see Ross, caught mid-stride on his way across the field. His head is tilted toward his watch, and there's a frown etched on his face. He looks bored and impatient, not like someone about to spring a trap. Then again, Ross is a very accomplished liar. I scan the rest of the field, searching without success for any sign of Jack. The idea that we could be the victims of a spinner's time skills is wildly unsettling.

"Why do you think Mr. Ross came instead of the chief?" I ask.

"I don't know." KJ stands up. "Does it matter? Chief probably had something more important to do than track down missing spinners."

I chew on a fingernail, ignoring the hand KJ holds out to pull me up.

"Ross got here awfully fast," I say. "Do you really think he would have had time to pick up Jack up from wherever he hides him?"

"Do you really want to find out?"

Misty rain fills the air outside of our shelter, the static drops hanging like a million shimmering beads. What if Jack *is* here? Would he actually hunt us down? When he threatened us that last night at the Center, Ross was standing beside him, and Jack had no choice but to cooperate. I think of him as he was when we first escaped the Center: thrilled by his new time skills, bright-eyed with enthusiasm to learn guitar, laughing as he flirted with a pretty girl. Jack likes to tease, but he isn't cruel. He's a trickster, not a killer.

I spit out a shard of fingernail.

"Let's look for him."

"Look for Jack?" KJ narrows his eyes. "That's actually a good idea."

I'm so startled by his reaction, I hit my head on a branch when I stand

63

up. "It is?"

"Yeah." KJ turns toward the empty field. "If we find Jack, we can bring him into a freeze and tell *him* our story about the other spinners being nearby. It's safer than talking to Ross, and he's sure to pass on the information."

I wipe my wet hands on my equally wet jeans. The plan I have in mind involves offering to help Jack get away from Ross, but there's no point in bringing that up if we can't even find him.

"I'll search the park," I tell him. "You look out on the street. Yell if you find him. Otherwise we'll meet back here."

The park looks like it did when we first got here: empty and wet. I check the other bushes around our hiding place, the covered spots in the playground, and the concrete public restroom, which is locked for the season. Up at the dog park, the men in fleece have been replaced by a thickset woman with dark braids and a pale-skinned man in a bright yellow rain slicker. There's a lab near them who's been frozen mid-prance, tongue lolling, its eyes glued to a tennis ball the man holds between his palms. The woman appears to be laughing.

I'm heading down the hill toward Ross so I can search his pockets to see if he brought a leash, when I feel tendrils of fear drifting through the air like a noxious fog. My foot skids on the rain-soaked grass, my arms windmilling to keep me upright. I know this feeling, and it's not natural. Ross is carrying a zapper.

I crab walk sideways until I'm out of range. Zappers are what I call chromoelectronegators, the wiper tool that will break a freeze if a spinner comes within ten feet of it. I can't sense it as strongly as I can when I'm the one holding a freeze, but the terror pouring out of it is still palpable. I press a hand to my chest and breathe deeply to still my hammering heart. I should have expected Ross would bring one. That man knows better than anyone the dangers of meeting with a spinner who has fully developed skills.

I jog back to our hiding place and wait impatiently for KJ.

"Any sign of Jack?" I ask when he finally turns up.

"No, but that doesn't mean he's not around."

I'm disappointed but not surprised.

"Ross has a zapper," I say.

KJ reaches into the bushes and starts digging around for the day packs. "All the more reason to leave."

"Wait." I put hand on his arm. "I know how we can stay safe from Jack and still talk to Ross."

KJ gives me a skeptical look.

"How?"

"Melt time and let me freeze it. I'll get just close enough to Ross for the zapper to break my control. As long as I stay within its influence, Jack won't be able to sneak up on me in frozen time. If he shows up in real time, *you* can freeze it and pull him away."

KJ shakes his head.

"You can't stand next to a zapper that long. The strain will be terrible."

"I'll manage. It's not as bad if I'm not holding time." I can tell from his expression that KJ's not convinced. "Come on, KJ, this plan is still our best chance. Barnard said he couldn't meet with us until tomorrow. Think of all our friends stuck the basement. How long do you think it will take until one of the wipers spots them?"

KJ shakes his head again, but in resignation this time instead of refusal.

"Be careful," he says.

"I will."

KJ pulls me against him and kisses me hard on the lips before turning to hide again in the damp shrubs. For a brief moment, I'm tempted to call him back, to take his hand and walk through the perfect safety of the freeze until we've left all these dangers behind. Instead, when I feel the shift in the air that tells me time is restarting, I immediately grab the strands and refreeze it. Then I square my shoulders and head into the middle of the field.

Ross waits, unmoving, paused in his trek across the grass. His skin boasts an artificial tan, and he's had his hair cut since I last saw him, the gray-streaked blond combed into a stylish sweep. His shoes look new, too, and more expensive than the ones he wore when we went on missions together. He seems shinier. More Ross-like.

I move closer, the pressure of the zapper building inside my head with every step. Menace invades the previously benign landscape. The blades of grass beneath my feet rise like tiny swords, the air tastes sour, and the clouds overhead promise dark omens. My head roils. It's as if time itself is writhing in terror, desperate to escape the zapper's pull. I force myself to keep walking until I feel the time strands start to snap. I take another step. Pain ricochets through my head. I stagger to a stop as the world begins to move.

Ross starts, placing a hand reflexively on his chest, where I can only guess he hides his zapper, and then his body relaxes and his face breaks into a slow smile. His teeth are bleached extra white. My mouth grows as dry as my legs are wet. I used to bask in the approval of this man's smiles, but now they hold all the appeal of a skull's grin.

"Dr. Barnard said he was sending the chief," I say. The chilling fear from the zapper has receded slightly now that I'm not holding a freeze, but I still can't stop my heart from hammering.

Ross gives a low, confident chuckle. "Don't you follow the news?"

A drop of water slips inside the neck of my sweatshirt and rolls down my back. It feels like a cold finger tracing the line of my spine. "What are you talking about?" I ask.

Ross taps the pocket of his uniform, which I now notice boasts a large gold badge.

"Lamar Graham was arrested two days ago," he says. "It turns out he's the one behind all those unsolved robberies. The mayor was so impressed that I finally broke the Sikes case, she named me the new chief of police." He laughs again. "Well, interim chief, but it's only a matter of time before it becomes official."

66

The lure of Ross's eternal schemes—once a shared fascination, now evidence of his corruption—distracts me from my carefully rehearsed speech about hidden spinners and desperate deals.

"You know Chief Graham isn't Sikes," I say.

"Do I?" Ross says. "Because Sikes stole a mess of diamonds over the weekend and left behind some pretty clear evidence that says otherwise."

"You *framed* the chief of police?"

"Now, how could I have done that?"

I don't have to answer. Both of us know exactly how Ross could have framed Chief Graham. Using Jack's time skills, Ross can frame anyone for anything.

"Diamonds, huh?" I say, trying to pretend his cunning doesn't rattle me. "Did you keep them?"

Ross smirks. A burst of anger at this man whom I once believed stood for justice overwhelms even the zapper's toxic emanations. My mind churns, searching for a way to hurt him. I settle on the only things that matters to him: his ego.

"Look at you," I say, drenching my voice in scorn, "with your fancy new title and big bank account. Too bad you're still just a bureaucrat working for a minor city. You don't have any real power. Not like Dr. Barnard."

"Dr. *Barnard?*" Ross scoffs. "You must think spinners are more important than they are if you believe anyone thinks Crime Investigation Centers are important."

"I'm not talking about the Center. I'm talking about the organization that runs them. That's who Dr. Barnard really works for."

Ross tilts his head. "The Central Office?"

"Not them." I make myself laugh. "The level above that. Kronos."

"Who?"

The surprise in his voice brings a thrill of vicious pleasure. It's rare that I know anything Ross does not.

"You've never heard of them?" I dredge up the few facts I actually know, filling in the gaps with tidbits I think will appeal to him. "They're the secret organization that's really in charge of controlling spinners. They have everything: money, power, prestige. Rumor is, they keep their own army of spinners who get them anything they want."

A mixture of greed and anger twists Ross's face, but my satisfaction is almost immediately quashed when he takes a few steps toward me. Fear from the zapper shatters my petty victory, turning me into such a quivering mess of terror that I have to bite my lips to keep from whimpering.

"Why did you come here, Alex?" Ross demands.

The trees behind him sway in a breeze that's gusting across the open field. Do their branches look more like elegant courtiers bowing to the wind or advancing demons straining to reach me?

"Dr. Barnard and I made a deal," I say, scrambling to recover my focus. "He said he'd stop the wipers from hunting KJ and me if I showed him where the other spinners are hiding."

"Please." Ross makes a dismissive gesture. "I know you'd never trade your friends for safety. Why are you really here?"

The muddy ground makes a squishing sound when I shuffle my feet. KJ was right that meeting Ross was a bad idea. Not because of the risk, but because I was never going to fool him. As well as I know Ross, he knows me even better.

"If you don't believe me," I say, "then forget it. I was having second thoughts anyway." I back away. "Enjoy telling Dr. Barnard that I got away from you. Again."

The fear that the trees are about to lunge for me lessens significantly as soon as I'm farther from the zapper. I glance around the park to plot my exit. The woman with the braids has left the dog park and is making her way down the hill. She's walking quickly enough that she'll pass me in a few seconds. I edge back another step. No sense in complicating things by letting myself be seen disappearing. My mind reaches out and touches the wall that still blocks me from time. As soon as the woman passes me, I'll leave the zapper's destructive orbit and freeze.

"Don't go yet," Ross says.

Fear shivers my skin as he reduces the gap between us again. I tense, ready to run. Ross stops walking.

"I am willing to make a deal with you," he says, "just not the one you offered."

I bounce on my toes. Time is a river locked beneath a thin crust of ice.

"What kind of deal?" I ask.

"You tell me where the other spinners are hiding, and I won't leak whose fingerprints were found at the scene of Austin Shea's murder."

Braid Woman is still too close for me to freeze without being seen.

"I'll think about it," I say.

"You better think fast." Ross moves a tiny bit closer, bringing the horror of the zapper with him. "I'm only going to make this offer once. There will be a lot more people than just wipers hunting for you if they know you're a murderer."

The crust in my head thickens as time recedes even farther. I stumble away, but Ross follows, keeping me inside the zapper's range. Fear fills the air like fog. Everything is too close: Ross, the zapper, the trees with their hungry arms.

"Find them yourself." I take another backward step, ankle wobbling as my foot lands on a patch of uneven grass.

"Oh, we will." Ross smiles. "Your help would just make it all happen a little faster." He inches closer. "You can't save the other spinners; you might as well buy a chance for yourself."

Terror is blurring the scene around me. KJ is too far away to be able to tell I've lost control of the situation. Run—I have to run, but I can't make myself take a single step. Ross glides toward me. It seems like his smile advances ahead of him, a Cheshire Cat crescent moon floating in the space between us. The mist of fear thickens, holding me in place. I squeeze my hands inside the sleeves of my sweatshirt until the pain of nails on skin burns through my panicked inertia. *Run.*

My feet peel away from the ground. I spin, pushing against the soft give of wet grass to fling myself away from Ross. Braid Woman has left the path to cut across the field directly behind me. I sprint toward her, away from the battering horror of the zapper. As soon as I get away from Ross, I will freeze time. I no longer care who sees me.

The block keeping me away from time loosens, and I strain for the invisible essence. Nothing happens. If anything, the flying seconds start to slip even farther out of reach, and the fear whispering in my ears grows louder. Which makes no sense. Ross is behind me; he's more than ten feet away, so the fear should be receding, not growing, unless—

I skid to a halt so fast my heels leave tracks in the mud. Terror fills the air, battering me, emanating not just from Ross, but from her, too. Braid Woman. She isn't walking anymore; she's bent in an athlete's crouch, her eyes fixed on me as she determines which way I'm going to run. Panic prickles across my skin.

Braid Woman is not a casual dog park visitor. Braid Woman is a wiper.

Ross makes a lunging motion. It's lazy, almost comical, the kind of playful swipe Aidan makes to scare the Youngers, except there is nothing playful about Ross. A smile curves the edge of his lips—he's *enjoying* this. I lurch away from him and feel my feet slip on the wet grass. When I scrabble for purchase, I find nothing. My legs buckle, and I hit the earth with a muddy splash.

"Grab her!" Ross calls.

I look up. Ross is at my back. Braid Woman is standing in front of me. I struggle to get up, my feet sliding, my hands unable to grip the soggy mass beneath my fingers. It smells like dirt and rot. The world is mud, and I will fall into it, fall forever until I am caught.

"Take the rope!"

KJ's voice. He's appeared suddenly, miraculously, behind Braid

70

Woman. In his hand is a rope, the end of which rests inches from my flailing hands. For a split second, his command makes no sense, and then his plan comes into focus.

I squirm forward, putting all my energy into one worm-like heave. Braid Woman looks down at me with an unreadable expression. She's bigger than she seemed from across the field, broad-shouldered with a high forehead. We stare at each other. She is close enough that I can see her eyes, dark and fathomless. Behind me, I hear Ross's footsteps sloshing toward me.

"Do it, X!" he shouts at the woman.

She extends her hand in my direction, slow and graceful as a swan. Her eyes don't leave my face. I snatch the rope. KJ has made a small noose at the end, and I shove my hand through it. My gaze is locked on Braid Woman's as the noose pulls tight. Something in her eyes flickers, and then she's gone.

Or I'm gone. I'm fifteen feet from her, lying next to KJ, who has his hand against my bare neck. My stomach feels raw, my wrist is burning where the rope has scraped it, I'm coated in mud, and time is frozen.

Hard, ugly gasping noises shatter the stillness. When I close my mouth, they stop. KJ kneels beside me, gently peeling the rope away from the torn-up skin on my wrist.

"What did you do?" I manage.

"Froze time," he says, tossing the rope aside.

"But they had zappers."

"I know." KJ touches my wrist with tender fingers. "That doesn't mean I couldn't stop time. The zapper would only break my freeze if I got close to them."

"But *I* was close to them. If you're near another spinner who's close to a zapper, it breaks the freeze."

"Not immediately."

"Right." I drag myself up into a sitting position, trying to put together the missing pieces. "How did I get *here?*"

71

"I dragged you. The hard part was throwing the rope close enough while staying out of range of the zapper. Once I finally got it to land next to you, I let time go and told you to take it."

"And when I grabbed the rope," I finish for him, "you froze time again, pulled me out of the zapper's range, then melted and refroze so I'd be in a new freeze with you."

KJ nods. I peek over my shoulder. Ross has his legs stretched wide, clearly running. Braid Woman is bent forward, one hand reaching down to the place I was lying an instant ago. Skid marks lead from the empty spot to where I'm sitting.

"I wasn't sure it would work," KJ says. "I was terrified that when I pulled, your arm would slip free of the noose." He touches my wrist again. The scrape is speckled with dots of blood.

"Sorry about that," KJ says. "I was picturing a hook, but all I could find was a clothesline."

My body starts to shudder as my adrenaline begins to subside. I look over my shoulder again. Even though I can barely feel it from here, I imagine the zapper's rays hanging like poisonous mist between my pursuers and me.

"A little rope burn is a small price to pay for my life." I reach for KJ and wrap my arms around him. "Thank you."

KJ's arms circle me. I both feel and hear his breath catch as he pulls me in close. I let loose a long rattling sigh. Safety, the kind I usually associate with holding a freeze, enfolds me.

"I guess that explains why Jack isn't here," I say. "Ross wouldn't have let a wiper see him."

KJ kisses the top of my head. I nestle into his chest and feel my adrenaline shakes fade away. Memories rise around me, memories of kisses and whispered endearments, too few and terribly precious. Why do we always have to be running from danger? I inhale KJ's unique smell, a scent as sweet as new grass, detectable even through the rain and the field's muddy stink.

72

"We should leave." There's strain in KJ's voice. I look up, see the pain of a time headache etched on his face, and scramble to my feet. How long did he have to hold time before he found the rope, much less successfully toss it that close to me while being battered by the zappers? Even now, we're close enough that the zapper must be pricking him with steady darts of fear.

I reach out and offer him my hand. KJ takes it and sucks in a deep, steadying breath. I can't feel it, but I know that the instant I touched his skin, my time skills melded with his, strengthening and supporting his hold. The two of us reclaim our stashed daypacks and hurry out of range, still holding hands. KJ's breathing evens out as we move farther from the zapper's pull.

"Mission accomplished, at least," KJ says, making an effort to imbue his voice with a cheer I can't imagine he really feels.

I shake my head.

"I don't think it worked. Ross didn't believe my story about trading everyone else for my own freedom. He suspects the whole meeting was a set up for some other reason."

Images of my near capture replay in my mind: the sound of steps squelching just behind me, the sensation of mud oozing between my fingers, and the taste of it on my lips. I feel the anchoring weight of wet denim and hear the infinite pause as I lay on the ground and stared into the wiper's unreadable face. What was the flicker in her eyes just before KJ pulled me away? It wasn't the triumph of someone about to catch their quarry. Was it hatred? Pity? Or something more complicated? What do wipers think about their job?

"I think we're far enough away," KJ says. "I'm going to release time."

The gray tinge to his usually warm brown skin reminds me how tired he must be. I scan our surroundings and head for a secluded spot. Both of us quickly change out of our muddy clothes before he restarts time.

"Come on," I say, when we regain the sidewalk. "Let's get you some caffeine to help with that headache."

KJ, who is way better at electronics than I am, uses the phone to find a minimart. After checking that Ross and the wiper are nowhere nearby, we step inside and roam the aisles, snatching up snacks that are both portable and filling—peanuts, pretzels—along with two Styrofoam cups of hot coffee.

There's a woman in line in front of us when we get to the cashier. KJ starts fiddling with the cell phone again while I adjust the groceries in my arms and scan our surroundings. The only other customer is a guy in the back, staring at the beer selection. I watch on the closed-circuit TV behind the cashier as he chooses a six-pack and moves on to the chip aisle. The woman in front of me finishes her transaction and walks away.

"Is that everything?" the clerk asks as I set our food on the counter.

"Yeah."

Just above the TV are a bunch of flyers tacked up on a bulletin board. They're printed in different colors, a jumbled mix of announcements for local events, pleas for help locating lost pets, and . . . my gaze skids to a halt on a pale blue flyer with the words HAVE YOU SEEN ME? emblazoned across the top. Below the words are photographs of three people: Jack, KJ, and me.

My stomach lurches. The photos must have been taken at the Center, probably snapshots Yolly or another staff member took on someone's birthday or a national holiday. My eyes flick between the photos and the live security footage of KJ and me standing at the counter. Just before we left Portland, I chopped my hair into a bob and dyed it red. KJ's hair is also shorter than it is in the picture, plus he's grown a goatee. But are these changes enough to fool anyone?

"That will be fourteen seventy-five," the cashier says. "You using a card?"

"Cash," I stammer. Over the cashier's head, the light on the security camera blinks steadily. Do the images get sent anywhere besides the store? My hands turn clumsy, my fingers fumbling as they try to separate a single bill from the awkward-to-explain clump filling the side pocket of my pack.

KJ steps on my foot.

74

"Alex," he hisses. I glance over at him. His face wears the stunned expression of someone who's been hit very hard on the head.

"I know," I mutter back. "I saw it, too."

KJ opens his mouth to say something else.

"Not now," I tell him.

My fingers tremble as I offer up a twenty. The cashier, a bored-looking guy with a pierced nose, doesn't seem to notice, but he could be faking it. Maybe he has a panic button like they do in banks and he's already summoned the police. I peep again at the flyer. There's smaller type along the bottom: *Missing since September 12. Call or text the hotline with any information. Up to $5,000 reward.*

My photo seems to grow larger, the image pulsing like neon. *Look! Look! Look!*

"Do you need a bag?"

I tear my eyes away from the incriminating flyer.

"What?"

The cashier raises an eyebrow. "A bag? For your purchases? It's five cents extra."

"Sure," I say.

"No," KJ says at the same moment. "We'll use the daypacks."

The cashier shrugs. KJ sweeps the food into his pack and hands me the drinks. My appetite has vanished, but I take them anyway. I try not to run as we head out the door.

"Do you think those are up everywhere?" I ask.

KJ blinks at me like I'm speaking Russian. "What?" he asks.

"The flyer. Didn't you see it?"

"Flyer? No." He shoves the phone at me. "I saw this."

I set our coffee cups on top of a garbage bin so I can read the small screen. KJ has pulled up a web page that shows today's schedule at a TV station.

Special Broadcast, the page screams. *Join us for this unprecedented event, when scientists from the Central Office for Spinner Studies announce the results of their world-changing research.*

I feel the blood drain from my face. Beneath the words is a picture. Two of the people in it are adults—a woman I've never seen and Dr. Barnard. The woman's smile is frosty; Dr. Barnard beams into the camera with pride. Between them stands a girl. I stare at the picture so hard I have to blink to make my eyes refocus. It's a tiny photograph, and she's wearing clothes I've never seen, but I still recognize her instantly.

I lower the phone and look up into KJ's shocked face.

"Shannon's *alive?*"

06 ◄◄

OUR SIMPLE PLAN, THE ONE THAT INVOLVES US BARELY TOUCHING down in Portland, implodes.

"We have to find her," I say.

"I know."

"And get her away from Dr. Barnard."

"I *know.*"

We're walking down a residential street. Slowly. KJ is focused on the phone, trying to find information about the broadcast, so he's barely paying attention to where he's walking.

"Got it!" He stops in the middle of the sidewalk and holds the phone out toward me. "They're broadcasting the show live from a studio on Sandy Boulevard."

"This must be Dr. Barnard's important event."

KJ hunches over the phone again. "The show starts at four, and we're supposed to be at the Springwater Trail by four forty-five. We'll have to grab her before it starts."

I chew on my thumbnail, a habit I was working hard to give up while we were at the refuge. "What do you think they've done to her?"

"I don't know." KJ tilts the phone, squinting at the photo of Shannon and Dr. Barnard. "She looks healthy, though."

"Maybe it's faked and they used an old picture," I say, even though I don't believe that. You can't share a room with someone for five years and not know every item in their wardrobe. Not with the size wardrobes we had at the Center.

"Maybe they drugged her." KJ starts walking again, eyes still glued to the phone. I grab his arm to keep him from crashing into a fire hydrant.

"What possible research can the Central Office be doing that they'd want to make public?" I ask.

KJ gives an impatient shrug and keeps scrolling.

"It just doesn't make sense." The nail I'm gnawing is down to a nub. "Central Office research is about how our skills work and how to kill us off more efficiently. Neither of those seems like something they'd want to advertise."

"Who cares what the Office is up to?" KJ waves the phone at me. "All that matters is getting Shannon away from them. Now that she's been there, she must realize how terrible they are."

The picture of Shannon smiling next to Barnard flashes past me as KJ swings the phone. Shannon was so eager to go back to Barnard, and at least in the photo, it doesn't look like she regrets that decision. I give up on my thumb and start on a different fingernail. What could possibly have happened to her at the Central Office that convinced her they were trustworthy? Did they brainwash her? A chill creeps across my skin. What if Shannon doesn't remember us? We could get her back and still have lost her.

"We need to find out what they're doing." I start moving more quickly down the sidewalk. "We have to hear whatever they're going to announce."

Puddles splash under my feet. It feels good. It feels like I'm smashing something.

"Alex, wait." KJ jogs a few steps to catch up with me. "We did what we set out to do. You talked to Ross and proved to the wipers that we're here in Portland. The only change we're making is going to get Shannon. If we walk part of the way in frozen time, I'm pretty sure we can make it to the truck before it leaves. We can all be safely back at the refuge by tonight."

I slam my foot into another puddle. Doesn't he realize there is no safety? And we did *not* accomplish what we set out to do. A wiper might have seen me here in Portland, but I don't believe they're going to stop watching the refuge. Ross's suspicion of my motives crushed that hope.

"Aren't you sick of always being in the dark?" I demand. "This is our chance to find out what they're doing."

"Our focus needs to be on our friends," KJ says. "They're our responsibility, not a bunch of free spinners we've never even met. Those people can help themselves. That's why they have a network."

"Finding out what the Center is up to *will* help our friends," I say. "It's not even that risky."

"We made a deal, Alex. No more fighting."

His words come out in short gasps. I remember how tired he is from holding time, and I stop walking to let him catch his breath.

"Please," I beg. "I know what I promised, but we're going to be there anyway. All I'm asking is that we hide somewhere and listen. We can call Lisa when we're done and spend the night here with Miguel. That's probably better anyway, since we have no idea what kind of shape Shannon will be in. The Springwater Trail is pretty far away."

KJ holds my gaze a long time. His jaw is clenched when he finally nods.

We start walking again without speaking. Briefly, I think about the refuge, but those sunbaked memories hold all the substance of a nearly forgotten dream. We're back where we started, scurrying down rain-soaked sidewalks with wipers nipping at our heels, and that sweet interlude feels like it never happened. Whatever KJ wants to believe, that pastoral refuge is a mirage. This urban landscape and this desperate fight, *these* are reality.

It's ten minutes to showtime by the time we reach the TV station. The studio occupies a windowless concrete building that takes up an entire city block. KJ and I circle around to the back, then idle with false casualness until the area is empty and we can duck behind some cars so I can stop time. We yank on various doors, looking for a way inside. The one off the parking lot is locked, but there's another door tucked in an alcove that opens, revealing a small lobby. KJ and I wipe our feet as well as we can on the thin welcome mat, then strip off our soaked sweatshirts and shove them into our daypacks with our muddy clothes. Reasonably sure we won't leave telltale drips, we cross the lobby, push open a pair of swinging doors, and enter the huge warehouse-like space behind it.

The place is dimly lit enough to feel gloomy, and the air is cool against my damp skin. Equipment litters the space: bulky cameras, tall light poles, and other more mysterious apparatuses. The only well-lit area is off to our right, so we thread our way through the mess toward its glow. There's a set here, designed to look like a particularly bland living room. It has a sofa placed at an angle with a coordinating armchair, both upholstered in muted colors. Along the back wall, a multipaned window displays a static image of the Willamette River flowing through downtown.

Dr. Barnard is sitting on the sofa next to the woman I recognize from the website KJ found. The armchair holds a pretty, overly made-up woman who must be the show's host. A half dozen people dressed in black are clustered around them, each frozen in the act of preparing for the upcoming show: dabbing powder on flushed cheeks, moving lights, adjusting microphones. A tall man with headphones draped around his neck has his arms raised in an awkward flail, caught in the midst of gesticulating. I'm guessing he's the director, because Barnard is looking up at him with an atypically attentive expression. Shannon is nowhere in sight.

I stop walking. Tension drifts toward me from the set, a fetid smoke oozing from across the room.

"There's a zapper in here," I say. KJ nods. Neither of us is surprised. The wretched things seem to be standard issue these days.

"Where's Shannon?" he asks.

"They must be bringing her out later."

KJ turns, clearly planning to expand our search. I grab the back of his shirt.

"Let's find a place to hide," I say. "If we talk to Shannon before they start, she might mess up the show, and then we won't learn anything."

KJ twitches his shoulders to release my hold, but he doesn't argue.

"Where do you think they'll go when they're done?" I ask.

"Parking lot, probably," KJ says. "Let's hide someplace where we can see both the stage and the exit."

We prowl around the oversize cavern. This place is the flip side to television's gloss, as if we've turned the whole thing inside out, exposing TV's unglamorous guts. There are cords snaking across the floor and ropes dangling from a nearly invisible ceiling. People wearing headsets lurk in corners, plain people dressed in dark clothing.

"How about there?" KJ says, pointing to a metal frame that's about equidistant from the set and the door leading out to the parking lot. It looks like a very tall storage rack. There's a pile of folding chairs stacked on the bottom level and a squat unused spotlight perched on the top platform, about ten feet over our heads. Beyond it, the line of a catwalk leads up into the darkness.

"Perfect," I say. "They can pass right underneath without seeing us, and even if they do, we can always climb up the catwalk."

We use the shelves to haul ourselves onto the platform. There's a tarp up here, which KJ shakes out so we can lie beneath it. The cover provides the dual purpose of camouflage and insulation from the chill. I prop up the tarp's front edge so we can see out, then let the world start again.

Lights brighten. The black-clad techs swarm the set like so many spiders. The director's voice booms out, instructing Barnard and the other guest on filming etiquette.

"Don't look directly at the camera," he tells them. "Try to act like this is just a regular conversation you're having with Cindy. Just relax and have fun."

81

I inch forward so I can see better. From up here, they all look like figures in a dollhouse. Barnard gives the director a measured nod that's the opposite of "fun." He's got on a nicer suit than he ever wore at the Center, dark blue with a crisp-looking white shirt. His right arm rests against his stomach at a stiff angle that might seem like nerves if the cast poking out the end of his sleeve didn't prove it's been broken. I smile to myself. Perhaps it's not evidence of my best trait, but the fact that I caused the accident that injured him gives me grim pleasure.

The woman beside Barnard is middle-aged with a round face and glossy black hair that's slicked back in a tight bun. She looks composed and, unlike Barnard, is paying very little attention to the director's instructions. She must have been on TV before.

"Everyone ready?" The director claps his hands, and all the techs scurry off the set.

"In five," the director says, pulling his headphones up over his ears. "Four." He stops speaking and uses his fingers to count the rest of the way down to one. Music starts, an energetic jazzy tune. The woman in the armchair turns to face the camera and plasters on a dazzling smile.

"Welcome to *News Tonight*," she says. "I'm Cindy Ramirez, and we are excited to bring you an exclusive interview with two of the senior scientists from the Tacoma Central Office for Spinner Research."

She turns toward her guests with an enthusiasm that makes me ill. No one should be offering admiring glances to the people in charge of killing us.

"Dr. Jeffrey Barnard," Cindy chirps, "is an internationally celebrated scientist known for his groundbreaking research on spinner physiology. For the past fifteen years, he was also the director of the Northwest Region's Crime Investigation Center, located right here in Portland, Oregon."

A camera swings in Barnard's direction, and Barnard, ignoring his earlier instructions, smiles at it.

"Our other guest," Cindy continues, "is Dr. Margaret Ellery. Dr. Ellery

82

is the Regional Director of Spinner Affairs and oversees all five of the U.S. Central Offices as well as the three in Canada."

"Regional Director of Spinner Affairs?" KJ whispers to me. "Have you ever heard of that?"

I shake my head. Something about Dr. Ellery gives me the creeps. There's a weird calmness to her that reminds me of a documentary I once saw about crocodiles. Dr. Ellery has the same controlled stillness that the crocs did while they lay in wait for their prey.

"We are so honored to have you both with us today," Cindy says. "Everyone knows spinners exist, but it's rare to have an opportunity to talk to the people who actually work with them."

"Thank you, Cindy," says Dr. Ellery without once glancing at the camera's beady eye. In contrast to the bubbly host, she speaks in a measured voice that makes her sound like a model of composed rationality. "We're pleased to be here. People don't hear much about spinners, because for the most part, there isn't much to tell. Spinners' lives are short and mostly devoted to keeping their unfortunate symptoms in check."

"Don't you want to leap off this thing and smack her?" I mutter to KJ.

"I think that would count as evidence of your unfortunate symptoms," he whispers back.

A nervous giggle rises up my throat, and I squeeze my lips together to keep it from spilling out.

"We understand," Cindy says, "that you're here to tell us about a major breakthrough in spinner research."

"Yes." Dr. Ellery clasps her hands in her lap. "It's a project we've been working on for many years, but we've only recently achieved consistent success."

"Before we dive in," Cindy says, "why don't you give our audience a little bit of background on spinners. For most of us, they're a pretty mysterious group."

"Of course." Dr. Ellery tips her head in a gracious nod, a queen acquiescing to her subjects' petty demands. I grip the edge of the platform. The words that pour from her mouth are as familiar to me as a fairy tale and as packed with half truths and outright lies: that we are mentally unstable, violent, and dangerous. These are the myths that condemn us without trial, the stories that are so ingrained in Norm society that no one ever questions them. To hear this slander spoken with such calm authority is like being forced to sit in a field that's thick with stinging nettles.

"Remind us," Cindy prompts, "exactly what spinners are able to do."

Ellery blabs on about how spinners move around while the rest of the world remains frozen, doing whatever terrible (though temporary) acts we please. I watch her mouth moving while picturing her jaw lengthening like a real crocodile's, complete with razor-sharp teeth and hideous skin bumps.

"A simple freeze is not their only dangerous skill," Dr. Ellery adds. "Spinners also have the ability to rewind time and view events in the past. By watching what has already happened, they have access to all kinds of private information. They can gather things like passwords and phone numbers or read confidential information. They can find out the location of hidden valuables or witness private actions that could be used for blackmail. Remember, these creatures are not sane. What they might do in frozen time, or with the information garnered from a rewind, is completely unpredictable."

Cindy gives an exaggerated shudder. "That is so sinister."

The word scrapes my ears like nails on a chalkboard. I wish I could deny all the doctor's accusations, but the uncomfortable truth is that I have done many of the things she described. I have used my time skills to rifle through private files and gain information, and I have suffered bouts of both paranoia and unchecked rage. Does that mean I am fundamentally dishonest? Are paranoia and violence truly part of my nature? I haven't had those reactions since I started taking the low-dose Aclisote Lisa prescribed, but if a drug is the only thing holding off those unwanted feelings, then which version of me is real?

My hands squeeze the edge of the platform hard enough to turn my knuckles white. I've only done illegal things in order to survive. I wouldn't have been forced to run and hide if the world just accepted me for what I am. I am not the amoral *thing* Dr. Ellery is describing.

"Isn't it also true," Cindy says, "that spinners can be useful? Until just a few days ago, we had a whole Center of them right here, working with the police. It seems like you could harness those skills for other kinds of good, too."

"Theoretically," Dr. Ellery concedes, "but the risks are unacceptably high. Science can only go so far toward mitigating the danger. Sometimes even the best medications are not effective."

Cindy crosses her legs—a signal, it seems, of a coming change in topic.

"All of this," she says, "gives special weight to the new research you came here to announce."

"This is it," KJ breathes into my ear. I ease my fingers out of their death grip on the platform's edge, and we both scoot a tiny bit forward.

"Let me turn the conversation over to my colleague," Dr. Ellery says. "This discovery is really Jeffrey's achievement."

Barnard straightens in his chair, his chest broadening as if he's inhaling a breath of pure pride. Prickles shiver across the back of my head. The information I've been so eager to learn is imminent, and suddenly I'm not sure I want to hear it.

"Thank you, Dr. Ellery," he says. "Before I announce the results of our research, I'd like to introduce a living example of our success: Shannon Callahan."

Beside me, KJ sucks in a breath. A man swings his camera to the right, and Shannon steps out of the shadows. Tears, hot and unexpected, spring to my eyes. Even though I saw the picture, I realize that until this moment, I didn't completely believe Shannon was really alive. I swallow down the lump in my throat. The girl walking onto the set is no Photoshopped trick or miraculously animated corpse. She's simply Shannon.

My one-time roommate takes a seat on the sofa next to Barnard. I lean so far forward on the platform that I'm in danger of being seen. Shannon looks not just undamaged but perfect. She's wearing pretty cream sandals and a dress that is clearly not a hand-me-down, a soft swirl of blue fabric dotted with tiny flowers. Her long blond hair shimmers in a way I've only ever seen in shampoo commercials.

"Welcome to *News Tonight*, Shannon," Cindy says.

"Thank you."

KJ has also moved forward beside me, staring down at Shannon with undisguised intensity. I squint through the studio's overbright lights. Someone has spent time doing Shannon's makeup. Features that were just pretty before have become beautiful. They've managed to still make her seem relatable, though. She looks like the kind of person half the world wants to be friends with and everyone else wants to date.

"Now, as I understand it," Cindy says, "until very recently, you lived in Portland's Crime Investigation Center."

"Yes." There's a rote lilt in Shannon's tone that makes me suspect she was prepped for the question. "I grew up in a Children's Home in Idaho and moved to the Portland Center when I was twelve."

"So you're a spinner," says Cindy.

"I was." Shannon smooths her skirt with her hands. Her smile is blinding. "But thanks to Dr. Barnard, I'm not one anymore."

KJ makes a muffled choking sound. I brush a drip of water from my forehead, not sure if it's sweat or rain. Even with my head out from under the tarp, I feel claustrophobic.

Down on the set, the camera swings toward Barnard.

"This is the essence of our breakthrough." Barnard's chest seems to be expanding even farther, as if it wants to burst from the confines of his jacket. "From now on, no one will ever have to be a spinner again. I'm very happy to announce that we have discovered a cure."

86

07 ◀◀

THERE'S A RINGING SOUND INSIDE MY HEAD. THE NOISE IS simultaneously overwhelming and muffled, like someone just hit a gong right next to my ear and knocked out my hearing. I look at KJ, who is repeating the word *cure* under his breath over and over, like he's not sure what it means. Barnard is still talking. I turn back to the stage and force my brain to process what he's saying.

"... actually a very simple treatment, though it did take some trial and error before we figured out exactly how to make it work."

Barnard's mouth keeps moving, but his next words are also lost to the ringing crashing through my head. How many spinner kids died in those trials? And errors.

"It's basically a type of gene therapy," Barnard is saying when I manage to focus again. "We take a sample of a spinner's blood and mix it with a reagent, which then works on the chromosomes in the sample. In layman's terms, the reagent 'eats' the mutation. After that, we inject the cleaned blood back into the spinner, and the active sample works through the rest of the bloodstream until all the unwanted elements are destroyed. The entire process takes about twelve hours for infants and forty-eight hours for a fully developed spinner."

"Was it painful?" Cindy asks Shannon.

"Not at all," Shannon says. "I just felt like I had a slight cold. I had some body aches for a couple of days and a very low-grade fever. Then the symptoms went away, and it was over." She laughs, a happy tinkling sound. "Really, the whole experience was rejuvenating. Dr. Barnard put me in a lovely private suite with a window overlooking a forest. I'd had a rough couple of days before I arrived at the Central Office, so I particularly appreciated the rest. With all the attention I got from the technicians, it felt more like a spa vacation than a hospital visit."

Beside me, I can feel KJ's body shaking. I reach out and rest one hand on his back. The quivering doesn't stop.

"What was it like living in a Center?" Cindy asks.

"There were some wonderful parts," Shannon says. "All of us kids were super close, and like any family, we shared a lot of good times."

KJ hunches forward, as if he's being reeled in by the wistful nostalgia in Shannon's voice. I listen to my former roommate's words with more skepticism. I have no doubt that Shannon genuinely loved the Center, but even for her, calling our upbringing "wonderful" seems like a stretch. How much of her speech has been scripted by the man sitting beside her? The one watching her with the proud expression of a ringmaster admiring his trained seal?

"When I wasn't out with a police agent," Shannon continues, "I worked with the Youngers—that's what we call the spinners who aren't old enough to go out on police missions." She smiles to herself, eyes unfocused as if she's recalling a particularly lovely private memory. "The Youngers are really the heart of any Center. So full of laughter and love."

"Tell us about a typical day."

Shannon starts describing the best possible version of Center life, highlighting the lessons and free time and skipping over the drudgery and stifling incarceration. The Willamette River view on the screen behind them fades as she talks, replaced with photos of our Center. A few of them I recognize as publicity shots that were taken for the occasional fundraising campaign. Others trigger vague memories of Yolly or one of the teachers snapping pictures with their phones. A photo of a younger, chubby-fingered Emma holding up a painting fades into an image of Aidan blocking a basketball shot Raul is trying

88

to make, followed by one of Angel harvesting tomatoes from the courtyard vegetable garden. A yearning ache expands in my chest—not for the place, but for the innocence of all of us when those photos were taken. Innocence of what our containment meant and of what the Center really was.

"But it wasn't all fun and games, was it?" Cindy prompts.

Shannon drops her eyes to where her hands rest in her lap. Barnard gives her shoulder an encouraging pat, as if he's settling her nerves, though from where I'm sitting, it seems Shannon has no nerves. She seems to be absorbing the camera's attention like a plant drinking in light.

"Some of the police work we did was pretty tough," she admits, "and kids can be so young when they start doing rewinds. You shouldn't be exposed to things like that when you're barely in your teens."

The images behind her switch to blaring headlines: MURDERER APPREHENDED, DRUG BUST SNAGS TWELVE, PROSTITUTION RING EXPOSED. The headlines are backed by grainy crime scene photos and scowling mug shots, unsavory people caught in distasteful acts.

"That wasn't the hardest part about living in a Center, though," Shannon says. "The worst part was the deaths. So many of us lost so young."

New photos replace the crime scenes: picture after picture of spinners who are gone. Steve. Alicia. Calvin. Each photo is rimmed in black, and I realize they are the memorial photos Yolly always put up when someone died. Anger burns through my nostalgia. How dare the Center use pictures of my dead friends to sell their "cure," especially when the Center is the reason they died in the first place?

"Thank you so much for sharing your story," Cindy says.

"I'm happy to." Shannon smiles. "I am so grateful to Dr. Barnard for freeing me from this terrible condition. To be given a chance at a normal life—you cannot imagine what a miracle that is. It's always been my dearest wish."

Shannon says these words directly into the camera. Is she thinking of KJ and me when she says them? A normal life. It's what I've always wanted, too.

89

Isn't it? My stay at the refuge made me think I might be able to go to college, even get a job, but that still wouldn't make me like everyone else. I'd still have to hide my real self. If I stopped being a spinner, I'd be free. No one would ever force me to wear a leash. No one would chase me. I'd never see that flash of disgust when people learn what I am. These are things I've always dreamed about.

So why do I feel like I'm about to throw up?

"Dr. Barnard," Cindy says, "what do you say to people who might doubt your results?"

Barnard straightens his glasses and makes a professorial *harrumph*.

"You can't tell the difference between a spinner and a normal person just by looking at them," he says. "But there are other methods." He describes the monthly blood work we all used to endure to test our chronotin levels. A photo on the screen shows one of the analyzers reading zero.

"I've tested Shannon's blood multiple times since she was went through the treatment, and there's not a trace of chronotin remaining in her system."

"What will happen to the spinners once they're cured?" Cindy asks.

"We're still working out the details," Dr. Ellery says. "Everyone at the Central Offices is committed to fully integrating former spinners into society. We want to make sure each child gets an education so they can gain useful skills. Some of the youngest children may even be able to reunite with their biological families. That's really the part of this that makes us most proud. From now on, expectant parents won't have to worry that their children may be defective. The centuries of family destruction caused by this terrible mutation are now over."

"That truly is a wonderful outcome," Cindy says. "I think Dr. Barnard is going to go down in history with the likes of Jonas Salk and Florence Nightingale."

Dr. Barnard beams.

"One final question," Cindy says. "What's going to happen next?"

"We have already started the process of reorganizing the five US

Central Offices so they can carry out the procedure," Dr. Ellery says, "and we've shared our findings with all the other Offices around the globe so they can do the same. The Northwest Office is obviously ahead of the others, so we're preparing for spinners from our regional Centers to come in for treatment right away. The spinners from the San Francisco Center are scheduled to arrive next week."

A picture of my own Center flashes through my head the way I last saw it, with neatly labeled boxes stacked by the door. Will the kids from the San Francisco Center be told what's going to happen to them? Or will they just wake up one day and not be able to access time? When that happens, will they be angry or relieved?

The show's director moves to the edge of the set, just out of range of the cameras. He holds up his fingers again, slowly counting down. Ten. Nine.

"Thank you so much for coming in to share this amazing news," Cindy says to the trio seated on the sofa. "We hope to see more of you as this fascinating new twist in the spinner story unfolds." The director is down to five fingers. Cindy turns to the camera. "After the break, we'll share our best pumpkin pie recipes, perfect for the upcoming holiday. Stay with us."

"That's a wrap," says the director.

A burble of activity takes over the set. Barnard stands up from the sofa and stretches. Black-clad techs detach microphones from collars. The director, headphones back around his neck, moves in to shake everyone's hand.

I squirm back under the folds of the tarp. It's full of dust, and I have to pinch my nose to keep from sneezing. KJ is lying very still. His body no longer shakes, but he wears the rigid expression of someone trying not to scream.

"Do you think it's real?" I whisper.

"It seems impossible, but . . . maybe?"

The ringing in my head has died down to a dull roar. It comes and goes, like the tidal rush of my own tainted blood beating against my ears.

"That was fascinating," I hear the director saying through the noise. "I

91

think our audience will respond really well."

"We appreciate you letting us come on your show," Dr. Ellery says.

I creep back to the edge of the platform and peek down. A tech is huddled with Cindy, presumably getting her ready for the show's next segment. The rest of the group is walking away from the set.

"They're coming this way," I murmur. KJ wriggles over to lie beside me.

"We'd love to do a follow-up piece," the director says. "How about something on our local spinners' post-recovery experiences?"

"We'll see," says Dr. Ellery. "It's important that we respect the spinners' privacy. Most of them are minors, remember, and their condition is a stigma they may not want to carry forward into their new lives."

Dr. Ellery and the director pass directly beneath us. Shannon is right behind them, walking shoulder to shoulder with Barnard. He must be the one carrying the zapper. Even though I'm not holding a freeze, when he passes by, I can feel its distorting rays. I force myself to breath in shallow sips. KJ has his fingertips pressed into the surface of the platform, poised to spring forward.

"You did a great job," Barnard says to Shannon.

"It was fun," Shannon says. "I'm so glad you chose me as the cure's ambassador."

The four of them move past us. As the stress from the zapper fades, the space it leaves behind fills with genuine worry. The group has nearly left the building, and they are still all together. How are we going to separate Shannon from her captors without being seen?

"We're going to lose them," I say.

The group stops at the far end of the building, about twenty feet away from where we're hiding. They exchange a last round of handshakes and mutual congratulations, and then the director hurries back toward the set, and Barnard opens the door leading to the parking lot. Sunlight streams in as Barnard exits and holds the door open for his companions. Dr. Ellery follows him out,

92

Shannon at her heels.

"It's now or never," KJ says. "Come on."

Air ruffles my hair as he rips off the tarp. KJ scrambles down the shelving, leaping when he's halfway down and landing in a crouch.

"Shannon," he calls. "Wait. We need to talk to you."

Shannon and Dr. Ellery both turn. Dr. Ellery looks startled. Shannon's face pales to white.

"KJ?" she gasps.

"Hi." KJ rises to his feet.

I climb down to stand at his side. Ellery's eyes land on me and immediately narrow.

"You!" she says.

She knows me? Her voice holds so much venom, I involuntarily take a step back.

Shannon sprints forward and hurls herself at KJ at the same moment Barnard rushes back indoors. I reach out and grab KJ's arm just as Shannon rockets into him. KJ embraces her, bringing my hand into contact with her bare skin. I yank the swirl of time to a screeching halt. The zapper's warning heightens. Shannon bursts into tears.

"You're here!" she cries.

KJ clasps the sobbing girl against his chest. "We thought you were dead."

"Dead?" Shannon lifts her face. "Of course I'm not dead. Why would you think that?"

"You were at the Central Office," I say. "They experimented on you."

Shannon's cheeks flush pink. She looks between KJ and me and seems to make a mental adjustment, then steps away from her former boyfriend and wipes away her tears.

"They didn't experiment on me," she says. "They cured me."

"Are you sure?" I ask.

93

Shannon turns in my direction. The happiness that lit her features when she saw KJ does not extend to me. I squirm, remembering the last time we saw each other. Her horror. My guilt. Somehow, I forgot those details after she was so miraculously resurrected. Except, of course, from her perspective, she's not resurrected. She's always been fine.

"Of course I'm sure." Shannon tosses her head. "Dr. Barnard took all the chronotin out of my blood. I'm cured. I'm no longer a spinner."

I've heard the word *cure* multiple times now, but it still seems implausible. Shannon is so much *herself*, how could such an essential part of her be gone?

"You don't believe me." She stretches out her arm. "Here. I'll prove it."

Her fingers hang in the empty space between us. Somebody manicured her nails so they are perfectly rounded and shiny with clear polish. Shannon's heart beats beneath her skin when I take her hand, a pulse as steady as a ticking clock, but there is nothing else behind it. It's just skin and bones and muscles. While a spinner's touch would bring another's power surging to the surface, Shannon's hand offers only the inert weight of a Norm's.

She wiggles her fingers.

"You can't sense it, can you?"

I move closer and place my hand on her arm, her cheek, the back of her neck. Shannon accepts my frantic touch with a complacent smile.

"There's nothing," she says. "Dr. Barnard ran my blood tests probably a hundred times. I don't have chronotin anymore."

"It's not possible," I say.

Shannon gestures to herself. "But it is."

I pull my hand back and cradle it like it's been singed.

"Don't you feel different?" I ask her. "Like something is missing? Like you're. . ." I stop before I say the word that rises to my lips: *less. Don't you feel like you're less than you were before?*

Shannon shakes her head. "I feel exactly the same."

"How do you know there aren't side effects?" KJ asks. "That's a big biological change. There may be risks."

"Dr. Barnard says there aren't," she says. "I believe him."

"How can you?" The zapper's evil buzz slithers around inside my head. Shannon's headlong rush left Barnard fifteen feet behind her, a big enough buffer to keep my time skills intact but not enough to avoid the zapper's effects. I move away from Shannon to gain more distance.

"Dr. Barnard lied about so much," I remind her. "The man was *poisoning* us."

"Oh, Alex." Shannon sounds disappointed. "Do you still believe that?"

"Of course she does," KJ says. "We both do. We've met adult spinners. It's proof our friends didn't have to die."

Shannon waves away the memory of our friends as if their premature deaths mean nothing. "I know there are adult spinners," she says. "Dr. Barnard explained that there are super-rare cases of spinners surviving postadolescence. The Center never told us because it's so unlikely and they didn't want us to get our hopes up."

My joy at seeing Shannon alive is getting spoiled by her willful stubbornness. Nuance is not her specialty. She sees the world in black and white, and Barnard, to her, is pure, shining white.

"You still don't accept that Aclisote is poison," I say.

Shannon raises her eyebrows. It's the exact same expression she used to wear when she was teaching the Youngers and one of them made an inappropriate comment.

"Dr. Barnard told me they still take Aclisote," she says. "Your rogue spinners."

"Free spinners," I correct her, "and yes, we take a little bit, but not the amounts we were getting before. The dosages the Center was giving us were lethal."

Shannon throws up her hands. "Now you're just splitting hairs. If you

95

don't want to admit that I'm right, that's fine. What matters is that you bring the others to Dr. Barnard so they can be cured."

The strain from being this near a zapper is not getting better. Its buzzing whisper tells me the dark spaces around us are filled with danger. I rub at the ache in my temple. *It's not real*, I tell myself. *It's not real.*

"What if the other kids don't want to stop being spinners?" KJ asks.

"Why wouldn't they want to be cured?" Shannon looks genuinely confused. "*Everyone* wants to be normal. Don't you?"

Do I? It's true that I've dreamed about blending in with the rest of the world. I've craved the shared experiences and the freedom that would come from acceptance, but now that the choice is actually before me, I'm not sure I'm willing to pay the price. The ability to control time is literally in my blood. Who would I be without it?

"Raul and Aidan are both excited about having expanded skills," I say, sidestepping her question.

Shannon's eyes narrow. "I thought you never told anyone else at the Center that your abilities changed."

"I didn't while we were there. We had this conversation a couple of days ago."

"You saw them?" For the first time since we started talking, Shannon sounds unsure. "But they got transferred to the Central Office in Dallas."

"Is that what Dr. Barnard told you?" I glance over her shoulder. From this angle, with the light pouring through the door at his back, Dr. Barnard is nothing but a dark shadow. Dr. Ellery, however, is lit by one of the studio's overhead lights. Her blank stare is aimed straight at me, her eyes lit with a gleam that feels like it could slice right through my freeze like a laser.

"Dr. Barnard lied," I say, dragging my attention back to Shannon. "Again. The other kids from our Center weren't transferred anywhere. KJ and I got them out the same day you turned yourself in. Don't you remember? We talked about doing it."

"We talked about renting a place somewhere out of town," she says, "and going back to get them later."

I struggle to remember the details of who knew what when. Even though it was only a few days ago, it seems like a lifetime has passed since we were all together.

"Our plans changed," I say.

"Then I guess no one told Dr. Barnard that you stole them." Shannon crosses her arms. "They probably didn't want to upset him while he was working."

"Dr. Barnard was there the night everyone escaped," KJ said. "He knows."

Shannon's crossed arms tighten.

"I'm sure there's an explanation," she says. "Dr. Barnard wouldn't lie to me."

The threat from the zapper is eroding my concentration and increasing my impatience with her refusal to accept the truth.

"He *did* lie to you!" My voice booms through the frozen quiet. "Over and over. You've admitted it. He lied when he told us all spinners die young. He lied when he said it was impossible to change things in frozen time. And he lied when he told you where our friends are. Just ask if you can call them at this other Center and see what he says. To Dr. Barnard, we will never be anything except specimens to experiment on. Why are you being so blind?"

Shannon's cheeks blaze red.

"Why are *you* so desperate to believe the worst?" she shouts. "Maybe Dr. Barnard softened the truth a few times, but he only did it so he wouldn't terrify a facility full of children. That man has never been anything but kind to me. He's letting me stay at his *house* while we're here. How is that treating me like a specimen? You just want everything to be some huge conspiracy so you can be a hero."

The unfairness of her accusation hits me like a slap. Anger sparks through the still air as we glare at each other, reigniting the jealousy and distrust that burned so brightly when we last met. I look away first. A week ago, I would have fanned that fire, but the days spent mourning her are too close, and the flames merely flicker before dying out.

"I'm sorry you believe that about me," I say.

Surprise cools the heat in Shannon's cheeks. She bites her lip.

"Why did you come here, anyway?" she asks.

"We came here to rescue you," KJ says.

"Even though you think Dr. Barnard is trying to kill you?" She sounds reluctantly impressed.

"We hoped you would want to come back and be with all of us," KJ says.

Shannon twists a fold in her skirt. "Where are the others?" she asks. "Are they OK?"

"For now." KJ takes a step toward her, a move that also puts him closer to the zapper. Time pulls at me, straining to break free.

"They miss you," KJ tells Shannon. "Especially the Youngers. They'll be really happy to know you're alive."

"I miss them, too."

The sadness in her voice melts the rest of my anger. Shannon may be dogged in her misguided beliefs, but I know her goal is the same as mine—she wants our friends to survive.

"When you go back to them," Shannon says, "will you tell them about the cure?"

"I won't have to tell them." KJ offers her a small smile. "Your interview will be broadcast on TV in a couple of hours. Everyone can make their own decisions."

"Right." Shannon looks around the cavernous studio as if she's forgotten where she is.

The zapper's insidious power sends fear crawling through the creases in my brain, slowly loosening my control of time.

"KJ," I say. "We need to leave."

He glances at me. I don't know what my face looks like, but he instantly comes over and takes my hand. Strength surges through the place where our skin touches. The fear from the zapper doesn't fade, but my ability to withstand it increases. I straighten my shoulders.

"You're leaving?" Shannon asks.

KJ reaches out his other hand. "Will you come with us?"

She hesitates, one foot in front of the other, as if she's been caught in a freeze.

"No." She steps back. "I'm staying here. Dr. Barnard needs me to be the cure's ambassador. He said that once we've got everyone cured, he'll help me get the training I need to become a teacher. This is the future. Our old life is over."

Shannon's voice sounds loud in the studio's silence, and her words seem laced with threat. *It's over, over, over.* I tug on KJ's sleeve, desperate to put more distance between me and the mind-sucking zapper. He doesn't move.

"Shannon," he says. "Before we go? I want to apologize for how I broke up with you." He grimaces. "Or didn't break up with you. I was a coward, and I didn't treat you well. I'm sorry."

Shannon turns her gaze up to the ceiling, and I wonder if she's trying not to cry.

"I'm sorry about how things turned out, too," she says. "I hope you . . . you both . . . end up OK."

A strand of time slips out of my grasp. I pull on KJ's hand, then start and stop time in quick succession to drop Shannon from the freeze. The strain on my skills lifts considerably. KJ and I turn away and head toward the exit on the other side of the studio, every step reducing my irrational terror and tightening my grip on time.

I look back once. Shannon stands where we left her, a wistful expression

99

locked on her face. Barnard is lost in the shadows behind her, but Dr. Ellery seems have moved closer. I hesitate for a moment, studying the woman's still face. The gleam of an overhead light makes her eyes look animated; even though I'm in a completely different location, they still seem to be trained on me. I shiver. Who is this woman? What is her real goal? Does she want to cure us or destroy us? If we live but no longer control time, is there really any difference?

08 ◄◄

SMEARED RAINDROPS AND WET LEAVES SPECKLE MARGARET
Ellery's windshield, partially obscuring her view of the studio's
parking lot. She squints through the distortion, paying special
attention to secluded nooks where someone might be hiding.
Where *spinners* might be hiding. The car's locks make a subtle
clicking sound as Dr. Ellery engages them. It's unlikely that the two
spinners stuck around after their conversation with Shannon, but
Dr. Ellery knows they are unpredictable creatures, and these two
have already proven themselves capable of unexpectedly
devious plans.

"What did they want from you?" Dr. Ellery had asked once
she, Barnard, and Shannon were in the parking lot.

"They wanted me to go with them." Shannon raised her
chin. "I refused."

"Good girl," Barnard said. "They're probably holed up in
another dirty squat somewhere. You're much better off staying
with us."

"I know."

Judging by Barnard's pleased smile, this answer was
enough to convince him of the girl's continued cooperation, but
Dr. Ellery's skepticism was validated when the former spinner
blurted, "Alex told me that the other kids aren't in Dallas. She

claimed she and KJ stole them out of the Center almost a week ago." Shannon twisted the fabric of her skirt. "That's not true, is it?"

"Of course not," Barnard lied, with what even Dr. Ellery had to admit was convincing sincerity. "How could Alexandra and Kaleel have snuck into, much less out of, our very secure Center?"

"It does seem unlikely." Shannon paused, then took a breath, as if girding herself for the question she wanted to ask. "Do you think, when we're back at the Office, that we could call them? Some of the kids might be scared. I bet they'll all feel better if I tell them about my own experience."

Barnard gazed at his protégé with a fond expression that made Dr. Ellery's lips pinch with distaste. Getting attached to a subject was never a good idea.

"Let's talk about it when we're back in Tacoma," he told Shannon. "I'll check with the doctors in Dallas and find out what their protocols are. If they agree it would be helpful, I promise I'll make a call happen."

Shannon smiled, but Dr. Ellery noticed that the girl's hand was still tangled in the folds of her dress.

Dr. Ellery adjusts the chromoelectronegator clamped to her car's dashboard and sighs. Barnard is a fool if he thinks his pretty pet will last very long in this ambassador role. The Central Office's Project Zed committee was right—using Shannon as the face of recovery *is* a good PR move—but the girl is problematic. She's seen too much, and as gullible as she's been so far regarding Barnard's soothing explanations, she's also obviously attached to the spinners she left behind. Eventually, she'll ask too many questions, and then, as usual, Dr. Ellery will have to step in and clean up someone else's mess.

Just like she needs to follow up on the fiasco at the park this morning. Dr. Ellery picks up her phone and scrolls through her contacts. She's still furious that Dr. Barnard didn't tell her about his phone call from Alexandra Manning until after they arrived at the studio. If she had known the girl was nearby, she would have had more security in place, and they might have captured the escapees. It's lucky for Dr. Barnard that his research is so useful. Otherwise she would have fired him on the spot.

Dr. Ellery finds the name she wants and hits the dial button.

"Xavier," a voice growls.

At least she answered with her real name. Agent Maria Xavier, a standard-grade Kronos security agent, is referred to by the other staff as Agent X, or even just plain X. It's an abbreviation Dr. Ellery finds irritating, with its allusion to superheroes, and today it seems particularly ironic. Allowing the Manning girl to escape capture yet *again* is not a mark in the agent's favor.

"This is Dr. Margaret Ellery. I need a full report from you on the incident this morning at Irving Park."

"Yes, ma'am."

The agent's voice is emotionless as she runs through the facts: the spinner's phone call to Dr. Barnard; his subsequent calls delegating the meeting to Chief Ross and requesting that the Central Office provide security backup; the public conversation and subsequent bungled capture. Dr. Ellery shifts in her seat. The tree overhead seems to have given up its fight against the season and decided to drop its leaves en masse. The car is starting to feel like a cave.

"You're telling me the girl disappeared in the middle of a city park? Did anyone see her?"

103

"Just the chief."

"How did you handle the cover-up?"

"When the girl vanished, I ran past the spot she disappeared from and purposely knocked the chief over, making sure he hit his head. I told him she dodged us and that our collision allowed her to get away."

Dr. Ellery pictures the scene. The distance between the agent and Chief Ross, plus the time between the girl's "escape" and the pair's collision, leaves a short but worrisome gap during which the police chief could have seen the spinner disappear.

"Did Chief Ross accept your explanation?" Dr. Ellery asks.

"I'm not sure. He fell hard enough to make him a bit woozy, but even so, it seemed like he accepted my explanation almost *too* easily. Given his previous experience working with Alex, I think there's a definite probability he knows, or at least suspects, that her actions during frozen time don't get erased."

Dr. Ellery drums the fingers of one hand on the car's steering wheel. This isn't the first concern she's had about the new chief. Ross found evidence proving that the former chief, Lamar Graham, is Sikes, but based on the thief's methods, Sikes is almost definitely a spinner, and Chief Graham is not one. Her staff got a DNA sample to check. Of course, Graham could have worked with a spinner accomplice. Or Ross himself could be part of the Sikes caper. Was the whole Portland police force rotten? Clearing out a compromised department, while possible, would take time. She spent months manufacturing the 2018 scandal that led to the overhaul of the Baltimore police force. Dr. Ellery's fingers drum faster. In her opinion, people who use spinners' skills for their own profit are almost as loathsome as spinners themselves.

"What did the Manning girl want with the chief?" Dr. Ellery asks.

"She said she would show him the location of the other spinners in exchange for freedom for herself and the boy, Kaleel Jabar."

"And the chief turned her down?"

"No," Agent Xavier says. "He played along until the girl got spooked and ran. He thinks she had some ulterior motive for the offer, though. He says Alex would never willingly give up her friends."

Honor among thieves? Impossible. Spinners have no honor, and the Manning girl has already proven her propensity for lies and violence. So why did she want a face-to-face meeting?

Dr. Ellery picks up the chromoelectronegator and double-checks that it's on. Agent Xavier was too far away to hear what actually passed between the spinner and the chief, which means they only had Ross's word regarding what she said. The girl could have said anything: lies, threats, even blackmail.

What if Carson Ross is a CIA informant? Dr. Ellery sets the chromoelectronegator back down on the dashboard and considers its reassuring beam. A time agent would be well placed to gain access, especially if he had a spinner to help him. The two of them used to work together, so if he is a double agent, the Manning girl would know, and she'd know about the CIA's desire to keep the spinners' secrets locked down. Add that to the fact that she escaped near-certain capture at the park, and the theory had definite merit. After all, it was far more likely that the chief aided her escape than that a couple of teenage spinners managed to outwit two trained professionals.

A small rustling sound on the other end of the phone tells Dr. Ellery that the pause in the conversation has grown too long. She clears her throat to reclaim her focus. Dr. Ellery has been counting on Portland's police department to play a critical role over the next few days, and if their chief is a CIA informant, it makes things a little more complicated. Not impossible, but she'll have to move more carefully than she planned. What is the old saying? Keep your friends close and your enemies closer.

"I have a meeting with Chief Ross tomorrow afternoon," Dr. Ellery tells Agent Xavier. "Until then, I want you to keep an eye on him. Tell him the girl is dangerous and you were assigned to provide him with extra security. If he has any further contact with her or any other spinner, I want to know immediately."

The phone's screen goes dark when she hangs up, and Dr. Ellery drops it into a slot on the center console. Nagging worry still itches at the back of her head. She frowns. It's not Ross that's bothering her, it's the spinner. Dr. Ellery squints at her windshield. The entire surface is now clotted with leaves, and she sees the Manning girl's face etched against them like an afterimage burned into her retina. Her frown deepens. When she glimpsed the girl in the studio, there was something about her that she recognized. Not her features—it was her expression of angry defiance that was so horribly familiar.

With a jolt, Dr. Ellery realizes who the girl reminds her of. Clarissa.

A memory surfaces, one Dr. Ellery hasn't thought of in decades: Clarissa at age nine, bursting into the living room where seven-year-old Margaret was reading to announce they were going to put on a play to entertain their mother when she got home from one of the grinding temporary jobs that kept the three

106

of them on the housed side of poverty.

Dr. Ellery shakes her head, trying to clear it, but the memory is stubborn, and the scene scrolls out across the darkened window like the reel of a long-forgotten movie.

"What play?" Margaret had asked.

"Beauty and the Beast." Clarissa bounced on her toes.

Margaret hesitated. *Beauty and the Beast* was her favorite story. She looked down at the book in her lap. Her teacher said she was a very advanced reader. She had said that if Margaret finished the book by morning, the teacher would give her a sheet of cat stickers as a reward. Margaret really wanted those stickers.

"Mommy will be home soon," she said. "We won't have time to learn our lines. We should do it tomorrow."

Clarissa, ever impatient once an idea took hold of her, shook her head hard enough to make her ponytail slap the sides of her face.

"No, we'll do it today. Besides, we can make time." A sly grin crossed her face. Diving across the room, she trapped Margaret's hand between her own. The world ground to a halt. "See?" Clarissa laughed. "Now we have forever to practice."

Margaret pulled her hand away. She hated freezes. They were terrifying places peopled with immobile statues wearing the blank stares of cadavers.

"Mommy said you're not supposed to do that," she said.

Clarissa shrugged. "So we won't tell her."

The room's total silence gave Margaret an unsteady feeling, as if gravity was no longer working right either.

"Let me out," she whined.

Clarissa gave her a pitying look. "Coward."

Time started again, but Margaret was alone. When

107

Clarissa reappeared a few seconds later, she was carrying something pink in her arms.

"Look what the lady downstairs has!" she crowed, holding up a frothy nightgown. "Isn't this a perfect costume for Beauty?"

The gown was long and had bits of lace sewn all over the bodice. Margaret clamped her hands under her legs to stop herself from stroking the silky fabric.

"Mommy says you shouldn't steal things."

"I borrowed it," Clarissa clarified. "I'll put it back."

Margaret shook her head. "You're being bad. I won't play with you."

"You sure?" Clarissa waved the pink nightgown in front of her. "Not even if I let you be Beauty?"

The silk made a shushing sound, as if it was whispering secrets especially for her. Margaret's hands reached for it before she could stop herself. Quickly, she stripped off her T-shirt and slid the nightie over her head. The silk caressed her skin, cool and slippery as a waterfall.

Clarissa disappeared again, reappearing across the room dressed in a fur coat. Margaret's eyes grew wide.

"Where did you get that?"

"A store." The coat was too big, and the sleeves fell past her wrists. Clarissa raised her hands level with her face and let out a snarl so realistic that Margaret shrieked. Clarissa laughed again.

"Come on," she said, "let's work on the first scene." The next instant, the coat was heaped on a chair, and Clarissa was holding out a piece of paper on which she had written out lines of dialogue. "I'll be the father." She flashed to the other side of the room, now dressed in a pair of overalls and a plaid shirt that weren't there a second ago.

A flicker of dread twisted in the pit of Margaret's stomach. Clarissa was starting to get giddy, the way she always did when she overused her skills.

"We should stop," she said.

"No." Clarissa glared at her. "We're doing this now. Say your lines."

Margaret read the first sentence of her script.

"Not like that," Clarissa said. "You have to memorize it."

"I can't."

Clarissa rubbed her temple. "You're not trying. It's easy. Watch."

"That's not fair," Margaret said when Clarissa recited every line perfectly. "You can just stop time and check the page whenever you forget."

"Come into the freeze with me, and you can learn yours, too."

"No."

Clarissa's brow folded into ugly creases.

"Why not?" She materialized inches from Margaret. "Don't you trust me?"

The yucky feeling in Margaret's stomach grew worse.

"You froze too much," she said. "I don't want to be in your play anymore."

Clarissa's face flushed crimson. "You have to. You promised!"

"I did not." Margaret wrapped her arms around her middle. The silk didn't feel like water anymore; it felt slick, even slimy. "It was a stupid idea anyway."

"Fine," Clarissa snapped. "I don't need you. I can play all the roles myself. Gimme the gown."

She lunged. Margaret lurched away just as her sister's hands closed on the nightie. The gown's thin fabric tore with a violent rip.

"Look what you've done!" Clarissa screamed.

"It wasn't me!" Margaret blinked back tears. "It was you. You're crazy."

Clarissa's eyes flashed like lightning before a storm.

"Take that back," she demanded.

"No!" Margaret yelled. The beautiful pink gown hung from her shoulders in impossible-to-fix pieces. "You *are* crazy! You're a disgusting, horrible, crazy *spinner!*"

The door to the apartment burst open. Their mother stood in the doorway, her body taut with strain. Her eyes swept over them, taking in Margaret's furious face and Clarissa, her hands full of torn pink silk.

The door slammed shut.

"Margaret," their mother said. "How could you? Everyone in the whole hall must have heard you."

Margaret burst into tears.

Twenty minutes later, after their mother had soothed Clarissa into an exhausted sleep, she came to where Margaret was sitting at the kitchen table, face buried in her book.

"You know you can't let your sister freeze that much," she said.

Margaret didn't look up. She had ten pages left, and she was determined to finish.

"It's not my fault," she said. "Clarissa's crazy."

Her mother reached into the back of one of the cupboards and pulled out a flattened cardboard box.

"Clarissa is not crazy," she said, rummaging in a drawer.

"She's a kind, clever girl with a condition that she hasn't learned to control yet."

"Then that's *her* problem."

Margaret knew she was being rude, but she didn't care. The sick feeling in her stomach was starting to come back. Her mother had located a roll of packing tape, and Margaret knew she didn't want to hear anything else her mother was going to say.

"It's our problem because we have to protect her," her mother said. "If people know what Clarissa is, they will turn her in to a Center, and she will die."

Margaret turned a page in her book. She didn't want to think about Clarissa, or Centers, or the plates her mother was putting inside the reconstructed box. She wanted to think about school, where things were calm and orderly.

Her mother picked up a glass and wrapped it in a dishcloth.

"Pack your things," she told Margaret. "We're going to have to move."

"Again?" The bad feeling in Margaret's stomach burned like it had turned to acid. "No! I don't want to."

Her mother sighed. "Nor do I. But someone might have heard what you said, so it's not safe here anymore."

"I *have to* go to school tomorrow." Margaret clutched the unfinished book to her chest. "The teacher is giving me cat stickers."

Her mother raised an eyebrow. "I think your sister's life is more important than cat stickers, don't you?"

"It's not fair." Anger boiled from the burning place in Margaret's stomach, flooding up her throat until it burst out of her mouth in rush of pure rage. "I *hate* Clarissa."

Her mother's hand flashed out so fast, Margaret felt the slap before she saw it coming.

"Don't *ever* let me catch you saying those words again," her mother hissed. "Clarissa is your family. That means she will always be your responsibility. Now, go pack your things."

Margaret pressed a hand to her burning cheek and marched from the room. Even if she couldn't say them out loud, the words were still true. She hated her sister. Clarissa ruined everything.

The interior of the car has turned nearly black. Dr. Ellery starts the engine and uses the windshield wipers to clear away the dying leaves. Light disperses the remembered images. She hasn't seen her sister in more than thirty years; why is Clarissa haunting her now? The past should stay where it is meant to be.

Dr. Ellery backs up, then guides the car onto the main boulevard. It's all the fault of that Manning girl. People keep saying that she's clever and kind to her friends. All those people are wrong. Dr. Ellery knows firsthand that manipulating time irrevocably damages people. Her mother believed Clarissa would learn to manage her skills, but her sister never did. Spinners are addicts, all of them, unable to control themselves in the face of their obsession. Getting rid of them is the best solution for everyone.

Traffic speeds up as Dr. Ellery's car hits the freeway. She depresses the accelerator, relishing the engine's deep purr. She will not let anyone else suffer as she did. Eliminating spinners eliminates chaos. She will find and erase all the rogue spinners, especially that supposedly clever brat called Alexandra Manning.

09 ◄◄

I LET TIME START AGAIN ONCE WE'RE TEN BLOCKS AWAY FROM the studio. It's cold out here. The rain has stopped, but the newly animated world includes a stiff breeze that presses my damp clothes against my skin.

"I'll call Lisa," KJ says, pulling out the phone. "We need to tell her we missed the truck and find out where this safe house is."

"And then what? We go back to the refuge tomorrow?" I yank on the straps of my daypack, pulling its slight bulk against my back in a futile effort to ward off the chill. "But we haven't fixed anything."

KJ stops walking.

"Alex, no."

I stare down at the pavement. My stomach feels like it's stuffed with worms and all of them are squirming around, searching for a way out.

"I know." My eyes trace a crack in the sidewalk. "It's just that we failed. At everything. The refuge is still under surveillance. Shannon is still with Dr. Barnard."

"Shannon is alive," KJ says. "That's what matters."

There's a catch in his voice. When I look up, I see that he's wearing the expression of someone who has realized the prison sentence he's been dreading has been lifted. I look away. Of course I'm glad Shannon's alive, but my relief isn't as pure as KJ's. Shannon's continued refusal to see the truth stings like a personal betrayal.

"I'd still feel better if she came with us," I mutter to the sidewalk crack.

KJ's peaceful expression shifts into something more wary.

"We made an offer, and she chose to turn it down. What more could we have done? Dragged her off, kicking and screaming? She just would have run again."

The wind picks up, making me shiver. I think about our conversation in the goat truck. I think about KJ saying he loves me and the feel of his finger against my lips. I think about my promise. The worms roil.

"What about our other friends?" I ask, without daring to raise my eyes. "The wipers are still searching for them. And Miguel still can't go home."

"Which isn't a problem we have to solve by ourselves. Alex, we're not alone anymore. There are adult spinners, a whole network of them. One of them will have a solution."

I press one hand against my churning stomach. KJ is right. Going to the safe house is the cautious thing to do. The smart thing. Miguel and his friend will have suggestions. My stomach gurgles. I press harder.

"OK," I say.

KJ calls Lisa while I bounce from foot to foot, trying to generate some warmth. His end of the call is pretty limited: *Portland. Fine. Yeah, a wiper saw us. Not sure. Too late. What's the address?*

Across the street, I see a woman crammed under a dripping awning so she can keep her cell phone dry while she talks. Could she be a wiper? I take KJ's arm and lead him down a side street. The woman doesn't pay us any attention.

KJ's tone changes.

"No," he says, "really, we're *fine* and yes, we heard the news. We went to the studio and watched it so we could talk to Shannon—that's why we missed the truck." Pause. "She didn't want to come with us." Another pause. "You can ask her yourself, she's right here." He hands me the phone. "It's Yolly."

114

The phone is still warm when I hold it to my ear. I can hear noise in the background, the low-level rumble of multiple people talking.

"Hello?" I say.

"Alex!" Yolly's voice would sound more familiar if it wasn't layered with concern. "You're both really OK? No one is after you?"

"Not at the moment," I say, trying to be funny, but Yolly makes little moan of worry, so I add, "Seriously, we're just walking through a quiet residential neighborhood."

KJ checks a street sign and points in the direction we should be heading. We both change course.

"You actually talked to Shannon?" Yolly asks me. "Is the cure real? Lisa heard the news through the spinner network. Everyone here is all worked up."

"It seems real, and Shannon is . . ." I catch myself before claiming one of us is *fine* for the third time. Yolly and Shannon were close; she deserves a better answer. "Shannon seems happy. She's always wanted to be like everyone else, and as far as I can tell, Barnard is treating her well."

KJ raises an eyebrow at me. I shrug.

"How is everyone over there reacting to the news?" I ask Yolly.

"Differently." The background noise fades. I suspect Yolly has moved to another room to get out of earshot. "Aidan thinks there's something fishy going on, Raul is adamant that he doesn't want it, Kimmi thinks it's awesome, Angel keeps changing her mind, and Yuki says she wants to talk to Shannon to find out what it feels like. Most of the Youngers are just parroting what everyone else is saying."

I picture all my friends crammed into Lisa's living room, a muted TV flashing in the corner while twenty voices overlap with twenty different opinions. Longing fills my chest.

"What is Lisa saying?" I ask.

"Not much. She's been on the phone or the computer ever since the story leaked." Yolly sighs. "When will you be back?"

"Soon." The word sounds like a lie, as do my assurances that we'll be careful, which I repeat about ten times before she finally lets me hang up. The street seems quiet afterward and very, very empty.

"How far away is the safe house?" I ask KJ.

"About a mile and a half," he says. "Lisa's calling Miguel to let him know we're coming."

The two of us walk for a while without speaking. Occasionally people pass us, busy with their own lives. I wonder what they see. Just two carefree kids strolling together? That dog walker who nodded as we walked by, or the group of schoolkids who barely acknowledged us—what would they do if they knew what we were? Scream? Call the police? Would any of them offer us help?

What if some of *them* are spinners? That man whizzing by on a bicycle, or the other man who just swore at him when the spray from the tires splashed his pant leg—either of them could be hiding the same secret I am. What will today's news mean to them? Will it make them happy? Will they want to be cured?

"Would you do it?" I ask KJ.

"Do what?"

"Be cured. Stop being a spinner."

We've reached an intersection, and KJ hits the walk button. *Wait*, a mechanical voice barks. *Wait.*

"First I'd need to know if there are any long-term effects," KJ says. "And if it lasts. There could be something in our DNA that manufactures chronotin, and even if it gets cleaned out, the body could make more, and—"

I make an impatient gesture. "Let's just assume it works. Would you do it?"

There's a pause. Cars whizz past us, hulking metal beasts galloping through an urban tundra. I rub one foot along the edge of the curb and feel like I'm teetering on a cliff.

"I guess so," KJ says.

My foot slips. I reach for a nearby telephone pole and steady myself against its rough side.

KJ tilts his head. "Wouldn't you?" he asks. "If we weren't spinners, we wouldn't have to hide or worry about the risks that come with controlling time. Remember that day Jack completely flipped out? I never want that to happen to me."

"Yeah, I guess, but . . ." Time swirls around me, ephemeral as mist and powerful as a tornado. I try to imagine never touching it again, never sinking into the utter stillness of a freeze, never feeling the security of knowing I am totally in control.

"We'd be so vulnerable," I say.

"True. But with nobody chasing us, we wouldn't have any reason to be afraid."

My hand smells like tar from the telephone pole. I rub it against my leg.

"Being a spinner is such a huge part of me. If that goes away, who am I?"

"You're Alex." KJ leans over and plants a kiss on my nose. "The smart, brave, special girl I happen to be hopelessly in love with."

The light changes. KJ takes my hand and steps down into the street. I follow him. For the first time, his kiss doesn't make me happy. What if the girl KJ is describing doesn't exist? I don't think I'm particularly smart, and I'm only brave because I know I can shield myself inside time. If my skills go away, what will be left behind that makes me special?

The safe house turns out to be a small blue bungalow on a quiet street in the Hawthorne neighborhood. KJ and I approach it warily. The house has a covered porch, its floorboards worn smooth from years of foot traffic. A well-used couch takes up space under one of a pair of picture windows. Next to it is an ornate metal sculpture that might once have been a birdbath but has been repurposed as an ashtray. Butts fill the bowl, sending out an ashy smell. KJ presses the doorbell, and I catch an answering buzz from inside. I check behind us. No one is out here except a cat, watching us from atop a retaining wall across the street.

The door clicks as multiple locks are unlatched, then swings open to reveal Miguel. He looks like he hasn't slept much since we last saw him. The chipper expression he wore the first time we met has been replaced by something more haunted, and the laugh lines around his eyes are deep with worry.

"Hey, there." Miguel scans the sidewalk as he motions us inside. "Come in."

We follow him through an entry hall and into a living room, where a uniformed man unfolds himself from one of the chairs. I flinch, instinctively reaching out for time, before recognizing that the uniform he's wearing says Emergency Medical Technician and not Portland Police Department. My mind unclenches.

"I'm Jamal," the man says as he rises to his feet. He's taller than Miguel and heavyset, with a completely bald head that shines like polished mahogany. "You must be Alex and KJ. I've heard a lot about you."

I grimace. "Not all good, I'm guessing."

Jamal laughs, and the cheery sound does a lot to reduce the tension squeezing my shoulders.

"I heard you're committed to helping your friends," Jamal says. "That's good enough in my book."

I duck my head at the compliment. Miguel motions for us to sit while Jamal goes to the kitchen, returning with a tray holding a plate of cookies and four mugs of steaming coffee. I take a cup gratefully, cradling its warmth in my cold hands.

"Lisa said you came here to distract the wipers," Miguel says. "How'd that go?"

KJ fills him in on our day while I sip my drink and study the room. It's

118

a welcoming place, filled with the homey scent of recent baking. The sofa and matching armchairs are covered in a dark red fabric that's both fuzzy and soft. On one wall, a fireplace sits between built-in bookcases stuffed with paperbacks. Framed photographs crowd the mantel, most of them featuring Jamal and another shorter man with sandy-blond hair. I run my eyes over the photos. Jamal and Blondie standing by a lake, holding up a pair of very large fish. Jamal and Blondie at a party. Jamal beaming at the camera while Blondie plants a kiss on his cheek. Blondie wearing a white doctor's coat and sitting on the blue house's porch sofa, a cigarette drooping from his lips as he stares out toward the street with a pensive expression. There's also a picture of a younger, thinner Jamal sporting a full head of hair, standing with a whole group of people in some dusty terrain. All of them are wearing army uniforms, and most are hefting serious-looking guns.

KJ starts talking about our meeting with Shannon. I try to focus on the conversation, but my attention keeps drifting back to the photos. There's something disconcerting about them. Our time at the refuge made the concept of free adult spinners real, but I'm not sure what to make of this man living in an ordinary house in the middle of a Norm neighborhood. The refuge was private, tucked in an out-of-the-way corner of the state. Jamal's life seems so *obvious* and, judging by the pictures and his career choice, completely public. It's hard to believe he could live like this and still be a spinner.

"Who *is* Dr. Ellery?"

KJ's question snaps my focus back to the conversation. Jamal is frowning at him, one hand rubbing the smooth globe of his head in a steady rhythm like it's a talisman that can ward off evil.

"Margaret Ellery," he says, "runs the Tacoma Central Office and oversees all the Centers in the US. We're fairly sure that she's also a high-ranking member of Kronos."

The word *Kronos* falls from his lips like a curse. Danger invades the cozy confines of Jamal's living room, as if even the mention of the organization

119

has the same effects as a zapper. I think of Dr. Ellery, that small, neatly dressed woman whose gaze seemed to pierce the dark studio to find me even during my freeze, and shudder.

"What exactly does Kronos do?" KJ asks. "They're not listed on any of the Central Office websites or any other official site I could find."

Jamal looks surprised that KJ has researched Kronos, a fact I didn't know either but should have expected. KJ always wants to understand how things work.

"Kronos has no official role with any of the Central Offices," Jamal says, "but they make policy and control everything from behind the scenes. They also play a critical role in maintaining the lie that spinners are dangerous. The group uses its substantial wealth and global influence to do things like make sure only anti-spinner politicians are elected and that spinner-friendly legislation gets quashed. They also produce a steady stream of propaganda to ensure that the public remains fearful, like that TV show that's popular right now—what's it called, *The Secret Life of Spinners?* That's got Kronos written all over it."

KJ frowns. "The organization must be massive."

"Surprisingly, it's not," Jamal says. "We think there are less than a hundred people who work directly for Kronos around the globe, managed by a small multinational board of trustees. The trustee positions are inherited, handed down through generations. Most of the families have been with the organization for centuries."

I sip my coffee, seeking comfort in its warmth. There's something ghoulish about an inheritance whose entire purpose is the suppression of a particular group of people.

"Is Dr. Ellery one of the trustees?" I ask.

Jamal shakes his head. "She's more like a liaison. Officially, she is the person in charge of the Offices, but in reality, her orders come from Kronos. At least, that's what we believe. Given the consistent treatment of spinners across the globe, it's logical that the same group is controlling it all."

"So this cure." KJ leans forward. "It will be used everywhere?"

"I'm sure it will." Jamal turns to me. "You talked with Shannon; you're convinced the cure is real?"

"Oh, yeah." My hand moves to my cheek, brushing the same spot where I touched Shannon's. "We were in my freeze, and when I touched her skin, I felt nothing." I drop my hand. "It was just like touching a Norm."

"We should post that on the network." Miguel scratches his chin. He hasn't shaved in a while, and the lower half of his face is dark with growth. "There's lots of buzz that the whole thing might be a hoax."

"Good idea." Jamal digs a silver laptop out from under a stack of newspapers heaped on a side table.

I watch his fingers dance over the keyboard. "Is this the same network Lisa mentioned? She said she was using it to try and find permanent homes for all of us."

"Probably," Jamal says without looking up. "Most English speaking spinners are part of a shared online message board."

"What are they saying about the cure announcement?" KJ asks.

"Mostly questions." Jamal taps out another flurry of keystrokes. "No one trusts the Central Office doctors. And lots of people are worried that we won't be given any choice about whether or not to undergo their new treatment."

"Of course we'll have a *choice*," Miguel says. "It's not like they can force us to come in. They don't even know where we are."

Jamal looks up. "They found the trawlers. And what about that big project we know they're working on? Project Zed."

Miguel makes a dismissive gesture that doesn't match the muscle twitching in his clenched jaw.

"It seems pretty clear to me that we know what Project Zed is now. It's the cure."

"Maybe." Jamal closes the laptop's lid with a soft snap. "But what about the part they're not talking about? They say they're going to cure all the kids living in Centers; no one has said a word about the free spinners."

Miguel fixes Jamal with a look that I'm pretty sure means something along the lines of *don't scare the children.*

"You'll have to forgive Jamal," he says, offering us the plate of cookies. "He spends all his time reading conspiracy theories."

The cookies are homemade, the batter thick with oats and chocolate chips. KJ shakes his head. I accept one but hold it between my fingers without tasting it. I have too many questions to fill my mouth with a hearty cookie.

"What are these theories?" I ask.

"They're not just *theories,*" Jamal says. "There have been too many rumors for them not to be true."

"But that's just it, isn't it?" Miguel says. "They're rumors."

"Is it a rumor that Mike and his roommates died in an unexplained house fire last week? Or that Jeanine's car went through a guardrail two days ago, even though she's the most cautious driver on earth? Why would they be hunting us down this aggressively if they mean to cure us?"

"It's rumor that those deaths are *connected,*" Miguel says, "and that they have anything to do with Kronos."

A smattering of crumbs drifts onto my lap, and I realize I'm crushing the cookie between my fingers.

"Wait a minute," I say. "Back up. How many free spinners has Kronos killed recently?"

The two men exchange a glance, and Miguel's scowl makes it clear he wishes Jamal had kept his mouth shut.

"The wipers' job has always been to capture free spinners," Jamal says, obviously choosing his words with care. "Their focus is on kids like you who escape Centers, but they also round up adult free spinners if we make ourselves known. Recently, a handful of spinners have died under suspicious

122

circumstances, but Miguel is right—we don't have *proof* that they're actively hunting us." His emphasis on the word *proof* makes it clear he thinks otherwise.

I drop the uneaten cookie into my empty coffee mug and stand up, kicking aside the daypack at my feet. "Can't you stop them?"

Jamal's eyes widen. "Stop Kronos?"

"Yes!" I pace to the end of the room and spin on my heel to stride back. "They're the ones running the Centers and the Central Offices, right? And they're the ones behind all the propaganda. So if we stop Kronos, we'll be free."

"It's not that simple," Jamal says.

"Kronos has support from the highest levels of government," Miguel adds. "It's all very complicated."

I turn again. "What about the CIA? Lisa said they were investigating Kronos."

Jamal gives a bitter laugh. "All the CIA cares about is whether Kronos has more power than they do to manipulate elections. Even if they manage to collect enough evidence to actually charge Kronos with vote tampering or blackmail, all that will change for us is that it will be the CIA running Centers instead of Kronos."

"Life for spinners under the CIA could be better," Miguel says. "Max is confident they wouldn't murder us outright. She thinks they want us to work for them, which means they'd have to—"

Jamal waves a hand to cut him off. "I know what Max thinks, but all of that is speculation. It's not like the CIA has a golden record on human rights."

I glance at KJ, who hasn't said a word in the last ten minutes. He's turning his coffee mug in his hands and staring down at the floor. I swallow a burst of frustration. How can KJ listen to this and not want to *act?*

"OK," I say. "Forget the CIA. What if we went public? Told everyone that Kronos has been manipulating the truth and fixing elections?"

"With what evidence?" Miguel shakes his head. "Kronos is very, very good at hiding what they do."

123

"What if *you*"—I stop pacing and point to Jamal—"a full-grown spinner, showed everyone the extent of your skills? The Norms would see that what they've been told about spinners is a lie, and then they'd question everything else."

Jamal holds up a finger. "Terence Hutchinson made his announcement onstage at Woodstock. Wipers dragged him away, and the whole thing was written off as a group acid hallucination." Another finger. "Gwendolyn Harris spoke the truth in the middle of Times Square in 1987. Later, it was 'proven' she was a street magician pulling an elaborate prank to try and jump-start her career." A third finger. "In 1999, Camille Torres collaborated with a reporter who published her entire story in the *Hartford Courant*. The article was retracted within hours. The editor lost his job the same day, and the reporter who wrote the story 'committed suicide' two days later."

"Kronos killed a *Norm?*" KJ asks.

Jamal nods. "Should I go on? Those are just a few of the people who have tried during my lifetime."

"What happened to them?" I ask, even though I'm pretty sure I know the answer.

"They disappeared."

I start pacing again. The living room isn't very big; it only takes a handful of steps to get from one end to the other.

"Doesn't your network have any other ideas?" I ask. "In all these years, hasn't someone thought up a way to fight back?"

Jamal lays a hand protectively on his computer.

"Of *course* people have thought about it," he says. "There are millions of threads on the network devoted to this very topic. There was even a serious plan a couple of years ago. We were going to hack into the Central Office's mainframe and download files to prove Kronos was murdering spinner children. Norms may be blinded, but the human race isn't inherently evil. If we could prove—really *prove*—that Kronons were killers, most of us don't think they'd

124

be allowed to continue."

"What happened?" I ask.

Jamal grimaces. "No one could get access. All our efforts to convince one of the on-site staff members at the Office to leak the information went nowhere. Three of our best hackers worked for months to get past their firewalls, and the only result was that the wipers managed to track them down. After they died, the idea kind of withered."

Frustration spreads like a rash across my skin. KJ believes the free spinners are going to take charge and fix everything, but from Jamal's description, it sounds like they've given up.

"Forget hackers, then," I say. "Someone should just go to the Central Office and download the information from there."

"That's a suicide mission," Miguel says, "not to mention impossible. Security is way too tight for anyone to break into the Central Office."

My circuit around the living room sends me past Miguel's chair, and he reaches out to take my arm.

"Sit down, Alex," he says. "There's no point in getting worked up over something you can't fix."

I yank my arm free. "So none of you are going to do anything?"

"We're doing something," Jamal says. "We're collecting information, and then we'll decide, as a community, the best strategy to keep ourselves safe."

He pats the laptop's silver cover. There's a sticker pasted on it with an EMT emblem and the words FIRST I DRINK COFFEE, THEN I SAVE LIVES. The living room that seemed so cozy when we first walked in now feels claustrophobic. The snug furnishings, the multitude of photographs—they all speak of someone entrenched, stable, and cautious.

"Collecting *what* information?" I snarl. "More rumors?"

"Alex," Miguel says, "you're not being fair."

"It's all right." Jamal holds up a hand to Miguel and turns to me. "Here's an example of what we're doing. There's a meeting happening here in town tomorrow afternoon that will be attended by Dr. Ellery, Dr. Barnard, and the new police chief. Our understanding is that they'll be discussing the follow-up to today's announcement, and we have an informant we're hoping will be able to pass on the gist of their conversation. Once we know their plans, we'll be able to take concrete steps in direct response to any threat, which is a much better strategy than rushing around in a fruitless effort to bring down the entire behemoth."

Our understanding. We're hoping. Gist of the conversation. It all seems so tenuous. There's a cure out there no one knows anything about, Kronos is picking off free spinners, and they're relying on a *possible* leak? I look over at KJ, hoping for an ally in my outrage, but he's still staring at the floor with enough intensity to bore a hole through it. I cross my arms over my damp chest. I can almost hear his voice reminding me of my promise and telling me how disappointed he is that I'm once again talking about fighting. Another shiver rattles my body. My sodden sweatshirt is a heavy weight dragging at my shoulders.

Jamal moves his laptop back onto the side table and stands up. "Lisa scheduled another goat delivery for Friday," he says. "You two will be able catch a ride back to the farm then. Let me show you where you'll be staying for the next couple of days. I've got some clothes downstairs you can change into. You'll both feel better when you're dry."

Being wet is the least of my worries, but it's clear the conversation is over, so I grab my pack and follow him and KJ out of the room. Jamal takes us down a short hall, pointing out a guest room he says is mine, before leading us downstairs into the basement. Unlike the refuge's storage-room décor, this space feels like an extension of the house. The walls are painted a soft cream, and there are three twin beds lined up against one wall, each with a handmade quilt.

"KJ, you can sleep down here," Jamal says. He shows us the bathroom and where to find clean towels, then opens a wall-length sliding door to reveal a closet stuffed with clothes.

"My house is basically an Underground Railroad stop for spinners on the run," he explains. "Sympathetic folks send me stuff all the time, so feel free to help yourself. There are plenty of sizes—just dig through."

"Thank you," KJ says. "We really appreciate you taking us in like this."

"It's what we do," Jamal says.

The warm coffee taste still coats my tongue, and the expansive collection of clothes, plus the promise of my own bed tonight, pricks at my conscience.

"I'm sorry." I twist the daypack's straps around my fingers. "I am grateful for everything you're doing. I'm sorry I was so rude upstairs."

Jamal's wide face softens into a smile.

"It's all right." His voice is gentle. "I know this is hard and scary. Just be patient, OK?"

When he leaves, KJ starts digging through the closet, holding up a series of sweaters to see if they'll fit. I flop down on one of the beds and stare at the ceiling. The stitching on the quilt tickles the back of my neck, and my wet sweatshirt makes it feel like there's an oversize toad squatting on my chest.

"You want to shower first?" KJ asks.

"KJ?" I sit up. He's still facing the closet, but even from behind, I can tell his shoulders are tense. "Do you ever get tired of running?"

"What do you mean?"

"Ever since we left the Center, it's all we've been doing. Running. Reacting."

"We're the ones who set up the meeting with Ross."

"Yeah . . ." I shake my head, frustrated by my inability to communicate what I'm feeling. "Sort of, but even that plan was just in reaction to the fact that the wipers suspected where we were. I mean, we should have our *own* plan. Take the initiative. Right now, it seems like they're always one step ahead of us."

"That's because they are," KJ turns around. He's holding a too-small green sweater against his chest like it's a shield.

"They don't have to be." I pick at a thread on the quilt. The patches are all shades of sunny yellow, and the stitching on the top is patterned like clocks. Someone somewhere cared enough to donate this especially for runaway spinners.

"Miguel and Jamal," I say, "they're too cautious. It's like you said in the truck. The free spinners have so much to lose that they're afraid to take any risks. They're just sitting back and *hoping* that Max or some other secret ally will *maybe* find out something useful when they could be figuring out how to listen to the conversation themselves, like we did at the studio. That wasn't even that dangerous!"

KJ lets the sweater droop to the floor. I try to read the expression on his face. Is he sad? Angry?

"I knew you were going to say this."

"I'm sorry." I drop my eyes back to the quilt. "I know I promised I'd let them take over." I twist the thread again, and it comes loose, partially unravelling the face of a stitched-on clock. I sigh. "There's nothing we could do, anyway. We don't even know where the meeting is going to be."

KJ clears his throat.

"We do know who's going to be at the meeting, though. If we could look at one of their calendars, I bet we could find out where they'll be."

It takes a second for his words to sink in. I look up. KJ is still standing in front of the closet with the sweater trailing from one hand, but there's a glint in his eyes now that has nothing to do with anger.

"Are you saying you agree we have to fight back?" I ask.

"I'm saying I know you'll never forgive yourself if you just sit here. Fighting for what you believe in is a big part of who you are, and if I love you, then I have to love that part of you, too." He balls up the sweater and tosses it to me. "I figure if you're going to go fight the big bad guys, my job is to make

128

sure you don't run off alone and do something totally half baked."

I don't think I've ever loved KJ more than I do in this moment. I want to leap across the room and cover his face with kisses. That blank stare he wore upstairs was not about his disappointment in me. KJ was making plans.

"We can't get into Dr. Ellery's calendar," I say, "since we don't know where to find her. And we can't go to Barnard's house because he keeps a zapper in his office. That leaves Ross."

"My thoughts exactly," KJ says. "We can run a rewind in his office. He's bound to check his calendar at some point."

"That should work," I say. "Ross might be carrying a zapper everywhere these days, but I doubt the whole police department will be stocked with them. We're not exactly their main focus." I shake out the sweater KJ tossed me. It's made of soft cotton and will fit me perfectly. "The harder part will be eavesdropping on the meeting. This one isn't going to be in some huge studio with lots of convenient places to hide."

"What if we don't try to watch it in person?" KJ says. "We could use surveillance equipment. I've seen ads for electronics stores that sell loads of the stuff."

This time I do leap across the room. KJ catches me in his arms as I hurtle into him. The warmth of his embrace chases away even the chill from my wet shirt. I raise my face and find his lips. The details of our plans, my frustration with the free spinners—all of it melts away in a wave of electric bliss.

"I love you," KJ murmurs against my mouth. His hands tangle in my hair, and mine stroke the back of his neck.

"I love your courage," he says, "and your resourcefulness, and how hard you fight for what you think is right."

I pull him closer. I want to absorb him into me.

"I could never do this without you," I tell him.

KJ gives a husky laugh.

"Of course you could." He kisses me again, deep and long. "I'm just the

129

guy holding the ladder steady down on the ground. You're the one scaling it."

"But we'll get there, won't we?" I pull away so I can look into his eyes. "We'll figure out how to protect our friends?"

"You lead the way." KJ crushes me against him so tightly my spine cracks. "And I promise I will do everything in my power to keep you safe."

I rest my head against his chest. Almost every minute since we left the Center, I've felt afraid. Even our brief respite at the refuge was tainted by the wipers hovering on its perimeter. I don't feel afraid now. I feel strong and filled with purpose. I am a spinner, and I'm going to fight. For all of us.

10 ◀◀

"YOU LOOK WEIRD," KJ SAYS.

We're walking downtown, it's just after nine a.m., and the sidewalks are crowded with people on their way to work. I brush a hand over the skirt I selected from Jamal's closet. My outfit, an unremarkable urban-teen-goth getup, is nothing like my usual jeans-and-a-sweatshirt ensemble, which is the point. The skirt is black and long enough to swing around my calves. The tights under it are black, too, as are the clunky boots, the down vest, the hair-covering beanie, and my eyeliner. Even my fingernails are painted the midnight hue.

"Bad weird?" I ask. "Or different weird?"

He tilts his head. "Different weird. I think it's mostly the lipstick."

I purse my lips and squint down my nose, allowing me to catch a glimpse of Jungle Red.

"Yeah, well, you look weird, too," I say. "Even without any lipstick."

Weird isn't really the word I would choose to describe him. KJ is wearing baggy skater pants, a brimmed hat, and sunglasses. Honestly, he looks really, really cute.

I take a gulp of the oversize latte I got to fend off any time-holding side effects. More than twelve hours without freezing, along with a carefully measured dose of Aclisote, has washed away yesterday's headache, but I know there's another one in my future. Our plans for the day involve a lot of freezing.

We spent most of last night pretending to watch a movie in the basement while talking through details. Our first problem was figuring out how

131

to get Jamal and Miguel to let us leave the house. We finally settled on telling them about our stolen money and saying we wanted to use it to get supplies for the refuge so that Lisa wouldn't have to sneak suspicious amounts of extra stuff into the house. The two men were reluctant but finally agreed that supplies were necessary.

Our next problem was how to get into police headquarters, home of Ross's new office. The website said the place had restricted access, which means we can't get past the lobby unless someone lets us in. Even with our low-level disguises, neither KJ nor I—whose faces are plastered all over MISSING signs— can realistically hang out in the lobby waiting for the door to open, so our plan is to loiter outside until we see an officer we can follow into the building.

We get to police headquarters at nine fifteen. It's a high-rise in the middle of downtown with police cars parked nose-to-end all along the block in front of it. The words JUSTICE CENTER are etched in the concrete over the entrance. KJ and I slouch casually into the park across the street and plop onto an empty bench. He sits at a slight angle so he can see the headquarters' front door, and I curl up beside him and lean my head against his shoulder. We're aiming for a look that is not so vagrant that someone will roust us but adrift enough that we'll be ignored. It seems to be working. Everyone who passes by avoids making eye contact.

"What's going on?" I ask after a few minutes. From my position, all I can see is the army of squirrels that dominate the park.

"No one in uniform yet."

A healthily plump squirrel dashes along the metal fence that marks the edge of the park, perfectly balanced on the narrow rail. When the sun lights its bottlebrush tail, the fur turns nearly blond.

"Hey, KJ, why do you think Shannon trusts Dr. Barnard instead of me?"

"Probably partly because it *is* you."

"What do you mean?"

"Shannon likes being special."

I nibble on the rim of my coffee cup, which is now smeared with Jungle Red.

"Wasn't she special enough at the Center? She always had boyfriends, she was Yolly's favorite, and the Youngers all loved her."

KJ glances down at me. "Is that really how you saw her?"

"How else should I have seen her?"

"She's always been jealous of you, Alex. Not just about me," he adds when he sees me squirm. "You're the smart one, the best at holding time, the one who got the agent everybody wanted to work for."

"Shannon didn't even like time work!"

"It doesn't matter if she liked it. Shannon needs people's approval. That's why she always had a boyfriend. And if holding time is what defines us and she wasn't very good at it, then in some basic way, she was failing. The only thing she got approval for was being the Center's good girl. That's why it's so hard for her to let go of the idea that they're helping us. I think when Barnard chose her as their ambassador, she felt . . . I don't know, redeemed, I guess. Like she finally beat you."

I stare at his profile, not sure if I'm more startled by KJ's conclusions or his insight. I thought I knew everything about him, and now it turns out he's secretly Freud.

"Did she tell you all this?"

KJ shrugs. "Some of it. The rest I just put together."

I take a swallow of coffee. Is KJ right? Is Shannon in denial about the truth and therefore angry about my perceived stubbornness, or is she angry at me and therefore in denial? If it's the latter, does that make her defection to Dr. Barnard more or less my fault?

KJ lays a hand on my arm. "Here comes a cop."

The mystery of Shannon recedes, and I roll to my feet, moving as calmly as my quickened heartbeat allows. A uniformed officer has reached the steps of the police building and is jogging up them. KJ and I hurry in the

133

opposite direction, slipping into a concrete public restroom between some trees.

"Think he's opened the security door yet?" I ask, breathing through my mouth to avoid the noxious urine-and-cleanser stench filling the dingy room.

"Let's try it."

I set my coffee on the sink. KJ stops time.

The Justice Center's lobby is spare; other than the metal detector at the entrance, there are just a few plastic chairs and one dusty plant. The front desk is protected by a bulletproof window, behind which sits a bored-looking woman with a peace sign shaved into her hair. A tall man stands in front of her. The freeze caught him gesticulating as he talks—one hand raised, the other held out to one side. To their left, the police officer we saw outside is halfway through the secure entrance that leads into the precinct.

"We're in luck." KJ gently pulls the door away from the officer's hand to make a gap wide enough for us to pass through. I duck under the man in blue's arm and step into the police department's inner sanctum.

The interior hallway is painted a depressing shade of industrial beige. Three bulletin boards hang near the door, all crusted with overlapping flyers: employee safety notices, announcements about upcoming neighborhood events, missing pet posters, and a long line of mug shots. I scan the boards until I find the lost children section. Our faces stare back at me. MISSING. REWARD. I lick my fingers and let them trail across our photo as we pass, pressing down to smudge the grainy ink.

A sign by the elevator tells us the administrative offices are on the third floor. We take the stairs.

The chief of police's office is empty, which we expected; if Ross was here, his zapper would have alerted KJ with its warning panic. Still, something inside me unclenches, and I realize how much I was dreading seeing Ross again. The new chief hasn't had the position long enough to make the room his, and the office has the unnatural tidiness of a place no one actually inhabits. A handful of pens in a wire cup anchors a small assortment of office supplies lining

134

one side of his desk, the bookshelf is empty except for some manuals, and the drawers, which we search, hold almost nothing. There's no half empty pack of gum, no stash of extra staples, no stray forks or crumpled tissues. The files we find are few and neatly ordered.

"He's not going to keep a paper calendar," I tell KJ. "We're going to have to look for the meeting info on his computer. Try rewinding."

Time runs backward, quickly at first as KJ backs us through the night, then more slowly as the events from yesterday afternoon being to unroll. I perch on the edge of the desk and watch as shadows flicker over the room. The computer lights up first. The image on it is faint, a shadowy version of an active screen superimposed over the dark real one. When the memory of the door opens, I jump up, even though I'm expecting it. The Ross that enters is a wisp of the actual man, but seeing him still brings a flash of rage.

Ross backs into the room and drops into his chair, swiveling to face the computer. KJ and I move to stand behind him, watching over his ghostly shoulder as he un-writes a couple of emails and makes a bunch of phone calls from his desk phone. Whatever he's saying plays out in reverse and is impossible to understand. Periodically, Ross pulls out his personal cell and checks it. KJ and I stand side by side behind his chair, reading the words that flash up on the computer screen.

"These aren't very helpful," KJ says after pausing the rewind for the fifth time to read an email. This one is to Officer Cannon, whom Ross is "so sorry" to inform that he has been let go. The smile that curves Ross's lips as he types is vindictive.

"Keep going," I tell KJ.

The rewind picks up speed. A female officer enters the room to talk to Ross. Even with unintelligible gibberish coming from their mouths, I can see how much Ross enjoys his new position. He's practically preening while they chat. The woman smiles at him and ducks her head. I cringe. Did I look that dazzled and stupid when I was working with him?

135

"How could I have believed Ross was a good guy?" I say.

"He was nice to you." KJ slows the rewind to watch Ross un-write a short memo, then speeds it up again when the note turns out to be a reminder to himself to pick up coffee filters. "Getting treated like dirt by ninety-nine percent of the population makes you vulnerable."

"You didn't fall for it," I say. "You always thought he was a jerk."

KJ shrugs. "Shannon wasn't the only person who was jealous."

"*Right.*" I fiddle with the pens in Ross's cup, rearranging them so they all lean the same direction. "You never cared that I had the 'best' agent. You told me you preferred rewinding traffic accidents to crimes."

"I wasn't jealous that he was your agent," KJ said. "I was jealous that he took so much of your attention."

My hands fall still. "You were?"

Morning sun—the real one, not yesterday's weak replica—shines through the window to light KJ's face. He's so beautiful. The smooth bronze of his skin, the regal arch of his nose, the shadow that accentuates the curve of his cheekbones. I could stare at his face forever and never get bored. And it's not just his face that I love. KJ is good in a way I'll never be. He's always so clear about what is right and wrong, while I flounder around, questioning everything.

KJ leans toward the computer. "There it is."

I drop the pens and follow his gaze. Ross's calendar flickers on the computer screen, a mishmash of blue squares stamped on a white background. The colors are faint, the words barely legible through the real-world glare. I push the desk chair aside and put my face right through Ross's misty shoulder so I can see more clearly.

"What's that one?" I point to a large blue rectangle with a heading that includes the word *conference.*

KJ shakes his head. "That's tomorrow. See?" He points to a different spot. "The calendar is showing the whole week, so we only care about this column. Wednesday."

136

I run my eyes down the section he's indicating. According to the schedule, real-time Ross is currently having coffee with someone named Hank Ramirez. At ten, he'll be at the city manager's office for a staff briefing, and at noon, he's having lunch with a Monica Duvall. My eyes skip forward to the afternoon.

"That one." I snatch up a pen and scribble the information on a sticky note: *2:30, spinner consultation, Fletcher Underhill.* "Who's Fletcher Underhill?"

"I think that's the location," KJ says. "The meeting after it says conference room B, and the one tomorrow says Seattle Hyatt."

"Rewind some more," I say. "Maybe he'll click on it and there'll be an address or something."

Ross un-types an appointment for Friday with someone named R. Sullivan. Then he checks his cell phone again. I'm still standing with my head halfway through his chest, so the phone's ghostly screen is right in front of my nose.

"Stop!" I tell KJ. The rewind halts. I adjust my position so I can better see what Ross is looking at. There's a map on his screen, and in its center, there's a small green dot.

"That's a tracker," I say.

KJ squints at the image.

"He's not tracking us." KJ points at a blue curve running along one side of the map. "That's the Willamette River. Whoever he's watching was on the west side yesterday afternoon. We were at Jamal's house then, in southeast."

"You think it's Jack?" I ask.

"Didn't Shannon cut his tracker out when she did ours?"

I touch the air where the green dot hovers, my finger passing through the spot where Jack is not.

"Ross must have put a new one in him." I shudder. I had a tracker until a couple of weeks ago. Knowing what I do now about the people who want to

137

find us, the idea of being fitted with a locating device is chilling.

"Do you think Ross told him?" I ask.

"Don't know." KJ starts the rewind again, inching time backward with his eyes fixed on the computer screen. "And don't care. Jack chose to work with Ross, and he knows exactly what kind of manipulative jerk he is. I don't see why Jack would expect the guy to treat him fairly."

The green dot quivers as it moves across the map on Ross's phone. It looks lonely.

"Don't you feel even a little sorry for Jack?" I say. "He wasn't in the best condition when he agreed to work for Mr. Ross. And he was super helpful when we first ran away from the Center. We wouldn't have had anywhere to stay if it wasn't for him."

KJ doesn't answer.

The map on Ross's phone disappears, replaced with a login screen. I watch Ross's fingers type in a code in reverse: *7565. Above the code is a white rectangle containing an email address: cross@gmail.com.

I glance at KJ. He's still focused on the computer, spooling out the rewind as he waits to see if Ross will reveal any more information. I slide the sticky note with the meeting details into my pocket and use another one to jot down the name of the tracking app and Ross's login information. I know Jack is a traitor, but he's still a spinner. He's one of us, and despite KJ's disapproval, knowing I can find him brings me comfort. We're not leaving Portland for two more days. Maybe we can visit him and give him some way to contact us, just in case he ever changes his mind about Ross.

"I don't think we're going to find anything else," KJ says, massaging his temple ten minutes later. He's rewound Ross's day all the way to yesterday at noon, at which point the new chief left the office without checking his calendar again.

"We can look up Fletcher Underhill on our phone." I set the pen and the unused sticky notes back where I found them on Ross's desk. "Come on, let's get out of here."

We leave the building the way we came in. Once outside, we return to the stinky bathroom and start time. I reclaim my lipstick-smeared coffee cup and take a long swallow as we step back outside. The coffee is still hot.

Optimism swirls through me along with the caffeine. Our morning's plan went off without a hitch, and stumbling on a way to find Jack is an added bonus. The day before us shines with possibilities.

"What do you think they're meeting to talk about?" I ask KJ.

"Jamal said it was probably a follow-up to the cure announcement. Maybe they'll say something about how effective it really is."

We make our way onto the sidewalk and blend in with the morning crowd. The city looks fresh, like yesterday's rain washed away all its usual grime.

"Maybe they'll talk about the process of shipping kids to the Office," I say, "and we can figure out a way to intercept them."

"And if we're lucky," KJ says, "we'll find out whether they bought your claim that all of us are still in Portland."

My new boots make a satisfying clunking sound as they smack the sidewalk. It feels good to have a plan. Whatever next step Kronos is plotting, for once we aren't going to be caught unawares. We're going to know what's coming, and we'll be able to share our knowledge with every spinner on the network. I sip my coffee and feel the invigorating caffeine spread through my insides. For the first time, we're going to be a step ahead. We're going to be prepared.

11 ◀◀

FLETCHER AND UNDERHILL TURNS OUT TO BE A LAW FIRM HEADED
by James Fletcher and Clarence Underhill. Their offices are on the twenty-
seventh floor of a very tall, grayish-pink building on the north end of downtown.
At 2:10—after spending the day buying spy equipment and skulking in the main
library—KJ and I hike up a very long flight of stairs that leads to the office. By
the time we reach our goal, I have a stich in my side, and we're both panting.
The sound is super loud. Even if time weren't frozen, the landing outside the
law office would be quiet. Thick carpet muffles our every step, the fibers so
plush that I'm tempted to lie down and rest my quivering legs.

"We should have dressed as couriers," KJ manages between gasps.
"Then we could have taken the elevator up here in real time."

My laugh comes out as a wheeze.

The law office's main doors are glass with the company name etched in
frosted letters across the front. They're not locked. The interior is decorated in
an earthy mix of khaki green, browns, and beige, as if the staff is pretending they
work in a really tidy version of the great outdoors. A coiffed woman sits behind
a reception desk, her manicured hands poised over a keyboard. Behind her is a
colorful painting with swirls that are vaguely reminiscent of salmon. The
receptionist is probably lovely, but the freeze caught her mid-blink, giving her
the droopy expression of someone about to nod off.

Directly across from the front entrance is a conference room,
sandwiched between a wall of glass and floor-to-ceiling windows that offer

dizzying views of the city below.

"You better not come here for a meeting if you're scared of heights," I say, making a beeline for the window. Buildings that look elegant from the street are surprisingly gritty when seen from above. Metal vents sprout from roofs like squat mushrooms, their edges sealed with messy splotches of black tar. The city itself looks tiny, the people ants, the cars miniature toys. Standing here makes me feel godlike, as if Portland is merely a plaything I can control. It seems fitting that Kronos chose this as their meeting place.

KJ opens his daypack and pulls out the surveillance stuff. I was worried that buying it would make the clerk suspicious, but the guy who helped us didn't even blink when KJ trotted out a story—which I thought sounded far-fetched—about how he suspected someone was breaking into his dorm room and downloading his papers. KJ and the clerk engaged in a very long and exceptionally boring conversation about the merits of various models before finally selecting a pen-shaped camera that can transmit a live feed with both sound and video to an app we downloaded on our phone. Since we don't have access to the building's Wi-Fi, we also got a portable router with a prepaid SIM card.

"Where should we put the stuff?" I ask.

We both survey the room. There aren't a ton of options. A polished conference table takes up most of the space, surrounded by a dozen throne-like leather chairs. On the right-hand side, a tall bookcase displays impressive tomes, spines stamped with gold writing, that look like they've never been opened. Next to that is a credenza with a collection of glasses and mugs, presumably to serve the soon-to-be-arriving guests. The wall opposite is bare except for a giant clock.

"The router can go here," KJ says, dropping down on all fours and peering under the credenza. I hand him the router, a slim thing about the size of a pack of playing cards, and KJ uses the duct tape we brought to attach it the underside of the furniture. I peer down at it from various angles to make sure it's completely hidden.

"What about putting the camera behind the clock?" I suggest.

"Nah, people look at clocks. They might notice the end poking out. What about along the top of the blinds?"

"Too risky. Someone might lower them if there's a glare."

We prowl around discussing options before finally settling on a potted plant on top of the bookcase. KJ stands on a chair, which I hold to keep it from rolling away, and pokes the end of the camera between the greenery, carefully arranging the plant's fronds so they don't block the transmission.

"What if someone decides to water it?" I say.

"Unlikely." KJ jumps down and studies his handiwork. "It's fake."

We find a bathroom down one of the halls and lock ourselves inside, releasing time so we can test our equipment. The image is impressively clear.

"Who knew spying was so easy?" I ask.

"Makes you wonder why Norms are so freaked about spinners," KJ says. "Seems like they can spy on each other just fine without our help."

I check my watch, and my stomach does a little somersault.

"It's two fourteen," I say. "The meeting starts in sixteen minutes."

I freeze time again, and we trek all the way back downstairs, then hide in the lobby bathroom to restart the world. The street is crowded with people, all theoretically busy with their own concerns. I slide on a pair of sunglasses but still feel way too visible.

"Where shall we watch from?" KJ asks.

We settle on a public plaza a block away. It's mostly brick with raised planters and is empty of visitors, except for a man curled up on a bench in a dingy sleeping bag. KJ and I find a second bench tucked between a lamppost and a large blue bike storage locker. I check my watch again.

"Eight minutes," I say.

KJ pulls out a set of headphones and plugs it into the phone, offering me one of the earbuds. We sit together shoulder to shoulder, staring at the tiny screen. Any passerby would assume we're just average teens numbing their minds with the latest trending videos. I hope.

A woman walks into the conference room first. She's holding a tray with a bakery box, a coffee urn, and a carafe full of ice water, which she carries to the credenza. Through the headphones, I can hear clinking sounds as she arranges the offerings.

"It's working," KJ says. I nod, not wanting to jinx our plan by crowing too much.

The glass door opens again, and a man with a briefcase walks inside. He's broad shouldered and dressed in a perfectly fitted dark suit. Black-framed glasses perch on his nose, and he thrusts his sizeable girth forward like it's a sign of his importance. He's talking into a headset, something about rescheduling a meeting for the next day, snapping out orders in a quick, impatient tone. The woman glides out of the room without any obvious acknowledgement on either side. The glass doors open once more, and the guy hangs up, slipping his headset into his pocket as he turns to greet the newcomer.

"Jeffrey," he says, transferring his briefcase so he can hold out his right hand.

Dr. Barnard steps forward eagerly. "You must be Clarence."

My stomach twists into an angry knot as the two men shake hands. Barnard is dressed in another crisp suit, his spine ramrod straight in a way that implies not discomfort but control.

"Is it OK if I call you Jeffrey?" Clarence jokes. He has a deep voice, cultured, like a classical music radio announcer. "Perhaps I should call you Dr. Barnard, you being such a hero and all."

Barnard is facing the camera, so I see the pride lighting his face as he chuckles.

"Jeffrey is fine." He gestures to the room. "Thanks for offering your space for the meeting."

"Not a problem."

"From what I understand," Barnard says, "your firm has been an invaluable resource for the Kronons."

"We're honored to have such a storied client. The challenges Kronos faces from a legal perspective are really quite fascinating."

"I'm sure they are," Barnard says. "Margaret told me Fletcher and Underhill has a dedicated staff attorney for cases involving alien abductions." He winks. "Fanning the flames of those rumors is such a useful way to keep the disappearance of rogue spinners off the public radar."

Clarence gives a modest bow. "We do what we can to support our clients."

The glass doors open again, and two women walk in. Dr. Ellery looks as slickly professional as she did yesterday, but now that I know she is part of Kronos, she seems different, like I can actually see evil radiating from her. I'm so distracted by her that I almost don't notice the woman who walked in behind her. Until I do.

"Move your head," KJ says, when I lean into the phone. "I can't see."

I point to the screen. "That's the wiper who was at the park with Mr. Ross."

KJ tilts the phone so he can see it, too. "You're right. That's weird. Why do they want a wiper at the meeting?"

The answer to his question becomes clear when the woman pulls a pair of small disk-shaped objects from her jacket pocket and sets one in the center of the conference table. KJ's head bumps mine as we both lean closer to the phone.

"That must be a zapper," I say. KJ nods.

I study the thing with the same horrified fascination I used to feel at murder scenes. The zapper has a small blue light flashing in its center, making it look like a miniature UFO. Even without being able to sense the thing's distorting emanations, the sight of it makes me feel vulnerable.

Dr. Ellery greets the two men. The wiper moves away from the table, scanning the room with narrowed eyes that flick over each piece of furniture

144

with efficient concentration.

"What do you think she's looking for?" I know she can't hear me, but I'm still whispering.

"I don't know," KJ says. "I'd guess she's making sure everyone is safe from attack."

"I don't see why. No one ever attacks *them*."

The wiper crosses the room toward the bookcase. Her expression is stony, and a feather of fear brushes my chest. Her cool brown eyes move methodically up and across the bookcase, assessing the items before her by whatever metric a wiper judges threat. For a brief instant, her gaze touches the plant. My breath stops. I'm certain she can see me, that she will somehow reach through the tiny camera and grab both KJ and me. But the next instant, she looks away, and I start breathing again.

Ross bursts into the room, tapping on his cell phone as he pushes the door open with one shoulder. Clarence congratulates him on his recent promotion, a compliment Ross accepts with what is obviously—to me, anyway—false modesty. KJ points a finger down his throat and mimes gagging. I manage a smile, but it takes effort. Ross has caused way too much damage for me to so easily mock him.

The group exchanges chitchat for a bit—comments on the rainy weather and complaints about a construction project clogging downtown traffic. Dr. Ellery and Ross both help themselves to coffee. Barnard takes a pastry. Clarence sets his briefcase on the table.

"Shall we get started?" Dr. Ellery asks after a few minutes. "Agent Xavier, please wait outside."

The wiper hesitates, and I wonder if she's worried that being even a few feet from her charges might put them in danger, but she turns on her heel obediently to take her place, sentry-like, just outside the door. The rest of the party settles around the table. Ross and Clarence Underhill take seats with their backs to the windows. Drs. Ellery and Barnard sit across from them.

"I wish he'd move over," I mutter, poking at the phone as if I can manipulate people through its glass surface. The lawyer, who is sitting closest to the plant, takes up most of the screen, and he's blocking my view of Ross. All I can see of my former agent is a slice of his profile and one hand, which is clicking the top of his pen with quick erratic jabs.

"Thank you all for making time to come to this meeting," Dr. Ellery says. "Especially you, Chief Ross. I know you're very busy settling into your new job."

"I'm happy to be here." Ross flashes his charming smile, the one with all the teeth. "All this news about a spinner cure has caused quite a stir. My team put together a strategy for the Q&A event at City Hall tomorrow afternoon, and I'm eager to go over it with you. Anything related to spinners always leads to some kind of protest."

"Think we should go to the Q&A?" I ask KJ. "We might learn something."

KJ offers a noncommittal grunt.

Dr. Ellery gives Ross a polite nod. "We appreciate your support, and I look forward to reviewing your strategies. What I'd like to focus on in this meeting, though, are the ways our two organizations might best work together in the coming weeks. We're launching some large-scale containment strategies, and our activities might have some overlap with traditional law enforcement."

Containment strategies? My thumbnail is in my mouth, and I bite down, an action I immediately regret. The nail tastes like polish, bitter and artificial.

"Before I say more," Dr. Ellery continues, "I'll need you to sign a confidentiality agreement, as the information I'm about to share is highly sensitive."

"Of course," Ross says, his smile widening. He's always enjoyed knowing sensitive information.

Clarence snaps open the briefcase and pulls out a sheet of paper,

146

explaining the details of the agreement to Ross, who signs without reading it while simultaneously blathering on about how honored he is to have earned their trust.

I nudge KJ. "How much do you think Kronos tells outsiders about what they do?"

"I think we're about to find out," KJ says. "They can't give away too much. If a lot of people know the whole story, you'd think eventually some of their secrets would leak out."

Dr. Ellery sips her coffee while Ross signs. When the papers are safely locked up in Clarence's briefcase, she sets her cup down on a coaster marked with the law firm's logo.

"Time skills," she says, clasping her hands in front of her, "as you are aware, are very damaging to those who wield them and lead to fatal time sickness. What the general public does not know is that there are a few very rare cases in which spinners do *not* get sick."

"What happens to them?" Ross asks with surprise that sounds natural even to me.

"When a Center identifies one of these abnormal spinners," Barnard says, "we transfer them to the Central Office. Assuming they are mentally competent, we provide them with work and a place to stay. Janitorial positions, mostly. Some of them live relatively normal life spans."

Ross's pen clicks. "That's incredible."

"This is pretty much the same thing they told Shannon," KJ says. "Makes sense that they'd have some sort of standard cover story."

Dr. Ellery clears her throat.

"What's even more incredible," she says, "is that some of these spinners—again, a very tiny minority—develop an anomaly where the things they move in frozen time occasionally stay that way."

I pick at the polish coating my thumbnail. If there were an Oscar for real-life acting, Ross would be a shoo-in. His voice conveys pure shock.

147

"How is that possible?" he asks.

"We're not sure," Dr. Ellery says, "but, needless to say, this is a dangerous ability, and it seems that it's not one the spinners themselves can control particularly well. It's also clear that the mutation goes hand in hand with higher levels of the mental illness we all know comes from spinning time—namely increased incidents of violence, paranoia, and hallucinations. This is a dangerous combination, which is why we've done our very best to keep this knowledge from the public. If people knew the truth . . ." Dr. Ellery shakes her head. "Well, you can imagine the mass hysteria that would follow."

My finger slips on the chipping polish, and my nail digs into the skin of my thumb. It hurts. There's something horrifying about listening to Dr. Ellery weave her grotesque mix of lies and truth. Take a fact, then bend it so that any glimpse of reality is twisted to fit their narrative of spinners as mutant beasts. The brilliance of their propaganda has never been so clear to me.

"That's pretty terrifying." The click of Ross's pen sounds like the ticking of a fitful clock. "I can see why it's important to keep this quiet."

There's a pause while the group lets Ross take in what to anyone else would be a stunning revelation. Clarence Underhill leans back in his chair, allowing me my first clear view of Ross. He's frowning down at the table, his face a mask of manufactured confusion. Or plotting—his brain must be working overtime to make sure he doesn't give away his preexisting knowledge of these facts.

"You're in a unique position from most the police chiefs we've partnered with," Dr. Ellery says. "Jeffrey tells me you've actually worked with spinners."

"Yes." Ross clicks his pen again. "I was a time agent for three years."

Dr. Ellery studies him with a cool expression. "What do you think of them?"

"Spinners?"

"Yes."

148

Ross gives his pen a series of rapid jabs. "I've made a point of not saying this out loud, but given the circumstances, I should probably be up front." He pauses, clearly thinking carefully about his wording, then announces, "Spinners have always made me uncomfortable."

"Uncomfortable?" I burst out, so loudly that the homeless guy across the plaza jerks in his sleep. "What is he talking about?"

Barnard seems to share my surprise, since he says, "I thought you liked working with spinners."

"I've always done my best to hide my discomfort," Ross says with an aw-shucks dip of his head. "Chief Graham gave me the assignment after my partner was killed, and I knew he had my best interests at heart. I didn't like to complain."

"Liar." Heat flashes over my skin. I want to rip the phone from KJ's hand and stamp on Ross's falsely earnest face. "Ross complained about Chief Graham all the time. And he loved working with spinners. He didn't see us as disturbing. He saw us as opportunities, assets to lure into his web so he could suck out our power like some kind of big fat thirsty spider."

"Alex." KJ makes a shushing noise. "I can't hear."

I adjust my earbud. Not that adjusting it will make anything coming out of Ross's mouth sound any better.

"I do feel sorry for the kids." Ross's voice oozes with false sympathy. "I know they can't help how they were born, but there's something so peculiar about their skills. It's like being near someone with a deformity. You try not to stare, but it's difficult to treat them as if they're normal."

"You certainly had us fooled," Barnard says. He's watching Ross with narrowed eyes. Barnard has never liked Ross very much. Maybe he'll call Ross on the garbage coming out of his mouth.

"I'm pleased I covered it up so well." Ross spreads his hands in a sheepish gesture. "That's actually one of the reasons my reports to you were so often late, Jeffrey. Being in those rewinds always left me feeling a little sick, and

149

stepping back into the experience to write it up took a bit of effort on my part."

"Well, that's a creative excuse for laziness," I fume.

"Gotta give the guy points for being clever," KJ says. "Not only is he making himself sound like someone unlikely to use a spinner for personal gain, he just bought himself some cover for his sloppy work habits. Barnard might have mentioned Ross's less-than-stellar qualities to his higher-ups."

I stare at KJ. "You *admire* Ross now?"

"Of course not," KJ says. "The guy's scum. I'm just saying he's clever scum."

I make a huffing noise and turn my attention back to the little screen.

"Now that you understand the threat," Dr. Ellery is saying, "I'd like to discuss our request."

Ross turns his face toward hers, the perfect eager listener.

"You must be aware that spinners sometimes slip through our net, either during the infant screening process or, more rarely, by escaping from a Center. Some of those people survive into adulthood. Our security agents work hard to track down these rogue spinners, but I'm afraid many of them remain at large. Luckily, we have recently achieved a breakthrough on that front."

I lick the back of my thumb to keep from chewing on it. I've picked most of the polish off, and the nail looks defenseless without its shield of black lacquer.

"The rogue spinners communicate with each other through an online network," Dr. Ellery says. "Our team has been aware of it for some time but hasn't been able to crack it. This changed two weeks ago. Our computer technicians now have full access to the data and have recently compiled a list of all the users' IP addresses."

KJ's hand clenches convulsively around the phone.

"What does that mean?" I ask. Unlike me, KJ actually understands computers.

"Having the IP addresses," he says, "means that Kronos can trace their computers. They'll be able to figure out the locations of all the free spinners."

I grab his arm, nearly knocking the phone out of his hand.

"Jamal was right," I say. "Spinners aren't going to be given a choice about the cure. We have to warn them!"

"Listen," KJ hisses.

I turn back to the screen. Ross is saying something congratulatory. Dr. Ellery brushes his words aside with a small cough.

"This is the part where we're asking for your assistance," she says. "It turns out Portland is something of a hot spot where quite a few of these creatures live. It is imperative that we collect them without announcing to the general public that adult spinners exist. We only have a limited number of security agents assigned to this area, so we don't have enough people to collect the spinners in a single simultaneous sweep. What we want from you is assistance in arresting the people we identify, along with the assurance that any spinners' disappearances will not be questioned too closely by your department."

Ross lays the pen he's been holding down on the table.

"You mean," he says, "the same way Chief Graham cooperated in covering up the death of Tito Marquez?"

There's a beat of silence in the room that sounds tense even through the earbuds. Dr. Ellery exchanges a glance with her lawyer.

"What happened to Agent Marquez?" I ask. I know Tito Marquez. He was Raul's time agent, and he saw a rewind in which I disappeared.

KJ shakes his head.

"The department's actions in that instance," Clarence Underhill says, "were deeply appreciated."

"I understand that it wasn't easy to convince the officer in charge to classify the death as a suicide," Ross says. "As *interim* chief, my influence won't be as effective as it could be."

My insides turn over, and for a second I think I'm going to be sick. "Does he mean Kronos killed Agent Marquez? Because he found out the truth?"

KJ's looks as nauseated as I feel. "I think so."

Dr. Ellery drains her coffee.

"Understood." She gives a curt nod in Ross's direction. "I'll speak to the mayor and tell her how highly we recommend you as a permanent appointee for the position."

Ross buries a smile in his own coffee cup.

"Once I am chief," he says when he sets the cup down, "I will be happy to do all I can to help you achieve your laudable mission."

"That's blackmail," I say. "Or coercion. Something corrupt." I wave my hand at the phone. "Can't we turn this tape over to someone?"

KJ doesn't raise his eyes from the screen.

"We're streaming this, not recording," he says. "The phone doesn't have enough memory to hold it all."

The homeless guy on the bench across from us groans in his sleep. Our day, which started with such promise, is starting to crumble. We set out to get information, but this isn't the kind of information I was hoping to hear. I wanted to know *their* weaknesses, not ours. This morning, the city felt like a shiny place, but now I see only dirt and graffiti and slashed hopes. The knowledge that was supposed to set us free only proves how completely we are trapped within Kronos's dark plans.

"What about the missing Center kids?" Ross's voice sidles into my ear, pulling my attention back to the video. "Has cracking the network helped you find out where they're hiding?"

Dr. Ellery nods. "That information was confirmed this morning. The whole group is on a goat farm in Eastern Oregon."

This time, the phone does slip from KJ's hand. I snatch it before it hits the ground.

"So the suspicions I shared with you were correct," Ross says, shooting a gloating look at Barnard. "Alex isn't hiding them in the city."

"The chatter we picked up," Dr. Ellery says, "tells us the spinners

152

arrived at the ranch the same night they escaped. We suspect Alexandra returned to the city, accompanied by her friend Kaleel, to mislead us."

"If we're lucky, the two of them have returned to the farm by now." Barnard strokes his cast. "Then we'll be able to take all twenty-three of them into custody at once."

The number twenty-three throws me for a second until I realize they're counting Jack. My desire to warn him gains importance. If the wipers succeed at the ranch, they'll see Jack isn't there, and the search for him will intensify.

"So you're going to scoop them up and take them to the Central Office"—Ross picks up his pen again and rolls it between his fingers—"where they'll be cured."

"A group of agents are heading out to the ranch as we speak," Dr. Ellery says. "They plan to collect the young spinners as soon as it gets dark."

"Why wait until dark?" Ross asks.

"Drone surveillance shows that the creatures are scattered between the house and a nearby barn," Dr. Ellery says. "That makes it more likely that one or two might escape when we round them up. In the evening, they'll likely be clustered together. In the meantime, we've cut power to the only cell tower that services the area and sent in our own people disguised as techs working on the problem. Without internet or cell service, no one will be able to warn them."

"I assume that means you haven't found the source of the leaks yet?" Barnard asks.

Dr. Ellery's mouth pinches in at the corners.

"No." She give another little throat-clearing cough and turns to Ross. "I understand that when you were a time agent you worked with Alexandra Manning?"

Ross nods. The sound of my name makes the open plaza we're sitting in seem dangerously exposed. I pull the beanie lower on my forehead, which only makes me feel more like a fugitive.

"Alexandra's recapture," Dr. Ellery continues, "is particularly high on our list of priorities. You see, Miss Manning suffers from the abnormality we just discussed."

"Alex . . . can change things in frozen time?" Ross gives his pen a particularly aggressive click. "I worked with her for months. There was never any sign of an anomaly. She even got sick at one point."

"That wasn't time sickness," Barnard says. "Just a regular flu. The symptoms are very similar, and I have to admit that even I was initially fooled. But there was another incident—perhaps you remember? Alex ran off when she had a day pass and came back very agitated, sporting injuries she couldn't explain. I completed more tests after that and realized that her condition had . . . mutated. I tried to take her to the Central Office so we could transition her to a safe location, but as you are aware, that didn't work out very well." He gestures to his arm in its blue cast.

Ross glances at Agent Xavier's dark shape on the other side of the glass doors. "I guess this explains how Alex got away from us the other day. The agent claimed I'd hit my head." His tone carries a hint of spite. He must have hated having to play dumb.

"If the girl contacts you again," Dr. Ellery says, "inform me immediately."

Ross gives his pen a particularly brutal stab.

"Don't worry, you'll be the first to know."

On the table, the zapper's light glares like an evil eye. I feel like it's watching me through the camera. I'm not surprised I'm on Kronos's radar, since they must know I'm the one who organized the others' escape, but that doesn't fully explain the pointedness of Dr. Ellery's interest. Her attention feels *personal.*

Dr. Ellery pushes away her empty coffee cup. "I think that's everything we need to discuss. Thank you again for taking the time out of your day to join us, Chief Ross, and even more for your promise of assistance. I'll make sure to talk to the mayor before I leave town."

The meeting breaks up, the participants shuffling around, exchanging self-satisfied goodbyes. When Ross asks for Clarence's card, the lawyer invites him back to his office like the two of them are new best friends. I lower the phone with a hand that's gone numb.

"I guess that's it, then," I say. "All the free spinners are going to get taken to the Central Office and be . . . neutered."

The worry on KJ's face reflects my own.

"It's not right," he says. "Rounding everyone up, forcing this cure on them. Miguel's livelihood relies on being a spinner."

"And what about our friends? Can you imagine being at the refuge when a dozen wipers descend on them like some nightmare SWAT team?"

KJ shudders. "Let's go back right now and tell Miguel and Jamal what we heard. If the spinners know what's coming, at least it won't be quite so terrifying."

A truck lumbers down the street behind us, making a sound like thunder.

"How are we going to warn them?" I ask. "They said the network's down and there's no phone service."

"Jeffrey," Dr. Ellery says, loudly enough that the word rises above the vague hubbub drifting through my earbud, "would you mind waiting a moment? There is one more thing I wanted to discuss with you."

I tip the phone back up to look at the screen. Ross and Clarence have left the room, and Agent Xavier still guards the door. Dr. Ellery is standing just below the fake plant, which explains why her voice sounds so loud.

"Of course." Barnard crosses the room to her side.

"Kronos needs to have final agreement from all senior Central Office staff," Dr. Ellery says, "on the protocol for the rogue spinners going forward."

Barnard frowns. "I thought we'd settled that."

The silence that follows lasts long enough that KJ raises the volume. Dr. Ellery clears her throat.

"No," she booms. I wince, and KJ stabs the volume back down. "You wrote a proposal that included some suggested changes. We've reviewed it internally and decided your ideas aren't feasible."

Barnard's frown deepens. "Why not? Everything is different now that we have a cure."

"The cure," Dr. Ellery says, with a testiness that implies she's said this before, "only makes sense for those who don't know that they could live past their teens without it. If spinners know that they can live full life spans *and* retain their skills, it's quite likely some of them will elect not to undergo the treatment."

"Who said anything about electing?" Barnard says. "When we bring them in, we can *force* them."

A leaf from the fake plant is blocking Dr. Ellery's head. It makes her look like a mutant character in a horror movie.

"The cure is a wonderful option for the future," she says, "and we are all very pleased with the success of your science. Thanks to you, we can fix spinners at birth and wipe out the condition completely. The plan for the existing deviants, however, will remain as it was set forth in Project Zed."

"Project Zed?" Barnard takes a handkerchief from his pocket and dabs at his upper lip. "But that policy stated that all the rogue spinners would be killed."

A breeze whispers across the plaza. The air whistles past my ears, making me feel like I'm falling.

Dr. Ellery draws herself to her full height, which isn't very impressive, but Barnard still flinches.

"I understand that eliminating a large group of people at once is distasteful," she says, "but I don't believe we have any other choice. These creatures have to be disposed of."

Barnard dabs his lip again. "If word of this gets out, the public backlash will be enormous."

"The backlash would be substantially worse," Dr. Ellery says, "if the rogue spinners revealed that it was possible for them to survive into adulthood *without* the cure. Exposure of a centuries-long systematic eradication of children—even abnormal ones—is not going to play well in the media."

Barnard reaches past Dr. Ellery and pours himself a glass of water. She steps aside to give him room, and I can see her face again. It's somehow worse to see her as human rather than as a headless ghoul. She looks so . . . normal. KJ reaches out to steady the phone in my hand, which is when I realize I'm shaking. How can someone who looks so ordinary be so inhuman?

"What about the escapees from my Center?" Barnard asks after he's gulped a few swallows of his water.

Dr. Ellery is making throat-clearing noises, which I've learned means nothing good.

"The escapees know about their capabilities," she says, "which means they are now just like any other rogue spinner. They will have to be eliminated."

The word hums through the tiny speaker, lodging in my ear like a trapped bee.

"Eliminated?" I repeat. As much as I've worried about my friends at the ranch, I realize now that deep down, I always believed they'd be safe.

KJ opens his mouth but can't seem to find any words.

"It's too bad we can't be up front about all of this," Barnard says. Even through the buzz in my ear, his tone sounds world-weary. "Humanity just doesn't appreciate the trade-offs that are required to ensure their safety."

Dr. Ellery picks up the zapper from the middle of the table, pockets it, and moves toward the door. Barnard follows, still muttering about the heavy burden of responsibility. The door swings open, then shuts with a nearly inaudible swish. I stare at the sunlight reflecting off the empty conference table. The bright glare burns my eyes, but I can't make myself look away.

KJ stands up and rips his earbud out.

"We need to tell Miguel and Jamal." His body quivers, as if he can

157

barely keep himself from racing down the street. "In person, in case their phones are tapped."

I'm barely listening. The light on the screen is blinding, wiping my mind clear of thoughts. All that remains is a blank canvas that's filling with snapshots of the people we left behind. Yuki brushing back her long dark hair. Aidan's teasing smirk. Emma and Molly cuddled under a blanket. Every image is ringed with a black border, a funeral portrait for a young life lost.

I press the button that turns off the phone's screen. One thought makes its way up through the haze in my head, a thought that blares like a banner headline.

"KJ."

He turns to me, then immediately sits down again.

"What's wrong?"

"It's our fault."

"What do you mean? *We're* not killing anyone."

I shake my head. "I thought that when we took them from the Center, we'd saved them from being experiments, but that's not true. If we'd left them there, they would have been taken to the Central Office, and they might have been cured, but they still would've lived."

Comprehension dawns on KJ's face. I watch it crumple and feel his pain like a lash added to my own.

"When we took them away," I say, "we didn't save them. The minute we told them the truth, we sentenced every single one of them to death."

12 ◄◄

THE ELEVATOR IN THE FLETCHER AND UNDERHILL SUITE PINGS TO herald the car's arrival. Barnard waves Dr. Ellery forward with a courtly gesture, but before he and Agent Xavier can join her, Chief Ross hurries into the hall.

"Dr. Ellery," he says, reaching out a hand to prevent the elevator doors from closing, "I was hoping I could have a quick word with you." He shoots a glance at Barnard. "In private."

Dr. Ellery takes in both Ross's easy smile and his calculating eyes. She rather welcomes a tête-à-tête with the new chief. Despite all his denials in their meeting, she's still not certain how much he knows. Or who he might work for.

"Of course." Dr. Ellery looks at Barnard, who is hovering just outside the doors, the security agent at his heels. "You don't mind, do you, Jeffrey?"

The way Dr. Barnard's lips tighten proves he most definitely does mind, but he steps aside anyway.

"We'll take the next one," he mutters.

"Thanks, Jeff." Ross claims the space beside Dr. Ellery with the confidence of a captain taking command of the bridge. Dr. Ellery presses the lobby button, using the motion as an excuse to increase the space between them. Arrogant men are high on her list of people she dislikes.

"What is it you wanted to discuss?" she asks as the elevator doors slide shut.

Ross flashes his snake oil salesman's smile. "I have a proposal I think your bosses might find interesting, something that would benefit both of us."

Her *bosses*? The elevator begins its descent. Dr. Ellery refrains from gritting her teeth and instead nods to show she's listening.

"You mentioned in our meeting," Ross continues, "that you have a limited number of wipers—excuse me, security agents—which seems like a liability at a time when you are trying to round up so many rogue spinners. I thought now that I'm on the inside, so to speak, I could take on a larger role."

The height of the building means the elevator has an express mode, allowing it to drop half the building's thirty stories in a single plunge. The pressure makes Dr. Ellery's ears pop.

"What kind of role were you thinking of?" she asks.

"Why don't you put me in charge of collecting the rogue spinners here in Portland? I can head up a team with some of your agents plus a few of my own officers, people I know I can trust to be discrete."

"And you think you would be equally as effective as my trained professionals?"

"I'm sure your agents are good, but the problem with them is that they are steeped in hatred for these people. The spinners know that, which makes it impossible for a wiper to win their trust. I, on the other hand, have worked with spinners a long time, and even if I didn't always like the job, I did develop a rapport with them. I might be able to get them to come in for the cure without any unexplained 'accidents.' Ask Dr. Barnard—he'll tell you I was the favorite. All the kids wanted to work with me."

Dr. Ellery considers this speech carefully, both the spoken and unspoken parts. Like the fact that this man who claimed to have hated working as a time agent seems to take quite a bit of pride in his role. Where exactly do his loyalties lie?

"It's a generous offer," she says. "I assume you would like something in return?"

Ross laughs like she's made a clever point.

"I am very intrigued by this organization you work for, Kronos. I did some research before our meeting, and I have to say there is very little to find."

Dr. Ellery struggles to keep the outrage off her face. The man talks about Kronos's ability to limit public information like he's impressed. As if some small-town cop has a chance of finding anything Kronos would prefer remains private.

"We like to keep our operations discrete," Dr. Ellery says.

"Understandable."

The elevator reaches the lobby. There's a handful of people there, waiting to access the higher floors. Dr. Ellery threads her way through the crowd with quick steps, forcing Ross to wait until they are clear of the other people before he speaks again.

"What I find most interesting," he says once they're alone, "is the question of what Kronos will do next. To accomplish what you have, you must control a vast network of influence. I assume you're not going to let all that go just because you've solved your initial problem."

"Actually, we are." Dr. Ellery directs their trajectory away from a knot of people clustered around a coffee kiosk. "Kronos is a very focused organization. It's one of the reasons we've been

161

so successful. No mission creep, as they say."

"Of course, of course. Very laudable." They take a few steps in silence. Dr. Ellery waits for Ross to work up to his next volley.

"Perhaps you haven't considered this," Ross says, "but it seems to me that there are many new directions Kronos could head in that are aligned with your original mission, all equally as laudable. Your goal is to make the world a safer place, am I right? Well, what could make people safer than things like ensuring good government?"

Dr. Ellery's suspicion that Ross might work for the CIA is starting to fade. What professional would fish for information as obviously as this bumbling fool?

They near the end of the lobby, and Dr. Ellery slows her pace, not wanting to have to remain in Ross's company once they leave the building. The man's egotism is breathtaking. Surely he cannot believe that his idea is original? It seems she has underestimated him. Not his capacity, no, the man is neither as clever nor as charming as he thinks himself, what she underestimated was the depth of his greed.

Dr. Ellery leads Ross toward an unpopulated sitting area tucked in a corner of the lobby. As much as she would enjoy turning him down flat, she needs his cooperation, at least for the next few weeks. Besides, it would be prudent to find out exactly what his true goals are. In her years of working with spinners, she has learned many things, and one of them is that people with an obsession can be dangerous.

"Why don't you give me a better sense of what you're picturing Kronos might be able to do," Dr. Ellery says as the two settle themselves on a pair of chairs upholstered in beige artificial leather.

Ross launches into an enthusiastic narrative, full of thriller-level intrigue designed to create totalitarian governments with "the right kind of people" in positions of power around the world, all of them indebted to Kronos. He clearly pictures himself as part of this group. Dr. Ellery listens with her features composed in a carefully neutral expression. None of Ross's ideas are even remotely feasible. Kronos is a precise blade honed to address one specific problem, a problem that's linked to a genuine threat everyone can appreciate. What Ross is suggesting is a cudgel intended to amass power under a single umbrella—an impossible dream, as untold numbers of aspiring dictators have learned, to their peril.

"Your plans are certainly . . . ambitious," Dr. Ellery says when Ross finally shows signs of winding down. "Given our experience with influence over the last few centuries, however, I'm not sure they are all achievable."

For the first time, Ross glances around to ensure their privacy.

"They would certainly be more achievable"—he lowers his voice—"if we had a little *help*."

He raises one eyebrow meaningfully. A chill wraps Dr. Ellery in its cold fingers. It's all she can do not to shudder.

"Are you talking about using spinners?" she asks.

Ross chuckles.

"Surely you never meant to destroy *all* the spinners," he says. "I mean, power like that isn't easy to come by, and it definitely would be handy. I was thinking a small cadre, maybe a half dozen, properly groomed and positioned around the world?"

Dr. Ellery clears her throat. There's a bad taste in her mouth, like she accidentally drank spoiled milk, and it's making her ulcer burn. Her suspicions were clearly wrong. Carson Ross is not a CIA informant. He is something much worse: a greedy egotist who has discovered the spinners' full capabilities and now doesn't want to let them go. He sees power without its cost. He is as depraved as the spinners.

Something in her face must reveal her distaste, because Ross's smile grows cautious.

"Of course, all these grand schemes are in the future," he says, "and they would require a great deal more discussion among your board members. Perhaps a trial run showcasing how I can be useful might help convince them to bring me into the conversation? As I see it, using spinners is an excellent strategy to achieve your immediate objectives. Dangle the promise of extended life in exchange for disclosing a hideaway or two—what spinner wouldn't leap at that? And it would help us determine which ones are the most amenable, too."

Us, he said. As if he were already part of Kronos. Dr. Ellery presses a discrete hand to the growing burn that's eating at her from the inside.

"It sounds like you might have some experience in this area," she says.

Chief Ross hesitates, eyes flicking between hers, like a nervous rat trying to decide his next move. Acting on her years of experience in extracting information, Dr. Ellery leans her head closer, dipping her voice to a conspiratorial level.

"Using spinners in the pursuit of a higher good *is* something that Kronos has allowed in the past," she says, "under the proper circumstances. That said, your plan might be more appealing to

164

my *bosses* if it had a more tangible element."

The hint of sarcasm coating the word *bosses* must fly right over Ross's head, along with the possibility that Dr. Ellery might be lying. Honestly, for a man enamored with international intrigue, he is surprisingly gullible. Either that or the possibilities presented by the spinners' power have turned his brain to mush.

"It's possible I might be able to access a rogue spinner," Ross says. "Not an adult—one of the missing teens."

Dr. Ellery's body grows instantly taut. "The Manning girl?"

Her voice is too eager. Even Ross must notice, because he cocks a curious eyebrow at her.

"No," he says, "a different one."

The burn in Dr. Ellery's stomach flares. She sits back, nodding at Ross to continue.

"His name is Jack Whiting." Ross moves his hand seemingly unconsciously to his pocket, where Dr. Ellery can make out the outline of his phone. "Someone on my staff just let me know that he's reached out. It seems he got separated from the others, and now he's looking to make a deal in exchange for his own safety."

"Do you think he knows where the other two are?" Dr. Ellery asks, pretending to be distracted by something going on across the room in an effort to make the question sound casual.

"You mean Alex and KJ?" Ross shakes his head. "No, that ship has sailed. They'd never trust him."

Dr. Ellery swallows her disappointment and shifts her attention back to the man beside her. The bitterness in his voice when he mentions Alex is palpable. Clearly there is history here.

"Jack could still be useful, though," Ross continues. "If he pretended to be alone, looking for safety, I bet someone in the spinner network would offer to help him, and then . . ." Ross winks instead of ending the sentence.

The sly look makes Dr. Ellery want to abandon the conversation entirely. *This* is his great idea? A baited trap? As if Kronos hasn't used this tactic for decades. The rogue spinners tread far too carefully these days to fall for something this obvious. Ross, though, seems ripe for it.

Dr. Ellery taps her lip and pretends to be deep in thought. "I don't know that using this particular spinner as a lure is a good idea. There are too many people searching for him. I believe your own department put up wanted signs."

"Yes." Ross frowns. "That was before I was in charge. I've already ordered them taken down."

Already ordered? She wonders if he is aware of the slip. Chief Ross would have had no reason to order the signs taken down if he only just now decided Jack could be useful. Dr. Ellery pretends to consider the situation, taking just long enough that she can tell Ross is getting uneasy.

"Chief Ross." She turns on her chair so she's facing him. "Let me be frank with you. I am perfectly willing to talk to my superiors about having you work more closely with our organization—even about the idea of you, shall we say, 'managing' a spinner yourself. The problem is that Kronos is a somewhat distrustful organization. They'll want to see proof of your commitment before they'll be willing to bring you in."

The eagerness that lights Ross's face is pathetic. "What kind of proof?" he asks.

"Turn this boy Jack over to the security agents."

Ross flinches.

"Kronos is an elite organization," Dr. Ellery says. "And we are highly discriminating about who we allow to join us. Let me have your spinner as a token of your commitment, and I can guarantee that you'll get the reward you deserve."

Ross pretends to consider her offer, but she can tell by the suppressed excitement making his foot tap against the tiled floor that he's already on board. It takes less than ten seconds before he turns to her.

"You've got yourself a deal," he says.

Ross holds out his hand. Dr. Ellery shakes it.

13 ◄◄

MIGUEL LOOKS LIKE HE'S GOING TO BE SICK. HE'S HUNCHED ON the sofa with his hands clenched between his knees. Jamal mostly looks angry. He's taken over my route from yesterday, pacing the small space between the living and dining rooms, stomping so hard that each step rattles the two mugs of coffee resting on a side table. At least Miguel and Jamal are too upset to be mad at us for lying about where we were going today.

I rub my forehead. KJ and I took turns freezing so we could get back here as fast as possible, detouring only to reclaim our spy equipment so Kronos couldn't discover we'd overheard them. Now a dull ache has woken up inside my skull, the soft pounding echoing the steady knell of minutes slipping away.

"Did they say," Miguel asks, "how long it would be before they invaded the ranch?"

"Tonight," I say. "After it gets dark."

"You think Max can help us?" Miguel asks Jamal.

"I don't see how." Jamal's shoes squeak as he spins back in our direction. "She's on a local assignment, so they won't be sending her out to the ranch."

Miguel stands up. It's an abrupt, jerky movement, and he bumps the low table beside him. The coffee mugs tip over, their contents spilling into a dark lake on the carpet.

"I'm going there," Miguel says.

Jamal steps in front of his friend, blocking his headlong rush.

"You can't," he says. "The wipers are already at the farm, which means

168

they've probably set up a perimeter. You won't be able to get near that house."

"I have to try," Miguel says. His voice is pleading. "With the cell tower knocked out, how else can I warn them?"

He and Jamal stand together, eyes locked. Some message passes between them, and Jamal sighs.

"You have a plan?" he asks.

"I'll drive out and park at McPherson's; they have that lot out back behind their barn. From there, I can run to the house in frozen time—the wipers can't have set up a perfect perimeter, and I'll find a gap. Then Lisa and I can take the kids out in small groups, like Alex did at the Center. McPherson's got that mobile home—he's let me borrow it before. I'll call him on the way down and make up some reason why we need it."

"Where will you take them?" Jamal asks.

"Prineville. We'll camp on Meg's land until we figure something out. She's been off the grid for years."

Jamal nods. "Use my car," he says. "They won't be looking for it. We can take David's."

Miguel clasps Jamal's hand in wordless thanks. His eyes are bright.

I get up from the sofa where KJ and I have been sitting since we got here. The camera and router I shoved in my pocket bang my leg when I move, physical reminders of the horrors we overheard. I yank the folds of my skirt so they don't tangle around my legs.

"We'll go with you," I tell Miguel. "We can help transport everyone."

"No," Miguel says. "You stay here. It's safer."

Safer? I almost laugh. In our current situation, the word has no relevance. Kronos has destroyed any possibility of safety.

"Those kids out there," KJ says, rising to stand beside me, "they're *our* family. We're going."

Miguel shakes his head. Jamal comes over and wraps an arm around my shoulder.

169

"Miguel can handle this," he says. "You going with him only puts more people at risk."

I look from one to the other. Jamal's chin is set, and Miguel's lips are pressed together so tightly they're flattened into near invisibility. Truth dawns—despite the brave words, both men know exactly how shaky Miguel's plan is. The chance that he'll manage to save anyone at the refuge is vanishingly small.

Miguel blinks and lurches off to the bedroom. Through the open doorway, I see him grabbing up shirts and toiletries and shoving them haphazardly into a duffel bag. I rub my toe against the spilled coffee spreading across the rug. The stain will never come out, but it hardly matters. Jamal can't stay here anymore. The room around me goes fuzzy, like I'm staring at the law office's conference table again, blinded by its vicious glare. This time, though, instead of feeling crushed by my own guilt, the light acts as a prod.

I bend to pick up the one of the fallen cups as an excuse to slide out of Jamal's shielding embrace. They might be right about us being no help at the refuge, but that doesn't mean I'm just going to sit here.

"What are *we* going to do?" I ask Jamal.

"We?" He moves over to stand near the fireplace. "There are a few other spinners living in Portland." He picks up one of the framed photographs sitting on the mantel. It's the party picture of him and Blondie. David. They're wearing New Year's crowns and have their arms around each other's shoulders. Bits of confetti are sprinkled all over their heads, and both their faces are lit with laughter. "I'm going to bike over and warn them in person. Then I'll head out to get David. He's working at the clinic today and is unlikely to answer the phone."

"And then what?" I ask.

"Then the four of us drive out to Prineville."

I clutch the empty coffee mug against my chest. "We can't just run away. We have to do something to stop this."

170

"What about posting a warning on the network?" KJ says. "We can say in the message that Kronos is reading everything so no one gives their plans away."

"The network went down an hour ago," Jamal says. "It happens sometimes, so I just assumed it was a random glitch, but now I'm guessing the wipers did it so we can't communicate with each other once they start rounding folks up."

"Let's go to the Central Office," I say. "We can set up a roadblock. Stop their cars from going in and then freeze time and take all the spinners away."

Jamal sets the picture down and gently buffs some dust off the mantel with his sleeve.

"We talked about this, Alex. Going to the Central Office is beyond risky. Kronos won't be sending those kids there without protections in place. You confront them and you die."

I make an impatient gesture. I'm sick and tired of people warning me about risk. *Everything* is risky.

"You two have already done plenty." Miguel emerges from the bedroom, his duffel bag draped over one shoulder. He's changed his shirt, but the buttons are done up wrong, leaving one end hanging down over his belt like a backward tail. "You've given us a warning. That's huge."

"It's not enough," I say.

"It's enough for now," Miguel says. "Our priority is to get everyone we can reach somewhere safe. After that, we can talk about what to do next. One step at a time, OK?"

"But we're out of time." I squeeze the empty coffee mug more tightly. "Don't you see? Kronos is planning to kill every single one of us. We have to face them."

"Alex," Miguel says. "You fighting Kronos is out of the question. I promised Lisa I'd keep you safe, so please stop pushing this."

I'm clutching the mug so hard its lip is digging into my chest. I picture the ceramic shattering and the shards slicing through my skin. But why should *my* blood be spilled? The sharp edge needs a better target. Like Dr. Ellery, with her neat hair and detached expression. She already believes we're violent; what is there to lose by proving her right?

KJ reaches over and eases away the mug I'm clutching, and as he does, he leans his head close to mine.

"Stop arguing," he whispers. "We'll talk after they're gone."

A surge of fierce joy at KJ's loyalty does more to release my grip than his coaxing hand. I twine my fingers around his, using bone and tendon to knot the two of us together.

"All right," I tell Jamal. He nods. The relief on both his and Miguel's faces at my false capitulation deals me a pang of guilt, but I don't look away.

"I'll be back to get you around six," Jamal says. His gaze drifts around the room, touching on his photographs, his collection of books, a painting bright with splashes of primary colors. "This house isn't safe. My neighbor across the street is out of town—the green house with the red door. I've been watching her cat, so I have her key. Pack your things and meet me there." He turns to Miguel. "What's your timing?"

"It will take me about two hours to reach the refuge," Miguel says. "Which means we should be on the road to Prineville by six fifteen."

"Good," Jamal says. "We should both be at Meg's by nine."

Miguel comes over and gives KJ and me each a quick hug.

"It's going to be fine," he says. "Just wait at the neighbor's for Jamal, OK?"

No, I think. KJ's hand presses mine.

"Yes," I say.

Jamal hands me a house key dangling from a ring decorated with an enamel cat charm. "Miguel and I have both used our phones to access the network," he says, "so we'll have to destroy them. No one should be able to trace yours, so if I'm not at back by six, call Max. She'll find a way to help you." He

172

tells us her number, insisting we memorize it rather than saving it in the phone.

Jamal turns to Miguel, and the two friends embrace, the tight squeeze of people parting for a long time.

"Good luck," Jamal says.

"You too," Miguel answers.

Miguel gives us a final wave and heads out the door. Jamal follows, his final words floating behind him like an empty promise. *Good luck.* I stuff the cat key in my pocket and lean into KJ's shoulder. Luck is a mirage. We're going to need something much more tangible than that if we're going to survive.

The house feels eerie after Miguel and Jamal are gone, as if the empty air is thick with static electricity.

I turn to KJ. "You agree that we have to fight back?"

"I agree that we have to try, but I'm setting limits. We've got to come up with a plan that's realistic and that will get us back here in time to go to Prineville with Jamal."

I picture being alone in a city awash with wipers with no place to sleep. I nod.

KJ looks at his watch. "It's ten after four, which means we have less than two hours." He drums a finger against the side of the coffee mug he pried away from me. "Going to the Central Office is off the table. Even assuming we could sneak in, which we can't, we don't know exactly where it is and couldn't get to Tacoma and back in time if we did. So we need a different way to stop Kronos."

I disentangle our hands so I can chew on a nail.

"Jamal said the best plan they came up with before was to steal information from the Central Office computers. What if there were another way we could find proof that Kronos was murdering spinners outright?"

"And Norms," KJ adds. His tapping finger sounds like a ticking clock. I look at my watch. It's 4:12.

"We know there's nothing useful at the Center." I walk over to the window and peek through the closed curtains. There's no one out there, just the empty street, looking blandly innocent in the afternoon sun. "I never found any clear evidence that they were poisoning us while we were there, and besides, it's probably cleared out."

"Dr. Barnard's house?" KJ suggests

"I doubt he saves anything incriminating, plus he keeps a zapper in his office."

The tempo of KJ's tapping increases. "What we need is an informant."

"Exactly. But who?"

Time swirls around us, slipping forever forward. Even without touching it, I am aware of each second as it slips away, stealing another moment in which we can act.

KJ scoops up the other fallen coffee mug. "It's going to be a long night," he says, carrying both mugs into the kitchen. "We should eat something."

I trail after him. "I'm not hungry."

KJ opens the refrigerator and peers inside. "We should eat anyway."

I open a cupboard and find a box of crackers. They are both whole grain and gluten free, and they taste like a mouthful of seeds.

"What about Dr. Ellery?" I say. "We could steal her phone and copy all her messages."

"How would we find her?" KJ opens a container of yogurt and sniffs it. "Plus, if we took her phone, she'd probably delete everything. You can do that remotely."

I finger the lump in my pocket. "We should have left the spy cam up at the lawyer's office."

"We could put it back." KJ closes the fridge. "But we don't want to have to watch it all the time. We need, like, a remote recorder or something." He pulls the phone from his pocket and starts poking at it. "I think the guy at the store told me about a model that might work."

The phone's glass surface winks in the kitchen's overhead light, flashing like a memory. I put down the crackers.

"KJ, didn't that guy say something about an app that, like, bugs your cell phone?"

"Not helpful. Clarence Underhill uses a landline in his office."

"I'm not talking about Clarence. I'm talking about Ross."

KJ stops typing and looks up. "Ross?"

"Ross promised to cover up Kronos's crimes, remember? That means Dr. Ellery, or someone like her, is going to call him when they're ready to close in on a spinner so they can tell him how to cover it up. If we could tap his phone, we could warn people *and* collect evidence of actual crimes."

A smile spreads over KJ's face. "That's a great idea. Think we could find him? What about his zapper?"

"We don't need to find him." I point at the phone "We can find Jack. I wrote down the access code to Ross's tracker app when we were in his office."

KJ's smile fades. "You think *Jack* will help us? The last time he saw us, we tied him up and locked him in a closet."

"He's still a spinner."

"Being a spinner doesn't make you automatically good any more than it makes you automatically bad."

"I know, but this is *Jack*." I hurry out to the living room and dig through my pack, searching for the sticky note where I wrote the tracker app information.

"Remember what he used to be like?" I call back to KJ. "Before he froze time so much that he got all whacked?"

"As I recall," KJ says, "Jack was always kind of a jerk."

The note is crumpled in the bottom of a side pocket. I dash back to the kitchen, waving the scrap of paper like a victory flag. KJ is leaning against the counter, arms crossed, a scowl wrinkling his brow.

"OK," I say, "yes, Jack can be a bit self-centered, and he probably isn't

175

very happy with us right now, but he can't be happy with Ross these days, either. What Jack wants more than anything is to be free, and working for Ross can't feel like freedom to him. The guy put a tracker in him. If we make it sound like tapping Ross's phone is to Jack's advantage, I think he'll do it. He'll like the idea of eavesdropping on Ross—it will make him feel powerful. Like he's not totally under Ross's control."

KJ still looks skeptical.

"Come on," I say. "At least let's see if he's somewhere we can get to."

KJ is still frowning, but he picks up the phone and figures out how to download the tracking app. I enter Ross's login and password, and a map of Portland materializes on the screen, centered around a small green dot. I zoom in, checking street names until I orient myself.

"That's Northeast Sandy," I say. "Not that far from the TV station. We can get there in half an hour, less if we freeze."

"You realize this is a long shot?" KJ says. "And that Jack is not going to be glad to see us? I don't want you to get your hopes up that this will be some happy reunion."

"It doesn't need to be happy. He just has to agree to help."

KJ nods and opens the fridge again. I go out to pack our things. There's not much—just the clothes we came in and our bottle of Aclisote. I divide the stuff between our two daypacks and hide the remaining wad of cash at the bottom of mine. I almost leave the spy equipment on the dresser, but instead I keep it in the pocket of my skirt. Maybe if Jack is super cooperative, I can get him to set up the camera so we can watch Ross, too.

When I get back to the kitchen, KJ is making us sandwiches. I watch his hands, strong and capable, as he slices thick pieces of cheese. My heart squeezes. I love everything about this boy. I love the way he spreads mustard so that it reaches every corner of the bread. I love the way his hair is starting to curl around his ear as it grows out. I love the scar on his left palm that he got when he was thirteen and he took apart an old radio to see how it worked. Yolly nearly fainted when she saw all that blood.

Doubt creeps through the ache in my chest, spreading out to fill the empty house. In my head, I hear KJ telling me I'm acting reckless because I don't believe I'm going to survive. *Is* my idea reckless? I know it's risky to go anywhere right now, but at this point, what isn't risky? What if our plan does succeed and Jack manages to plant a bug in Ross's phone? I cast my mind forward, trying to envision what will happen after we get into a car with Jamal and David, but no picture emerges. The furthest I can get is the image of a dark windshield and a car barreling through an endless night.

I set the two daypacks on the floor at my feet.

"I think I should go alone," I tell KJ.

He looks up. "What?"

"It doesn't take two people to talk to Jack, and you only want to do this to support me. There's no reason both of us have to take the risk."

KJ sets a slice of bread on top of each sandwich, lining them up so the edges match exactly.

"I'm not going with you just to support you." He opens a drawer and pulls out a plastic bag. "I've thought about this a lot. When I said I wanted to let the free spinners take charge, I thought they could protect us. I saw the refuge, and then the cure, as ways that things could be different for us. I thought our lives could be simpler. But I was wrong." He places the sandwiches into the bag, then turns to face me. "Spinners will not survive unless Kronos is destroyed. I want you to be safe because I want you in my life, but that kind of safety is gone now, and ignoring that is just wishful thinking. Our only chance now is for every one of us to fight in the best way we know how. We have to trust ourselves to save ourselves."

Tears burn my eyes. Tears for me, for him, and for the injustice of the world we were born into. I don't let them fall.

"You know," I tell him, "that no matter what we do, the chances are pretty good that we're not going to make it."

177

"I know." He moves forward and pulls me close against his chest. "But you are the best of us. If anyone can pull something off, you can."

I bury my face in his sweater. Through the wool's prickly fibers, I can smell the sharp tang of KJ's fear. A tear slides down my cheek, but only one. KJ's arms tighten around me. We stand together, sharing a handful of seconds out of however many are left to us. KJ once told me that the average American lives seventy-eight and a half years, which equals 2.47 billion seconds. He's right that I don't believe all those seconds will be mine, but he's wrong if he thinks I don't want them. Standing in KJ's embrace, I have never wanted anything more in my entire life.

We leave our daypacks at the neighbor's house and walk to the spot where the green dot rests on the tracker map, eating the sandwiches as we go. We decide it's smart to save our freezing skills as much as we can, in case we need them later. The residential streets we pass through are disconcertingly normal. Sunlight shines through leafy tree canopies, children shoot basketballs in front of their homes, and people look up from weeding their gardens to smile at us. It's hard to reconcile the quiet ease of a Wednesday afternoon with the terror creeping toward anyone who carries chronotin in their blood. I want to shake the people around us, shatter their complacency and scream out the threat that lurks in the shadows. But the threat is fickle. There are no shadows for the Norms. For them, it's just a regular sunny day.

The tracker app places Jack at a store called Everyday Music. It's a stand-alone one-story structure next to an aging office building with a prominent FOR RENT sign. We reach it a little before five. KJ pushes the crosswalk button, and I chew my bitter-tasting nails and study our target while we wait for the light. The store's windows are plastered with posters depicting album covers. On the roof, a huge white billboard announces, *We Pay Cash for Any and All Used Vinyl, CDs, and DVDs.*

The light turns green. KJ steps into the crosswalk, and I hurry after him, shooting sidelong glances at the cars idling nearby. All the drivers' faces are blanked out by the glare of the setting sun on their windshields, and I'm grateful when we leave their menacing presence for the shelter of the store. Not that being inside is a lot better. There's a woman with neon pink hair working the front counter who looks up as we enter. She's talking to a customer, but her eyes travel over us for longer than seems necessary. I skulk down the nearest aisle. A song with mournful lyrics plays from the speakers, the singer's voice half drowned by the thrashing beat of angry drums. The air smells like dust and old dreams.

I pick up a random album, holding it in front of me as if I find the cover interesting.

"Where is he?" KJ whispers.

"I don't know." I slide the phone from my pocket and check it behind the shelter of the album. "The tracker says he's still here."

Pretending to be curious about the rest of the store's inventory, I turn in place and search the premises. Each section has a black-and-white sign hanging over it, identifying a musical genre: rock, R & B, classical, pop. There's another staff person stocking records in one of the bins at the far end of the store and a handful of customers roaming the aisles.

KJ elbows me. "Look over there. The blond guy."

The staff person I skimmed over is nodding as he listens to something through a pair of headphones while he works. His hair is bleached nearly white, and he's wearing thick plastic-framed glasses, but the set of his shoulders and the way his head bobs gives him away. Jack.

KJ and I wend our way through the store. The sight of Jack brings back a lifetime of memories. Jack snickering with Aidan in the back of a classroom. Jack teasing me about loving time work. Jack bent over a bus map in the squat where we hid after our escape from the Center, making sure I understood the route I needed to take on what turned out to be a foolish trip to search Dr. Barnard's house. Jack, freaked out from overusing his skills, his clenched fists

179

stained with blood.

I reach his side.

"Jack?"

He looks up. Under the platinum hair, his familiar dark eyes widen.

"What are *you* doing here?" he asks.

There's anger in his voice. I smile at him anyway. He doesn't smile back. KJ catches my eye and lifts his eyebrows in an I-told-you-so look.

"We're here to make you an offer," I say to Jack.

"About what?"

I glance around the store.

"Is there somewhere private we can talk?" I ask.

Jack removes the headphones and sets them on a hook on the side of the bin.

"Why should I listen to you after what you did?" he says. "You left me leashed inside the Center. What did you think was going to happen to me?"

"What *did* happen," KJ says. "Ross covered for you and got you out."

Jack rounds on him.

"You didn't know that for sure. I could have been caught."

"Come on," I say. "You weren't exactly the hero that night. You were about to turn us over to Ross; what do you think *he* would have done to *us*?"

"I told you that night," Jack snaps. "One of us was going to die, and it wasn't going to be me."

"Turns out it wasn't any of us," KJ says.

Jack and KJ glower at each other. My mouth tastes sour with disappointment. Even though KJ warned me, I had higher hopes for this reunion.

"We didn't come here to argue about the past." I glance around the store again. The clerk up front is now focused on a sale, but one of the customers is casting us curious glances. How loudly have we been talking? I move closer to Jack and lower my voice.

"What we're offering," I say, "is a way to gain leverage over Ross. And to stay one step ahead of the wipers."

Jack crosses his arms over his chest, clearly debating whether or not to refuse right off the bat. Curiosity must win, because his arms loosen.

"We can talk in there," he says, jerking his head toward a door I hadn't noticed along the back wall. The sign over it says STAFF ONLY.

"It's OK," Jack says before KJ or I can protest. "Ross got me a job here." He grins. "The owner owes him a favor."

Pride rings through his voice, and I realize he has mostly agreed to talk to us because he wants to show off. It makes me want to shake him. Jack believes he's safe, and he has no understanding of how tenuous that safety is.

Jack struts through the staff room door as if he owns the place. KJ and I follow more cautiously. I make sure no one is watching before ducking into the back room. The space inside is mostly filled with shelving holding everything from office supplies to crates of vinyl. It's brightly lit and unexpectedly tidy. Neatly lettered signs identify the records by genre, and the floor looks recently swept. There are no windows, but a softly glowing red sign marks an emergency exit.

Jack marches right through the main room to a smaller one in the back. This space is more cluttered. A tattered sofa sits against the back wall, fronted by a table and three chairs. In the corner is a tiny kitchenette. Coffee cups fill the sink under a sign with a picture of a troll that says, WASH YOUR DISHES OR ELSE!

"So," Jack says, turning to face us, "what's your big offer?"

"You know how Dr. Barnard discovered a 'cure'?" I say. Jack looks at me like I've stated something too obvious to merit a response. "Well, the wipers are stepping up their hunt. They've hacked a spinner network, and now they're tracking down all the free spinners. Anyone who knows the truth about our real abilities is going to be killed."

Jack leans back against the sink and crosses his arms again. "I'm not seeing how this is any different from how it's always been. Wipers kill spinners. Fact of life."

KJ makes an irritated sound, which I choose to ignore. Jack isn't exactly being encouraging, but at least he no longer sounds angry. I take that as progress.

"The wipers are more focused now," I tell him. "Before, they just wanted to make sure no one found out the truth. Now their goal is total elimination."

Jack raises an eyebrow. "Still not seeing what this has to do with me."

"This isn't about you," KJ says. "It's about Ross."

A slight relaxation in Jack's stance tells me we've finally caught his interest. I hurry to explain.

"Ross is working with Kronos now—with the Central Office," I tell him. "We want you to download a listening device onto Ross's cell phone. KJ can show you how. That way we'll know when they're going to attack someone."

Jack fiddles with the plastic frames hiding his face. "I don't know," he says. "Ross wouldn't be happy if he found out. I don't think I want to piss him off."

Hope leaps in my chest. Jack has never liked being controlled; forcing him to tread on eggshells is the wrong way for Ross to gain his loyalty. I choose my next words carefully.

"What's it like living with Mr. Ross?" I ask.

Jack snorts. "I don't live with the guy. I live in an apartment he rented for me. Which isn't as cool as it sounds. Ross likes to keep tabs on me, and he—" Jack glances at KJ and stops himself. "It's way better than the squat, though." He give a shrug that does little to improve my impression of his living situation. "Where have you two been hiding out?"

"On a farm," I say; there's no reason now to hide the truth. "Out in Eastern Oregon. It's run by some free spinners as a shelter for runaways like us. All the kids from the Center are there. Or they were."

My voice catches.

182

"What happened?" Jack demands.

"We just found out the wipers are on their way to round them up."

Jack makes an odd choking sound, like he just took a punch to the gut. "I thought you were taking them somewhere safe."

His tone is accusing. I force myself not to look away. "I thought so, too."

Jack takes off his glasses and rubs at a spot behind his ear. "Will they be cured?"

"No," I say. "They know too much. One of the free spinners is trying to rescue them, but I don't know if it will work."

Jack nods like he expected me to say this. Without the glasses, he looks more like the boy I grew up with: younger and more vulnerable.

"Will you help us?" I ask.

Jack adjusts his weight against the sink, searching for a more comfortable position. "What was the farm like?" he asks.

The question makes me smile.

"It's way out in the boonies," I say. "And it was kind of hectic with so many of us there. You wouldn't have liked all the chores, but it was a happy place. Peaceful. The landscape is beautiful in a stark kind of way." I shake my head, dispelling the memory of what is gone. "Even though it turned out not to be true, the place felt like a beginning. Being all together like that made us feel so much stronger."

An odd expression crosses Jack's face. He's staring down at the glasses in his hand, which he must have squeezed hard enough to break off one of the plastic arms. The black shard lies in his palm, long and thin as a dismembered spider's leg.

Jack looks up, our eyes meet, and I suddenly remember a time years ago when the two of us were Youngers and Jack found a pen lying on the floor in a hallway. It was an expensive pen, the kind advertised by sulky men in the glossy magazines that sometimes showed up in our donation bin. We both knew it was Dr. Barnard's. Jack started clowning around—chewing the pen like a cigar, waving it through the air like a sword—and I was laughing at him, when he accidentally dropped it and a piece broke off. With a crawling sense of horror, we both heard the distinctive clip of Dr. Barnard's footsteps coming down the hall. Jack stared toward the sound, immobile. He was already in trouble for some recent misdemeanor and was likely looking at a week in solitary for this new infraction. The footsteps came closer.

Without a second thought, I snatched up the pen, hiding both pieces behind my back as Barnard asked if we'd seen his pen and we both claimed ignorance. I remember the heat on my face from the lie and the feel of the broken shards clutched in my hand. Jack never thanked me, but I didn't expect it. At the Center, covering for each other was automatic.

Jack shuffles his feet.

"I . . ." The word barely leaves his mouth before he stops. Something in the air between us shifts. Jack's hand closes over the broken frames, and his gaze darts from me to KJ. His eyes narrow.

"How did you find me?" he asks.

Disappointment and frustration mingle with a vague sense of dread.

"We saw an app on Ross's phone," I say. "You know he's tracking you, right?"

Jack wraps his arms around his chest.

"It's for my own safety," he says. "In case I get caught."

"Ross doesn't do anything for someone else's good," KJ says. "Not unless it's for his good, too."

Jack shrugs.

"Don't you want to be free?" My tone is angrier than I intend, and I see the answering flash in Jack's eyes.

"Free?" He gestures around the shabby room. "I'm already free."

"No one else is." I feel our plan slipping away and struggle to contain my rising anxiety. "If we can record Ross covering up crimes for the Central Office, he'll go to jail, and we might be able to get rid of wipers entirely. Stop being selfish for one minute and help us so maybe we can *all* be free. Permanently."

I know this is not the way to convince Jack, but I can't help myself. The ugliness in the room spreads like a sheen of oil, threatening to catch the spark of our old resentments.

Jack smirks. "Same old Alex. Always thinking you're going to save the world. Well, I don't need you to save me. I've got the chief of police on my side now. He's the best protection anybody could want."

I shiver. There's something ominous about Jack's words. My eyes flick around the staff room again. It seemed cozy when we first came in, in a run-down sort of way, but I don't really see the appeal anymore. Now the fact that it doesn't have windows seems really unnerving. KJ seems to be thinking the same thing. He's rubbing his hands together and casting nervous glances toward the door. I wish Jack hadn't closed it. Someone could be out there. I nibble on the edge of my thumb. We should have had this conversation in frozen time.

KJ wriggles his shoulders, as if he's adjusting a daypack. "I told you this was a long shot," he says to me. "Come on, Alex, let's go. We tried."

The idea of leaving fills me with overwhelming relief. I move with KJ toward the door. There's something about this place that's making me uncomfortable. Even the coffee maker seems to emanate a kind of warning. My chest feels tight, and my breath—

Which is when it hits me. This particular sensation of fear is too familiar not to recognize. Someone very near to us has a zapper.

"KJ," I say, but his face has gone slack, and I know he's realized it, too. I grab his hand and snatch at the time strands. Nothing happens. It's like stepping into a cloud—I can see time moving, but there is nothing for me to hang on to.

"They're too close," I say.

I stare at the closed door. No wonder Jack changed his mind about trusting me. Fear wafts between the cracks, black as smoke and just as deadly.

185

How could we have been stupid enough to let ourselves get trapped back here?

"What's out there?" Jacks whispers. He's only been near a zapper once, and at the time he had no idea what it was. I doubt Ross has enlightened him.

"Wipers," I say.

We all face the door. KJ puts his hands on the back of a chair, and I claim another one. They're not great protection, but holding them feels better than just standing here unarmed. The terror around me is so strong I feel nauseated. I want whoever is out there to come in just to cut the suspense.

The door opens, and I change my mind. Two figures stand there, horrible creatures with shaggy heads, their jaws gaping . . . I scream, and one of them turns in my direction. I squeeze my eyes shut and reopen them. The panic-induced vision clears. They're not monsters—they're men. Big men dressed in dark colors. The one in back has a neck so massive it bulges over his collar. The one in front has a tattoo of barbed wire inked around his throat. He's holding a zapper up high like it's some sort of magical talisman, which I suppose from their perspective, it is. The thing has no effect on them, while I can barely breathe for the absolute terror squeezing my chest.

The five of us hold this tableau for the time it takes the two men's heads to swivel from one of us to another. I grip the plastic chair so hard my knuckles turn white. KJ's breath is jagged. Jack has backed into the corner, sweat shining on his pale cheeks. A stab of pity slices through my fear. Jack has no idea his emotions are being manipulated, which is going to make his terror worse.

Tattoo Man steps forward. In the hand not holding the zapper, a leash dangles, its clasp hanging open like hungry jaws.

I measure the distance between us. If I throw the chair, will I hit him? It's hard to think with the waves of panic threatening to swallow me. I lift the chair a couple of inches, weighing its heft. The man opens his mouth.

"Well, well, well," he says. "It looks like we hit the jackpot. I was told there'd only be one back here. Now, which of you is Jack Whiting?"

Jack's face blanches so white it's a miracle he doesn't pass out.

186

"What do you want?" he squeaks.

"You're a spinner," Tattoo Man says. "We're taking you where you belong—away from humans."

"I'm not a spinner." Jack's voice sounds strangled. "None of us are. I work here. The manager knows me."

"You're not spinners?" Tattoo Man moves closer, lifting the zapper and holding it toward Jack like he's about to impale him. Jack whimpers.

"If you're not spinners," Tattoo Man says, "then why are you all so scared?"

Neckless settles himself against the door frame, his bulk blocking the exit as solidly as a boulder. "Three for the price of one," he says. "That's going to make the boss happy."

Tattoo Man waves his fear-inflicting instrument again. A buzz radiates from it, a horrible sound like a million bees stuffed into my head, filling the space where thoughts are supposed to take root. I bite my lip to try and force myself to concentrate. We need to get through the door. If I run straight at Neckless . . . the idea dies before it's fully formed. The man is huge. Running into him would be like running into a wall.

Jack starts spluttering excuses, telling the men they're wrong and this is all a mistake. KJ inches closer to me until his arm is pressed against mine. I lean against him in a futile search for comfort. Tattoo Man moves toward Jack. He's tucked the zapper in his pocket, and he's holding out the leash like it's a whip and he's a lion tamer. I half expect Jack to snarl at him. Instead, Jack swings his fist at the older man. The man dodges out of range with the grace of someone who has been attacked before.

"You don't want to do this," Jack says. "You don't know who I am."

Tattoo Man drops into a fighter's stance.

"Sure I do," he says. "You're a filthy spinner, and I'm going to take you down."

KJ nudges my shoulder, pushing me toward the corner opposite Jack. I

187

try to take a step, but my legs are trembling so badly it's like walking on cooked spaghetti. I don't even know what part of the fear is real and what is manufactured by the zapper. Not that it matters. This is definitely a situation that merits a lot of fear.

"I'm not a spinner!" Jack's voice is high. "Call my uncle—he's Carson Ross. Police Chief Carson Ross!"

The wiper laughs. "That's the fun of catching spinners," he says. "They always tell such crazy lies."

"It's true," Jack says. "Ross wouldn't want you to do this."

"Really?" Tattoo Man's smile is like a hungry python's when he sees a very small mouse. "That's funny, since he's the one who told us where to find you."

My stomach drops. Jack moans.

The wiper moves faster than seems possible, given his bulk. There's a blur, and then both Jack's arms are pinned behind his back. It's not even the leash holding him, just plain old handcuffs. Only after he's immobilized does the man snap the leash around Jack's wrist. Lazily, like it's an afterthought.

KJ nudges me again, this time with so much force I stumble in the direction he's pushing, dragging the chair I'm holding with me.

"We can't get out," I murmur under my breath. "The other one is blocking the way."

"I know," he mouths. He's still carrying his chair, so I pick up mine, too, and inch over a little farther, lifting the chair above the tiles so it doesn't scrape the floor. Neckless, perhaps noticing our slight movements, straightens up and digs around in his pocket.

"We've only got one other leash," he says. "We'll just handcuff the girl. Keep your chromo on so she doesn't try anything."

KJ leans his head down so his lips brush my ear.

"Be ready to run," he whispers.

Run where? The words scream through my head, but there's no time to ask. KJ has snatched the chair out of my hands and spun back toward Jack.

"Jack!" he shouts, hurling the chair across the room. "Quick, catch!"

Jack's head snaps up. Tattoo Man swears and ducks. The chair misses Jack completely, slamming instead into a shelf over the sink. Mugs cascade onto the counter, exploding into ceramic shards like tiny bombs. Neckless adds his own curses to Tattoo Man's colorful display. I stare at the mess. Whatever KJ planned hasn't done a thing. Jack is just as bound as he was before, and we're still trapped. Tattoo Man straightens with murder in his eyes. Neckless steps out of the doorway, turning his thick body toward the commotion.

"Now!" KJ yells. His own chair is in his hands, and he's charging at Neckless.

Time stops. Not literally, only in the way Norms sometimes use the phrase. I have no power to shelter me from vanishing seconds, but there is an instant, a fraction of a nanosecond, in which a choice has to be made, and the starkness of it makes the instant stretch into an eternity.

Neckless has turned away from the door. Beside him, there is a sliver of an opening just big enough for me to glimpse freedom beyond. And beside me is KJ, nearly airborne as he lunges at the ogre's back. KJ's wild flight is not going to hurt the giant man. It's not even going to stop him. But KJ's momentum will, for one precious moment, open that sliver into a gap wide enough for someone to dash through.

Some*one*. Just one. Just me.

"Run, Alex!"

He's screaming, the words flying knives because we both know what they mean. I will escape. Me, the person KJ believes has a chance of pulling off a miracle, the one he promised to protect. KJ will be caught. And if I don't do anything, both of us will die. It's the worst choice ever, and it isn't even a choice. If I don't run, the only future for all three of us is death.

The pointy ends of the chair legs sink into Neckless's beefy back. The hulking man, warned by KJ's shouts, has started to turn around, but it's already

189

too late. The weight of KJ's body, increased by his desperate lunge, sends Neckless staggering a few steps away from the doorway.

The muscles in my legs burn as I dive through the opening. My feet move so fast I don't even feel the linoleum under my toes. Neckless's furious face flashes past me. His mouth is open, his hand raised to shove KJ and the chair to one side. It's a glimpse, the barest image, and one I know will replay forever.

I hit the ground in the storage area and keep running. Ahead of me, the red light of the emergency exit sign beckons. I throw my body at the metal bar that opens it at the same moment I throw my mind around the time strands whipping past me. My mental grip closes. The door swings open, the alarm silenced before it even starts, and I burst out onto the sidewalk.

Concrete scrapes a layer of skin off my palms. My hands burn. I'm panting, my breath mingled with sobs so that the only noise in this frozen world is a horrible choking sound. I kneel on the ground just long enough to catch my breath, and then I go back. The door, which I was not touching when time stopped, remains open. I step over the threshold and peer into the storeroom. The space pulses with threat. Across the room, I can make out the dark outline of Neckless's body, KJ right beside him. Beyond them, Jack cowers in the far corner. I step a tiny bit closer. A buzzing sound grows in my head, and instantly the time threads start to shred. I back away. Tremors of combined terror and frustration wrack my body.

There has to be *something* I can do. I edge around the storeroom, just out of range of the zapper's time-stripping rays. In the corner I spy a mop. I grab the handle, weighing it in my hands. Maybe I can hook the end under KJ's belt and pull him toward me, dragging him out of reach of the zapper the way he did for me in the park. The wood feels soft in my hands, its rounded handle smooth from the touch of hundreds of workers. I creep as close as I can stand to while still holding time and stretch the mop across the space between KJ and me. I'm at least three feet short. I lean closer. The buzzing sound grows so loud,

190

the vibrations shatter my concentration. A rush of sound rises through the cracks of returning time, and my head screams with the pain of ricocheting strands. I leap back, snatch control again, then lean against the wall, panting into the returned silence.

Sweat pours off my forehead, the salty dampness indistinguishable from the tears coursing down my cheeks. My head throbs from the assaulting zapper. I'm not going to be able to hold this freeze if I stay here very much longer. Even if I could find a rope to replicate KJ's rescue, I would never be able to pull him through the small space between Neckless and the door frame. Jack, in his corner on the other side of the room, is utterly unreachable.

The mop slides from my grip and hits the ground with a hard smack. I scream into the silent world, venting my fury at an uncaring universe.

"It's supposed to be *us*, KJ, not just me! This is not how it was meant to happen!"

KJ hovers before me, frozen in the moment of his sacrifice. I swallow my heartbreak and scrub the tears from my cheeks. KJ believed in me, and he gave me a chance. He gave all of us a chance. However dim that flicker of hope is, I cannot let it go to waste.

14 ◀◀

THE SUN'S UNMOVING RAYS HANG IN THE AIR WITHOUT ENOUGH strength to warm my body. I stumble down the sidewalk away from the music store, moving blindly through an unmoving city. A dozen blocks away, I duck into a coffee shop, grab someone's to-go cup from the counter, and lock myself in the bathroom. I release time and leave quickly. The coffee is hot and burns my tongue.

I rub my knuckles against my throbbing head, as if the motion can somehow force my muddled thoughts into order. I need reinforcements and a place to think. The neighbor's house. Jamal. I'll talk to him again, tell him about our idea, and find another way we can make it work before we run away. Jamal has to help. He *has* to.

I reach a street corner and stop walking. Do I go left or straight? Neat houses offer blank stares, their doors closed and windows curtained.

How long do I have to save Jack and KJ?

The wipers will take them to the Central Office—that's a drive of about two hours. They'll probably start their "treatment" as soon as they get there. The first time KJ got sick, Barnard injected him with enough Aclisote that he was knocked out immediately. If I hadn't unhooked him from that IV drip, I doubt he would have lived through the day. I gulp more of the scalding coffee. How many hours does that give me? Twenty-four? No. The pain in my head twists. The most I can count on is probably twelve. I check the time on my phone. It's 5:17 p.m.

The caffeine does a tiny bit to reduce my headache but nothing to ease my desperation. I steady both hands against the warmth of my cup. Fear is not an option. Hesitation is not an option. The seconds KJ has left are relentlessly slipping away, seconds I can't control no matter how often or how long I freeze them.

A breeze gusts through the air. Mingled with its soft rustle comes the lilt of a child laughing. The sound is faint, and even as I search for its source, it fades. The loss feels personal. That laugh could be Emma's or Yuki's or any spinner's. Even mine. The wind whips harder, and I zip my down vest against its chill. KJ and Jack are not the only people being abducted tonight. All over the city, the state, maybe all over the world, the scene I just witnessed is being played out. The only difference is that in most cases, one person will not escape.

I still have the phone, and I pull it out to check the map, orienting myself so I can get back to Jamal's. When I left the Center, all I cared about was finding a safe place for KJ and me. When I broke back into the Center, my goal was to free my friends. Neither effort truly worked, because neither effort addressed the real problem. I turn toward my goal and start running. KJ was right when he said this thing was bigger than us. If we are going to survive, we need to fight the source.

We have to stop Kronos.

I'm gasping by the time I near the safe house. I jogged most of the way, but I also managed to get turned around, and the phone tells me it's past six. What did Jamal think when he discovered we weren't at the meeting spot? Did he wait? One more block. A stitch burns in my side. I dig my fingers into the ache and try to take deep breaths the way Yolly taught me years ago, except I'm panting already, so deep breaths aren't really an option. I dash across the final street and turn the corner.

Two police cars are parked in front of Jamal's house, the lights on top sending flashes of blue skittering around the block. I skid to a stop so fast I nearly trip off the curb. A cop stands on the safe house's porch behind a line of yellow police tape, talking into a cell phone. As I watch, another officer passes him, carrying Jamal's laptop. Across the street, neighbors dawdle in small groups, gaping at the unfolding drama like it's a scene from a tawdry television show. Among them is yet another cop, head bent as he asks someone a question. The ache in my side stabs more deeply. The house they are standing in front of is the one where we were supposed to meet Jamal, and that door, too, is blocked off with tape. Does that mean Jamal was there when the police came? I force myself to idle for a few minutes, pretending only a mild interest in the officers' actions, before turning away and slowly, casually strolling back the way I came.

If Jamal did avoid capture, where did he go? How will I find him? He already threw away his phone. Seconds flash past me, each one taking KJ further away. I need someone else who can help and there's only one option: Max. I yank the phone from my pocket, dredge up her number from memory, and dial.

"Alex?" A voice answers before the phone can ring twice.

"How did you—"

"Jamal told me you might call. Where are you?"

"Near his house. There are cops here."

"I know." She speaks quickly, each word snapped out like an order. "I'm parked around the corner, on Twenty-Eighth at Main. A silver Ford, license plate 157HJF."

The connection cuts off. I check the sign on the nearest corner: SE 28th AVE. I hurry down the street. The Ford is half a block ahead.

A police car heads toward me from the other end of the street. Its flashing lights aren't on, which somehow seems more ominous, as if it is cruising the area rather than aiming for a particular destination. I lower my head, staring at my phone until I'm standing right next to Max's car. The cop drives past me. I bend and peer through the passenger window. The car is empty.

I snap upright. Before the idea that this might be a trap fully forms in my head, a figure darts from the shadows. The next instant, an arm is around my waist and I am welded to someone's side.

"Don't make any noise," a voice hisses in my ear. "If the cops see you, I'll have to turn you over to them."

I twist my head around to see my captor. It's a woman. A tall, dark woman with a headful of braids.

Agent Xavier.

I choke back a scream. The wiper is holding me so close that I can barely move, and her hand is wrapped around my wrist. I can't freeze without taking her with me. I push against her bulk and fail to create more than a millimeter of space between us. Horror crawls over my skin like a trail of fire ants. I can't get captured, not now.

"Stop struggling," she says. "Someone will notice us."

"Why would you care?" I hiss back at her. "You *work* with the police."

"Not this time," she says. "I'm here to help you."

"Help me?" I try again to twist out of her hold. Fail. "You're a *wiper*."

"I came here because of Jamal, not Kronos. He sent me here to intercept you."

The sidewalk we're standing on does a weird wobbly thing, like it has suddenly turned into a roller coaster.

"*Jamal* sent you? He's helping the wipers?"

"No, you idiot. I'm helping *him*."

The grip soldering me to her side loosens the barest amount—not enough for me to escape, but it allows me to turn and look her straight in the face. The expressionless mask she always wears has slipped. Behind it burns something angry and raw. The expression is terrifying and also reassuring. No one could look like that and lie.

"Who are you?" I ask.

"My name is Maria Alicia Xavier," she says. "Jamal calls me by my initials."

If the sidewalk is a roller coaster, we just went over the steepest drop, the one that feels like falling off a cliff.

"*You're* Max?" I ask.

Agent Xavier's—Max's—arm is still wrapped around me, though at this point, given the wobbling sidewalk, her grip feels more steadying than restraining.

"I thought you worked for the CIA," I say.

"I do. We're investigating Kronos. I'm their plant."

"The CIA rescues spinners?"

The hand gripping my wrist twitches. "No."

"I don't understand."

Max glances around, searching the surrounding dark with an intensity I recognize from the meeting we watched this afternoon.

"I'm going to let you go." Max motions toward the car parked in front of us. "You can run, or you can get in the car, and I will answer your questions."

I study the modest vehicle. It looks innocuous enough. The exterior is dull with dust, and the roof is scattered with leaves from the tree overhead.

"If I was going to leash you," Max says, "I would have done it already."

The pressure holding me in place releases, and I automatically take a step back. Max strolls to the other side of the car and unlocks it. I look down the street. Another police cruiser speeds by, turning toward the no-longer-safe house with a loud squeal. I get in the car.

The seats inside are worn. It's not a new car. The interior smells like spearmint gum, and there's a starburst crack in the corner of the windshield.

"OK," I say, not letting go of the door handle. "Explain."

Max rests her hands on the steering wheel but makes no move to start the car.

"Fifteen years ago," she says, "I was a sniper serving in Iraq. Jamal was in my unit. I didn't know he was a spinner. None of us did. The two of us were together when an IED exploded in front of the jeep we were in. I blacked out in the accident, and when I came to, Jamal and I were both on the side of the road, bruised but alive. Jamal had stopped time to get us out, a fact that I was, of course, unaware of. All I knew was that he'd saved my life. It made a bond between us. After my service was over, I was recruited by the CIA. I worked in the undercover unit, and when the assignment came up to infiltrate Kronos, I took it. Like most people, I distrusted spinners, and while I had concerns about the reach of this shadowy and powerful organization, I wasn't against their work. Then one day, the target I was assigned to hunt down turned out to be Jamal."

For the first time, I catch a hint of emotion in the wiper's voice.

"Until that point," Max continues, "I'd believed everything I had been told about spinners: that they were unnatural, insane, and only semi-human. But I knew Jamal, and finally understanding how he had managed to save me forced me to rethink those assumptions."

I study Max's profile. Late afternoon sun slants through the windshield, its harsh light stripping her features bare. What was it like for her, a wiper, to be forced to see a spinner as a fellow human being? It's a scene that's hard to imagine. Then again, here I am, a spinner, starting to consider trusting a wiper.

"What exactly does the CIA know about spinners?" I ask.

"Everyone in the Agency knows that the Centers use Aclisote to suppress the full extent of your powers, but they don't know that Aclisote can kill. Agents are all told that only a small minority of spinners live past adolescence. They know that adult rogue spinners are being killed, but those numbers are small and fall under the category of acceptable loss. I suspect there are people at the top of the organization who are aware Kronos is practicing all-out genocide, but I think they have chosen to turn a blind eye because it's convenient. They may not approve of Kronos's methods, but they certainly appreciate the results. All of them believe spinners are dangerous."

I rub the aching spot on my temple.

"You know the truth," I say, "and you're still working as a wiper. You're still hunting down spinners."

The look Max gives me is cold.

"The CIA's objectives are larger than any individual. Besides, the CIA made it clear when I accepted this assignment: people don't quit the Order of Kronos. If you serve long enough, they let you retire. But you can't quit. Especially not if your reason for leaving is a loss of faith. The Kronons are ruthless in their efforts to keep their secrets. Even with the protection of the CIA, I'm not confident they won't find me."

"Does Jamal know?"

She shifts uncomfortably. "That I'm working as a wiper? No. He just knows that my position with the CIA allows me access to information. I do more when I can. I did my best to keep the other security agents misdirected when you and your friends first escaped. And I let you get away at the park the other day."

I'd say she *sort of* let me get away. If KJ hadn't found that rope, I am quite sure I'd be in the Central Office by now. Or dead. Which makes her what, a wiper with a conscience? Or a true sympathizer whose ability to help is limited by her own precarious position?

"Did Jamal get away?" I ask.

"His name has not yet appeared on the list of spinners that have been captured."

Max may be Jamal's friend, but no one would mistake her tone as friendly. I peer up at the sky. The sun slants toward the horizon, a ball of light tangled in the branches of the neighboring trees. If Miguel's plan worked, he should be driving away with an RV full of spinners right now.

My palms feel damp. I rub them over the fabric of my skirt.

"What about Miguel?" I ask. "Is he on the list?"

"The wipers intercepted Miguel before he arrived at the refuge."

There's a small hole in my skirt. My finger catches in it, and I hear it rip.

"We need to find another way to warn Lisa," I say. "There's still time.

198

The wipers aren't going to the refuge until it gets dark."

"It's too late," she says. "When Miguel got captured, the security team was instructed to move up the timing of their attack. All of the escaped spinners were captured, along with the other residents of the premises." Max's fingers flex against the steering wheel. "There was a struggle. A door had to be blasted open. Two of the targets were killed in the explosion."

The tear in my skirt exposes the blackness of the tights underneath. I fix my eyes on the gap. The hole looks like an opening into a vast bottomless pit.

"Who died?" I ask.

"Two females, both age ten." Max speaks without emotion, as if the facts she's relaying do not involve actual people. "The report identified them as Emmaline Smith and Molly Evans."

The world turns dark. I can hear their voices, Emma's high and eager, Molly's slower and gentler. Emma always picks the cucumbers out of her salad because she thinks they taste slimy. Her favorite movie is *My Fair Lady,* and she knows the lyrics to every single song. Molly sucked her thumb until she was eight, even though everyone teased her about it. She prefers pajama pants to jeans, taught herself how to knit from a book, and once did ten perfect cartwheels in a row after Aidan said she couldn't.

How can they be dead?

Max is still talking, but her voice sounds far away, as if it is reaching me through layers of interference. I shake my head in an effort to clear it.

"Project Zed," she says, "has officially begun. The spinners from Goat Hill Farm are currently being transported to the Central Office in Tacoma. They are expected to arrive at approximately ten p.m. Warrants have been put out for the arrest of every spinner Kronos has identified, and forces are closing in on locations across the country."

The air inside the car feels thick. Max's words fade out again. *I am in the basement with my friends, crouching in the inky dark. Footsteps creak*

199

across the floorboards overhead. Someone whimpers. The basement's dank smell is laced with the sharp tang of sweat. Terror from a zapper slides through the gaps in the wood. Lisa and her children start to scream.

I grip my knees through the folds of my skirt. Molly and Emma are only the first who will die. KJ is next. And Jack. Then Aidan. Yuki. Baby Rosie. Yolly. My hands start shaking. I can't think about the rest of them, or I will never get out of Max's car. I will dissolve into this worn seat, leaving nothing but ash.

"It will be best for you," Max says, "if you run. Kronos has no record of your whereabouts. If you lay low, you may be able to survive."

Survive. The word is hollow. What is survival if everyone I love is dead? What is life if I can never show my true self? Every free spinner will be murdered. New ones will have their skills snuffed out at birth. This is not a future. This is a bleak plane that offers nothing but existence. My fingers dig so deeply into my knees that I can feel them bruising. It doesn't hurt. Why would it? If everyone is gone, then nothing matters.

I shut my eyes against the darkness closing in around me. I push away the fear and the sorrow and the horror, isolating my thoughts until my mind is as clear and sharp as a knife. When I reopen my eyes, the sun has slipped farther toward the horizon. The streaks that remain scrawl a bloody haze across the sky.

"Is it true that the CIA is trying to stop Kronos?"

"The CIA is very close to having enough evidence to prove that Kronos has influenced government policies—both foreign and domestic," Max says. "Once they have enough data, they will move to dismantle the organization."

"What will happen to spinners?"

"Before the launch of Project Zed, I thought the CIA would be more lenient than Kronos in its treatment of spinners. I expected them to continue the long-term incarceration but not the overt poisoning. Now I believe that there are people in the CIA who have known about Zed for years and are delaying prosecution until Kronos has finished their grim task. This way, the spinner 'problem' will be resolved without the Agency having to sully their reputation. They can act shocked in retrospect."

"That's cowardly."

Max shrugs.

"If the CIA received undeniable proof that Kronos was killing spinners," I ask, "wouldn't they be forced to act?"

"They would, yes, but the CIA is a large bureaucracy." Max's hands flex on the steering wheel again. "Acting quickly for them means weeks of sorting new data and working up a strategy. That's not fast enough to save your friends."

I consider the streaks staining the sky. There are trees blocking my view, and their branches look like arms holding back a fiery mass.

"There must be proof on the Kronos computers," I say. "If I found something specific enough, it would at least stop them from killing off the spinners at other Centers."

"Our best people couldn't hack into their computers," Max says. "You don't have those skills. You have no chance."

My despair returns in a rush that threatens to overwhelm me. I grip my knees even harder and picture a box, a big one, made of metal with huge iron locks. I shove every doubt and fear and all my grief inside it until the only thing left is a single objective: stop Kronos.

I turn to Max with a face that feels as expressionless as her own.

"I won't try to hack their system. I'll get the information directly from Dr. Ellery's computer in the Central Office."

"You can't." She says it like it's a fact, not an opinion.

"Why not?"

"The Central Office is designed like a fortress. It is surrounded by barbed wire–topped concrete walls, and there are multiple security checkpoints to enter the grounds and the building. All the checkpoints are protected by chromoelectronegators, and people require clearance higher than mine to get past the building's main lobby."

I consider this. Perhaps sensing my lack of deterrence, Max adds, "Even if you could get in, you'd still need physical keys to get inside her office and a password to access her computer."

"Can you get me a broken leash?" I ask. "One that looks normal but doesn't block my skills?"

"I could rig one."

"Then those things won't be a problem." Stealing keys is easy in frozen time, and I can find passwords by rewinding. I reach into my pocket and take out the spy cam. "I can set this up, too. If I put it in Dr. Ellery's office, it's sure to catch something incriminating."

Max's eyes narrow. "Even assuming you could get in, your chance of success is near zero. And if you did download any files, there is no way they won't catch you, which means you will be killed."

I shrug. It's calming, not feeling anything. KJ was right. Without the distraction of trying to survive this endeavor, the road ahead is blazingly clear

"The way I figure it," I say, "I'm going to die either way. I'd rather die knowing I've done everything I could to fight Kronos."

Max nods as if conceding a point.

I lift the edge of my down vest and pick at the threads along the seam. When they give way, I stuff the tiny camera and the portable router inside the gap. The router is bulkier, but the down is thick enough to hide the lump. I knot the threads to keep the gap from widening and work through more strategies.

"My chances would be better if you help me," I say.

I'm not really asking. I'm just calculating the odds, and having someone—anyone—on my side increases them.

Max studies me with her emotionless eyes. "What kind of help are you talking about?"

I dredge up the limited knowledge I have about computer files. It's just barely enough to cover the basics. "I need someone to send the files to."

Max's fingers tap the steering wheel in a slow rhythm.

"If the CIA knows I'm acting without their approval," she says, "I will lose my job. If Kronos figures out that I helped you, they'll kill me."

I meet Max's gaze. Her empty eyes don't scare me anymore. I understand them now. Max has as little to lose as I do.

"If I don't do this," I say, "a lot of people are going to die. You will be one of the ones sent to hunt them down, and their deaths will be on your head. If I succeed, you can leave Kronos forever."

Max's face doesn't change. I smooth my skirt over my legs. The temperature is starting to drop, and the change in the weather feels bracing. I wait for Max's answer while my mind churns through the problems laid before me. The Office. The computer. Passwords.

"All this is theoretical," Max says. "You still don't have a way into the Central Office."

"Yes, I do."

Max actually looks surprised. "How?"

I clasp my hands in my lap. The sun has fully sunk now, leaving a dim twilight that leaches the color from the street around us. Which doesn't mean it looks black and white. The world outside may be stark, but it's painted in myriad shades of gray. Gray is the color of subtleties. It's a color that can shift and change. Gray is the color of hope.

I turn and face the wiper sitting beside me.

"I'm going to go to Dr. Barnard," I tell her, "and turn myself in."

15 ◀◀

MAX DROPS ME OFF AT THE END OF THE ROAD NEAR BARNARD'S
house. She'll call her supervisor as soon as I'm gone to sign up for an extra shift,
something Kronos has already asked their security agents to do given the
current level of activity. She'll mention her location, which should make her the
obvious choice when the call comes in asking for someone to drive a spinner up
to the Central Office. Max also had me memorize an email address and
explained how to attach computer files to a message and send it out. I gave her
the password to the app that links to the surveillance camera. All the stuff in
between—moving around the Office and staying alive long enough to access
Dr. Ellery's computer—is up to me.

Barnard's house looks exactly like I remember it: the same quiet street
and neatly trimmed trees, and the same maroon front door that radiates anxiety
from the zapper tucked away behind it. The only difference is that this time,
darkness shrouds the front porch. In fact, the whole front of the house is dark;
only one upstairs window—a bedroom, as I know from my earlier break-in—is
lit up. I hesitate on the sidewalk at the base of the front steps. What if Barnard
isn't home? The twist of worry this thought brings fades almost immediately
when a shadow moves across the bedroom's opaque shade. The figure is too
slight to be Barnard's, and a fact I'd forgotten drops into my head. Shannon is
here.

My plan reshuffles. Shannon knows nothing about the capture of our
friends. She doesn't know that Molly and Emma are dead. Grief momentarily

takes my breath away, and I have to grasp the cold metal of Barnard's railing to ground myself back in this moment. Shannon loved those girls, and they loved her. She deserves to know what happened to them. She is also someone who knows too much, and even if she refuses to believe me, I have to warn her that she might not be safe anymore.

I let go of Barnard's railing and head around to the side of the house. Unlike the last time I was here, I don't bother with any precautions. I don't hide before stopping time. I don't waste my freezing strength picking the lock. Covering up my skills no longer seems relevant. I stop time in the middle of the sidewalk, jump the fence around Barnard's back yard, and smash his living room window with a rock.

The zapper oozes horror from the study at the back of the house. I can see Barnard at his desk through the open door, his broken arm resting in front of him, the fingers of the other hand hovering mid-type over his computer. The room glows in the tawny beams of his desk lamp. I turn the other way and walk up the stairs. The zapper's effect fades. I open the door to the guest bedroom and find Shannon bent over a suitcase, frozen in the act of tucking a pink cardigan next to the pretty sandals she wore on the TV show.

I sit on the bed beside her open bag and let time go.

"Hey, Shannon," I say. "Please don't scream."

Shannon springs backward. The sweater flops out of her hands, its carefully folded arms splaying out across the bed like a startled starfish.

"Sorry," I say. "I know it's rude to appear like this."

"Rude?" Shannon pats her chest. "It's things like this that make people hate spinners."

I don't remind her that hardly anyone knows spinners can do this.

"Sorry," I repeat. "I came because I have to tell you something."

"Where's KJ?" she asks, craning to look over my shoulder as if KJ might pop out of the closet.

"That's part of what I need to tell you," I say. "The wipers have KJ. He and Jack should be at the Central Office in"—I check the time on my phone—"thirty-seven minutes. Everyone else is on the way there, too, though they won't get there until later tonight."

Shannon stares at me.

"They're all going to the Central Office?" she asks. "The one in Tacoma?"

I nod. Shannon moves back to the bed and plucks up her crumpled sweater.

"Why aren't you with them?" she asks.

"KJ distracted one of the wipers so that I could escape."

Shannon folds the sweater into precise thirds, smoothing the soft cotton until it lies perfectly flat. The rest of the words I came here to say sit on my tongue, ugly painful facts that can never be taken back once I say them. Forcing my mouth to shape them feels cruel, as if saying the words out loud will make them real. Except they're already real, and nothing I say or don't say will change that.

"Emma and Molly are dead."

Shannon's head jerks up. There's a beat of silence so complete the world might have frozen, and then her lips press into a thin, angry line.

"Don't say things like that," she snaps. "They're not funny."

"I'm not trying to be funny."

Shannon hugs the carefully folded sweater against her stomach. "What happened?"

"The wipers killed them when they rounded up the others. It was an accident—they died when a door was blasted open—but the others will all be killed, too, once they reach the Office. I'm not sure you're safe anymore, either. The Center's bosses are killing every spinner who knows the truth about what we can do."

Shannon opens her mouth, and I hold up my hand. "I know. You don't believe me."

She closes her mouth. The two of us look at each other.

"Do you remember," I ask her, "the first night we spent as roommates? I was barely ten and scared to be in a Center for the first time. As soon as the lights went out, I pulled the covers over my head and cried. You hadn't been there more than a few months, and you were what, eleven? But you got out of your bed and came over and tried to give me a hug. I told you to leave me alone." I smile at her. "You didn't, though. You went back to your bed, and you sang to me—for hours, it felt like—a crazy made-up lullaby about penguins and kittens floating in a boat. The chorus was something like *rock, rock, rock you to sleep, the water is deep, don't make a peep.*"

The song never had much of a tune, and my singing skills don't add anything, but the words from long ago still fill the air with a painful sweetness. Shannon's lip trembles.

"You remember that?" she says.

I nod. "I'm sorry I dragged you away from the Center when you didn't want to leave. I'm sorry for all the times I was rude and even more for the times I yelled at you. I know I haven't been a very good friend. I'm prickly, and I get obsessed with things, even ones that don't matter. You're different. You've always known what's important. You know how to love people and how to take care of them. I don't need you to believe that the Center is a bad place, but please believe that everything I am doing now is because I love our friends and want to help them. I'm trying to be more like you."

"I don't know what I . . ." She bites her lip. "Look, I do believe that you mean well. The thing is. . ." The look she gives me is apologetic. "Everything you've said is a theory. You don't have actual proof. I've *been* to the Central Office. I've met the people there, and they didn't treat me like a lab rat or torture me. They cured me. Maybe Dr. Barnard has lied about some things, but I'm sure there are reasons, even if neither of us knows what they are. You can't be right that the Center is going to kill everyone. You just can't. It's too monstrous."

Her tone is pleading. I don't argue. Shannon smooths the sweater again.

207

"Why did you come here, anyway?" she asks. "To Dr. Barnard's, I mean."

"I want to go to the Central Office."

"You do?" The sweater tumbles from Shannon's arms again, flopping into another crumpled heap. "Why?"

"To find proof."

Shannon doesn't say anything.

I gesture to the half-packed suitcase. "Are you going back there?"

"Yes. In the morning." Shannon twists a strand of her hair around her finger. "Are the others really on their way there right now?"

I nod.

"Then I'll ask Dr. Barnard if he'll let me go with you tonight." She picks up the sweater, not bothering to fold it this time before tossing it into the suitcase. "They'll feel more comfortable if I'm there to greet them, and you'll see for yourself about the cure. Everyone in the Central Office is super nice."

We walk downstairs together. Zapper fear blossoms as we near the landing. It's less intense now that I'm not holding a freeze, but I can still sense the faint, persistent hum of dread emanating from Barnard's office. Shannon, oblivious, walks straight toward it. I grit my teeth and follow.

"Dr. Barnard?" Shannon says.

He looks up. When he sees me standing at Shannon's side, the slightly bemused expression on his face switches to alert in less time than it takes to blink.

"Alexandra?" Barnard leaps up from the desk, eyes darting to the small UFO-shaped zapper flashing on his desk.

"Hello, Dr. Barnard," I say. "I'd like to go to the Central Office."

"You *want* to go?" Barnard adjusts his glasses. He edges around the desk, peering past me toward his living room with suspicion. When he sees the glass all over the floor, he backs up a few steps.

"I'm sorry I broke your window," I say. "I wanted to talk to Shannon, and I wasn't sure you'd let me do that if I knocked on the door."

Barnard stares at me, clearly looking for the tricks in my words, but there are none, because everything I'm saying is true. It makes this encounter so much simpler than my previous talks with Barnard.

"Why do you want to go to the Office?" Barnard asks.

"You have KJ," I say. "I want to be with him."

"Ah."

He sounds both uncomfortable and reassured. Instead of scanning the room for an army of attacking spinners, he leans against his desk. His relief is short-lived.

"So it's true?" Shannon asks. "KJ is at the Central Office?"

Barnard's gaze flicks to her, then back to me. "He's on his way there, yes."

"Why didn't you tell me?" she asks.

The slightest hint of accusation tinges her voice. I turn to survey the glass on Barnard's floor so he doesn't see me smile.

"I just found out myself," Barnard says. "I was going to tell you in the morning, after he gets settled in. Remember, I warned you that sometimes the treatments don't go as smoothly as yours did."

My smile fades. Same old Barnard. I shouldn't have underestimated his ability to make up a backstory to provide cover when KJ inevitably fails to rally.

A faint frown creases Shannon's brow.

"What about the other kids from our Center?" she asks. "Alex told me they were on their way to Tacoma, too. She also said Molly and Emma were . . ." Shannon can't seem to manage the word *dead*, so she finishes with, ". . . that they're missing."

"Missing?" Barnard's voice is a perfect imitation of benign confusion, but I notice that instead of looking at her, he's focused on shuffling some papers on his desk. "Not that I'm aware of. I don't know where Alex would have heard such nonsense, but as I've already told you, the whole group was transferred out

209

to Dallas a week ago."

Shannon nods. She looks more confident than she did when we talked in the bedroom, presumably reassured by Barnard's soothing lies.

"Well, Alexandra," Barnard says in a falsely hearty voice, "I have to say your arrival is unexpected. Welcome, but unexpected. I'm sure the Office staff will be delighted to see you."

"And I'm delighted to be going. I hear such good things about the cure." I smile at him—a wide, tooth-baring grimace. Barnard's cheer quails beneath it. "Are we all driving together? It will be just like old times."

Barnard backs away a little farther, his good arm cradling the one encased in the sling.

"I'm afraid my traveling with you isn't going to be possible," he says, reaching for a cell phone lying on his desk. "Protocols."

Protocols. Right. After his last two failures to bring me in, I'm betting Kronos told him flat out he wasn't allowed to take me anywhere.

"Is it within protocols for Shannon to go with me?" I say. "She promised me she would."

Barnard hesitates, one finger hovering over the phone. I can read his thoughts as clearly as if he were speaking them out loud. On the one hand, having me arrive with Shannon is going to complicate their efforts to shunt me into a death chamber. On the other, having me show up peaceably will be a huge coup for him. If he refuses and this turns into a tussle, he'll have a hard time explaining his behavior to Shannon. Worse, if I make a fuss and run, Barnard will be forced to admit to Dr. Ellery that he lost the chance to capture me three times in a row.

He turns to his protégé.

"Do you really want to go now?" he asks her. "It's late. You can always meet Alexandra there in the morning."

"I'd like to go with Alex." The look Shannon gives me hovers somewhere between exasperation and pity. "I think she'll feel less scared about

210

the cure if I'm there. Let me just run up and finish packing."

She heads back upstairs. Barnard waits until she's out of earshot before asking, "What did you tell her when you two were alone?"

"What I've always told her: the truth. Don't worry, though, she still doesn't believe me. For whatever misguided reasons, she trusts you, and she's happy to be your ambassador."

Barnard gives a satisfied nod. He slips the zapper in his pocket, then crosses over to a cabinet, from which he removes a leash.

"You don't mind," he says, "if I put this on you while you're in transit?"

I hold out my arm and am proud to see it isn't shaking. "I expected nothing less from you."

The buzz from the zapper explodes in my head when he comes close. He picks up my arm, then turns it from side to side, studying the rope burns slashed across my flesh. I will myself not to flinch. When he places the leash around my wrist, its touch is both familiar and horrifying. I reach for time, brushing it through the zapper's impenetrable haze as I watch the leash snap shut.

Barnard returns to the cabinet and starts rummaging inside. I rub the metal band that's pressing against my raw skin. Max better get here soon to swap it for a fake one. Wearing this thing makes my brain fuzzy.

Barnard turns around. In one hand, he holds a vial of pale liquid.

"What's that for?" I ask.

"It's Aclisote."

He moves toward me. I back away.

"I know what it is," I say. "I'm asking why I need it. I'm leashed. What's the point of suppressing my skills?"

"Have you forgotten the last time I put you in a car?" Barnard holds up his broken arm. "I haven't. This will make sure you don't try anything like that again."

The Aclisote sloshes in the vial as Barnard holds it out to me. I force

211

my brain to think through the leash's mind-numbing buzz.

"This is different," I say. "Last time I didn't want to go. This time I'm volunteering."

"So you say." Barnard waves the vial in front of my face. "If you are truly cooperating, then you won't mind drinking this. You're giving up your skills, so what does it matter if you can't use them before you get cured?"

The vial is so close to my face that I can smell its cloying chemical scent. Any argument I make will only add to his suspicion, and the more he doubts me, the more he'll warn the Office staff to watch me extra closely.

I take the vial from him and hold it up to the light. It's just viscous enough to look cloudy.

"How much are you giving me?"

"Ten cc's," he says.

My stomach flips. That's almost double the dose I was taking at the Center and ten times the nominal amount Lisa prescribed. I bring the vial to my lips. Is just this one dose enough to suppress my skills? It's probably not enough to make me ill. He wouldn't dare make me sick in front of Shannon. I channel a blank Max expression and toss the Aclisote into my mouth.

Barnard watches my throat until he sees me swallow, then takes the empty vial from me and sets it on the edge of his desk before picking up his phone again. I touch my lips and spit half the drug down my sleeve. Moisture soaks the inside of my arm, but the sickly-sweet taste of Aclisote still coats my tongue. I can feel the rest of the liquid sliding down my throat like thick slime, working its way deeper into my body. The sensation feels a lot like dread.

"Dr. Ellery," Barnard gloats into the phone, "I have Alexandra Manning."

The combined interference from the zapper and the leash makes my head throb, but if I get too far away from Barnard, I won't hear what he's saying. I hover in the corner of his office, pretending to be interested in a collection of awards lined up on a shelf. A particularly large silver one reads FOR SCIENTIFIC

212

ACHIEVEMENT.

"Yes. She turned herself in to get the cure. Uh huh. I'd like to arrange transport tonight. No, with Shannon. Shannon insisted."

A smaller award, this one gold, says FOR SERVICES RENDERED. There's a symbol above the words that looks like a scythe. Next to it is a framed photo of a group of people that includes Dr. Ellery. I pick it up. Would it ruin my charade of cooperation if I "accidentally" smashed it?

"I don't see why it matters, won't any agent do?" A sharp edge tinges Barnard's voice. I put the photo down.

"Well, that's going to be a problem," he says.

I cast a surreptitious glance at the time. It's been twelve minutes since Max dropped me off. Hasn't she called in her location? What if she did, and they've already assigned her somewhere else?

"No, she *can't* stay until tomorrow," Barnard says into the phone. "I have nowhere secure to put her. Yeah, I'll hold."

The buzzing in my head ratchets up to a roar. Stay here? Overnight? The imaginary box where I banished my emotions strains at its bonds. I'm hyperaware of minutes ticking by, all of them completely out of my control. The box starts cracking, leaking images that sneak through the fissure.

I'm in the refuge's basement. Yolly has her arms wrapped around cowering children. Yuki and Aidan are creeping through the darkness, searching for something heavy to block the entrance. I can hear the wipers pounding on the door, feel the blast of an explosion, sense a thousand sharp edges flying through thick still air, see Molly falling . . .

I slam my mind closed again. My mouth tastes like blood and dust. I grip the edge of the shelf in front of me, willing the images to stop.

Barnard stands behind his desk, phone clamped against his ear.

"That's excellent." He sounds relieved. "Thank you."

My fingers feel melded to the edge of the shelf. I hold very still, barely breathing while I wait to hear my fate. Barnard hangs up the phone.

213

"Someone will be here to pick you up in five minutes."

Relief washes through me. I pry my fingers away from the shelf and move into the darkened living room, away from the zapper's horror vibes. Max must have called in after all. I move over to stand in front of the smashed rear window, letting a cool breeze dry the panic-induced sweat from my cheeks. Maybe there is some antidote to Aclisote Max knows about, something that will reduce the drug's impact.

Footsteps rattle behind me, and I turn to watch Shannon trot down the stairs. Her face is flushed, and she's carrying her bag in one hand.

"Thank you for letting me stay in your home, Dr. Barnard," she says.

"Happy to have you," he answers. "We all appreciate the fine work you're doing as ambassador."

Shannon blushes even pinker under the praise.

I face the window again and take a deep, calming breath to ease my nervous energy. The elements of my plan line up in my head, marching forward with the single-minded purpose of a trail of ants. The new leash, the drive, my arrival at the Office.

Barnard's doorbell chimes, and I hear his footsteps as he hurries over to answer it.

The hard part is going to start once I'm inside. Shannon said they administered her treatment in a private room, so I assume they'll do the same for me, at least while she's watching. Once they put me there, I'll stop time and find Ellery's office. Nothing electrical works when the world is frozen, so the rest has to happen in real time, but I won't need very much of it. An hour should be more than enough.

Voices drift toward me from the door. I hear Barnard saying the words *subdued* and *cooperative*. Shannon reaffirms her willingness to go with me. I move away from the window, taking time to mask any expression so no one suspects I know Max. I turn around, and my heart stops.

There are three people standing in the doorway. Barnard is looking at me with impatience; Shannon is wearing a happy smile. The third person's gaze is hungry. My heart starts beating again, each pulse a throb of pain. It's not Max. It's Carson Ross.

"Hello, Alex," he says. "I hear you need a ride."

The plan in my head splinters. The shards rain down, sharp and deadly as shrapnel. Max's leash—everything hinges on that broken leash. It takes all I have not to let my panic show on my face. Ross is watching me with narrowed eyes. I know this expression. When I used to work with him, he looked like this when he talked about Sikes. He said *justice* when what he really meant was *vengeance*. I believed in him then. I thought his intentions were good. Now I understand what really drives him. It's greed.

"What are you doing here?" I ask.

Ross's smile is as cold as an arctic night.

"It seems all the regular security agents are busy with more important assignments tonight," Ross says. "But as it turns out, I'm attending a conference in Seattle in the morning, so I was already planning to drive north tonight. Dr. Ellery called to ask if I would drop you off in Tacoma on my way."

I cringe. Shannon stands beside him, swinging her suitcase, seemingly delighted to be getting a ride from someone she knows, but the chill of Ross's smile fills my veins with ice. How can Shannon not recognize Ross's deadliness?

"I appreciate you going out of your way," Barnard says.

"It's no bother," Ross says. "Alex and I have always shared a special relationship."

I clutch at the leash binding my wrist, the one I set my arm inside so willingly. Calm—I must stay calm. I bow my head to show my meek submission while really hiding the thoughts racing through my brain. My plan is still possible. I'll just have to modify it.

Really? whispers a voice in my head. *Without access to time, you'll be as helpless as a Norm. How will you get to Ellery's office? How will you rewind to find out her password?*

215

The buzz from the leash, the fright from the zapper, the scattered fragments of my strategy—all of them combine to send my thoughts skittering in a million directions.

Barnard opens his front door, and everyone steps out onto the porch. Clouds block the stars, turning the night sky into a ceiling of black and filling the air with the electric scent of coming rain. Ross heads down the stairs toward his car. Shannon picks up her suitcase and starts thanking Barnard again for his hospitality. My toes tingle. I'm leashed, but I'm not restrained. I could take off, find a bolt cutter, remove the leash, and run far, far away. The tingling in my toes makes it hard to hold still. I peer into the dark, judging the distance between the police cruiser parked at the curb and the open sidewalk beyond it.

Ross reaches the street and turns to look back at me. Maybe he senses my doubts, or maybe he just wants to gloat as I walk into my doom. I put one hand on the railing. Get in the car, or take off and save myself?

Something moves in the shadows at the bottom of the stairs. A feral cat, or maybe a raccoon. Either way, it's wild and unwanted. I grip the metal railing. If I run now, I will be like that creature: a lost, lonely thing creeping stealthily through the shadows. Chased away. Despised. I don't want that. It's not what I—or any of us—deserves.

I start down the stairs. Ross's face comes closer, his eyes shining with triumph. I keep moving. I don't know where Max is, and I don't know how I'm going to carry out my plan with this leash clamped to my wrist, but the only chance I have to change anything lies in the Central Office's mysterious halls.

I take the final step. The sidewalk feels firm beneath my feet. My fate is as blank as the night sky, and I walk into it with my eyes wide open.

16 ◀◀

ROSS PUTS ME IN THE BACK OF HIS CRUISER AND HANDCUFFS MY unleashed wrist to a metal bar. We both know this is unnecessary. Ross isn't carrying a zapper tonight, but the leash still blocks me from accessing time. The additional restraint is just an added insult to underline my captivity.

Shannon rides in front. Ross told her my imprisonment is standard practice for rogue spinners, making this statement with a helpless shrug that implies he'd do otherwise if he had a choice. Liar. Even if those are the rules, Ross wouldn't follow them if he didn't want to. Shannon looks uncomfortable with my confinement but doesn't speak up, a disheartening confirmation of her confidence in the Center.

We drive. The freeway provides a monotonous line of cars streaming by on endless concrete. Within fifteen minutes, we've crossed the Columbia River into Washington State. Green highway signs flit past: HAZEL DELL, LONGVIEW, CHEHALIS. I've barely spent any time outside of Portland, so the names mean nothing to me. Five minutes later, it starts to rain, the heavy drops filling the car with a low-level drumming that drowns out the possibility of talking, not that any of us are so inclined. Shannon stares out the window, seemingly mesmerized by the water-smeared lights of the passing cars. Ross drives with one hand while simultaneously answering messages on his phone. The car lurches as he passes a truck with an aggressive swerve.

I pull up the fragments of my plan, trying to adjust the pieces to fit my new reality. The core of my strategy—downloading the files—remains intact,

217

but moving around inside the Central Office will be much harder if I can't do it in frozen time. I visualize the room Shannon described in her TV interview, the private suite with a view of the forest. Her agreement to escort me suddenly takes on greater importance. Surely, with Shannon as my shield, combined with my professed cooperation, they won't kill me as soon as I get there. Which means I'll have time, and as long as I have that, there's still hope. Somewhere in the Office, there has to be a key to unlock the leash or a tool to break it. Right?

Ross cuts off another driver, who responds with a series of honks. The loud blasts echo the panic rising in my chest. My plan is flimsy, impossible. The double bracelets of handcuff and leash feel like nooses growing ever tighter around my wrists. I take in steady lungfuls of air to stop myself from screaming. KJ trusts me. He believes in me. I can do this. *I have to do this.* I repeat the words in my head over and over, desperate to block my doubts. The car races northward. *I have to do this.*

It's late when we pull off the highway. It feels like it should be midnight, but the clock on the dashboard tells me it's only nine. I calculate in my head. KJ and Jack have been at the Office for approximately two hours. The kids from the refuge are still an hour away. I shake myself out of my stupor and refocus on the scenery flashing past. I know Tacoma is a city not far from Seattle, but when people say the Central Office is "in" Tacoma, they must mean it's nearby, because the exit we take is hardly urban. Within a minute of leaving the highway, there are no buildings in sight, and five minutes after that, we're winding our way up an isolated two-lane road bordered on one side by thick pine forest and the other by a cliff.

Ross makes another stomach-churning turn that hugs the drop-off much too closely. I grab the metal bar my cuff is locked to. I'm just starting to consider how ironic it would be if I died in a crash before we even arrived when the car turns deeper into the woods and lights appear along the side of the road. I blink into the sudden brightness. A tall concrete wall runs along the right side of the car, its top edge snarled with curling strands of barbed wire. We reach a

218

gate, and the car slows.

Artificial zapper fear shimmers the air in front of us. They must be using some super version, because the discomfort feels as strong as it does when I'm controlling time. Ross pulls up to a security booth at the entrance and rolls down his window. The rain has stopped, and the air outside carries the gritty scent of wet asphalt.

"Good evening," Ross says.

A clean-cut man in a tan uniform leans out of the booth to survey us.

"Name and reason for visit?" he asks.

"Portland Police Chief Carson Ross," Ross says. "I'm delivering Special Ambassador Shannon Callahan and a rogue spinner, Alexandra Manning. Dr. Ellery is expecting us."

The guard picks up a tablet and scrolls through it, presumably checking the accuracy of Ross's statement. I grit my teeth and try not to itemize all the ways the zapper-infested entrance reminds me of every picture I've seen of the gates of hell.

"IDs?" the guard asks.

Ross digs his wallet out and hands over his badge and driver's license. Shannon also provides ID. Hers hangs from a lanyard and has her picture stamped on the front and an electronic strip along the back. I wish they'd move faster. The gate is starting to transform in front of my eyes, its metal bars morphing into a host of jeering faces, hairy ones with long ugly snouts. The guard scans both ID cards with a handheld device before returning them. When he peers into the back of the car, his eyes burn like bubbling lava on the verge of erupting. I whimper.

"Would you like the chromoelectronegator's emissions reduced while you drive through?" he asks Ross.

"No need."

The guard shrugs. "Drive on in."

The gate in front of us clicks before swinging open on silent hinges.

Ross accelerates through it, and terror engulfs me. Jackals lunge at the car, teeth bared, sharp and gleaming. I scream. The sound ricochets around the car. Then the jackals are in the car with me, jaws open. They're going to sink their teeth into my flesh and eat my beating heart. I scream again, writhing, desperate to escape the horror. Something clanks. Pain lances my wrist.

And then it's over. I slump back in the seat, shaking and damp with sweat. My arm hangs from the handcuff Ross attached to me, my wrist bright with blood from trying to wrench myself free. From far away, I hear Shannon's voice asking if I'm all right.

With a huge effort, I straighten my shaking limbs. Ross watches me in the rearview mirror, a sadistic smile twitching his lips.

"I see why nobody ever gets out of here," I mutter. Ross grins.

Shannon turns around in her seat so she can see me. Her eyes are round.

"What happened?" she asks.

"It's the zapper," I say. She looks blank. "Didn't that happen to you when you arrived here the first time?"

"No," she says.

I brush my sweat-soaked bangs off my forehead.

"Alex has been off Aclisote for a very long time," Ross tells Shannon in a voice nowhere near low enough for me to miss the words. "You know how unstable spinners get."

Shannon studies me. Bites her lip. Looks away.

I use my skirt to wipe away the blood dripping down my forearm.

The car crosses a well-lit parking lot and pulls into a space marked VISITOR. I crane my neck to see out the window. The Central Office looms over us, a fortress of glass and steel promising I will never escape. Rain-wet windows glitter like unblinking eyes. The parking lot is a concrete moat, and the tall evergreens are sentinels guarding the perimeter.

Mad drumming starts up in my chest again, and it takes all my effort to keep from screaming.

Shannon stretches as she gets out of the car. Ross joins her, taking time to chat with her as he retrieves her luggage before finally returning to release me from my back seat prison. When he unlocks the handcuff, I step from the car without looking at him. The outside air is cold. A breeze rustles the tree branches, making them whisper as if they are sharing secrets.

Ross makes an impatient gesture.

"Go on," he says to me.

The Central Office's entrance gleams with light. Shannon picks up her bag and practically skips toward it. She seems energized by being here, as if the presence of this slick facility reaffirms her faith in Kronos's good intentions. I touch the fresh bruises blossoming around my wrist and trail behind her

The front door opens into a vestibule. A set of chairs with ice-blue upholstery are clustered on one side, surrounding a low sharp-edged table that offers neither magazines nor any other type of entertainment. Built into one wall is a gas fireplace with flames rising from an artistic pile of white glass beads; the fire offers no warmth, since it's trapped behind glass. It's hard to imagine anyone ever sitting here. Despite the furniture, it's not really a reception area; it's just a decorative security measure.

We move toward a wall of floor-to-ceiling glass—thick and presumably bulletproof—that blocks access to the building's interior. The sole entrance is a swinging glass door with another uniformed guard standing in front of it. Everyone goes through the same process as we did at the outdoor security booth—Ross states his name and purpose, and he and Shannon hand over their IDs. The guard studies each ID with care, and then she, too, scans them with a machine. Over her head, the steady eye of a security camera glares down at us. Finally, the glass door swings open, and we file through it. There's a zapper posted over this entrance, too, but it's not as strong as the one outside. I hold my breath and force myself to walk past it. It feels like stepping through a shower of acid. Heat flashes over my skin as I cross the threshold, but the discomfort eases once I walk away. I exhale with a shudder. Fingers crossed there aren't any more of these horrible things set up inside.

Dr. Margaret Ellery is waiting for us in the atrium on the other side of the barrier. She's wearing a tight smile and a navy suit. Even though it's way past normal work hours, her makeup is flawless and her clothes appear freshly pressed. When she sees me, her eyes gleam. Fear dries all the spit from my mouth. I'd never heard of this woman until a couple of days ago, and I've only seen her twice, but the sight of her makes me feel like the walls are closing in around me. Margaret Ellery is the Central Office personified, distant and clinical and ruthless. She holds the fate of all of us in her carefully manicured hands. In her presence, even Ross fades. He may be my personal nemesis, but he is only a pale moon of evil in the face of this burning sun.

"Chief Ross." Dr. Ellery steps forward to shake his hand. "I appreciate you going out of your way to escort our charge here." She gestures in my direction without turning her head, as if I'm no more than an errant package.

"My pleasure," Ross says.

I shuffle my feet on the polished concrete floor and check out my surroundings. The atrium rises the full height of the three-story building. The ceiling is glass crosshatched with metal beams. The sky arches beyond it, its darkness impenetrable thanks to the blazing light emanating from a trio of chandeliers that jab downward like so many shining spears. I hunch my shoulders. The space seems designed to make visitors feel both small and vulnerable.

"Since I'm here," Ross says to Dr. Ellery, "perhaps you'd be willing to give me a tour? I'd love to see all the good work you're doing firsthand."

It's possible she hesitates, but politeness covers any resistance.

"Of course." Dr. Ellery turns to Shannon. "I'm sure you're tired after your trip. The cafeteria is still open if you want a snack before you head upstairs to settle in."

"Thanks." Shannon glances in my direction. "What about Alex? Can she come, too?"

Dr. Ellery offers her the bland smile of a professional host. "We'll send a tray up to the medical wing for your friend," she says. "We need to get her checked in."

The leash shackling my arm drags like a ten-ton weight. Everything is suddenly moving too fast. I grasp for the steps of my plan, but it's like trying to pick up grains of rice that have scattered across the floor.

Dr. Ellery beckons, and a woman I hadn't noticed glides over from where she's been standing off to one side. She wears green scrubs and a lanyard like Shannon's around her neck.

"Alexandra?" she says to me, checking the name on the clipboard she's carrying. "I'm Jean. I'll be your technician. Won't you come with me?"

My feet are rooted to the floor. This is the point at which my vague plans are supposed to solidify into action, but my mind is as blank as the atrium walls. The spear-like chandeliers stab down at me from the ceiling. I'm not even in their lab yet, and already I feel like a specimen pinned under a microscope.

Ross watches me with that triumphant gleam back on his face. I'm pretty sure mine has turned pale. I touch my wrist, tracing the fresh scratches from my attempt to rip myself out of the handcuff. The only shred of a chance I have of pulling off any kind of coup lies in making sure Dr. Ellery and her allies think I'm going to cooperate, so I gather every bit of self-control I can muster and face the technician.

"OK," I tell her, then turn to Shannon. "You'll come and visit me later, won't you? Before you go to bed?"

"Sure," Shannon says.

"It would be better to wait until morning," Dr. Ellery says. "Jean will be checking Alexandra's chronotin levels and going through the other preliminaries. It might take some time. You remember the process, don't you, Shannon?"

Shannon nods obediently, and my hope shrivels. Her watchful eyes are my only protection here. If they aren't going to let her see me tonight, what

223

guarantee do I have that I'll live until morning?

The tech takes my arm. It's a struggle not to yank myself free.

"If you see KJ," I call to Shannon in a final desperate effort to shake her out of her complacency, "tell him I said hi, OK?"

Dr. Ellery frowns. The serenity on Shannon's face flickers. She turns to the doctor, but I can't hear what she says because Jean is already leading me away. Her grip on my arm grows firmer as she propels me into a long tiled hall.

After the openness of the atrium, stepping into the hallway feels like walking into a tunnel. The walls are stark white, and the doors we pass are all closed. Framed pictures of artfully composed nature scenes hang at regular intervals: streaks of sunlight streaming through a verdant forest; a close-up of a small three-leaved flower; a mist of spray rising from a tumbling waterfall. They are photographs printed on metal, the images too clear and the colors overbright. Here, even nature is unnatural.

We pass by more doors, differentiated only by discrete room numbers. What's behind them? Sleeping quarters? Offices? Labs? I picture spinners wilting in hospital beds and metal slabs holding partially dissected cadavers. We turn down a second hallway, then a third. Fluorescent bulbs hum softly over our heads. I try to memorize the room numbers as we pass them, but the jumbled thoughts clogging my head make it impossible to retain anything. I should run. Cooperate. Scream. Wait.

Jean stops in front of a room marked as 37A, which looks exactly like every other door we've passed. She swipes her ID through the card reader, and I hear an answering click.

"Here we are," she says as she pushes the door open.

Horror makes me stumble as I cross the threshold. The space we're standing in is not the cheerful private room Shannon described when she talked about her cure. This is a windowless barracks that mirrors every nightmare I've ever had about the Central Office. Jean maneuvers me inside, letting the door close behind us with a heavy clunk. Inside, another tech is waiting. He's a man, a muscly one, with a wide nose and cold eyes. A scythe, twin of the one I saw on Dr. Barnard's award, is tattooed on the side of his neck. Heat and cold flash simultaneously across my skin, and for a moment I think I might pass out. A half dozen twin beds line each side of the room—basic metal frames and thin mattresses wrapped in taut white sheets. Every bed is crisscrossed with a set of thick canvas straps. Stuck on the wall over each one is a card printed with a familiar name: Yuki, Angel, Lisa, Rose. Alexandra.

My dream of resistance drifts away from me like rising fog. I was a fool to come here. Jamal, Miguel—everyone—was right that this place is impenetrable. How did I ever think that I, a lone girl, had any chance against a massive institution like Kronos? Imagining I would find some crack that would allow me to slide through their lair undetected was ludicrous. They have always been ahead of me—not by steps, but by miles.

"What is this place?" I ask, although it's hard to speak with a tongue that feels glued to the roof of my mouth.

"We're expecting quite a few spinners to arrive this evening," Jean says. Her grip on my arm has turned steely. "We thought we'd treat you all at the same time. This room is for the females."

There's an IV stand next to every bed. Bags of liquid hang at the ready, needle-tipped rubber tubes dangling from them like the lanky arms of murderous jellyfish. I try to swallow, but my mouth is too dry.

"You said you were just checking my chronotin levels tonight." It's a stupid protest. I knew when she said it that she was lying.

"There's no point in putting off the procedure," Jean says. "Aren't you eager to be cured?"

We're standing just inside the door. I reach behind me and try the handle. It's locked. The muscle-bound man shifts his stance, a small movement that still implies threat.

"Shouldn't we wait?" I ask. The beds in this room look like so many graves waiting to be filled. "I'm tired. Yolly always told us you should be in tip-

225

top condition before trying any new treatment."

"You're going to be fine," Jean lies without even a hint of hesitation. "You'll see."

We move across the room. I feel as if I'm in a dream, watching myself from outside my body. What's the point in fighting? I walked in here willingly. There are two of them, the door is locked, and there are no windows. I lie down on the taut sheets when they tell me to. Straps wrap my chest, squashing my vest's puffy down into distorted lumps. Other straps bind my hands and feet to the bed's metal frame. Hands remove my shoes, take the phone from my pocket. I look up at Jean's calm face.

"Do you think it's right to kill us off?"

"No one is killing anyone." She says the words like they're memorized. I shake my head, the only part of my body I can still move.

"Do you believe what you're saying? Do you even know what you're doing?"

There's a sharp prick as a needle slides into the back of my hand. Poison drips into my veins, keeping pace with the tears sliding down my cheeks.

"Why?" I ask.

Jean leans over me and I see the glint of fanaticism behind her eyes.

"Because you are dangerous." Her breath carries the fetid smell of something that's been locked away for a long time. "You are a threat to society, and you need to be contained."

"We're people," I say.

"No, you're not." She straightens. "You're spinners."

They turn the lights out when they leave, blanketing the room in darkness. The only illumination comes from a thin line leaking under door, and that faint glow only throws the rest of the room into deeper pitch.

I stare up into the black. It's over. I am completely alone, and the only people who know where they've put me are my enemies. Tears drip down the sides of my face and slide into my hair. Somewhere in this cursed building, KJ is also lying in the dark. Couldn't they have shown a fragment of mercy and put us together? His face swims above me, a mirage etched over a nightmare. I taste the memory of his lips. A sob wracks my body. Maybe this is the better ending. KJ gave himself up so that I would have a chance. To know that I wasted what he lost his life for might be more than he could bear. At least in his thoughts, for as long as they last, I will still be out there fighting, alive and free.

17 ◀◀

TIME MUST BE PASSING, BUT BLANKETED IN THE LEASH AND THE Aclisote, I can't feel it. Here, there is only despair. The early signs of fever lick my body with alternating heat and chills. The straps chafe through the layers of sheets and clothing. The IV bag hanging over my head feels like it's pulling on my arm. How fast is the drip? How long will it take? Will I still be conscious when the others arrive from the refuge? I sink my awareness inside my body and search for signs of sickness. Is my face flushed from crying or fever? Is the twist in my stomach from hunger, nausea, or fear?

A beam of light streaks across the ceiling. I twist my head and see a figure silhouetted in the doorway. A technician, presumably, coming to check my decline. The door shuts, and darkness closes in again.

"Alex?"

The voice is a whisper, far too anxious to come from Jean.

"Shannon?" I try to sit up and am rewarded with an immediate reminder of the canvas straps.

The overhead lights flicker on. I squint. Shannon runs toward me and throws herself to her knees at the side of my bed. She looks like she's been crumpled. Her blouse is crossed with wrinkles, and stray strands of hair frizz around her forehead.

"Alex!" she chokes out. Anything else she meant to say gets lost in a storm of sobs. I struggle again in a fruitless effort to sit. Shannon's face is mottled red and white—red from crying, white from the shocked pallor underneath.

"What happened?" I ask.

"It's KJ. He's sick, as bad as he was at the squat. And Jack . . ." She hiccups, trying to subdue the sobs shaking her body. "I think he's dead."

A thousand tiny swords prickle my skin as the blood drains from my face.

"You saw them?" I ask her. "What did you do?"

"Do?" She looks confused. "I tried to wake them. I shook KJ's shoulder, and he made this sort of moaning sound but didn't open his eyes. When I tried Jack, he just . . ." She shudders. "He just flopped."

The lights over my head are blazing, but the room feels as if it's growing dark. There are shadows everywhere: in the corners, under the beds.

"That's not the worst part." Shannon starts crying again. "It's the room they're in. There are beds for everyone, all the boys from our Center." Her voice rises. "Dr. Barnard said they were in Dallas."

"He lied."

Shannon clutches my shoulder. Her eyes are glazed, and I'm not sure she's heard me.

"I asked Dr. Ellery if I could see KJ. She said it wasn't a good time, that KJ's treatment wasn't going that well and he needed to rest. It doesn't make sense—I mean, KJ hasn't been here for more than a couple hours. Why have they even started treatment?" Her grip on my shoulder tightens. "I didn't know what to think, so I went to the cafeteria. The only people there were a couple of technicians. I didn't want to talk to anyone, so I kind of hid in a corner, and I heard them talking . . . and they said . . ."

Shannon starts crying again. The shadows in the room inch closer.

"They said what?" I prompt her.

"One of them was complaining about having to work extra shifts because of the bus that's coming with all the new spinners, and the other one said at least they weren't in the morning crew, because then they'd be expected to deal with all . . ." Shannon gulps. "All the ca-ca-cadavers."

229

The word seems to release something in Shannon. Her body goes slack, the hand gripping my shoulder loosens, and she wilts toward the floor.

"What's happening?" Shannon moans. "The staff didn't do this to me. I was in a really nice room. There were flowers. And they cured me. They *did*."

"I know they did," I say, trying very hard to be patient as she works through her shock. "And they will cure others, but they're not going to cure us. They can't afford to. We know what spinners can do. We know that they have murdered us for years, and they know we won't keep quiet."

"I didn't believe you," Shannon sobs. "I *wanted* you all to come here."

Shannon's cries turn into wails, and my patience thins to nonexistence. I thrash the few millimeters my restraints allow.

"Shannon, if you want to help them, you have to stop crying and untie me."

She sniffs, blinking at me as if she has just noticed I'm not lying here by choice.

"What are you going to do?" she asks, fumbling with the restraints holding down my arms. Her hands are clumsy, and I can barely keep from yelling at her to hurry up.

"Stop the poison." One of my arms bursts free of the straps. I reach over and rip the IV from my hand. "At least it will buy us a little time."

I don't add that it will probably be *very* little time. A tech could come in and reattach KJ's IV minutes after I take it out. And mine. Blood seeps up from where I yanked out my IV, the drop a rich dark red. When I dab it with the sheet, another bead rises in its place.

Shannon removes the straps across my chest. I sit up, leaning over to free my feet.

"Come on," I say, swinging my legs over the side of the bed. "Show me where they are."

I stand up, and the whole room spins. I stumble, reaching back to lean on the mattress to steady myself. I'm sick. I know I'm sick. The only question is

230

how sick. Bile rises up to bite the back of my throat. I swallow.

"Are you OK?" Shannon asks.

"No." I push back to standing. "But I'll make it."

I take a step forward. It's wobbly, but I neither vomit nor faint, which feels like an accomplishment. The tiles under my bare feet are cold. I focus on the chill instead of the heaving in my belly.

Shannon leads the way across the room and swipes a card over an electronic reader to unlock the door. I turn off the lights before she cracks it open, and we both peer up and down the hallway.

"How far away are the boys?" I whisper.

"They're right next door," she whispers back, pulling the door wide enough to slip out. I slide through behind her. The glare of the fluorescents feels uncomfortably bright.

"How did you find them?" I ask as we tiptoe down the hall. "And how did you get in?"

"I took this from the cleaning crew." Shannon holds up the card she just used to unlock the door. The top is stamped with the word JANITORIAL, and a dark-haired woman smiles up from the picture on the front. "There was a map on the cart showing all the rooms, and these two were the only ones on the lab floor marked 'Do Not Clean.'"

Shannon swipes the card through the reader to open the boys' door. I gape at her like she's just turned into a frog. *This* is the girl who once chastised me for shoplifting food so we could eat?

"You *stole* someone's key card?" I ask.

"I couldn't think what else to do." Shannon's lip trembles. "I hope she doesn't get in trouble."

The door swings open, and my shock at Shannon's dip into lawlessness vanishes as quickly as it flared. The room looks exactly like the one we just left, except the names tacked up over the beds are all boys'. Aidan. Raul. Simon. Miguel. Jeremy. I scan the tightly made-up beds until I find the ones I'm dreading, the two at the end of the room that aren't empty.

I'm at KJ's side before I've even consciously decided to move. His skin is ashy. Sweat dots his brow in irregular splotches. I touch my hand to his cheek and feel its heat.

"KJ?"

No response, only labored breaths leaving his lips in short gasps. My heart craters. The sound is agonizingly familiar. How many hours did I spend in the squat, listening to him struggle like this?

Shannon kneels beside me and takes his hand. She's sobbing again, her tears now underscored by a soft keening noise. The sound echoes in my ears, a siren's call luring me to join her. The fever creeping through my body weakens my resolve. I want to sink into the floor and lose myself in grief, too. I want to curl up on KJ's bed so that neither of us dies alone.

I squeeze my wrist, digging my fingers into the bruises and steadying myself against the pain. I can't give up. To give up is a betrayal of everything I believe in. Everything I—and countless other spinners—have fought for. Died for. KJ traded his freedom and most likely his life so that I can stand here, unbound and able to fight. I gather the slivers of the plan I built with Max. The outline is pale as a shroud, but the shape contains the scaffolding of hope.

I lean down and rest my fever-warmed cheek against KJ's burning one.

"I love you," I whisper into his ear. He doesn't move.

"I don't know if I can save you," I tell him, "but I promise I will do everything I can to stop Kronos."

A tremor passes through KJ's body. Maybe it's only the fever, but I feel the trail of it flash between us, and I accept it as his blessing.

I straighten up and focus on the tasks before me. Key, passwords, camera, files. Minutes drift around me, unseen and unknown but counting down nonetheless. I look at the leash lashed to my wrist. Any minute now, a technician could come bursting into the room. I need to move. But first . . .

KJ's arm flops like overcooked pasta when I free it from the straps. His

232

hand is wet. I touch the spot and bring my finger to my nose: Aclisote. KJ's hand, the sheet beneath it, and the plastic tube leading to the IV bag are all wet with Aclisote. I trace a line of liquid up the outside of the tube. Partway up, my fingers find a bump in the line. I peer closer. There's a hole, tiny and rough at the edges, the kind of hole a mouse might make if it tried to chew through the hard rubber. A mouse or a very weak boy.

"That's my guy," I whisper as I pull at the tape holding the IV in place. The needle slides smoothly from his vein, but a bead of blood still rises from the spot. He doesn't flinch. The tiny hole hasn't diverted enough Aclisote to stop him from getting sick, just enough to keep him alive. Very carefully, I rest the needle against the back of his hand, then reapply the tape to hold it down. Anyone who looks closely will see that the IV isn't attached, but a casual glance might keep him temporarily safe.

I tuck KJ's arm back under his restraints and cross the room to Jack. It's quiet over here. No labored breaths strain his chest; no fevered thrashing disturbs his stillness. I place one hand on his forehead. The skin under my palm is cold. Shannon was right. Jack is dead.

Something huge and ugly lurches in my chest. How much Aclisote did they give him? It was only a few hours ago that I talked to him. I stroke his head. The hair, white-blond where it should be dark, feels too soft for a boy who always tried to be so tough.

"Goodbye, Jack," I tell him. "I'm sorry."

It doesn't feel like enough. I shut my eyes and let my mind fill with memories. Not the recent ones when Jack was angry and scared, but earlier ones, when he was a restless kid, eager to grab the short life he'd been offered. I picture him wrestling with Aidan in the common room, flicking peas across the cafeteria at Raul, bragging about the wild adventures he had when he scored a day pass and spent an afternoon outside. I remember his concern the day I got beaten up by Sikes's men, the joy he took from playing with time, and the way his face lit up when he talked about music. The memories flash through my head, a frail

233

echo of the boy who created them. They're not enough, either—not enough as a memorial or as a life—but neither mourning nor bitterness is a luxury I can indulge in right now.

I let the images fade and lift my hand from Jack's cold brow.

"Come on," I tell Shannon. "We have work to do."

The keening falters. Shannon looks up.

"What do you mean?"

"Will that key card open the doors in the administrative wing?" I ask her.

She wipes her nose with the back of her hand. "I think so. Why do you want to go there?"

Instead of explaining, I hold up my wrist. "First, I need you to get me a key for this leash."

Shannon adjusts the sheet over KJ. There's a splotch of Aclisote dribbled on the white fabric, and she rubs at it as if she can somehow erase the spot. A quiver of impatience rattles my body. Doesn't she realize how little time we have left?

"I don't know if I can do that," she says. "I'm not brave like you."

"You *are* brave." I force myself to keep my voice level as I cross the room again and kneel at her side. "You stole the key card, didn't you? And when we were at the squat, you snuck Aclisote to KJ."

Her eyes fill again. "That wasn't helping, that was hurting him."

"Yes." I jam my hands between my knees to control my impatience. "But you didn't think so. You fought for what you thought was right, even though it meant hiding what you were doing from Jack and me. That's brave."

Shannon doesn't say anything, but I can tell she's listening, because her whole body is tense with attention. I press my knees together so tightly my fingers sting.

"They're all on their way here, Shannon," I tell her. "Yuki and Angel. Aidan and Raul. Plus hundreds of others we've never met." I wave a hand, gesturing at KJ's tormented body and Jack's still one. "You don't want them all to end up like this, do you?"

"No," she says, so softly I barely hear her.

I hold my breath, waiting. Shannon takes the key card from her pocket and turns it in her hand. When she speaks again, her voice is small but steady.

"Where would I find a leash key?"

Shannon is gone for what feels like hours. I wait on the bed in the room where they bound me, unwilling to raise anyone's suspicions more than necessary by staying with KJ. While I'm waiting, I use the needle hanging from the IV to pick the hem of my vest. The bulky fabric sticks to the needle, which drips liquid still trapped in the tube all over my hands, but it still does the trick. From the vest's padded interior, I pull out the objects I smuggled inside. The spy cam and portable router fit easily in my hand. I roll them around on my palm. I could place the camera here. Broadcasting the death of a half-dozen spinners has to look bad for Kronos, doesn't it? No. I slide the surveillance equipment into my pocket. Spinners dying during treatment is too common an occurrence to raise a red enough flag. It would be easy for Kronos to explain these deaths away as merely treatments gone inexplicably wrong.

The door to the room opens. I crouch on the floor next to the bed, clutching the dangling IV needle in a pitiful attempt at self-defense. Shannon hurries inside, partly hidden behind a big laundry cart she's pushing in front of her.

"I found it in the hall," she pants, parking the cart just inside the door. "I thought we could use it to sneak you out."

I stand up, dropping the needle onto the tiled floor.

"Shannon," I say. "That's perfect."

She beams.

"I found this, too." She holds up a leash key. "It was in one of the supply

235

closets."

I offer her my wrist, and she unlocks the leash. The band falls from my arm, and I take what feels like the first deep breath I've had in hours. Nervously, I reach out for time and feel a surge of relief when my mind connects. The strands rush around me, seconds dancing past like they are welcoming me. I sink my mind into them and will them to stop. They do, though it takes effort. Between all the Aclisote swimming in my veins and the low-grade fever, my grasp on time feels tenuous.

I take two steps and let time go. A once-familiar swirl momentarily dizzies me. The next instant, I'm back where I was when I froze time, standing next to Shannon. It's what I expected, but I'm still disappointed. They've already given me so much Aclisote that nothing I do during frozen time is going to stick.

"I can't change anything," I tell Shannon. "But I can scout the route. Where's Dr. Ellery's office?"

Shannon's eyes go wide, but she doesn't question me.

"The administrative suite," she says. "On the second floor. If you go back toward the main lobby, there's a stairwell to the left of the elevator. Do you remember how to get there? It's two lefts and a right. When you get upstairs, the admin suite will be directly in front of you."

Shannon unlocks the door with her card, and I stop time again, then wait a few moments until I've steadied my hold on the reluctant strands. Even with the extra effort, the peace surrounding me bolsters my resolve. This is my domain, and the only place where I will always feel safe.

The hall outside is still empty. I start down it, the padding of my bare feet hardly disturbing the freeze's perfect calm. Left. Left again. I'm jogging, matching the pace of my feet to the urgent beating in my chest. I skid around the corner for the final right turn.

Two men are standing in front of the elevator. One has his mouth open and his left hand raised in some kind of gesture. Both wear white lab coats.

"Murderer," I tell the talking man. His frozen face doesn't budge; I doubt he'd react that differently if I accused him in real time. I grab his raised hand and bend his fingers into an obscene gesture. It's a childish impulse, but one I think Jack would approve of.

The stairwell is where Shannon said it would be. I race upward, the metal edge lining the lip of each step biting the exposed skin on my feet. The second-floor hallways are unlit and echoing with emptiness. Ahead of me is a door marked ADMINISTRATIVE OFFICES. I try the handle. It's locked, but there's a swipe pad next to it that looks just like the ones on every other door in the building.

"I'll be back," I murmur. There's no need for me to make the return trip. Time slips from my grasp as easily as exhaling. The world blurs.

"There are only two people out there we have to avoid," I tell Shannon when I'm standing by her side again. The swirl of returned time has given me back my breath, so I'm not even panting from my mad dash. The only evidence of my freeze is the whisper of a headache starting up in the back of my head.

"They're by the elevator," I say, "but by the time we get there, they should be gone."

"OK." Shannon twists her hands together. "I guess we should go, then."

I lean into the laundry cart, grab the handful of sheets lying at the bottom, and toss them onto the floor. I stretch one leg over the side, then stop. Shannon's face hovers before me, all pale cheeks and bedraggled hair. I take my leg out.

"We can't do this," I say.

"What do you mean?" Shannon peers into the basket. "Won't you fit?"

"No, the idea is a great one. I meant that we can't do it."

Shannon frowns. "Why not?"

"If the Kronons find out you helped me," I tell her, "then they'll consider you a traitor. They won't let you live, Shannon."

She doesn't flinch.

"I already thought of that." She shrugs with exaggerated nonchalance. "They're going to figure out I'm the one who stole the key card. I mean, who else here would help you?"

I study the cart. If Shannon doesn't help me, I'll have to sneak around by myself. I could scout ahead before I make each turn, but it's still a lot riskier than hiding in the cart. I chew my lip. Shannon might be right about Kronos figuring out her involvement anyway, but she might not. All that blond innocence might go a long way toward protecting her, at least until she can get out of here. If she goes with me, though, she'll have no chance at all.

"You've done enough," I say. "More than I expected. Go back to your room now and—"

Shannon shakes her head before I can finish the sentence.

"They're my friends, too." Her fingers are knotted together, but her voice is steady.

"I won't let you," I say. "Too many people have already died because of me."

The expression on Shannon's face hardens. I recognize it as the one she used on the Youngers when they tried to shirk their daily chores.

"If you do this by yourself," she says, "you'll be less likely to succeed, right?"

Reluctantly, I nod.

"You're not the only one who gets to play the hero, Alex. This is my choice." She points at the cart. "Get in."

The list of protests crowding my tongue withers under the combined pressure of Shannon's stubbornness and the mounting seconds I can now actively feel slipping past us. I climb into the cart. The bottom is cloth, and I distribute my weight carefully to avoid ripping it. Shannon drops the sheets on top of me until I'm covered. They smell like bleach.

"Here we go," she says.

We bump our way down the hall. One wheel must be crooked, because the cart keeps veering to the right. Shannon grunts as she struggles to shove the overloaded thing forward. I try to judge how close we are based on the number of turns. Left. Left. Right. The cart slows, and I hear a soft click as her finger stabs the elevator button.

"Shannon!" someone calls out cheerily.

I curl my arms against my chest, terrified I might be making non-sheetlike dents in the cart's cloth side.

"Hi, Jean."

Shannon sounds weirdly perky, but Jean hasn't known her very long, so maybe she won't notice. I hold my breath, a strategy that makes my heart gallop so fast I'm afraid I'll pass out.

"What are you doing with that?" Jean asks.

"Just helping." Shannon giggles. "I'm so used of being part of the team at the Center, it's hard for me to sit around and do nothing."

"You're our ambassador now." Jean sounds disapproving. "That's an important job. You don't have to do this kind of work anymore."

"Sorry, I won't do it again."

The laundry cart is rocking very slightly. Shannon's leg is pressed against the side, and I can tell that it's shaking.

"Where are you taking that thing, anyway?" Jean asks.

"Landry room."

"The laundry room is downstairs. You pushed the up button."

"Whoops." Shannon giggles again. "I guess I got confused. All these halls look the same."

There's another soft click as one of them presumably hits the elevator's down button. The quiver in Shannon's leg quickens. I hold as still as I can, taking tiny little sips of air.

"Drop the cart off and go back to your room," Jean says. "It's getting late."

"Yes, ma'am."

239

The elevator bings, and I hear the doors open. The cart lurches as Shannon starts to wrangle it inside.

"Let me help you with that," Jean says.

No! I scream in my head. If Jean moves the cart, she's going to notice the extra weight.

"I've got it." Shannon manages a herculean shove that rockets the cart all the way to the back of the elevator, slamming my shoulder into the wall. I bite my lip to smother a gasp. Shannon positions herself between the laundry cart and Jean.

"What floor?" she asks, which must mean Jean has followed her into the elevator.

"Three."

The elevator starts to rise. At the second floor, no one gets off. We rise again.

"Thanks for the directions," Shannon gushes when the doors open a second time.

"No problem," Jean says. "Get some sleep. You look a bit frazzled."

"I will."

The door closes, and my stomach drops as we sink downward. This time, when the elevator bings, the cart rolls forward.

"We're here," Shannon pants.

I pop my head up out of the cart.

"Do you think Jean suspected anything?" Shannon asks.

"You did great." I clamber over the side of the cart, spilling sheets in my rush to get out. "Come on, let's get inside, quick."

Shannon digs the stolen key card out of her pocket and swipes it across the reader. There's a click, and I release a sigh of relief when the door opens. Shannon bundles the sheets back into the cart, and the two of us work together to maneuver it out of the hallway.

The administrative wing matches the rest of the facility: lots of white walls and chrome. The room we're standing in is set up like a meeting room, with a table in the center surrounded by chairs. Doors ringing the interior walls open up into five private offices. The whole area is dark, but I stop time anyway to make sure no one is here.

"They're all empty," I tell Shannon after I've searched them.

She nods. Now that we're actually in the Central Office's inner sanctum, her nervousness has returned. She's pulling on her hair, wrapping the end of her braid around her fingers with an anxious twist. I, however, am bouncing with the possibility of success.

Dr. Ellery's office, identifiable by the burnished nameplate tacked outside her door, is tucked in the corner, with views overlooking both the parking lot and the forest beyond. I shut the door, then turn a cord that closes the blinds before flicking on the light. Dr. Ellery's workspace looks more like a glass-topped table than a desk, and the only things on it are a computer and a phone. The room around it is equally sparse. There's a black desk chair, a chrome filing cabinet, and a bookcase featuring more art than books. Dr. Ellery favors Asian designs: a curving white vase, a framed pen-and-ink drawing of bamboo, a bronze statue of a geisha. All of it looks expensive. The only things that seem out of place are two large paintings hanging on one wall, heavy ancient-looking things in gilded frames.

I move to the desk and shake the computer mouse, making the screen light up and revealing a blank page with a sign-in box in the center demanding a password. Along the bottom edge is a digital clock announcing the time: 9:37. My stomach flips. The other spinners will be here in less than half an hour.

"Now what?" Shannon asks.

"Rewind," I say.

Time stops only after I wrench at the strands, and I have to rest for a bit before I can gather enough energy to pull them backward. Our wraithlike selves leave the room, and then there is nothing to watch except the numbers on the clock ticking backward—a challenge, since the rewound numbers are

241

superimposed over the real ones. I increase the speed until the clock hits 9:02 and Dr. Ellery backs through the door. The memory of her presence brushes over me as she reaches the desk. I shiver. I've been in thousands of rewinds, and this is the first time I've felt what Norms always describe when they're in one: that watching past images flicker by is like being in a room full of ghosts.

Dr. Ellery settles into the chair and clicks a few buttons—it must be a log off command, because the screen flips to a word processing program. Then she slides a cell phone out of her pocket and reads a message. *They're here*, the faint words say. She sets the phone on her desk, and a moment later I heard the echo of the phone's notification chime.

I move over to the window and part the blind. The shadow of Ross's car is parked below us. I watch myself scurry with tense steps away from the building, then duck into the car backward. He closes the door, then turns to stand beside the car, staring up at the building. The smile he's wearing is the satisfied grin of a world conqueror.

I speed up the rewind, pulling time backward as Dr. Ellery un-writes some emails and periodically speaks gibberish into the phone. When the clock has wound back to six thirty p.m., Dr. Ellery starts un-opening a bunch of the computer's programs. I slow the rewind. The last program blinks shut, and the screen switches over to the sign-in page again, the box in the center filled with black dots. I lean forward eagerly, forcing the seconds to rewind at a crawl as I watch each movement of Dr. Ellery's fingers.

&...H...W...)...

My eagerness dims. How am I going to remember this? A pen—I need a pen and a piece of paper. I smack the desktop in frustration. Why didn't I think of this before? I stop the rewind. Dr. Ellery's pristine glass desk holds no pens or paper, so I run to the office next door and grab a thick blue marker stashed by a whiteboard. Hurrying back to Dr. Ellery's office, I scribble *&HW)* on the glass surface of her desk, then restart the rewind so I can transcribe the rest of the symbols as she types

242

0...9...I...H...8...Z

The dots vanish one by one. Dr. Ellery shakes the mouse, and the screen goes black. I stop the rewind again and study the collection of letters, numbers, and symbols scrawled on the desk. Great—a password that appears to be completely random. I smack the desk again. Why couldn't she use something easy to remember, like Dr.Ellery.Rocks? I read the password over three times, say it out loud four more times, then let time go. There's a moment of dizziness, and then I'm standing on the other side of the desk next to Shannon. The ghost of Dr. Ellery is gone, as is the password I scrawled on the glass. The marker is also missing.

&HW)09IH8Z

"Is it over?" Shannon asks.

I sprint into the other office. *&HW)09IH8Z. Z?* Or was it *C?* I grab the marker and a sheet of paper and run back. *&HW)09IH8 . . . Z? C? D?*

"Did you get the password?" Shannon asks.

The random string is crumbling in my head.

"Shhh," I snap at Shannon, scribbling as fast as I can recite the password in my head. *&HW* . . . was the parenthesis open or closed? *09IH8,* and then that *Z* or *C* or *D. C*—I think it was *C.*

I grab the mouse and type in the characters, then delete them and reenter the string when I remember that what I wrote down is backward. *Incorrect password* flashes on the screen. I clench my teeth.

"What does the password mean?" Shannon asks, head twisted around as she tries to read my scribbles.

My teeth clench harder. "I don't know," I mutter.

I enter the sequence again, this time starting with *D.*

Incorrect password.

"Damn it!" I stab at the delete button and start banging out another slightly different combination.

"You better be careful," Shannon says. "You might lock yourself out."

243

My finger hovers over the enter button. "What?"

"I heard KJ say that once," she says. "It's, like, a security thing. If you enter the wrong password too many times, it stops working, and you have to wait awhile before you try again."

My jaw hurts from clenching it. I study at the mess of characters. I think they're right this time, but if they're not . . . The clock on the desk says 9:38. Where was Jean going when she ran into Shannon? How much longer do I have before someone notices I'm not strapped down in my room?

I lift my hands off the keyboard and rewind time again, rushing backward to get to the relevant hour. Dr. Ellery enters the room, un-writes emails and un-dials phone numbers. I screech time to a halt, barely stopping it in time to catch the part where she types her password. & . . . H . . . W . . . I follow along with the symbols I wrote in real time, correcting them as I go. The parenthesis is right, but the final (first) letter is Z, and she hit shift when she typed the 8, so it's actually an asterisk.

Time swirls back to the present, and I re-scribble the corrections before I type in the password. There's a pause, a tiny moment that feels like a century, and then the screen magically unlocks. I collapse into the desk chair with relief.

"You did it!" Shannon says. "That was so fast!"

I crumple the paper with the password on it and shove it in my pocket. "Fast" in this context is relative, and there's a headache starting behind my forehead that would argue I was nowhere near fast enough.

"That was the easy part," I tell Shannon, then briefly outline the task ahead.

"How will you know which files you need?" Shannon asks.

The question whines like a gnat in my ear. I perch on the edge of Dr. Ellery's desk chair, resisting the urge to shout *I don't know* at her. The computer's screen shimmers in front of me, a solid blue that gives away no secrets. I move the mouse in vague circles. Except for a handful of video games I never played, the Center didn't let us use computers. What did Max tell me to do? I sink into the memory, picturing the car's worn seats and the smell of spearmint. Our conversation drifts back to me slowly. It seems like it happened days ago rather than hours. Email—I have to send Max an email and attach as many files as I can find.

Assuming Max is even out there to read them.

I push away my worry about things I can't control and find the email icon. A few clicks, and the program opens, populating the screen with messages. My eyes roam down the list of subject lines. *Meeting request, Revised Draft, Morgan Study, Updated results, Facilities, Lunch?, Contact for ELT.* The mouse drifts from one to another. Are any of them important? I don't know what most of the subjects even mean. I scroll down farther, and my heart sinks. There are probably thousands of incriminating words somewhere in this mess, but the list is endless. The clock in the corner of the screen flickers as another minute ticks forward: 9:39.

Shannon is hovering so close to my shoulder that I can hear her breathing.

"Which message are you looking for?" she asks.

"I'm not." I push up the sleeves of my sweater. "I'm looking for files. I just need to set up a way to send them."

I study the screen and find an icon that says New Message. *Click.* A blank message pops open, and I carefully enter the address Max said to send things to: Incognito987@gmail.com.

"Who's that?" Shannon asks.

My fingers twitch, making me type an *h* instead of *g.*

"A friend." I correct the address. *You there?* I write in the subject line. I hit send and open a new message to the same addresses. *Find the paper clip,* Max said. Another screen pops up, this one with folders, just like Max described. I wipe my palms on my skirt before picking up the mouse again. OK, I found the files. Now how do I figure out which are the right ones?

My fever is making the room feel overly warm. Dr. Ellery's office windows are sealed shut, and the air in here feels heavy, as if all the passing seconds are filling up the space, elbowing for room as they pile up around me. The clock flickers again: 9:40.

I click randomly on a folder that says Admin, and a whole new list of folders appears: *Agendas, Board Meetings, Corporate Docs, Deliverables.* The words dance across the screen, growing more and more meaningless as I scroll through the endless list. I close Admin and start searching through other folders. Where would Dr. Ellery store evidence of Kronos's murderous intentions? Shannon bounces on her toes behind me, making the floor creak with every movement. The clock advances: 9:41, 9:42. My quivering fingers keep scrolling, each folder stuffed with subfolders brimming with files. How can I possibly know which ones might be worth sending?

The computer makes a soft ding. I jerk so hard I accidentally attach a file called Office Supplies to the email I'm sending Max. The screen with the folders vanishes, and I see that a new message has appeared in Dr. Ellery's inbox. The sender is Incognito987. I dive for the message.

Where are the files? Have you set up the video? I'm not seeing anything on the app.

My relief that Max is out there is almost instantly obliterated when her message sinks in. The video! I whirl around so fast I pinch Shannon's toes under the chair's rolling wheels. She yelps.

"Shannon." I dig in my pocket for the spy cam and portable router. "I need you to set this up." I turn the devices on as I explain to her what they are. "Hide the camera somewhere that will give a good view of this room, and hide the router near it. The camera has to have this part exposed." I show her. "Can you do that?"

"Yes." Shannon takes the surveillance equipment and starts roaming around Dr. Ellery's office, seemingly as eager to have something concrete to do as I am to have her stop breathing down my neck.

I turn back to the screen and hit reply.

246

Setting up camera now. Where should I look for files?

I don't know how to type, which means finding the right letters is slow. Waiting for Max's response takes even longer. The clock advances.

Try any folder that talks about project notes, especially Project Zed. Also see if you can find their original charter, maybe in org docs? If you can find lab results, send those. And field notes could be useful, or anything about special agents.

Project Zed. Field notes. Special agents. My hand cramps from the speed of my clicks.

"I hid the camera on top of one of the paintings," Shannon announces, appearing back at my side. "The one with the cherubs."

"Great." I click on another folder and see something called Project Notes. That's like field notes, right? I hit the attach button, and the folder's name appears on the email. Send.

Shannon stands behind me for a while, then paces to the window, which she abandons seconds later to peruse Dr. Ellery's shelves. I dig through more folders. Agents, one says. I send that, too, then open another folder called Research. Dozens of subfolders litter the screen. Alpha, Amino 1, Amino 2, Amino 7, Barclay. The folders' dates stretch back years, all the way to the dawn of computers, probably. The sight of them makes me queasy. How many deaths are locked in those innocuous icons? I scroll down. The list is endless.

"Alex!" Shannon calls. "They're here!"

"Who's here?"

"The kids from the Center."

Shannon's restless pacing has brought her back to the window, where she's peering through a partially raised slat in the blinds. I attach the entire Research folder to an email, hit send, and jump from the desk to join her. A big yellow bus is parked outside the front entrance, its open doors flanked by Dr. Ellery and a man in a uniform who must be the bus driver. Standing on the bus's first step is Aidan.

247

"We should get away from the window," I say. Shannon nods. Neither of us moves. More people are stumbling off the bus now: Raul, Yuki, Angel, Oliver. Aidan has one arm in a sling and a bloodstained bandage wrapped around his head. When Yolly steps off the bus, holding two Youngers by the hand, Shannon moans.

Lisa and Miguel exit the bus last. Miguel is holding Jeremy's hand tightly; Lisa carries Rose in her arms. The little girl is clinging to her mother's neck, her hair is mussed, and she looks as if she's just woken up. Each of them wears the glinting band of a leash, and they all look dazed.

Bile rises up from my stomach to burn the back of my throat. I want to bang on the glass, scream at them all to run, but run where? There's no escape from this foul place.

"Who are they?" Shannon asks, pointing down at Lisa and Miguel. She's whispering, even though there is no way the people below can hear us.

"The couple that took us in," I say. "Remember I told you we went somewhere safe? They're both spinners. Adult spinners."

Two technicians emerge from the building. They brush past the dazed spinners being ushered inside and head for the idling bus. Each of them is pushing a gurney. A buzzing sounds starts in my head. It's like the drone that comes from a zapper, only louder and more rhythmic, like the crashing of very large waves. One of the techs yanks open a panel in the bus's side to reveal a storage cavity. There's no luggage under that bus. What the techs drag out of those shadowed depths are two child-sized body bags.

A tsunami of static crashes inside my head. The manufactured horror from a zapper is nothing compared to the real agony of those two snuffed-out lives, ended for no reason besides one organization's finely honed hatred. Tears blur the scene below me, as if my body wants to protect me from what I'm seeing even though it's already too late. Nothing will ever erase the heartbreak of those small crumpled bags.

I lower the slat and turn my back to the window. Shannon's face is paper

248

white. All the facts I've told her about the fate of our friends seem to be hitting her at once. Believing someone's words is different from watching the truth being dragged out of a bus.

"Have you found the right files?" Shannon asks, a new edge hardening her voice.

"Working on it." I wipe my cheeks with the back of my hand.

"You better hurry," Shannon says. "As soon as they take everyone to that room, they'll see that you're not there."

"Right." I go back to the desk and snatch up the mouse. Shannon follows me.

"See if you can find out what Dr. Ellery is saying to them," I tell her, more to give her something to do than because I think it will make much difference. "But don't let anyone see you."

Shannon nods and marches out the door. I shift my focus to the computer. There are two new messages in Dr. Ellery's inbox. Both of them say the same thing:

Error. Email not sent. File size too large for server.

I squeeze the mouse. Files can be too big? Instead of banging my head against the desk, I email Max.

Help then fifieles anrento going thriguh. Theyre tobig. what do I do??

My fingers are moving too fast to manage coherent typing. I send the message anyway because correcting it will take too long. Then I wait. Chew on the side of my thumb. Try to imagine what might be happening downstairs. Will Dr. Ellery pretend the others are going be cured? Offer them some hope to keep the group from panicking? Or are techs descending on them right now, sedating the whole group so they can all be dragged off en masse? I strain my ears for any sign of struggle. The Central Office is as silent as a tomb.

The clock turns: 9:53.

"Come on," I mutter, waving the mouse around the screen. "Max, where are you?"

249

A now-familiar ding sounds softly, announcing a new message. It's not from Max, but I click on it anyway.

Incognito987 invited you to join a shared file.

What in the world? Another ding.

I sent you a link so you can upload the files, Max writes. *Just drag the file icon into the website. If you shrink both programs, you can see the pages side by side.*

The words dance in front of my eyes. What is she talking about? Uploading, shrinking pages, dragging files? My heads swims, the simmering fever reminding me of its presence. I smack the mouse against the desk. It's KJ who should be here, not me. He's the computer guy. I should be the one lying in the dark.

"They're still in the lobby," Shannon says, rushing back into the office. "I heard Dr. Ellery say something about checking them in one at a time. How are you doing?"

I fling a hand at the screen. "I don't know what this means."

My voice betrays me by wobbling. Shannon returns to her spot by my shoulder.

"I do," she says.

I pinch the bridge of my nose to stop the treacherous tears from falling. "You do?"

"Yeah." Shannon leans over me and clicks a small square at the top of each screen, dividing the programs so they only fills part of the space. "You can drag a file over like this." She shows me.

"How did you learn that?" I ask her, taking back the mouse.

"I had to stay in bed for a couple of days while I was being cured. One of the techs showed me how to use a computer so I could watch movies."

I gulp in a shaky breath and start digging through the folders again, trying to remember where I found the files I selected before. Research? History? My attention drifts out of the admin offices and creeps down the stairs. In the

250

lobby, the techs will have selected someone. They'll be walking that person down those empty white halls. Any minute, they will open the door to the death room. And when they do, they'll see that I'm not there.

I drag a folder over like Shannon showed me. It appears on the shared site, along with a thin rectangular bar. *One minute remaining*, it says.

"What's that?" I ask Shannon.

"I think it's loading?" She doesn't sound sure. "Just keep adding more."

I send an email to Max: *Is this working?* Then I grab more files and drag them over. More bars appear, each one with a longer timeline. *Three minutes remaining. Five minutes.*

A harsh beeping sound rips through the air. It's loud and insistent, and it's not stopping. At the same moment, a message flashes up on the computer, overlaying both the email and the upload screens. The words are in a box with a thick black border around it.

ALARM SOUNDED. SECTION 43. SECURITY BREACH.

Shannon claps her hands over her ears. "What *is* that?"

Fear fills my stomach, cold as ice and twice as heavy.

"I think they figured out I'm missing."

I click on the *x* in the corner of the warning message. The black-framed box vanishes, but the alarm doesn't pause. I lean closer to the screen and keep searching. My fingers feel stiff, each click of the mouse slow and awkward. The first file I added now says *upload complete*, but it's the only one so far, and I don't even know if it's anything worthwhile.

I'm running out of time.

The screen in front of me dissolves into a random mess of black-and-white dots. I blink and force myself to focus. The files all look the same, and their names are nonsense. I start grabbing folders, dragging anything that seems even remotely relevant onto the upload page, not even checking to see what the subfolders might contain. The alarm's beeping lances my brain, turning my thoughts into Swiss cheese. Thin bars fill the screen, their contents inching into the electronic void. The bars keep growing longer. *Seven minutes remaining. Nine minutes remaining. Twelve minutes remaining.*

"I'm going out again to see what's going on," Shannon says.

"OK," I say without looking up.

I grab a folder called Project Gamma. Did I already upload that one? I drag it over anyway. The list of uploading files is so long now, I can't even see the beginning, so I can't tell how many have gone through. Did I add so many I overloaded the system? Maybe the whole thing is going to crash. The beeping continues. Max hasn't answered my email.

Shannon bursts through the door.

"Someone's coming!" she gasps, one hand pressed against her chest as if she's trying to keep her heart from exploding out of it.

I reach for time. The rush of it encircles me, beckoning with its secret comfort. I bring it close, soaking in the power like a sip of restoration. We have to run, to hide, to get—

Time slips back into its groove. Stopping it isn't going to help. This work has to happen in real time.

"What are we going to do?" Shannon's voice quivers with fear.

"Go to one of the other offices." I open another subfolder. Accounts, it says. I drag it over. "Look for somewhere to hide. I'm right behind you."

Shannon runs. I look at the list of files I've uploaded. Is that enough? I open one more directory. There's something there called History. I grab it, then see another one called Charter. Isn't that one of the things Max asked for? I drag both of them into the shared site.

Somewhere much too close, a door opens. I let go of the mouse. There are footsteps crossing the conference room. Another door opens, this one even closer. I hear an indistinct voice rumble and then another one, answering. My heart starts hammering, its pace a double-time counterpoint to the horrible beeps of the alarm. Someone is working their way through the suite, checking each office methodically. I slide out of the office chair and tiptoe over to click

252

off the light. The room doesn't go dark. The computer on the desk is glowing like a homing beacon, calling to whoever is out there.

I race back to the desk, slam the email program closed, then the search menu, leaving only the file sharing program running. The light doesn't dim; if anything, it gets brighter. I run my hands along the edge of the screen until they land on a power button. Will this turn off the screen or the whole computer? I need something to block the light. The room holds nothing except fragile art and the useless glass desk. Maybe I can stuff the monitor somewhere? I heave the heavy plastic box off the desk and feel the tug of a power cord dragging it back down. The only way to move it is to unplug it, and that means stopping the file transfer.

A man's voice rings out from one of the other offices, loud enough this time that I understand what he's saying.

"Found one!" he calls.

The computer slips in my hands.

"Which one did you find?" another man asks.

The computer is falling. I make a wild, juggling grab, which stops the thing from crashing down onto the glass desk, but only because it lands instead on the outspread fingers of my right hand. Pain radiates up my arm as the computer grinds against bone. My eyes water.

"It's the ambassador," I hear the first man says. "Guess Dr. Ellery was right to suspect her."

Through the walls, I can hear Shannon whimpering. I slide my hand out from under the computer and cradle my aching fingers. Bars still fill the screen, the uploads inching forward at a snail's pace. *Eight minutes remaining*, says the bar at the bottom. How much information has actually gotten out? Will any of it provide proof? *Move*, I will the creeping files. *Faster*.

"Alex can't be far away," says the second voice.

My mental urging falters. I know that voice. Carson Ross has joined the hunt.

Footsteps patter on the floor outside Dr. Ellery's office. It's death, pacing toward the room like a hungry beast waiting to claim me. I back away from the door until I'm mashed against the window blinds. Declaring my willingness to sacrifice myself sounded simple at the time, but now that the end is closing in around me, something much deeper and more primal is tearing its way to the surface, and I am aware of exactly how much I do not want to die.

The undimmed screen continues to light the room. My eyes travel over the empty desk, the single chair, the carefully decorated shelves. There's nowhere to hide in this stark space. The floor on the other side of the door creaks. Terror flushes my body, and without thinking, I reach for the only safety I know. Time stops.

Silence brings a thin veneer of calm. I cross the room and open the door. Ross stands, frozen, on the threshold. Even though I expected it, the sight of him is still shocking. Everything about him is so familiar: the blue eyes, the sandy hair brushed back from his forehead, even the way his head thrusts forward ahead of his gait, as if his eagerness to get where he's going is pushing him faster than his feet can carry him. One of his hands is held out, fingers curved in the act of grabbing the doorknob. The way his hand hovers makes it look like he's offering me something, except his palm is empty, and all he has to offer me is death.

I shove his stomach so I can move him aside enough to get through the door. His body is heavy, and all I manage to do is bend him over a little, but it's enough to let me out of the room. I slither past him. His body curves over me like he's bowing, not in allegiance but in mocking salutation. *Run all you want,* he seems to be saying. *There is no escape from me.*

The room behind him is blinding. Shannon and I never turned on the overhead lights, which now beam down like unnecessarily bright spotlights. The white walls gleam. The chrome sparkles. I squint against the glare. The doors to the all the offices are open, so I only have to turn my head to find the other searcher. He's a big man wearing the same tan uniform as the security

254

guards and he's bent over to peer behind the wooden desk in the office where I found the marker.

My bare feet pad across the carpeted floor. Shannon is curled up underneath the desk, her arms wrapped around her knees in an effort to make herself smaller. Her face is tipped up toward her pursuer, wearing an expression of pure terror. Time squirms against me. I struggle to keep control, though what does it matter? There is nothing I can do to alter what's happening before me.

I kneel on the ground beside my friend and take her hand in mine.

"I'm sorry," I tell her.

The words sound hollow. I've said them too many times in the last few days, and the sentiment, however heartfelt, has worn thin.

I stand up and cross over to the window. The blanketing clouds have broken up, allowing a clear view of the sky beyond them stretching out into infinity. I lean my head against the window's smooth pane and stare up into the void.

KJ loves space. The summer he was fifteen, he tried to map the movements of the stars. He'd stay up late every night so he could draw the constellations, then stagger around all day in a sleep-deprived stupor. He had this theory that the power to freeze time fades away over the vastness of space, and that if you could somehow travel through frozen time into the deepest reaches of the universe, you'd find stars continuing to shine and far-off planets still spinning. He theorized that this dissonance could explain some of the universe's anomalies.

Above me, a light a zillion miles away twinkles. How far *does* my power reach? I know that when I stop time, the freeze extends to the rest of the world, but does it really reach the moon? The stars? The whole universe? It seems inconceivable that I can control what happens far beyond any place I can even imagine. No wonder Kronos fears us. The power I wield has repercussions beyond anyone's comprehension. The irony is that for all my power, I am also terribly insignificant, one tiny being lost in the enormity of a vast and complex

255

web. I have stopped time on countless occasions; now it's going to stop for me.

The ache in my crushed fingers has lessened, but a growing pain pulses in my head. Time is whispering its desire to run free. Soon the whisper will grow into a persistent scream, and there will be nothing I can do to hold it back. I could stand here for the equivalent of an hour—maybe two, or even three—but when I let time go, I will be back where I started, stuck in the moment when a door is about to open to reveal Carson Ross. My skills will not be able to save me this time, nor will KJ or Shannon. I will face Ross alone, stripped down to what I really am: an unremarkable sixteen-year-old girl. It's what I've always been, really. Someone born with unusual genes and raised in exceptional circumstances, but still just a girl. Just me.

The chill of the windowpane isn't helping to ease my headache. I exhale onto the glass and write my name in the fog my breath leaves behind. Is it better to be killed by a stranger or by someone you once loved? There's an intimacy to death. Love and hate, they say, are two sides of the same coin.

My name fades as my breath evaporates. For an unmeasured moment, I stand there, holding fast to my own power, the freeze's comfort, and my vanishing freedom. Then I let it all go.

18 ◀◀

THE ALARM IS SCREAMING AGAIN. WINDOW BLINDS PRESS against my back, and my fingers throb, their damage newly fresh. The flush of terror washing over me the instant I froze time continues its course across my skin. This time, I resist the urge to flee. Instead, I hold on to the tranquility of the distant stars, and when the doorknob rattles, I turn toward it. I don't want Ross to discover me cowering.

He flicks on the light when he enters, and when he sees me, he smiles.

"I was hoping I'd be the one to find you."

"Hello, Mr. Ross."

"I have the missing patient," Ross says over his shoulder.

From outside the office, the other man calls, "I'll be right there to help you secure her."

"There's no need." Ross winks at me. "I'm a trained police officer. She's nothing I can't handle."

"I'll take this one downstairs, then," the man says, "and let Dr. Ellery know you've got the target."

There are sounds leaking from the other office—erratic shuffling noises mixed with faint cries for mercy. I try very hard not to picture what's happening. If I let myself imagine Shannon's terror right now, I will lose the thread of calm that's holding me together.

Ross walks toward me, his steps bouncing with ghoulish eagerness.

"What are you doing back here all alone?" he asks. "It seems like an odd

257

choice of a hiding place."

"Just doing a little research," I say, hoping that if I acknowledge the computer screen's betraying glare, he'll be less likely to investigate.

"Research?" Ross comes closer. "It's a little late for that, I'd say. *You* are the research subject now."

"Is that what you're calling murder these days? Research?"

Ross rounds the desk and, completely ignoring my attempt at diversion, peers at the computer. His eyebrows rise. "Where are you sending these?"

I don't answer. Someone chooses this moment to cut off the alarm, and the abrupt silence makes my lack of response seem especially significant.

Ross clucks his tongue. "Dr. Ellery is going to be very angry with you," he says.

He reaches for the computer, and I hold my breath. I think he's going to start closing down the files, which, given how many there are, might allow a few more to get through, but he does something much more effective. With a quick tug, he pulls the power cord out of the back of the computer. There's a soft click, and the light from the screen winks out.

"It doesn't matter," I say, not sure this is true. "Enough files have already gone out. Pretty soon everyone is going to know how Kronos operates."

Ross frowns at the now-blank screen. I rock back on my heels and smile at him with false assurance.

"You don't have to go down with them," I say. "They think you hate spinners and that you have no idea they've been poisoning us, which means you can steer clear of the whole mess. If you stop them from killing us tonight, I won't tell them that you lied. Choose our side, act shocked about what Kronos is doing, and you could be the hero who saved hundreds of children from unnecessary death."

I can tell he's considering my suggestion. Ross is always eager to pursue the angle that works out best for him. The pauses between my heartbeats feel interminable. Time might not be stopped, but between beats it's stretched as

258

thin as a piece of taffy.

"Kronos getting in trouble isn't going to hurt me," Ross says. "As you just pointed out, I'm not aware of their plans. In fact, throwing a little chaos their way might work in my favor. Kronos put me in charge of rounding up the remaining spinners, and without them breathing down my neck, it will be easier for me to select the best replacement for Jack."

The possibility of him siding with us, while slim, still hurts when it slips away, though not as much as his callous dismissal of Jack.

"I don't think a spinner helper is going to be an option for you anymore." I spit the words out like a curse. "After the CIA reads the files I sent, they'll know all of us can change things in frozen time. You won't be able to use us to commit your crimes."

A muscle in Ross's cheek flexes. When he speaks again, the jocular tone that has colored our conversation since he walked in is replaced by annoyance.

"Do you really think that a dumb brat like you is going to change anything by sending a few files to the CIA?" He dismisses the silent computer with a contemptuous flick of his wrist. "Everyone hates spinners. No one will care if you all die."

His words hit home. Is he right? I think of the two thugs who trapped us in the music store and of Jean with her fanatic's gleam. Are they typical Norms? Or is the world populated with more people like Yolly and Max?

"Even if I did consider saving the spinners," Ross continues, "I'd make sure that you weren't one of them." He moves closer and slides a finger under my chin, forcing me to look him straight in the eye. "I'm about to turn you in for the second time today, a move that is sure to make me quite the favorite with Kronos. Thanks for that tip, by the way. It's because of you that I figured out they were worth joining." The smile that flashes over his face is the opposite of charming. "How does that make you feel, *partner*?"

My musings about the moral compass of Norms vanishes in an unexpected burst of sorrow. Being Ross's partner used to make me proud. Ross and I, working together to make the world a better place. Except his world turned out to be inhabited by only one person—Carson Ross—while my world encompasses dozens of people. Hundreds. Thousands.

"What happened to you?" I ask him. "You used to believe in justice. You used to want to help people in need."

The fingers gripping my chin pinch.

"Your death will be payback," he says, "for all the things that you took from me."

"What have I ever taken from you?"

"We were supposed to be a team," Ross says. "I gave you all that power, and you stole it for yourself."

"You gave me nothing." There's danger in his eyes, but I don't care. What can he possibly do to me that Kronos isn't planning to do already? "Time has always been mine."

"Yeah?" Ross's breath feels hot against my face. "It might be yours, but you don't have very much of it left."

He releases my chin and instead latches onto my arm. Fear scrambles my brain, and the room breaks into pieces. There's the desk, the bookshelves, the paintings on the wall, but each item appears to me in a separate flash. There's no continuity, no sense that the parts make up a whole. I let my knees sag, hoping my slack body will loosen Ross's grip. Even if running from him only sends me to Jean, now that I'm in his grasp, I realize I've answered my own question. A sterile death at the hands of a technician is better than spending my final moments under this man's rain of hate.

The door in the outer office bangs open, and Margaret Ellery strides in, her suit still unwrinkled and her jet hair perfectly tucked into a neat chignon. The sight of her expands my fear into a yawning terror that hollows my insides.

"You found her." She gives me a look weighted with loathing. "Excellent. Thank you."

"You're welcome." Ross hauls me upright. "She was in here. I caught her trying to send files from your computer."

Dr. Ellery starts.

"Don't worry," Mr. Ross says. "I unplugged it."

Dr. Ellery ignores this reassurance, brushing past us to inspect her silent machine. She mutters something short and angry, then snatches up her desk phone and stabs in a number, tapping her foot impatiently until someone picks up on the other end.

"Courtney," she snaps into the receiver, "check the server's backup file. Make a copy of all the activity on my computer from eight thirty p.m. until now. I want it printed out and on my desk in twenty minutes."

She slams down the receiver and scowls at me.

"This sort of invasive and illegal behavior," she says, "is why you and your ilk need to be controlled."

"Controlled?" I ask her, pushing the word through the fear clogging my throat. "Or killed?"

She doesn't blink. Her eyes are like a banked fire, cool control set over seething coals.

"Alex." Ross gives my arm a shake. "Show some respect. Dr. Ellery has offered you and your friends a cure, not a death sentence. You should be grateful."

Dr. Ellery picks up the phone again.

"Thank you for stepping in to help with the search," she tells Ross. "I'll have Jean come and get her."

"I can escort Alex." Ross pulls me against his side. "The two of us have . . . a history. Seeing her finally get the medication she needs would be a relief."

Dr. Ellery's forehead puckers. There's something almost comical about this polite charade, the two fiends dancing around these niceties—or there would be, if they weren't arguing about who gets to lead me to my death. At least it seems unlikely that Ross is going to win. The Central Office is Dr. Ellery's realm, and she won't want anyone to witness me dying.

261

Witness. The room around me abruptly snaps into focus. How could I have forgotten about the spy camera?

I rest a hand on the edge of Ellery's desk and steady myself on its slick surface. Shannon said she hid the camera above the painting with the cherub. Without moving my head, I shift my gaze to the wall where the two pictures hang. Both are old-looking, vaguely religious, and framed in gilt. The one on the left shows a bearded man wearing draped fabric, sitting on a throne, holding a scythe in his left hand and an hourglass in his right. Chronos, presumably—their namesake, the god of time. The second painting also shows Chronos, but in this one, his scythe hovers over a boy who's resting in his lap, a very young boy with a pair of wings sprouting from his back. A winged baby. A cherub.

I scan the edges of the ornate frame. The camera's black head pokes up from the corner, its tiny red eye aimed almost directly at where we stand. A seed of hope takes root in the empty space terror left behind. Max is there on the other side of that light. However tenuous the connection, there is someone sympathetic in this room. Max is watching me. No, she's watching *us*.

I switch my attention back to the conversation going on around me. Ross has changed topics and is now yammering on about some extra officers he's identified to help Dr. Ellery with this "influx of troubled spinners." Dr. Ellery looks annoyed. Jean isn't picking up her call, which seems to be increasing her irritation.

The glass desktop under my hand has grown slippery with my sweat. A video confession will make a stronger case than just computer files, which means that if I can get Dr. Ellery to say something explicit about killing off spinners, it's less likely the CIA will be able to dismiss the evidence. Heat flushes my skin again, but this time it's excitement rather than fever.

Dr. Ellery hangs up the still-unanswered phone.

"I told you," she says to Ross in a frosty tone, "the trustees will discuss your offer. Until then, I suggest you refrain from moving ahead." She reaches a hand toward me. "I need to get this girl in for treatment. I hope you won't mind if I don't see you out?"

Ross's hold on my arm tightens, and I shrink back against him. Leaving this office means leaving the camera. But how can I get her to confess anything with Ross standing here? Dr. Ellery still believes he is ignorant of their darker methods. Unless he goes away, she isn't going to speak freely.

My arm is starting to ache from the intensity of Ross's grip. I look down at the fingers clenching my arm, then up at Dr. Ellery's icy glare, and the ghost of an idea sends out a tentative root. My two enemies don't seem to be friends. Despite Ross's assurance that he's about to be brought into Kronos's heart, the evidence implies otherwise. Dr. Ellery has been speaking to Ross this whole time with barely controlled annoyance. It's only his phenomenal ego that is preventing him from realizing he's being dismissed. I study the tight line of Dr. Ellery's mouth. Ross knows way more than she thinks he does, and from what I know of her, that fact will make her at least as angry with him as she is at me for stealing her files.

I straighten my shoulders.

"You don't have to pretend I'm going in for treatment," I tell Dr. Ellery. "Mr. Ross knows you're going to kill me."

Dr. Ellery's head swivels in my direction. "Excuse me?" she says.

"He knows the Center has been overdosing us with Aclisote," I say. "He also knows that without those drugs, any one of us can change things in frozen time."

Dr. Ellery's lips thin to near invisibility.

"She's raving," Ross says. "I have no idea what she's talking about."

"Of course you do." I twist around to look at him. "You're the one who took me off Aclisote in the first place."

The sheen of sweat that gleams on Ross's forehead gives me a surge of confidence. I turn back to Dr. Ellery.

"The reason he took me off Aclisote was so that I could work for him. He was using my skills to advance his career."

263

"I think you've said enough, Alex." Ross shakes my arm so roughly it makes my teeth rattle. "All you're doing is proving to us that you're sick."

The harsh line of a frown slashes through Dr. Ellery's cultivated calm like an exclamation point. I push harder.

"You know what's sad?" I ask her. "When Mr. Ross took me off Aclisote, I was so naive that I thought he wanted to extend my life because he cared about me. He promised me we were going to make the city safer, but what he really did was have me freeze time so he could slice Austin Shea's throat while he slept."

Dr. Ellery nostrils flare, and her breath hisses through them in short bursts. I sneak a glance at the hidden camera. The tiny red light stares back, unblinking. I can almost hear Max behind it, telling me that Dr. Ellery hasn't said anything incriminating. All she's done is not deny my accusations.

Ross takes a step backward while simultaneously pushing me in front of him, offering me to Dr. Ellery like a sacrifice.

"You're right," he says to her. "You should hand Alex over to your technician. She's clearly disturbed. I don't have to go with her."

Dr. Ellery faces him, her expression ominous.

"Is this true?" she asks.

"She's raving . . ." he starts.

Dr. Ellery holds up a hand and cuts him off.

"After I got away from him, he got hold of Jack," I tell her. My voice is level. Conversational. Definitely not raving. "That's why he was able to turn him over to you. Ross put a tracker in Jack so he could follow him with an app on his phone. I'm sure if you scan Jack, you'll find it. Mr. Ross has been grooming Jack so he'll work for him. Or he was." My voice catches. "Now that you've killed him, Jack won't be able to help anyone."

Ross starts. "Jack is dead? But he just got here."

Dr. Ellery's face mottles. Grabbing up the phone again, she dials a few numbers.

264

"Security," she snaps into the phone. "Send Marco to the admin wing. Now."

I wipe my palms on the fabric of my skirt. The camera's steady gaze hovers in my peripheral vision. No one has said anything definitive, and both of these people have way too much practice at worming their way out of trouble for vague accusations and innuendos to stick. Someone needs to confess.

Dr. Ellery slams the phone down with a bang. I search my brain frantically for inspiration. The door to the hall seems poised to burst open. Time is running out. As soon as security gets here, they'll take me away, and my chance will be gone.

Ross rounds on me.

"Is Jack the one who told you all this nonsense?" He makes a choking noise that I think is supposed to sound like a laugh. "He must have done all those things himself, and now he's trying to pin them on me. That boy has always been devious. Spinners are terrible that way." He holds me out to Dr. Ellery again, his voice deepening to underline his meaning. "That's why I agreed to help you. As the police chief, you know, the way we discussed?"

Dr. Ellery crosses her arms over her chest.

"I don't think your help is going to be necessary."

"Really?" Ross smirks. "What about the rogue spinners you're rounding up? Having the police look into all those *unexplained disappearances* will be very awkward for you."

"Are you threatening me?" Dr. Ellery's face turns livid.

Ross, apparently realizing he's gone too far, holds up his free hand. "Not threatening," he says. "I'm just reminding you of our agreement."

The office door bangs open again. A man walks in, the same beefy-armed guy who stood watch while Jean injected me with poison.

"You called for security, Dr. Ellery?" he asks.

Dr. Ellery points to Ross.

"Take him away, Marco."

"Take . . . me?" Ross sounds incredulous. "You don't believe those things Alex said, do you?" He shoves me toward the security guy with so much force that I stumble. "Take her. *She's* the one you want."

Dr. Ellery grabs my arm and yanks me out of the way.

"Take *him* away," she repeats, dropping my arm like it's dirty and pointing to Ross. "I want him escorted off the property. *Far* off the property."

Rage twists Ross's face, but the emphasis in Dr. Ellery's words distracts me from his anger. She's looking meaningfully at Marco, and I catch him giving her an infinitesimal nod. My throat feels like I just swallowed an ice cube. I think of the road that leads to the Office: the remote forest, the dark rain-slicked asphalt, and the sheer cliff falling to eternity on one side. I think of what Jamal said about his friend: *Jeanine's car went through a guardrail two days ago, even though she's the most cautious driver on earth.* The coldness in my throat sinks down into my chest. Ross is more prominent than the anonymous Jeanine, but Ross is not a cautious driver. No one would question it if he drove off a cliff.

"You're going to regret this." Ross, too furious to notice any innuendo, brushes past the bulky Marco so he can walk to the door without the indignity of encouragement. "The second you or your minions harass any citizen in my jurisdiction, I'm going to be all over you. Don't forget I'm the chief of police."

"Not yet." The look Ellery gives him is withering. "Marco, make sure I don't see this man ever again."

The chill sinks into the pit of my stomach. I take an involuntary step forward. "What are you going to do to him?"

Dr. Ellery ignores me.

The security man follows Ross as he stomps out to the conference room. Ice seeps into my veins, spreading its frozen trail throughout my body. Mr. Ross is a thief and a murderer. He brought me here to be killed. But watching someone walk to his own death, unaware of what's happening? It's hideous.

"Wait!" I call out. "Mr. Ross!"

266

He doesn't turn his head. The door closes behind the pair of them with a final snap.

"You're going to kill him, aren't you?" I back away from Dr. Ellery. "That man, Marco, he's going to get Mr. Ross to crash his car somehow."

"I don't see why you care." Dr. Ellery opens a carved box on her bookshelf and takes out a leash. "That man is a self-serving cheat."

"I know that, but . . ." I sort through the emotions rattling through me. I hate Ross. He betrayed me. He's a bad person. But still.

"It's just *wrong*," I blurt.

Dr. Ellery moves toward me with the careful tread of someone approaching a wild animal. I back away.

"Why are you doing this?" I ask her.

"Because spinners destroy everything they touch."

I flinch. This woman is mad. She just ordered the death of a Norm. A *police officer*. My plan to get her to talk washes away under a wave of horror. I move away from her on legs that wobble.

"I'm not hurting anyone," I try to say, but my voice comes out in a whisper.

Dr. Ellery takes a step closer. I suppress a whimper. It's not the leash I fear—I know my skills won't save me. It's what the leash means. Captivity, the forced march back to the barracks, the steady drip of poison in my arm. My heart thunders in my chest, the frantic beat of the caged beast Dr. Ellery thinks that I am.

"You're unbalanced and evil," she says. "Left alone, you all go crazy."

"We don't have to go crazy." Terror makes it hard to shape the words. "Aclisote can control it."

"But you *don't* control it." Dr. Ellery rattles the leash dangling from her fingers. "You just admitted that a man died because of your skills. Helpless, in his bed, with no chance of fighting back."

Her words awaken my nightmares: the dim house, my silent tread on

267

the stairwell, and the shock of finding my one-time hero standing over a man who would never wake up again. Guilt rises in me like corroding sap. All the good I've tried to do, all the running around and searching for evidence, has meant nothing in the end. I have saved no one.

Dr. Ellery is getting closer. I lower my head so she won't see the tears pricking my eyes.

"It's those freezes that corrupt you," she says. "Those blank spaces with their terrible silence." She shudders. "They incubate evil."

A single tear escapes from my eye and slides down my cheek. I brush it away. There's a voice whispering in the back of my head, a very small voice that is still somehow louder than all the ugly words Dr. Ellery is flinging at me. *She's wrong*, the voice says. There's nothing evil about a freeze. A freeze is just a moment that gets extended. It's a blank canvas that carries no moral weight at all. Time isn't good or evil. It's people, and what they do with time, that matter.

Dr. Ellery takes another step toward me. I scuttle sideways until I'm on the opposite side of her desk. The wide surface yawns between us, the glass as clear and uncluttered as the sky outside. Time doesn't define who *I* am, either. I am just a girl. My genes gave me a unique trait, but like any trait, there's no morality tied to it. I'm no better or worse than anyone else because I can stop time. Just like the Norms, I'm better or worse than other people because of my actions. Goodness is a choice any of us can make.

A shadow flickers across the surface of the desk. I adjust my focus, and the glass turns opaque, its surface mirroring the room around it. Dr. Ellery is there, her reflection upside down and distorted by an imperfection in the glass. My own image is clear. I stare at it, taking in the red hair, the brown eyes, and the curve of my chin. *I know you.* I am a person who chooses love and friendship over fear and hate. A person who fears death and still accepts it. A person who is both brave and reckless, who wants to make a difference in the world, even if a lot of people in that world hold me in contempt.

I am more than just a spinner. I am Alexandra Manning, human.

I lift my head. Margaret Ellery stands across from me, a triumphant smile twisting the corners of her cold mouth. My fear of her swarms me like a thousand venomous bees. I let them land. I let them sting. I absorb the pain until all the poison washes away.

"I didn't kill Austin Shea," I say, believing the words for the first time. "Carson Ross did."

She smirks. "It was you. You caused it with your unnatural abilities. The world isn't safe with people like you in it."

"Is that why I have to die?" I ask her. "Because I'm more powerful than you are?"

Her smile slips. "You're not powerful. Freezing time is cheating. It lets you sneak around behind people's backs."

The voice in my head is no longer a whisper. It is strong, and it wants to be heard. I take another step to the side, forcing Dr. Ellery to follow me and ensuring that her face is caught by the spy cam's beady eye.

"Freezing time isn't what got me here." I gesture around her office. "Everything I did—escaping the bed you tied me to, walking through the halls, sending those files out—all of that happened in real time."

"Which just proves my point," Dr. Ellery snarls. "Spinners are dishonest and sneaky."

Her words are the darts that have pierced my soul a thousand times, but today those darts skitter away as harmlessly as if they were bouncing off concrete. This woman doesn't know *me*. She knows a fairy tale about scary beasts that she's told herself so many times that she might even believe it.

"Any Norm can lie," I say. "Or steal. Any Norm with a gun can kill someone with no more warning than Austin Shea got."

Dr. Ellery lunges for me. I leap away, keeping the desk between us.

"I've *seen* spinners hurt people," she says. Her voice is rising. "Innocent people. For no reason. Society can't manage with that kind of threat."

"And I've seen Norms hurt people for no reason. I worked for the

269

police, remember? Society manages with all kinds of threats. Diseases. Natural disasters. We don't slaughter everyone who knows how to box just because they *might* punch someone. That's barbaric. As long as spinners use their skills responsibly, why shouldn't we be allowed to keep them? People should be judged by their actions, not their abilities."

Dr. Ellery's face flames red, as if the heat that filled my cheeks has transferred to hers.

"You are a freak. A monster."

She swings for me again, a furious snatch that's easy to sidestep.

"I'm a teenager," I tell her, "who wants to hang out with my friends, and go to school, and one day have a job and maybe even a family. That's it. All I want is the chance to live a normal life like everyone else."

"You can never be normal! You have to die. All of you."

There's a vein beating in Dr. Ellery's temple. Her hair has slipped from its chignon, the dark strands waving around her neck like furious antennae. I set my hands on the desk's surface and feel the coolness of the glass soak through my fingers.

"Why do you hate me so much?" I ask her.

The color in Dr. Ellery's face deepens to near purple. "Because you are the worst kind of spinner. You think you're special, but you're not. You're defiant. Crazy." She leans closer to me. "You're just like *her*."

Surprise interrupts my instinct to recoil. "I'm just like who?"

"My sister." The words leak from her in an angry hiss. "Clarissa."

My jaw drops.

"Your sister was a spinner?" I ask. "What happened to her?"

Dr. Ellery's eyes are glazed, lost in some internal reverie.

"She died."

"How?"

Dr. Ellery gives her head a sharp flick, as if she's brushing off an irritating tickle.

"Like you will," she says. "Strapped to a bed in a Central Office with an IV dripping into your arm."

She reaches for me, and I stumble back, as much to get away from her words as to escape her.

"Kronos took your sister? And now you *work for them?*"

"They didn't take her. I gave her to them."

My mouth opens. Closes.

"You turned in your own sister?" I manage. "Knowing that they would kill her? And you're calling *me* a monster?"

Dr. Ellery's eyes flash. There is no hiding the fire in them now. The flames rage like an out-of-control inferno.

"I had to do it." Her voice is shrill. "Clarissa was crazy. Dangerous. Spinners corrupt everything. They destroy families. Kronos understands that. They know I did what had to be done."

She lunges, fast as a striking cobra. This time, I don't try to avoid her. I know the game is up. Not my game—hers. The leash cinches my wrist, its cold embrace bringing the inevitable dull buzz, but for once the sound doesn't cloud my brain. I know exactly what I need to do.

"Look up there." I gesture with my chin because Dr. Ellery is restraining both my hands. "At that painting. Do you see that red light? Up in the corner? That's a video camera, and it's been transmitting everything you've said since you walked into the room."

Dr. Ellery whips around so fast she nearly yanks my arm from its socket. The silence that follows is almost as comforting as the one in a freeze.

"You're lying," Dr. Ellery says.

"No. I'm not."

Dr. Ellery lets go of me so she can stride over to the painting and rip the little camera from the frame. It lies in her hand, a small black piece of plastic, totally unremarkable and utterly powerful. Like me.

"You don't need to control time," I say, "in order to spy on people."

Dr. Ellery's fingers clench around the small device. She's squeezing it tight enough to muffle the transmission, but not enough to crush it. Even Dr. Ellery doesn't seem to be able to think fast enough to decide if destroying the thing will work in her favor.

"Who is watching this?" she demands.

"The CIA," I say. "That's where I sent the files, too. The ones I pulled off your computer."

The vein in Dr. Ellery's temple throbs.

"There's nothing here that we can't explain," she says. "I don't know what you think anyone is going to do with the information."

The leash buzzes in the back of my head. The sound is the hum of thunderous applause, it is the cheers of spinners all over the world, it is the crash of breaking chains and the rasp of a rusty key. There's a low-grade fever burning in my body, bruises on my arm, scabs ringing my wrist, and a crushing headache pounding inside my skull. Zapper-protected walls have me trapped in this fortress, and my right arm is shackled by a leash, yet I have never felt freer than I do right now.

I look Dr. Ellery square in the face.

"Justice," I tell her. "They'll offer justice."

19 ◄◄

DR. ELLERY LOCKS ME IN A SPARE OFFICE WHILE SHE MAKES A series of phone calls. One of them must be to Marco, because he shows up after a while and marches me to the boys' room, opening the door just enough to shove me inside before slamming it shut again. Jack's body has been removed, but KJ lies where I left him. His straps are gone, presumably due to Shannon, who sits on a bed she's pulled up next to his, wearing the resigned expression of a deposed queen. I cross the room and join her. The IV bag hanging over KJ's head is empty, and a damp patch on the bed affirms that what was left in it leaked out. I rest a hand lightly on his sheet-covered chest. KJ's breathing is labored but steady.

"What happens next?" Shannon asks once I've filled her in on everything that happened after they took her from the admin office. I shrug. The reality of KJ's limp figure has crushed the triumph I felt in Ellery's office, leaving behind a tiredness so deep I feel like I could sleep for a month.

"Max is sharing all the information I sent her with the CIA," I say. "Hopefully, someone will think it's worth acting on."

"Will it take a long time?"

"Max said a few weeks."

Shannon looks down at KJ. "When do you think they'll come for us?"

"Soon."

Shannon gives a long, weary sigh, seemingly as far beyond tears as I am.

"Do you know where the others are?" I ask her.

273

"I think they put them all in the girls' room. There was a lot of noise in the hallway before you came in."

KJ's body twitches, his head tosses, and he mutters something incomprehensible. I wipe away the sweat beading on his brow, and he calms. I don't know how long we have, but I'm grateful we get to spend the time together. Outside the room, I know people are working frantically: reading my emails, checking to see if the spy cam was really filming, and feverishly redesigning their plans. Inside the room, the only noise is KJ's soft breathing. I pick up his hand and trace a finger along the lines of his palm. One of them is his life line, though I don't remember which one. I choose the longest and follow its curving path. Exhaustion drifts over me like a damp mist that sinks all the way to my bones.

"I'm sorry," Shannon says.

I rouse myself enough to look at her. "Sorry for what?"

"I'm sorry that I didn't believe you."

The line on KJ's palm ends when it reaches his wrist. The skin there is paler than the rest of his arm, and I move my finger from the shallow crease to the green-blue vein just beyond it.

"I'm sorry," I say, "that I kissed KJ while you were still dating."

She sighs again.

"That *was* a crappy thing to do," she says, "but I nearly killed him because I didn't want to believe that the people I trusted could be evil. In the grand scheme of things, I'm pretty sure that's worse."

She brushes her hand over the sheet covering KJ's chest, straightening the creases. Her gesture reminds me of our time at the squat, when Shannon purposely kept me away from KJ so she could feed him Aclisote. For a moment, the old anger sparks inside me, but it quickly fades. There is so much that is wrong about our lives and about what people have done to us. What Shannon did was wrong, too, but her choice was made out of love, while the Kronons' decisions are based on hate. What do I have to gain by holding a grudge against

274

Shannon for what she did? There is enough bitterness in the world without adding mine.

"I understand why you did it," I tell her. "And KJ forgave you. That's what matters, isn't it?"

Shannon shakes her head. "It matters that you forgive me, too."

Beneath my fingers, KJ's pulse beats steadily. I take Shannon's hand and rest her fingers against the reassuring rhythm.

"We're spinners," I tell her. "We stick together."

"But I'm not a spinner anymore," she says.

I lean sideways until my shoulder rests against hers.

"To me you are."

We sit like that, shoulders touching, sharing KJ's heartbeat. I don't feel particularly sad. I don't even feel scared. I've accomplished what I set out to do. Time passes, eternal and unalterable, the seconds and minutes progressing at the pace they were meant to proceed.

The door to the room rattles.

I jolt into wakefulness. My eyes are crusty, and my neck has a crick from propping my head against the wall. Shannon is asleep, her head cradled in my lap.

"Who has the key card?" someone says. The sound is muffled.

Adrenaline shocks away my sleepiness. I jostle Shannon's shoulder. There's another bang against the door, this one louder. Shannon jerks upright.

"What's going on?" she asks.

"They're here," I say.

The door bursts open, and a horde of people pours into the room. Noise shatters the quiet, a riot of thumping feet and overlapping words. My body turns rigid, and Shannon curls herself against me, whimpering. I wrap one arm around her, searching blindly with the other for KJ's hand, which fell from my lap while I was sleeping. The scene before me is senseless with pandemonium. The stink of antiseptic wafting from the hallway, the squeak of leather shoes. Light bounces off the dull metal of a gun. Someone says my name. I stretch out my hand to the other bed. KJ—I have to reach KJ. I won't let him die alone. I won't—

"Over there!"

Heads swivel in our direction. Shannon buries her face in my shoulder. The world tilts, steadies, and the swirl of images slowly gains meaning. I blink. The swarm of people settles into five, three of them in uniform.

"They're alive!" The voice is loud. And familiar. It's also filled with joy.

My searching hand drops to my side. These people aren't Kronons. They're not from the CIA, either. At least, not all of them. The man in front is Miguel. Behind him is Jamal, and next to him stands Max.

"Alex!" Miguel reaches us first and wraps me in breath-squashing hug. "Thank god. Are you all right?"

"Yes," I manage, too stunned to come up with anything more descriptive.

Miguel lets me go, and he, Max, and Jamal introduce themselves to Shannon. The room churns with activity. More police officers have arrived, and one is snapping photographs of the beds with their tacked-up name tags, the IV stands, us. Shannon pats at her sleep-rumpled hair. I put up a hand to block a camera's flash.

"No photos of the kids," Max snaps in her gravelly voice, placing her body between me and the documenting cop, who backs off obediently.

"You're here," I say, which isn't a question, but Jamal answers it anyway.

"The video," he says. "The one you took in Ellery's office. Max uploaded all the files you sent to an open website, and she livestreamed the video, tagging all of it as leaked CIA files. That video is playing *everywhere*: all the news outlets, YouTube, Twitter. People are horrified."

KJ, in the bed beside me, mumbles something in his sleep. I find the hand that eluded me before and lace my fingers through his.

"Are you saying," I ask, "that Dr. Ellery's confession worked?"

"It wasn't Dr. Ellery." The smile Jamal gives me is blazing. "It was you."

Behind him, the photographer has moved over to a now-unlocked medicine cabinet, where she's snapping endless pictures. The light from her flash explodes in my peripheral vision like a series of small bombs.

I rub my eyes. "I don't understand."

"Your arguments in defense of spinners." Miguel shakes his head in admiration. "They were pitch-perfect. You were eloquent, so calm and assured, and Dr. Ellery was so . . . not. Most Norms have never seen a spinner, much less heard one advocate for themselves." He smiles at me. "I'm not saying public opinion has turned on a dime. There's still a whole lot that people need to process, but your words are making a lot of Norms rethink their prejudice."

"Max gets some credit, too," Jamal adds, giving his friend's shoulder a playful jab. "Deciding to make it all public was a risky gamble, but it paid off brilliantly. Those files you sent provided enough evidence to prove Kronos's history of systematic annihilation, and thanks to Max, it's available to anyone who wants to read it. Combine that with a video that's creating a huge swell of public sympathy, and it means the CIA has to act immediately. If they wait, they'll be seen as child-killers."

I shift my attention to Max. The CIA informant/wiper/double agent's face is lined with tiredness, but there's a lightness about her, too, as if she's taken her first deep breath in a long time.

"What happened after you dropped me off at Dr. Barnard's?" I ask her. "You didn't pick me up."

I don't mean the words accusingly, and she doesn't seem to take them that way.

"I called in my location," she says, "just like we discussed, but dispatch said there was an emergency capture across town, and they assigned me there. I watched from the car as the police chief took you away. I knew your chance of success was tiny, but it was tiny to begin with, and I decided that either way, I was done. When Jamal called to find out where you were, I told him

277

everything—that I was undercover as a wiper, that you were planning to infiltrate the Central Office, and that I was going to help you. He, David, and I met at my apartment, where I set up the computer and waited for your files. After I posted them, I sent the link to my boss at the CIA, and when we saw it was all going viral, we got in the car and headed up here. The order to invade the Central Office came in while we were driving."

I rub the crick in my neck, trying to knit all these new facts together. "So, all these people"—I gesture around the room—"they're CIA?"

"Some are," Max says. "Others are local police we pulled in as backup. They've already got Dr. Ellery in custody, and the feds have ordered an immediate halt to research at all five Central Offices, pending further investigation."

I shake my head. My brain feels cloudy. I know everything she's telling me is good news, but I can't quite follow it all. Viral posts. Custody. Immediate halt. Further investigation. Shannon huddles beside me on the bed, looking as dazed as I feel.

"KJ is sick," I say, gesturing to his still form. "They overdosed him on Aclisote."

Jamal opens his mouth as if has more to say, then looks at me and closes it. He squeezes my shoulder.

"Got it." He says something to Max, and both of them stride from the room.

Miguel bends down, pressing his fingers against KJ's neck to take his pulse.

"Where's Lisa?" I ask. "And your kids?"

"In the room next door," Miguel answers. "They're fine—they all are. Except. . ." He straightens, a shadow crossing his face.

"I know," I say, saving him from having to tell me. "About Emma and Molly. Max told me."

My words seem to shake Shannon into full consciousness.

"It's really true?" she asks Miguel. "That they're . . ."

"Gone." Miguel nods. "I'm so sorry."

I expect her to burst into tears, but instead, she gets up off the bed. "I want to see the other spinners," she says.

Miguel studies her a moment. Her face is pale but set. He nods.

"I'll take you."

I hold tight to KJ's hand as I watch the two of them thread their way through the bustling room. A part of me wants to go with them, but my body is shaking with adrenaline-crash tremors, and I can't seem to make it stop.

Time turns unpredictable. Rather than moving forward steadily, or even stopping and starting in familiar ways, it seems to be skipping, and I keep missing the transitions. A tall woman wearing a headscarf is standing by my bed. I'm pretty sure she introduced herself, but I have no idea what her name is. She pops a thermometer in my mouth and checks my pulse. Officers come and go, their voices jarring in the once-empty space. "Are you the one who was cured?" one of them asks. I shake my head. My mouth tastes like plastic. When I wipe the back of my hand across my lips, I realize the thermometer is gone.

More people come over and ask me questions, though they don't always wait for an answer. Somehow, I am both the center of attention and completely outside of everything happening around me. I pick up KJ's hand again and focus on the beats of his pulse.

Time wrinkles again. A new man stands beside the bed. He's wearing blue scrubs and is dragging a gurney along beside him.

"This is KJ?" he asks.

Panic jolts through my daze. I clutch KJ's hand against my chest.

"Who are you?" I demand. "Where are you taking him?"

"It's all right." Jamal appears at the man's side. "This is Dr. David Levine. He'll take KJ to his clinic and give him the help he needs there. You can trust him. I promise."

"Are you a spinner?" I ask David.

279

"No," he says, "but I'm on your side."

He smiles at me, and I realize I recognize him. He's the blond man in Jamal's photos.

"Can I go with you?" I ask.

"Of course," David says.

Jamal helps David transfer KJ onto the gurney, and the four of us head out of the building, Jamal's bulk a useful tool as we push our way through the mess of people cluttering the hallways. Every time someone tries to stop us, Jamal waves them off with a protective glare.

"I have special clearance from Agent Xavier," he keeps announcing.

I'm not sure what this means, but it seems to work. Interference melts before us, clearing a path to the door. I keep one hand clutched tightly around the metal bar at the end of KJ's gurney even though David is doing a perfectly good job guiding it forward without my help.

The Central Office's lobby looks decidedly less intimidating than it did when I arrived. For one thing, its pristine elegance has been spoiled by all the people tromping through it; for another, the zapper that guarded the space has been turned off, and the room's sharp edges have transformed into the mundane outlines of regular furnishings. Jamal, David, and I pass unchallenged through the propped-open security gate and out the front door to where an ambulance waits in the parking lot. David slides the gurney into the back and motions for me to follow him inside.

"I'll meet you at the clinic once I know the others will be taken somewhere safe," Jamal tells me from the sidewalk. "A couple of hours, maybe."

I nod. The doors slam shut. David directs me to a seat and then reaches over to unlock my leash.

"That better?" he asks.

I take in a deep breath, shaking the cloudiness from my brain.

"I'm going to give your friend an IV drip," David says. "It's just saline." He holds up an IV bag with the words 0.9% SODIUM CHLORIDE printed in bold letters on the front. "I want to flush his system. When we get to the clinic, I'll give him a blood transfusion. That will help get the Aclisote out of his system faster."

"Will he lose his time skills?" I ask.

"No, the cure process is more complex than just a transfusion." He settles into the seat across from me and snaps on a seat belt. "Don't worry. I've treated worse cases than this. He's going to be fine."

The driver must have gotten in the ambulance because the engine thrums, and it pulls away from the curb. David busies himself hooking up KJ's IV, moving with a quick efficiency that seems completely unaffected by our swaying passage. I reclaim KJ's free hand and hold it in my lap, stroking the soft skin on the inside of his wrist. From where I'm sitting, I can see out the small windows in the back of the ambulance. Dawn is starting to break through the trees. The newborn sun lights the stark walls of the building we've left behind, staining the exterior with a shaming flush of pink.

The ambulance barely slows as we near the front entrance. The gates don't look like jackals now. We pass without fanfare, and I watch the opening I never thought I would pass through again recede. Within seconds, the entire facility has vanished, and we're surrounded by a thick forest of trees, their leaves turning greener with each growing ray of morning sun.

"We did it." I say the words to myself, softly, like I'm trying them out. "We stopped Kronos."

KJ turns his head. His eyelids flutter.

"Alex?" he mumbles.

"I'm here."

"Where are we?"

David leans over his patient, shining a light in each of his eyes.

"We're in an ambulance." I lift KJ's hand and hold it against my cheek. "It's taking us to a spinner-friendly clinic. You're going to be OK."

KJ blinks against the light, and David gives a satisfied nod.

"You can talk," he tells me, "just keep him calm."

He turns in his seat and starts tapping information into a laptop, leaving me as alone with KJ as one could in such a confined space.

KJ strokes the side of my face. His fingers are warm and surprisingly steady given his condition.

"What about you?" he asks.

"Me? I'm fine. We all are. KJ, the Office is closing. Everything's going to be different now. I made a video with the spy cam, and Max put it on the internet, and . . ."

KJ gazes at me with a baffled frown. A thousand words flood my mouth, but I remember David's instructions about "calm," and I swallow them down.

"We won," I say. "I'll tell you all the details later."

This imperfect explanation must be enough for him right now, because he doesn't push for more. Instead, he grips my hand and asks, "Does this mean we're going to live?"

I kiss his fingers.

"For as long as anyone else does," I say.

KJ smiles. His eyes flutter closed again, and he sinks deeper into his pillow. I watch the steady rise and fall of his chest. Outside, a police car races by, its siren wailing like a mourning cry for all the souls lost to the Central Office. Someday, I want to find out the details of everything that happened in that bleak place. I want all their sins made public, and I want to make sure that the thousands who died are recognized.

KJ sighs in his sleep, a gentle breath that carries no hint of tortured nightmares. I stroke his sweat-spiked hair. KJ is right. Questions can wait. What's important is that we are together and that we are alive. This fight isn't over, but right now, there is no room for anything in my heart but love.

20 ◄◄

LATE NOVEMBER SUNSHINE STREAMS THROUGH THE WINDOW, ITS
golden warmth protecting the refuge's kitchen from early winter's chill. I scrub
bits of egg off a wide frying pan, enjoying the feel of hot soapy water sloshing
around my hands. Beside me, KJ is loading the dishwasher. The random clatter
of cutlery makes a homey counterpoint to the Mozart violin concerto drifting
from the radio on the shelf over our heads. Miguel always turns the classical
station on as soon as he wakes up, and usually no one thinks to turn it off until
midday when Aidan—who is in charge of lunch prep—switches the radio to
something louder with a much more pronounced beat. Lisa occasionally
protests that the lyrics of his preferred songs are inappropriate, but she rarely
changes the station. Usually before she gets that far, a kettle shrieks, or Jeremy
zooms into the room demanding matches to test the rocket he and Raul are
making, or Yuki announces that one of the goats has gotten into the vegetable
garden again. Life at Goat Hill Farm is a balancing act in a swirl of controlled
chaos.

"How's the remodel going?" KJ asks, reaching across me to grab the
dishwasher detergent.

"Good," I say.

I've been spending a lot of time recently working with Miguel to
convert the basement into three small bedrooms. It turns out I really like
building things. I enjoy thinking about how spaces fit together and appreciate
the precision of the actual work. I also like the physical aspects of construction.

There are still too many nights when I wake up in a cold sweat from dreams in which someone is chasing me though the Central Office's blank hallways, reaching for, yet unable to access, time. I've learned that being tired helps keep the nightmares at bay.

"The new bathroom won't be totally finished by the time the others get here for Thanksgiving," I tell KJ, setting the clean frying pan in the dish rack and reaching for a mixing bowl, "but at least the toilet should be functional."

"That will make Angel happy," KJ said. "She threatened never to come back if she had to run upstairs every time she had to pee."

I laugh. One of the surprising outcomes of Kronos's collapse—to me, anyway—was that thousands of people offered to take in a spinner kid. The Society for Spinner Rights dove into reference checks, and after a few tumultuous weeks of arguing with various officials about what our rights actually were, all of us got settled into foster homes. Those who opted for the cure, which ended up being about half of all the former Center residents, were placed with Norm families, while the rest of us were quietly funneled into spinner households. Raul, KJ, Yuki, Aidan, and I live here at the refuge. At this point, every spinner is being monitored—even the free ones, whose identities Kronos publicized in a final act of spite. Each of us has a caseworker, a therapist, a lawyer, and a medical team, all paid for with assets the government seized from Kronos's accounts. We have to check in with our caseworkers every twenty-four hours, need permission to go farther than five miles from our homes, and still have to wear leashes if we're in public—though for own safety, we are allowed to keep the leashes covered. We all have cell phones, too, which KJ has pointed out means they can track us, but given that pretty much all Norms also suffer that particular indignity, it's hard to protest too hard.

The one exception to the travel ban is that once a month, all the former residents of the Portland Center have permission to get together at the refuge for a weekend. It's an event we all look forward to, and for all her complaints, no amount of bathroom hiking would make Angel miss our reunion.

284

"What's your plan for the day?" I ask KJ.

"Aidan and I are harvesting the last of the alfalfa," he says, "and I'm hoping there will be time to work in the garden." He glances out the window. "There hasn't been any frost yet. Lisa is skeptical, but I think we can squeeze in one more crop of lettuces if we plant them in the greenhouse."

I trail my sponge through the rainbow-hued bubbles filling the sink. Despite the restrictions imposed on us, I'm often freshly stunned by the possibilities in our lives. The fact that KJ can plant seeds, knowing that he'll be here to watch them from the time they push their way up from the soil until they unfurl into full-fledged plants, still feels like a miracle I don't quite trust.

"It's supposed to get warm later today," I say. "We should go on a picnic for lunch."

KJ leans one hip against the dishwasher. "Just the two of us?"

"We could bring Rosie, if you want." I widen my eyes in mock innocence. "You know how much she loves picnics."

KJ slips an arm around my waist.

"Isn't noon close to her nap time?" he asks, bending to nuzzle my neck.

Soapy water drips on the floor when I accidentally drop the sponge. I make a half-hearted effort at ridding my fingers of bubbles before running them down the length of KJ's long back. He pulls me closer.

"You know"—KJ kisses the soft spot just below my ear—"Miguel got permission to take me to the DMV tomorrow for my driver's test." His lips brush my earlobe. "I was thinking maybe on Friday . . ."

"There you are." Lisa bustles into the kitchen. KJ straightens abruptly, turning to inspect the dishwasher's dial as if he might have set the machine wrong. I hide my flushed cheeks by bending to the floor to recover the errant sponge. I adore the refuge, but living in a four-bedroom house packed with nine people does not create a lot of opportunities for romance.

"I'll finish these up." Lisa waves a hand at the small pile of remaining dishes, either polite about or oblivious to what she interrupted. "Alex, you need to get moving. Your interview is in five minutes."

"Oh, right!" The recovered sponge plops into the water with a sudsy splash. "I didn't realize it was time already."

A week ago, Shannon convinced me to talk to a reporter from the *New York Times*. She promised me the interviewer, a guy named Sam Lyons, was friendly to spinners and that none of the questions would be "challenging."

"You can't bury yourself in that refuge forever," she lectured me. "You're the one in the video, and everyone keeps asking about you. Besides, I can't be the only person representing us in public. The world needs to hear other perspectives if they're truly going to understand what we've been through."

She's probably right, though her complaint about being the sole voice didn't sound completely genuine. From what I can tell, Shannon loves her role in the spotlight. She lives in Portland these days with Yolly. She's kept her job as a spinner ambassador, but now she works for the Society for Spinner Rights, starring in their media efforts to reshape public opinion about spinners. Her specialty is giving presentations at schools about tolerance and the damage done by stereotyping. Yolly got hired by the state's new Spinner Transitions Office. She and Shannon often travel around the state together to check on how everyone is settling in. They both seem really happy with their new positions.

I give the mixing bowl a final rinse, then shake my hands free of the dishwater.

"Do you want me to be in the room with you during the interview?" Lisa asks, handing me dish towel.

"No, thanks." I reach for the towel. Instead of letting go, Lisa grasps my hand through the terry cloth.

"You don't have to do this alone," she says.

Her grip on my hand is tight enough to be uncomfortable. Lisa is such a *mom*, and I'm so not used to having one. Her worrying about me is an unexpected gift, but it can also feel a little suffocating sometimes. I shoot KJ a beseeching glance, and he nods imperceptibly.

"I'll sit with her," he says.

Lisa releases the dish towel, and my hand, with obvious reluctance.

"Remember," she tells me, "Sam Lyons agreed that this would only be a five-minute interview, and you're not obligated to answer any questions you don't want to. If he asks anything that makes you uncomfortable, just say no comment."

"I know," I say. "I'll be fine."

Lisa takes over my spot at the sink while KJ and I head into the living room, where the refuge's land line is. We're using it because Lisa insisted that the interviewer not be given my cell number.

"You could be nicer to her, you know," KJ says when we're far enough from the kitchen that we can't be overheard.

"I'm nice."

"You're polite," he says. "That's different."

I shrug, feeling a bit stung. Twice, Lisa has invited me to do things with her one-on-one—once to go out to lunch, and once to go to a salon to fix my half-grown-out dye job. Both times, I claimed I had homework.

"I know she wants to do the right thing by us," I say. "And I appreciate everything she's done, I really do. It's just . . . I guess I don't understand what she wants from me."

"Lisa doesn't *want* anything from you." KJ sounds both frustrated and a little bit sad. "She cares about you. Just like Yolly does. And Miguel, and everyone else."

"It's not the same." The sun in the living room is very bright, and I squint my eyes so I don't have to meet KJ's. "I know Yolly cares for us, but let's face it, taking care of us was her job. Jamal, David, Max—even Miguel—I understand why they like me. We all worked together to break Kronos. I earned their affection. But what do I have to offer Lisa?"

KJ shakes his head. "Love isn't something you earn. It's something you

287

give. All Lisa is asking from you is that you accept her affection."

The phone on the other side of the room starts ringing before I can come up with a response. I hurry to answer it, grateful for the interruption.

"Hello?"

"This is Sam Lyons. Is this Alex?" The voice on the other end is deep, warm, and, as Shannon promised, friendly.

"Yeah." I settle into my favorite armchair, the one with the patchwork pillows, next to the big window that overlooks the backyard. KJ takes the chair across from mine. I set the phone down on the table between us and hit the speaker button so he can hear.

"It's a pleasure to talk to you," Sam says, the speaker turning his voice a bit tinny. "I know you've turned down a lot of other interview opportunities."

"I prefer to stay out of the public eye."

I don't mention how hard Max and Miguel have worked to keep my personal information private. It helps that I'm still a minor. Max manipulated the video from Dr. Ellery's office before she livestreamed it so that my face was blurred. Miguel insisted that only my first name was released to media, and he makes sure nobody knows where I live. This interview request, like all the others, came through my attorney.

"Let's dive in, shall we?" Sam says. "These past few months—they've been pretty life-altering for you."

I adjust the pillow to a more comfortable position behind my back.

"Every spinner in the world has seen their life change since September," I tell Sam.

"Sure, but the changes you've experienced are particularly dramatic. You were in the middle of it all."

KJ gives me a thumbs-up in support of this statement. I wave his hand away. "I guess."

"The more the world learns about Kronos," Sam continues, "the more we all understand how much they manipulated public opinions. As one of the spinners impacted by their efforts, how do you feel about the consequences the people involved have faced?"

"My goal was to permanently stop governments from murdering spinners. That seems to be happening, so to me it's a win."

"And yet, so many of the individuals involved in the scandal are still free. The entirety of Kronos's Board, including their leader, Antonio Romano, managed to disappear, as did a large part of their financial empire."

I nod, forgetting for a second that Sam can't see me. Kronos has always been more of a vague menace than a group of actual people to me, and the leaders' disappearance has done little to make them more real. Jamal worries that they will return in some new form and take up their ancient fight. I worried about that for a while, too, but KJ sides with my therapist, who encourages me to focus on stuff I can control. This is one of a number of things I'm working on.

"The only Kronons I met were the Central Office staff in Tacoma," I tell Sam, thinking of a photo I saw online of Dr. Ellery's face glaring from a mug shot. Despite my therapist's best Zen teachings, I can't help the surge of vindictive pleasure the memory brings. "All of *them* are in jail."

"Not *all* the people who've been implicated are in jail. Dr. Barnard has yet to be charged for any crimes, and he's still held in high regard for his work on the cure. He claims that when he prescribed lethal Aclisote dosages, he was merely following the treatment plan set by the Central Office. Do you believe his statement that he was unaware of Kronos's agenda?"

My never-very-successful efforts at Zen slide into the catastrophic failure category.

"Dr. Barnard is lying," I snap. "He knew exactly what he was doing. I've told the investigators that more than once. Developing a cure doesn't make him innocent of personally killing hundreds of teenagers."

"Your friend Ms. Callahan takes a much more neutral stance. She says it's for the courts to decide Dr. Barnard's guilt or innocence."

"Shannon is a very forgiving person. I'm not."

KJ must have stopped time for a bit, because he's suddenly holding up a sign that says, BARNARD IS A LYING SACK OF GARDEN DUNG. Along the bottom, he's drawn a row of blobbly creatures I think are supposed to be slugs, each carrying a placard that says BARNARD with a big red X over the name. I let my anger go and grin at him.

"Let's talk about Carson Ross," Sam says.

The smile on my lips fades. KJ catches my eye and mouths *no comment.* I shake my head to tell him it's OK, though it's really not. Even now, almost three months since I first discovered Ross's true character, the mention of my one-time agent's name still makes my gut clench into a complicated knot of anger, betrayal, and loss.

"Carson Ross's assassination," Sam continues, "and the subsequent revelations about all his misdeeds were particularly shocking chapters in this already-horrifying story. His behavior toward you—framing you for Austin Shea's murder, forcing you to break the law for him, turning you over to known killers—is a significant part of his crimes. Do you believe his death was a fair consequence for his actions?"

The slugs on KJ's sign take on a more militant vibe. Ross's downfall got almost as much press in the media as Kronos's collapse did. Jamal has gone on many bitter tirades about people caring more about the murder of one Norm police officer than the loss of thousands of spinners. Miguel's perspective is that anything that puts Office staff in jail is a good thing. I lean more toward Jamal's view, but I also can't see Ross's death as fair. If murder is wrong, doesn't that apply to every case, even ones where the victim deserved it? What is justice if penalties are selective?

"Ross's death isn't the one I mourn," I tell David, sidestepping the deeper questions. "The people I miss are the friends I grew up with: Emma, Molly, Jack, and all the other spinners whose lives were cut short."

Saying their names casts a too-familiar pall over the cheerful living room. I've said them on purpose, wanting to bring their presence into a conversation that feels overly focused on the lurid details of headline crimes. All of us Center spinners were raised to expect early deaths, and my voice doesn't crack anymore when I talk about my lost friends, but saying their names still hurts. KJ crumples his sweet, silly drawing, and we both look over at the bookcase on the other side of the room. Yuki has been making commemorative collages, and her artwork now covers most of the top shelf. I focus on my favorite, the one she made for Jack. Yuki layered pictures from Jack's time in the Center with objects representing things he loved: the cover of a much-played video game, a coiled guitar string, an excerpt from a magazine article about Kobe Bryant, a list of the songs he listened to the most. Yuki even pasted in one of the twenty-dollar bills Jack and I stole from the armored truck— perhaps not his most honorable moment, but representative of what was probably the last day when Jack was truly happy.

The silence in the room grows heavy. Sam, probably worried I'm about to cut off the call, rushes to change topics.

"Can I ask you about that famous video?" he asks. "I think most of the world has watched it at this point. What were you thinking when you recorded it? Did you expect it to have the kind of impact that it did?"

Thoughts of Jack recede as my mind reels back to that day in Dr. Ellery's office. The memory is mostly a confusing jumble: the fire in Dr. Ellery's eyes, Ross's exultant laugh, the ache of my smashed fingers, and the taste of fear drying my mouth. I watched the video once—or I started to—but I immediately broke into a sweat, and when Lisa saw how pale I was, she made me turn it off. I have no interest in ever seeing it again.

"When Shannon set up that camera," I say, "neither of us had any idea Max was going to broadcast the feed live. I was just hoping the CIA would get the evidence they needed to prove Kronos was plotting to kill us."

"And by Max, you're referring to the national spinner liaison officer, Maria Xavier?"

"Yeah, sorry," I say.

291

Max and the CIA parted company the day after she saved us, and she moved to DC not long afterward to take the new liaison position. Officially, she chose to leave the Agency, but Max said they never would have let her keep her job. By posting the video, she'd gone rogue, and even though the action made her a hero, the CIA doesn't keep operatives who act without approval from their superiors. Max told me she's glad for the change; her discomfort with the CIA's priorities would have made it hard for her to stay.

"Ms. Xavier is the real hero of this story," I tell Sam. "If she hadn't posted everything publicly, my friends and I wouldn't be alive today."

"I don't think she deserves *all* the credit," Sam says. "You're the one who risked your life by voluntarily entering the Central Office. I've seen an awful lot of media calling you the spark that started a revolution."

KJ holds his hands next to his head, then slowly expands them to signify my ego exploding.

"Thanks," I tell Sam, aiming a kick at KJ's leg, "but I was more desperate than brave. And I was lucky I had friends."

KJ mimes wincing in agony from my kick, then swings his leg around to trap my knee between his shins. I smother a laugh.

"Despite the new public sympathy," Sam says, "there's still a lot of controversy about how the world should deal with spinners going forward. One of the more controversial topics is how to use the cure. There's a lot of support for requiring all spinners to take it."

KJ and I exchange a glance. This is a topic we've all discussed. A lot. I let my leg relax inside our tangled limb embrace and spout the answer I've prepared for this inevitable question.

"I think the treatment is a great option for those who want it, but I also believe it should be a choice each individual makes on their own."

"Are you considering it for yourself?"

"No."

I look out the window. Raul and Jeremy are in the field outside, herding

292

the goats into a newly fenced-in section of grass to graze. It's a daily ritual that always makes me smile. The two of them dart around the pack, waving their arms and yanking on the animals' horns with cheerful enthusiasm while the goats mostly ignore them. Progress only happens because every few minutes, one of the spinners stops time and drags the frozen—and therefore malleable— lead goat toward the enclosure, which startles the goat but makes the other ones amble in the right direction. From my perspective, it looks like both the goat and the giggling spinners keep teleporting around the field.

"Being a spinner doesn't define me absolutely," I tell Sam, "but it *is* a big part of who I am. I have no interest in changing such an essential piece of myself, and I don't believe anyone has the right to demand that I alter the way I was born."

A rustling-paper sound leaks through the phone line; our time is almost up.

"Let's end our conversation on a cheerful note," Sam says. "The Society for Spinner Rights has set up a website where spinners and their families can submit DNA and search for matches. Quite a few spinner children around the country have been reunited with their birth families. Is that something you're thinking of doing?"

A half dozen of the goats trot through the fence into the enclosure. Raul gives Jeremy a high five, and the little boy's face lights with pride. I rub a finger across the armchair's faded upholstery. Family is another topic KJ and I spend a lot of time talking about.

"Maybe I will one day," I say, "but I'm not ready yet. I feel like I already have a family, and I'm not sure I need another one."

"Are you talking about your foster parents?"

I wriggle my foot, newly aware of how tightly KJ is holding on to it. When I said I had a family, I meant my friends, but Sam's question makes me rethink my answer.

"I guess I'm talking about home." I rub the armchair again, its fabric soft

293

from the touch of so many hands. "The kids I grew up with will always be my family, but we never had a home until we got here. Our foster parents and their kids, they're helping us create a new kind of family. New to me, anyway. I can't see any blood tie replacing that."

Across from me, KJ smiles.

"What do you see in your future?" Sam asks. "Assuming you're allowed to keep your skills, it seems like the sky is the limit for spinners in terms of careers. People are talking about all kinds of workplaces that would benefit from employees who could manipulate time: the police, obviously, but also sports referees, entertainers, any position that requires contact with explosives or tricky electrical connections, not to mention emergency personnel. Surgeries could be done without using anesthesia. People with life-threatening injuries could be transported to a medical facility instantaneously. There's even talk of companies wanting to keep spinners on staff simply to help them meet deadlines."

I throw my hands up in a what-do-I-know gesture that only KJ can see. He's the one who should be answering this question. He has enrolled in a virtual community college and has already mapped out two years' worth of classes that will lead him to a degree in electrical engineering.

"I'm still pretty much taking things day by day," I tell Sam. "I'm taking classes at the local high school—online, of course, until we're allowed to be out in the world without a horrible, buzzing leash—but I have a great tutor. I should be able to earn a high school diploma by next summer. I'm hopeful that if that new legislation passes, I'll be able to go to college at some point."

"Have you thought about what you want to study?"

"Medicine, maybe, or public policy?"

KJ raises a quizzical eyebrow, a response I deserve. Every time someone asks me what I want to do with my life, I come up with a different answer. Yesterday it was architecture.

"I don't know," I amend. "Thinking that far ahead is new for me."

In the background of the open phone line, I catch the sound of a soft ding. I check my watch. The call has lasted five minutes exactly; Sam must have set a timer.

"Alex," he says, "it's been a delight talking to you, and I hope we have an opportunity to speak again. I want to tell you that I am personally rooting for spinners to be allowed to keep their skills, and I am so happy for you that this whole thing is over."

"Thanks," I say, "but I think you're being optimistic. I doubt this 'thing' will ever truly be over."

We exchange a little more goodbye chitchat, and then KJ reaches over and hangs up the phone. I stretch my arms over my head.

"That wasn't too bad," I say.

KJ turns in his chair, disentangling our feet so he can look at me.

"Did you mean what you said just now?"

He sounds super serious. I lower my hands back into my lap.

"Which part?"

"The part where you said none of this would ever be over."

I trace a finger over my right thumbnail. I've been trying really hard to stop biting my nails and have mostly succeeded. Only this one thumb shows signs of anxious gnawing.

"Well, it won't, will it?" I smooth the nail's rough edge. "I mean, I don't think things will go back to how they used to be. I don't think anyone is out to kill us off anymore. But . . . we'll always be spinners, you know? Norms are always going to be afraid of us."

"I agree that things aren't settled," KJ says, "but they have stopped being a crisis." He hesitates. "Don't you think that's enough?"

He sounds so nervous that I look up at him. He's watching me, a smile flickering on the edge of his lips, like it's not sure it's allowed to stay.

"Enough for what?" I ask.

"Enough for you to feel like you can stop fighting. Enough for you to

295

truly believe that there's a future. For you. And for us."

Through the window, I see that Lisa has joined Raul and Jeremy by the goats. The three of them are feeding kitchen scraps through the fence to the now safely corralled herd. Jeremy, eager to reach one of the less aggressive animals, tries to climb the wire fencing, which immediately bends beneath his weight. His little body teeters, but only for a second, because both Raul and Lisa step forward to stabilize him. Jeremy leans back against them, secure in their support and apparently oblivious that he was ever in any danger. Lisa laughs. Sun shines on Jeremy's bright hair. The goats gobble their treats greedily.

I think of KJ telling me that all Lisa wants from me is to accept her affection. Can life really be that simple? I shift my gaze to the rolling hills spreading out beyond them. There's no Portland fog to obscure the view out here at the ranch. The sky is blue and clear, and I can see all the way to the distant horizon.

"I think," I say, bringing my attention back to the boy in front of me, "that there will always be things worth fighting for, but not in a reckless life-or-death kind of way. We won our chance to have a future, and I intend to cherish every minute of it."

KJ hands are suddenly full of flowers. It's Jeremy's trick, the one he showed me when I first came to the refuge, where you remember your pose when you stop time and return to the exact same position before you start it again. We've all played with it, though KJ must have been practicing, because this effort is particularly seamless.

"For you," he says.

He holds the flowers out. They're chrysanthemums, their round balls of petals the warm orangey-yellow of tiny suns. He must have grown them in the greenhouse. I flash back to my thoughts in the kitchen about KJ's assumption that he'll be here to see the seeds he planted mature, and for the first time, I start to understand his faith. We spinners are like those plants, timid shoots thrusting our heads up into a hostile environment, sheltered only by a temporary

296

construct. Wind could damage the greenhouse walls; winter's ice might come early; there could be mites, or a water shortage, or any one of a million other unexpected disasters. But KJ is right to believe that the plants will thrive. Plants are hardy, and so are we.

"Alex." KJ clear this throat. "I was wondering, assuming I pass the test and that Miguel lets me take the car, would you like to go into town and have dinner with me on Friday?"

I accept his flowers and bury my nose in the soft petals. They smell rich and earthy and very much alive.

"Kaleel Jabar, are you asking me out on a date?"

His nervous smile flickers again.

"Only if you're ready," he says. "As you've pointed out, our future is still a huge question mark."

When is anyone really ready for an unknown future? I reach out with my mind and stroke the strands of time flowing between us, binding us to this instant even as the moment rushes past. Touching the ephemeral essence fills me with a familiar sense of both power and peace. I consider resting my hand on KJ's and freezing time so that we can share what happens next in our unique brand of perfect privacy. I don't. I want our future to happen in real time, not in the stolen moments in between. It's true that there are a million hard things that might happen to us, and there are a million things we'll each have to decide. There are some choices, though, that I've already made, and I don't want there to be any chance those changes won't stick.

The chrysanthemums are covering half my face, but I don't think it matters. I'm pretty sure my smile is brighter than any sun.

"I would love to go on a date with you." I slide off my chair and climb into my boyfriend's lap. "But Saturday might be better. I was thinking I'd ask Lisa to help me fix my hair."

KJ's smile steadies. I set the flowers on the table and put my arms around his neck, burying any doubts he may have about my dreams for the future with a long, deep kiss.

Acknowledgements

Getting this book into print has been a labor of love, and as so often in love, it included some heartbreak. The final draft was also written during the pandemic, a sentence which I hope will one day soon be read with only the vague associations that come with distant memories. Perhaps these were not entirely unfortunate writing conditions. While there are no malevolent organizations in the shadows plotting my demise, writing while stressed did allow me a deeper affinity for Alex's troubles than I may otherwise have felt.

Unlike the first two books in the *Rewind* trilogy, this final volume is self-published, which was an adventure I never planned to undertake. I learned a lot in the process, and took on tasks I failed to fully appreciate when I had a publisher (what *is* the best line spacing for a novel?). I also received help from many people. Rebecca Davis and Suzy Krogulski at Boyds Mills & Kane offered developmental edits, as did the talented Alison Cherry, who also provided detailed copy edits. Ann Kollrack, Sarah Stevenson, and Diana Tesh did a final comb through for typos. Boyds Mill additionally allowed me to use the beautiful cover design they created for the book. Thank you all. Your hard work turned this from a decent manuscript into a polished novel worthy to stand with its predecessors; your kind words kept me going when I was tempted to give up on the entire undertaking.

Thanks are also due to Vannessa McClelland, Sonja Thomas, Fonda Lee, and Curtis Chen, who read an early draft and offered both helpful advice and writerly support. My family, especially my husband, put up with many, many hours dedicated to plot dissection with admirable patience.

Most of all, thanks to every single person who ever told me they liked my books. You are the ones who make it all worthwhile.

www.carolynodoherty.com

299

3 1491 01404 6217

CPSIA information can be obtained
at www.ICGtesting.com
Printed in the USA
LVHW090429110721
692397LV00001B/117